G000090194

Iscariot

In memory of Charlie McDade

To Pat and Joe and Michael with love

ISCARIOT

TOM PHELAN

BRANDON

First published in 1995 by
Brandon Book Publishers Ltd
Dingle, Co. Kerry, Ireland

British Library Cataloguing-in-Publication Data
is available for this book
ISBN 0 86322 212 9

This book is published with the assistance of
the Arts Council/An Chomhairle Ealaíon, Ireland

Author photograph by Vincent Colabella
Cover design by the Public Communications Centre Ltd, Dublin
Typeset by Koinonia, Bury
Printed by ColourBooks Ltd, Dublin

Acknowledgements

I would like to thank the following people who helped me while I was writing *Iscariot.*

Joanne Hourigan reported on the flora and fauna in Ireland's early springtime. Anne-Marie Hourigan supplied historical information. Kathy Stubing, RN, and Jerome Ditkoff, MD, explained things anatomical and medical. Seamus Deegan and Angelo Ippolito helped with the psychology. Mike Daly supplied technical information. C.F. gave me an interesting explanation. Joan Clarke read the raw manuscript. My sons, Joe and Michael, manned the spell-checker on the word processor. My wife, Pat, listened as a new version of the plot was run past her every week for three years; she edited the entire manuscript and was my agent for this book and for my first, *In the Season of the Daisies* .

Chapter 1

Wednesday in the Fifth Week of Lent – 7.20 a.m.

THE ONE THING the priest hated doing was giving out holy communion.

Most communicants stuck out their tongues and waited for the circle of bread to fall from his fingers like a gleaming snowflake. But there were the few snappers and suckers who, like greedy fish, snapped the blessed bread with their long lips and left the priestly fingers glistening with saliva.

For a man who had no compunction about gutting a fish or paunching a rabbit, Father Keegan's aversion to other people's saliva bordered on the pathological. On the terrazzo floor inside the altar rails he shuffled along, reaching in and out of the polished ciborium. He kept glancing to his right, looking for the silhouettes of the snappers and the suckers.

The Gilligan woman was the worst, with her great upper lip and protruding chin. She was an ugly lamprey hiding behind a rock, waiting for her prey. Every time the priest recognised her profile in his peripheries, his memory provided him with the remembrance of the time he dislodged her upper dentures as he snatched his fingers away from her descending horse lip. The sight of those stained choppers and the sound of their clattering onto the silver-plated paten which the altar boy was holding under her chin, stirred droplets of acidic sweat in the pores of Father Keegan's body. He had used his alb to get rid of Mrs Gilligan's spit, but the glare which he had blasted at her had gone unnoticed. She had been too taken up with the recovery of her false teeth. As the altar boy strove to keep the paten level, Mrs Gilligan's thick, embarrassed fingers had pushed the ugly things to the edge. In one great grasp she had recaptured the dentures and, in one great slamming of her hand to her mouth, had made them disappear.

But Maura Gilligan had learned nothing, and she still lunged and snapped.

It was Wednesday in the fifth week of Lent, and Father Edward Keegan was in his thirty-second year of sidling along the inside of this particular set of altar rails. For the first two years of his priesthood he had been loaned to a parish in Manchester diocese in England. When he came back to Ireland, he had been sent to the village of Davinkill, an outpost of the parish of Duneamon. It was unheard of for a priest to be left in the same place for so long and Keegan's fellow clerics never tired of trying to tease out of him the reason why succeeding bishops had not transferred him. Even when his colleagues hinted that the authorities had buried him in Davinkill to support a nest of secretly sired brats, Keegan had not satisfied their adolescent inquisitiveness.

A new silhouette moved into the corner of Father Keegan's eye, and his brain flashed a warning to his body. But it was only Paddy Dillon, he of the one long front tooth, coloured like a piano ivory exposed to turf smoke for a hundred years. Paddy Dillon was neither a snapper nor a sucker. He was ugly, with sour and meandering wrinkles, hairy nostrils, hairy ears and breath strong enough to stagger a stallion. Every morning Dillon had fresh cuts between the swaths of beard he had missed with his razor.

As he neared Paddy Dillon, Father Keegan took a deep breath, then held it as he carefully placed the communion wafer beneath the toothy stalactite onto the longest and narrowest tongue in the parish. The priest was repelled by the tongue; it reminded him of the red, glistening connecting rod of a plunging bull. Keegan found it easier to look at the dull blackness of a horse's penis than at the the rawness of a penis that looked like a freshly scraped and oil-dipped carrot. Every time he travelled into the countryside, he risked exposing himself to the sexual activity of the indigenous animals. Even on the streets of the village it was not uncommon to see dogs at it, the hindquarters of the all-consumed male pumping as much out of nervousness born of the fear of being interrupted by a hob-nailed boot, as by the instinctual drive toward orgasm. And there was a deeply buried image in Keegan's memory of a man's penis bobbing in the light of an oil lamp, the penis glistening with the blood of the raped vagina from which it had been hastily removed.

Despite the images which Dillon's tongue evoked, Father Keegan was always relieved to see him at mass. Paddy Dillon was the local pyromaniac; he was also an alcoholic, and the village thief. One December,

Dillon had got into the presbytery by breaking four panes of glass, and the wood in which they were set, with a shovel. He had made off with an armchair, making his getaway with the loot in the priest's wheelbarrow along the main street. The local Guard had not had to call upon his Holmesian talents to track down the criminal, and Paddy Dillon had eaten Christmas dinner in the slammer, as he had planned, the misery of his equally demented wife and children forgotten.

When he neared the end of the altar rail, the priest brought his mind back to his sacred duty. He placed the host on Mrs Culliton's non-threatening tongue. There was a stain on her head-scarf, the same one she had been wearing to mass for the last two years. How could she not notice it? – the stain, black like the blackness of old axle grease. Father Keegan believed Mrs Culliton would be serving her family and the community better if she stayed at home in the morning and washed her litter of six boys.

The priest's peripheral vision sent out another alarm, and he stopped breathing. Two places beyond Mrs Culliton was the one-eyed head of the knacker and gravedigger John O'Brien, that disposer of carcasses both human and animal. It was the anticipated odour perpetually upwafting off John O'Brien which had closed down Keegan's pulmonary system. When John O'Brien cut up animals which had died of sickness or accident, the smell of the decaying meat permeated his clothes and skin – even his breath had the smell of death.

The priest placed the consecrated host on O'Brien's tongue, and wondered, as he had wondered many times before, how Maura Gilligan and John O'Brien could fornicate with each other, she being so ugly and he being so smelly. Both sinners tried to disguise their voices when they came to confession, but his stench and her breathy saliva rattling against the wire-mesh divider betrayed them every time. They must have given up sex for Lent, Keegan thought, because since the beginning of the penitential season, both had been attending daily mass and receiving communion. There would be more than one resurrection celebrated on Easter Sunday.

With the soft sibilance of the altar boy's slippers trailing him, Father Keegan made his way back to the other side of the sanctuary and to a fresh row of communicants. He appeared to be looking at the green and black terrazzo as he swished along in the purple vestments of Lent. But the shapes of the kneeling people were flashing by in the corner of his right eye as he scanned the line for snappers and suckers.

Father Keegan was in good shape for his fifty-seven years. His back was still straight, keeping his frame stretched to its six feet and two inches. He had lost none of his hair which, although nearly white, still maintained its short, sharp-crested waves. His spectacles were rimless, even though their style was one of long ago.

The priest looked clean. He smelled clean. He felt clean. He liked the feeling of being clean. The uncleanliness of the general populace made his cleanliness stand out like a house on fire in the dark.

The sacerdotal sphincter tightened as Keegan neared the end of the altar rails. The shape of Maura Gilligan's hat in the corner of his eye had that effect on him.

When he had not seen her in her usual place in the first row of communicants, he had thought she had decided to come to the second mass at noon. He had also hoped that she was sick, maybe even dead in her bed at home, reeking of dog dung. Instead, here she was, lubricating her lips for her lunge at the Lord. Keegan began to prepare himself mentally for his encounter with the lamprey.

Mrs Gilligan was kneeling in the seventh position from the end of the line and, until he had given her communion, Father Keegan knew he could think of nothing else. He wished he could overcome the aversion which was so pronounced in his dealings with this woman.

Father Keegan began to shuffle his way back along the line, the well-trained altar boy keeping one step ahead of him. The flesh of the priest's lips and nose began to work itself into a defensive posture as his tormentor's hat approached. Because he was aware that this involuntary contraction of his facial muscles was apparent to the casual observer, Father Keegan felt vulnerable, the way he felt vulnerable when somebody was standing behind him at a poker game.

Of their own accord the priestly eyelids squeezed forward, and Father Keegan looked out on the world through blurry slits. By the time he reached Mrs Gilligan the world had faded from sight, and there was nothing left except for the hairy lip and chin, the wide, wet tongue protruding, the tips of the yellowed dentures hanging there, already caught in the grip of gravity and slowly slipping down. With the anxiety of a child escaping the closing jaws of a nightmare's monster, Father

Keegan delivered the body of his God into Mrs Gilligan's glistening interstice, and his fingers came away from the encounter without a trace of the communicant's bodily fluids on them. It was going to be a good day.

The feeling which coursed through the priest's body was similar to the satisfaction of winning a Sunday night poker hand, especially when that vacuous Monsignor Johnny Rabbet had a lot of money and self-assurance in the pot. So relieved was he, that Father Keegan was unaware of the identities of the next half-dozen parishioners. It was only when he gave communion to Dervla Donaghue that his mind came back to what he was doing. His index finger brushed against Mrs Donaghue's lower lip, and he was aware of a new sensation, one which was faint, wispish and thoroughly pleasant. But then Dervla Donaghue reminded him of Tony Donaghue and Tony Donaghue reminded him of Kit Foley. Their names shot a thin line of anxiety through his being and, like a needle slipping its way through a tomato, it disturbed the pleasant feeling as effectively as a breeze blowing away the taunting perfume of a passing woman.

Keegan continued down the line, his hand flashing between the gleaming ciborium and the open mouths.

It had taken him many years to put a name on the elusive pleasantness which Dervla Donaghue stirred up in him. The name had fallen out of the dark one night when he was lying awake, without his even being aware he had woken up.

Secure contentment. That was it! And around the edges of the feeling was the faintest tinge of sexual excitement. He had never given voice to this stirring of the flesh. And, most certainly, the priest had never spoken to Mrs Donaghue, or anyone else, of the erotic shadings in the penumbra of the secure contentment.

Above all things, Father Keegan was discreet in word and deed. As the repository of the sins and secrets of the parishioners, he was only too well aware that the walls of all the houses in the village were full of peepholes. The peepholes were not the ones bored through wood or concrete. They were the holes in people's faces. It was through these holes that people often spoke ill of each other, and in speaking ill of each other they revealed many secrets. There was a more dangerous dimension to the peepholes which came into being in the atmosphere of one-upmanship which existed late at night in the public houses. Then the peepholes were not only enlarged, but the magnifying glass of alcoholic exaggeration was slipped incautiously across the openings.

Father Keegan, like all the other residents of the town, knew at a glance who frequented the public houses. Those who took a pledge at the time of their confirmation not to drink wore a pin in their left lapel. The Pioneer pin was the great class divider in Davinkill, and the Pioneers lived in dread of the enlarged talk which emerged from the drunken peepholes in the pubs. The only fear the drinkers had was that the Pioneers' daily prayer for their conversion would be answered.

The sins and secrets which Father Keegan heard in the secrecy of the confessional were often encountered at a later date in the form of gossip on the streets of the village. This supported his views about the peepholes, and it fostered his paranoia about discretion. If he himself had an overwhelming need to externalise a feeling, he did not express it in words. Instead he wrote it down and immediately burned the paper. This, he believed, was as good as lying on a psychiatrist's couch.

In the top of his eyes, Father Keegan saw Saint Willie Gorman approaching the altar rail, saw him limpingly emerge out of the shadows of the nave into the edge of the chancel's brightness. As he placed the consecrated host on a flat, white tongue without noticing the face of the owner, Father Keegan wondered if there was a place in the Guinness Book of World Records for Saint Willie Gorman's limp. From five feet nine inches, Saint Willie Gorman shrank to four and a half feet with alternating steps, and then sprang back again to his apex. It had to be the deepest limp in the world. It wasn't that Saint Willie Gorman had been born that way or that one of his legs had been shot off in the war. There was something wrong with his back, something which no doctor had ever pronounced on, because Saint Willie Gorman accepted all of life's ills as visitations from God.

Saint Willie Gorman had spent six years of his youth in a contemplative religious order, where he had developed his own peculiar brand of piousness. He had also developed deafness in one ear. The affliction had proved to be a sign from God that the future saint did not have a vocation to the priesthood, for how could a monk with one deaf ear hear confessions in confessionals designed for priests with two good ears? The vocation to priesthood had been abandoned for a vocation to sainthood. The deafness had eventually caught up with his other ear, and Saint Willie Gorman was now without hearing. But, lest anyone think he was annoyed with the God who had so mercifully granted this handicap, the Saint beamed out on the world through an idiotic grin. He perpetually looked as if he had just had a satisfying bowel movement, or had just heard that some man in Dublin, whom he did not know, had won a million pounds. In his quest for sainthood, Saint Willie Gorman depended so much on the will of God that he was rat-arsed poor, and he, his wife, five daughters and two sons lived in divine squalor.

In the top of Father Keegan's eyes, Saint Willie Gorman grinningly disappeared as he came to rest at his four-and-a-half feet height and waited his turn to kneel at the altar rail.

Along the line of opening and closing mouths, Father Keegan sailed like a dutiful bee visiting clover. He only wished he possessed the enthusiasm for the tongues which the bee had for the stamens. The altar boy's gleaming paten floated from chin to chin, ever ready to catch a falling host; never touching the chins or wattles of the communicants, nor collecting bodily oils or flecks of dead skin. Since whatever landed on the paten would have to be disposed of later by being scraped into the chalice and washed down Father Keegan's gullet on a flow of water, the priest appreciated the altar boy's steady hand.

Keegan was mildly surprised to see so many people in the church on this blustery morning at the end of March. The faith was alive in Davinkill. Despite all the backbiting the people engaged in, their Catholic faith was the glue which held them together. It gave them a social unity, enabling them to face any obstacle thrown across their path. Whether it was a disastrous wet harvest, an epidemic of blood murrain or an invasion of the village by proselytising Jehovah Witnesses, their common beliefs brought them through.

When the priest administered the Blessed Sacrament to the last communicant, he silently sighed. He had escaped Gilligan's grasping, disease-laden lips, and he had avoided the saliva of all the lesser suckers and snappers.

He turned away from the communion rail and ascended the altar steps, the front of the alb clutched in the crook of his left pinkie, hitching it up to avoid tripping. With a little cymbal-like clash he placed the lid on the ciborium, pushed the sacred vessel through the nun-embroidered silk curtains hanging inside the tabernacle, genuflected, stood up and locked the tabernacle doors with the gold-plated key. Automatically following the rubrics he had learned in the seminary, and which had been polished to a high sheen with years of practice, the priest purified the altar boy's paten, the chalice paten, his own fingers and the chalice.

Without consciously directing them, his fingers dressed the consecrated golden cup with purificator, pall, veil and burse. When the awareness of what he was doing came to him next, Father Keegan was standing in front of the missal with hands outstretched in an attitude of prayer. He continued to move and bow and pray until, finally, he raised his hands toward the ceiling, and called down God's blessing on the standing congregation. It was in the lifting of his arms in this last blessing a year ago that Father Keegan had unexpectedly felt the first restrictions of age in his upper limbs. He had always thought he would feel the first encroaching limitations of age in his golf swing.

Kicking the hems of his soutane and alb out from under the toes of his shoes, Father Keegan came down the altar steps. With the stem of the covered chalice grasped in his left hand and his right hand flat on top to keep the burse from sliding off, the priest's sweeping eyes picked out Dervla Donaghue in the nave; immediately he saw Kit Foley lying in the damp morning grass where he had left her, her bent right knee making a little tent out of the tail of the sergeant's overcoat. With the same urgency he would use to beat a stinging wasp to death, Father Keegan shook Kit Foley out of his thoughts. He did not know that every time he reinterred Kit Foley in his memory, his head slightly snapped in and out of alignment; nor, for all his knowledge about the village and its inhabitants, did he know that the people of Davinkill spoke often about his nervous twitch, and speculated, sometimes using their scatological and sexual imaginations, on the reason for its frequency.

When he reached the bottom of the steps, the priest turned back to the altar and waited for the altar boys to stand. They all genuflected in unison, and Father Keegan followed the double line of boys off the altar. It was because he had been thinking of Kit Foley that he remembered Ken Considine was on today's list of house-bound communicants. He frightened himself when he felt the word "shit" slipping through his lips.

Chapter 2

Wednesday in the Fifth Week of Lent – 11.30 a.m.

EXCEPT FOR HIS clothes, his stereo system, his CD collection and five books, Frank Molloy had brought nothing out of New York. Whatever else he had winnowed from his life's accumulated baggage was somewhere at sea marked with the address of the Davinkill post office. He had offered the left-overs to the girls, and what they had not taken he had given to the Salvation Army.

Standing in the front door of his newly acquired cottage on Wheat Mill Lane, and surveying the almost-empty sitting-room, Molloy felt a pang of regret at having been so generous with his worldly goods.

The three pieces of second-hand furniture in the sitting-room did as much to emphasise its bareness as to furnish it. The couch on the right wall needed a coffee table. The faded white wall above the couch cried out for a picture of something, anything. The table at the front window, with one of the kitchen chairs pushed under it, lent an air of monk's-cell-starkness to that corner of the room. The bookcase on the wall opposite the couch held the stereo, the compact discs and the five books.

The bare floor, with its wide planks and prominent, worn nail-heads, reminded Molloy of the classroom floors in the convent school, where he had learned that the Roman Catholic Church is beautiful, pure and right.

After closing the front door Molloy put his helmet and gloves on a shelf in the bookcase. The blue and red anorak landed on the arm of the couch. His fingers touched a succession of buttons which lit up small red lights on the amplifier and disc player. As he turned back toward the front of the house, the room filled up with the opening bars of a Haydn symphony.

He went to the monk's table and pulled a loose sheet of stationery toward him. Without sitting, he read through the four paragraphs he had been doodling with for the last few days. His lips pursed as he came to the last line. "Shit!" he sighed, and with a flick of impatience he pushed the paper away. The far edge lifted into the air and the sheet became airborne. Like a leaf with no aerodynamic planes, it floated haphazardly to a graceful landing under the table. Molloy stared at the paper for a few moments before sauntering the length of the sitting-room to the kitchen door at the far end of the couch.

The furniture in the kitchen was as sparse as in the rest of the house. A round table and three chairs stood under the hard plastic shade of the ceiling light bulb. He went over to the stove at the end wall of the house. After testing the kettle for water he switched on one of the electric rings.

The built-in cupboard to the right of the stove held all his crockery, flatware and food. Following a habit-formed routine, which had taken all of three days to shape, he took out a mug, a tea bag and a spoon. The sugar bowl was already on the table, had been in the same spot since the table and the other furniture had been delivered from the second-hand shop in Glin.

The kettle groaned briefly before settling down to the business of getting to a boil. While he waited, Molloy gazed through the curtain-less kitchen window. Wheat Mill Lane ended just outside the house, and weeds and grass had grown up in the last few feet of packed gravel.

With hands clasped behind back, he let his eyes drift across the lane to the distant greens of the Commons Golf Links. Half a mile away two golfers were approaching the tenth hole. One was wearing yellow trousers. Molloy thought of the telescope and the other stuff he had mailed to himself before he left New York. He pictured the boxes in the dark hold of some big ship ploughing the Atlantic, nobody in the world, besides himself, aware of their existence.

Beyond the golfers, the Van Gogh trees at Mrs Gilligan's house bent to the wind. As he gazed, Molloy heard the sounds of raucous crows and he thought of Maura Gilligan. With five dogs, she had appeared out of nowhere this morning as he was starting his bike. Molloy had not been prepared for her probing inquisitiveness. He had only escaped when he had pointedly told her for a second time that he had an appointment to keep.

Frank Molloy was a quarter of an inch short of six feet. His beard was short, and as white as the hair at the sides and back of his other-wise bald head. Much to his chagrin, his face was as red as the red face of the stereotypical Irish drunk. Wire frames held bi-focal lenses on a nose inclined to be bulbous. He had big hands and he wore size eleven shoes on his fifty-eight-year-old feet. He was not fat, nor was he thin.

Molloy let his eyes lose their focus on the golfer in yellow. As he stared, and saw nothing, his mind wandered to his brother, Gregory.

Why am I avoiding him?

Because facing you, Gregory, is going to be a pain in the ass. You'll be saying one thing and I'll be saying another, and neither of us will hear. I, the star from which you were the beneficiary of reflected glory, fell out of the sky, and landed in a pile of shit. Well, Gregory, I am here. I am alive and I am home.

Frank Molloy struck the window frame with his fist. The glass rattled. He strode out to the sitting-room, to the monkish table at the window. Pulling the pad toward him, he grabbed the pencil and, without sitting, he engraved his angry words, his angry face hot.

"I'm back in Ireland, Gregory. I'm living in what was the Duggan house on Wheat Mill Lane." He underlined "living" until the paper tore.

The kettle began to whistle, but Molloy didn't hear it, nor did he hear Haydn's violins playing against each other. He remained bent over his proclamation, anger pounding its way up the back of his neck. His chest rose and fell in tempo with the raging breath in his noisy nostrils. Then he thought of Padrake, and he wondered if she'd have approved of what he'd just written. He knew she wouldn't. And as he thought of her, his anger for Gregory lent itself to the rage he still felt for the man who had killed his wife. For a few moments the rage increased until the whistling of the boiling kettle finally intruded, its raucousness blowing the torment around in his head like a breeze moving fog around in a thick hedge. He lifted his head, and as his eyes glanced past the window he saw the golf players looking in the rough for a lost ball. He went back to the kitchen. He was getting the milk from the small refrigerator when there was the sound of gravel crunching under wheels on the lane.

Gregory? He doesn't even know I'm here. Shit! Not that woman again.

Abandoning the mug of steaming tea on the table, he strode across the kitchen with the milk carton in his hand. Before reaching the window he had his mind made up not to be polite to Maura Gilligan. He looked out.

It was not Gilligan's car.

Praise be to God for small parcels!

A young woman, tall, her tanned skin the most immediately noticeable thing about her in this island of pale-faced natives, stepped out of the car. She was wearing a white pants suit which immediately distinguished her as a non-resident of this land of drab women's clothes. She was elegant. She was beautiful. She was graceful. Beside Maura Gilligan's pile of steaming shit, she was a diamond scintillating in a thoughtful setting. The parts of the female body which draw men's eyes were not overstated, but they were certainly obvious.

Saint God!

As she left the car to approach the front door, Molloy turned from the window. After putting the milk on the table he rubbed the palms of both hands along the hairy sides of his head as he went to meet her.

Old goat!

When he was halfway across the sitting-room, wondering how such an exotic bird had come to land outside his house, he heard the knocking on the door.

Randy old goat!

By the expression on her face when she saw him, he knew the exotic bird had landed in the wrong place. Her jaw dropped in surprise or disappointment, or shock.

Old fool!

Her shoulder-length, dark and silken hair rippled with the movement of her head.

"Oh!" she exclaimed, bringing her hand to her face. "She's dead!" She covered her lips with her fingers.

"If you're talking about Miss Duggan, yes, she died a few months ago." The moment he had spoken, Molloy wondered if he had been too blunt. The woman's face was every bit as attractive as her body had been from a distance.

"Oh! God!" she gasped, as tears threatened to brim out over her lower eyelids. Before Molloy could react, she said in a surprisingly calm voice, "It's just the shock. I wasn't expecting her… I'm not related to her." She dabbed the spilled water off her cheeks with a sky-blue handkerchief.

"Come in," Frank Molloy invited, and without hesitation the woman stepped into the house. She was wearing white sandals. Even her feet were brown. In her left hand was a small gift-wrapped package.

Chapter 3

Wednesday in the Fifth Week of Lent – 12.30 p.m.

BY THE TIME he gave the last blessing of the midday mass, Father Keegan had had enough of rituals for one day, rituals which brought him into close proximity with dirty bodies giving off unpleasant smells. It wasn't that the priest had to have blue water in his toilet bowl before he could have a bowel movement, or that he had to use a cloth to grasp the knob of the bathroom door. It was just that the odours which wafted off human bodies repelled him. He was repulsed by the feel of the plugged pores and dirt-filled wrinkles under his hands when he blessed, anointed, communicated, wedded and absolved. Above all, he was repelled by the primeval smells rising from the beds of the sick and the old and the dying.

Father Keegan had rated the housebound parishioners. At the top of a very steep graph line, in his clean, airy and geranium-scented bedroom was the well-groomed and washed Kevin Bannon. At the bottom of the graph line was Ken Considine, whose boudoir had not had a change of air since it first became a sick room, and in which dwelt a never-empty, florally decorated, porcelain chamber pot. To keep himself ahead of an avalanche of overwhelment, Keegan divided the home visitations into groups, each of which contained two of the best and two of the worst habitations. This morning, after the early mass and before his breakfast, he had sat beside Considine's reeking bed, the mattress a fifty-year-old filter saturated with the residue of forceful farts, the sheets grey from age and lack of detergent. Once again he had heard the insanely scrupulous scratchings as the penitent tried to resurrect the death of Tony Donaghue, even though Keegan, as his confessor, had forbidden the former policeman to ever mention it again. When he had given absolution to sins too venial to have been confessed by a nun, Keegan had stood away from the bed and stretched his arm to its limits as he communicated the old galloot. Considine, who was not so old at all, was dying because he didn't want to live. He didn't want to live because he believed he had been cursed by God. The air never felt as sweet as when the priest stepped out of Considine's house.

Now, as he picked up the covered chalice, Keegan realised he was experiencing a vague and unidentified feeling of relief. But before he had stepped off the praedellum, he had pinpointed the source of his relief; Ken Considine had looked so bad this morning that the priest had called Pain-in-the-arse O'Leary, MD, and told him Considine was very weak. It looked like the policeman's long struggle to die would soon pay off.

As he reached the middle step in his descent to the sanctuary floor, Keegan's eyes swept the people in the church like a watchtower beam sweeping a barbed-wire perimeter. Like a moth to flame, his eyes were drawn to the Molloys, Elisabeth and Gregory. But he only saw Gregory because of his nearness to his wife. Elisabeth Molloy was the priest's aesthetic joy and delight. Keegan's ordering of the people in the parish according to their cleanliness put Elisabeth Molloy in a category of her own. From his worshipful position Keegan conferred on this idealised woman qualities to which she had no entitlement. He could no more fantasise making love to her than he could imagine himself in bed with the Virgin Mary.

Like a flat stone hitting still pond-water, his pleased eyes bounced off Elisabeth Molloy, and then glanced off the repulsive face of Maura Gilligan.

What's she doing here again? I hope to God she hasn't found Jesus.

When his foot touched the terrazzo floor at the bottom of the altar steps, Father Keegan swiveled back to the altar on the ball of his right foot. He had been making this particular move since the day of his first mass because, many years before it had become a forgotten habit, this was one of the minutiae which had attracted him to the priesthood. The Father Kelly of his youth had always swiveled this way, and the boy, Eddie Keegan, had seen the chasuble swinging out from the body of his childhood idol, like the gown of a graceful, distant and mysterious dancer.

While he waited for the altar boys to stand and find their equilibrium before he genuflected with them, Keegan's gracefully moving chasuble found its own peace with gravity. It hung from his shoulders with the deathly stillness of a forgotten battle banner hanging in the dark corner of an English cathedral.

Following the priest's lead, the altar boys genuflected and the Clarke boy lost his balance again, had to put his hand to the floor to keep himself from toppling over. Father Keegan waited until the boys had lined up in two rows and, as he followed them to the sacristy, he was reminded, as he always was when he was paying attention to what he was about, of Santa Claus driving his double lines of reindeer across the sky on Christmas Eve.

Around the corner of the high altar the lines of boys wound and, as if a hidden switch had been tripped, the sacristy door in the back wall of the sanctuary opened in front of them. As Father Keegan passed through the opening, the nun-sacristan, who was standing behind the door with her hand on the brass knob, bowed her head to the celebrant. While the priest acknowledged the nun with a sideward nod, the thought floated through his mind that in a few minutes she would be putting the Clarke boy through his paces until he could genuflect without falling.

While the boys, like the well-trained circus animals they were, merged into one line in front of the vesting bench, the nun silently slid across the floor behind them. With their hands joined at their breasts, they waited and watched. Together, priest and boys bowed to the crucifix above the wide bench. Then they all straightened, pirouetted and bowed to each other. The priest said, "Thank you, boys" while he was still bent over. The altar boys turned and shuffled into their own sacristy through the nun-held door. They immediately burst into chatter like a flock of birds warmed by the rising sun.

Father Keegan slipped his upper limbs into automatic gear. His fingers, hands and arms removed the sacred vestments while his mind drifted off as languorously as a gas-filled balloon floating with a summer's breeze. A plate of bacon and eggs drifted past and stirred his saliva.

From the earlier mass, Dervla Donaghue's face floated into focus, her eyes closed in pleasure as she received her Lord into her body, and the priest remembered how his finger had touched her lower lip when he gave her communion. A genetically inherited feeling sparkled its way around a coil of nerves in the pit of his stomach, but the priest shut down the source of the energy with the decisiveness of the snapping jaws of a steel animal trap.

Father Keegan's attention to his duty returned as his fingers were undoing the knot on the long strings of the amice. He flipped the rectangle of blessed linen over his head, folded and tied it into the shape of a rolled-up scroll with its own strings. When he leaned forward to place the amice in its pigeon-hole he became aware that someone else was in the sacristy. His blood boiled.

Although Father Keegan wore his cassock under the liturgical clothing, and wore his trousers under the cassock, his sense of decorum demanded privacy when he was denuding himself of the vestments. For someone to see him in the process of vesting or divesting was to him the same as being seen in his underwear.

The fact that the amice was the last piece of the liturgical dress to be removed did not mitigate his embarrassment, because it was possible the intruder had been present for some time; had probably been there when his alb was up around his shoulders, his rear end exposed like the derriere of an undressing woman with the hem of her dress up around her shoulders; the intruder had probably been there when the widow, Dervla Donaghue, had been in his mind.

Trying to control the anger which he knew was visible on his face, the priest turned to confront the interloper, knowing that the identity of the Peeping Tom would either dampen or inflame his anger.

His anger flared when he turned around.

It was Mrs Gilligan, she of the grasping lips and loose dentures. She was standing inside the door which opened onto the sanctuary, her decrepit hat at a ridiculous angle, her eyes glittering with eagerness in her rubicund face, a scuffed leather bag in her red hands, her sagging breasts looking like half-filled sacks of oats tied around her belly.

The moment their eyes met, Mrs Gilligan spoke. "Frank Molloy's home and he bought Bessie Duggan's house on Wheat Mill Lane, Father."

"Lay people are not allowed to come into the sacristy through that door!" Father Keegan flatly stated.

"I thought you might like to know, Father."

"Lay people should not even walk across the sanctuary."

"He moved in a few days ago, but I didn't know who it was till yesterday. He got furniture from Kelly's in Glin."

"When you leave, go out through that door there!" Father Keegan pointed to the door leading to the boys' sacristy. "The next time you want to talk to me, wait till I go back into the church." He spun around to the vesting bench, the blood pounding at his temples, the image of Gilligan's voracious tongue slurping around in his head.

"Yes, Father."

In his throbbing ears, the sound of her feet scraped across the floor. When he heard the door to the boys' sacristy opening, he glanced up. Gilligan's back was framed in the open doorway and, as she turned to pull the door after her, Keegan saw the wobbly Clarke boy ascending out of a genuflection, the nun-sacristan standing in front of him like a lion tamer. The priest looked back at his fiercely interlocked fingers resting in the pile of discarded vestments.

He knew it was Gilligan's tongue, as much as her unannounced intrusion, that was the cause of his anger. He had always seen her slobbering as a symbol of the viciousness of her gossip. But there was something else; Keegan was afraid of Maura Gilligan. He hated the woman. He hated her poisonous braying.

Father Keegan took a deep breath and disentangled his white knuckles. He had laboured for years under the fear that Gilligan would discover a chink in his armour and process it through her gossip machine.

Taking another deep breath, Keegan pushed himself away from the vesting bench. He went to the free-standing wooden coat rack near the entrance to the boys' sacristy. As he reached out for his overcoat, he heard what Gilligan had come to tell him. He paused in the act of taking his coat off its hook.

"Frank Molloy!" he said to himself. He was still distracted by Gilligan's appearance, and the name he repeated to himself was only a sound until he said it a second time. He suddenly shivered as if he had emerged from a summer surf into a brisk wind.

Thirty-four years ago, when Father Keegan had left his own town of Mullingar for Manchester, Frankie Molloy had been joyfully and triumphantly sent forth by his village as a newly ordained priest. With the pride of the people of Davinkill bearing him up, and their gifts of money bearing him down, the missionary had left his parents' farmhouse for the shores of southern England. With the glow of his first blessing shining in their eyes, the people had waved him away as their gift to the Society for the Propagation of the Faith. He was theirs, our

Father Frankie, their proxy saviour of souls in distant lands.

Frankie Molloy and Eddie Keegan had spent eleven years forging a friendship during their stays at boarding school in Winter Hill, and in the seminary in Carlow. But their relationship had begun to die within three years of ordination when Frankie came home to visit his family and had returned to England without seeing Keegan. Frankie had stopped writing, and rumours started coming back from across the Irish Sea and then from across the Atlantic; rumours of flight from England to America; rumours of abandonment of the priesthood; rumours of marriage outside the Church and unbaptised children; stories of failure at jobs and stories of many addresses lived at for brief periods. As a friend of the Molloy family, and as the priest recently appointed to Davinkill, Father Keegan knew the stories were not rumours. In a rudderless voyage Frankie Molloy had drifted from one mess to another.

Then one day Frank's brother, Gregory, had told Father Keegan that the Molloys would not be humiliated any further by the prodigal son – Frankie had been told he was cut off from the family. Father Keegan had lived in Davinkill long enough to know that the reason for the abandonment of Frankie was small-town pressure. As painful as it was to cut their son out of their lives, the Molloys' continued acceptance in the community was easier once it became known that they had suitably punished their wayward child. The relationship with the son-priest, which had reflected glory onto the Molloys and given them a special standing, was the very same relationship which was now bringing shame on them, and giving them a place in the village hierarchy reserved for the truly unfortunate, the unlucky, the near-lepers. After all, it wasn't just his family he had let down; he had thumbed his nose at all the people of Davinkill and at the generations which had preceded them for seven hundred years; the dead generations which had suffered at the hands of the Protestant English for holding onto the very faith Frankie had so shamelessly thrown to the wind. If their God was made in the image and likeness of the Catholics of Davinkill, Frankie Molloy would burn in hell for all eternity, a close neighbour of Elizabeth I.

Frankie's mother could not even surreptitiously write to her son, nor receive letters from him, because Mary Scully, the postmistress, read the address on every piece of mail going through the post office. But Mrs Molloy, up to the day she died, always had a fresh letter to Frankie in her handbag, just in case she unexpectedly found herself in another town.

As Father Keegan left the sacristy and headed back into the church to make his thanksgiving after mass, he decided he would visit Gregory and Elisabeth Molloy. They should be told this piece of news before their children brought it home from the school playground.

Chapter 4

Wednesday in the Fifth Week of Lent – 12.00 noon

WHEN THE YOUNG woman stepped into Frank Molloy's house, stepped in under the strains of the Haydn symphony gently tumbling out of the speakers, she stood inside the door and went through the shock routine all over again: the hand to the face, the gasp of "Oh! God!"

"I guess it's not like you remember it," Molloy said.

She turned to him: "You're an American!"

"I lived there for many years," Molloy replied, but the woman was looking around the room as if she wasn't listening. Molloy's eyes fell down along her body.

Good Christ!

"With the piano gone, it's not the same. She has to be dead with the piano gone. It was a part of the house. Lord! It's always a shock when someone..." Again the fingers went to the mouth and she turned to look into Molloy's face. "I'm sorry. I was expecting Miss Duggan to open the door, and when I saw you I knew she was dead. She used to teach me. I'm Mary Delaney. My family lives over in Gannonbeg."

"I don't think you got that tan or those clothes in Gannonbeg," Frank Molloy smiled. He held out his hand. "I'm Frank Molloy, the returned native."

Mary Delaney took his hand in a firm clasp. She smiled a mouthful of even, white teeth.

"I'm a returned native, too, but I'm only visiting. It looks like you're staying."

"That's the plan, but I'm not sure if anyone can ever go home again."

"Sounds like you've just read Thomas Hardy and Thomas Wolfe." Mary Delaney's blue eyes sparkled.

Frank Molloy didn't respond immediately, and he twisted his eyebrows into question marks.

"*Return of the Native, You Can't Go Home Again.*" Mary Delaney blushed as she realised she might be showing up her host's ignorance. Her face relaxed when Molloy responded.

"You must be either a teacher or a serious student."

"Neither," she laughed a laugh of relief. "I'm a musician with a lot of time on my hands. My music teacher introduced me to literature."

"Would you like a cup of tea?"

Mary Delaney waved off his offer with a flutter of the right hand. "Oh, I don't want to bother you. I'm on my way home from the airport, and I was only paying my respects to an old teacher." She held up the small package in her hand.

"You won't bother me," Frank Molloy declared. "As a matter of fact, I just made some tea for myself."

Mary Delaney accepted, and Molloy led her to the kitchen.

"Do you like Haydn?" she asked from behind, and again it took Molloy a moment to change his mental gears. Before he could answer, she had stopped at his disc collection and was speaking again. "The locals won't be crowding in to listen to this stuff. Copland and Haydn aren't well known in this neck of the woods." Then she saw his five books, read the titles aloud. "*Light in August. Ulysses. The Brothers Karamazov. Moby Dick. The Plague.* Anyone who has these must have a whole library hidden away someplace. Melville is a pain in the butt."

"Four or five pages of Melville in one day is enough for me," Molloy said.

"I ploughed through a hundred pages of it once. I got the feeling Melville was constipated. Another one who gave me the itch was the guy who wrote *The Scarlet Letter.* I only read about twenty pages, and I did that out of guilt. Miss Duggan gave me her copy the last time I was home. Maybe she knew she was going to die. Where's the rest of your books?"

"They're scattered around New York by now. I gave them away. Books make heavy baggage."

While they waited for the kettle to boil, Molloy learned that Mary Delaney was a cruise-ship musician who sailed out of Miami. The ship visited islands with saints' names in the Caribbean: Thomas, Martin, John, Vincent, George, Nicholas.

"So that explains the tan and the clothes." Molloy pushed the sugar bowl across the table.

The woman's blouse was open to a modest depth; no cleavage in sight. "And how do you explain Joyce and Faulkner and Mozart and Copland and the Haydns – Mike and Joe?" she asked.

"I used to teach literature in a small college in New York," Molloy responded, "and I picked up the musical taste somewhere along the road. I'm afraid when it comes to music I'll always be listening at the door; intellectually, the music is beyond me."

"It can be learned." Mary Delaney poured milk into her mug. Silence came upon them as she stirred the tea, the spoon touching the side of the mug rhythmically as if she were keeping time to music in her head. It was only then that Molloy noticed the subtle make-up. He also saw her tiny diamond earrings, the rings and bracelets for the first time. Molloy had never been good at noticing the props used to enhance appearances, unless the props were screaming.

"Miss Duggan died about two months ago," he said. "I heard she died alone."

"She would have!" Delaney put her spoon on the saucer. "She had no relations except for a vague nephew in South Africa; the explorer, as she sarcastically called him." The exotic bird put her elbows on the table and held the steaming cup near her chin. She sipped. "Miss Duggan was inclined to be garrulous. Most people thought she was a bit mad."

"Was she?"

"She was odd, but I don't think she was mad. She lived alone for most of her life. If you have no one to bounce your ideas off, to tell you that your behavior is a little off centre, you can end up being eccentric. I have an uncle living by himself and he repeats conversations he has with his horse." Mary Delaney smiled at Molloy. "His horse is very good at forecasting the weather." She raised her dark eyebrows.

Molloy smiled. "She told ghost stories – Miss Duggan?"

"Ha!" Mary Delaney put her cup on its saucer. "But she only told one. How did you know?"

Molloy made a vague gesture in the direction of Maura Gilligan's house across the golf links. "There's a neighbour. She suffers from a disease that activates her vocal box when she sees another human. I think the word 'labile' could be applied to her speech patterns."

Mary Delaney smiled. "It was the ghost story that made people think Miss Duggan was mad. She was obsessed with it. She told it to me before my first piano lesson, and she repeated it at least once a week for the next ten years. 'An unvaried pall of cloud muffled the whole expanse of sky from zenith to horizon, the moon a celestial ship, sailing in blinding flashes across the wind-torn vault.' It was all told in quaint language that was hard to understand. Every child she taught heard the story. She only told it to children because the older people wouldn't listen to her. It was about the Foley girl, the one who was murdered around here years ago. At least that's what we all believed, assumed, her story was about."

After his earlier encounter with the abrasive Maura Gilligan, Molloy felt he was basking in warm sunshine on the first spring day of the year. "Miss Duggan must have looked forward to seeing you when you came home," he said.

"I didn't visit her every time I came. To be honest, when you answered the door I was relieved as well as shocked. She was a difficult person, especially as she got older. Her brain had become stuck in a groove. The ghost story and something she was guilty about got all mixed up, or so it seemed. And she was so religious!" Delaney brought the flat of her hand down on the table in exasperation. "Everything was plastered with religion, like a slice of bread with too much butter. It became very difficult to listen to her. And you have listened enough to me." Delaney picked up the gift-wrapped box in her long, brown fingers. "Do you like macadamia nuts? They were for her. They're yours by default."

"Take them home to your mother."

"I'm afraid macadamia nuts would be too hard for my mother's teeth and too sophisticated for her tastes." Mary Delaney stood up. She ran her brown hands down her white front as if brushing away crumbs. "As well as that, they're coated with chocolate, and chocolate and Tonnerys don't mix."

Before he knew he had heard the name Tonnery, Frank Molloy's heart gave a twitch.

"Tonnery?" he said. "I thought your name was Delaney." Molloy took the mugs from the table and brought them to the sink.

"My mother was Mary Tonnery from Davinkill. She married Charlie Delaney from Gannonbeg. None of the Tonnerys can eat chocolate."

God of the Protestants! I once had my hand in your mother's knitted knickers. And she was wearing them at the time.

As he turned back from the sink, Molloy asked, "Do you find it difficult when you come home?"

Mary Delaney pushed the chair under the table. "How do you mean?" She flicked her head, and her silken hair fell into place like water finding its own level.

"Do you get impatient with people, with your family?"

"God, yes. The first thing I'll do when I get home – no I won't even wait till I get home. I'll stop the car and do it on the side of the Davinkill Road – I'll take off this make-up, and the ear-rings and the bracelets." She touched her right ear. "The hints and the winks and the nods and the outright jeering! You'd think I was a prostitute." Mary Delaney's eyes flashed. "You can see how pissed I get thinking about it. Excuse me! And it's not only the make-up and the jewellery. I never let an accent leak into my speech. And there's certain words. One time I said 'pregnant' in my mother's kitchen when some neighbours were over. After they left my mother said, We don't use that word – meaning pregnant. She couldn't even bring herself to say it. Of course sex doesn't exist in Ireland."

Frank Molloy smiled. "Maybe we should start a support group for returned exiles. There's a fear of the foreign and the exotic here. I've decided I'll have to get new clothes – Irish ones. Browns or navy blues. These are too stand-outish." He looked down at his red shirt and blue jeans. "You're welcome to use the bathroom to get rid of your make-up."

"Oh! That's thoughtful of you. Thanks." Mary Delaney put the macadamia nuts on the table. "These are yours."

Frank Molloy showed her into the bedroom. Mary Delaney glanced around at the barrenness and said nothing. Molloy opened the bathroom door and went out to the sitting-room to wait.

He was gazing at the angry note to his brother Gregory when she rejoined him. He couldn't see any difference in her appearance.

"At least the bathroom is the same," she said. "Thanks for your hospitality."

"You're welcome," Molloy responded. "Come in again if you're ever on the Davinkill Road. We can support each other against the slings and arrows of the local xenophobes."

"The outrageous xenophobes." Mary Delaney giggled as she stepped past Molloy who was holding the front door for her. He walked with her to the car and opened the door.

As she was about to get in, Delaney put her hand on the top of the car. "I'll write out Miss Duggan's ghost story and send it to you. It's part of the house and you should know it."

"I'd like that," Frank Molloy said. "Keep it to one page and I'll hang it in a frame inside the front door."

"Are you making fun of me?" Mary Delaney asked. Her face turned pink.

"No. Of course not. I'd like to find out the names of all the people who ever lived here, and something about them – what they worked at – things like that. Did they ever kill anyone, or steal a sheep. The ghost story will be how Miss Duggan is remembered. Maybe you could write down anything you know about her."

"All the crazy things? Like visiting the beech tree every Tuesday night to hear the ghost?"

"What ghost?" Molloy's voice was full of glee. "Is the house haunted?"

Mary Delaney waved his enthusiasm away with a limp flick of her wrist. "I think you'd like if it were." Then she turned her back on Molloy and pointed. "Do you see that tree out on the golf course near the Davinkill Road?" The sun suddenly slipped out from behind a small racing cloud. At the same time the two lookers brought up their right hands to shade their eyes. "Miss Duggan said she could hear the ghost of the Foley girl crying near the tree every Tuesday night." Still with her back to Molloy, Mary Delaney swung her pointing arm to the left of the tree. "Do you see a clump of bushes over there? Well, there used to be a little garden there. Her brothers planted flowers and took care of them for a while. That's where she was killed, and Miss Duggan claimed she could hear her ghost every Tuesday at a certain time – seventeen minutes to eleven."

"She was very precise – the ghost," Molloy observed.

As if on command the two of them lowered their shading hands at the same time. "So was Miss Duggan, and she was also convinced she could hear the cries of the Foley girl."

"Who killed her?" Molloy asked.

"The black man. That's the only name I ever heard for him. He was some guy who had come here from up the country to work – you know, he was black Irish. But he drowned himself in the river. I think it was the newspapers that called him the black man. But that all happened before I was born. It must be more than thirty years ago."

"You don't happen to know who owned the house before Miss Duggan?"

Her elbows on the top of the car, Mary Delaney turned to Frank Molloy. "No, I don't. But there's a man in Davinkill who would know – John O'Brien, the gravedigger. Everyone knows him. He's also the local knacker."

"John O'Brien," Molloy said. "I remember John O'Brien. He used to be a stonemason one time, but he had an accident."

"The same one." Delaney said, "He lost an eye and gave up the masonry years ago. Is this how you're going to spend your retirement – finding out who lived here before you?"

"Hopefully I'll have time to do other things. But yes. It's the kind of thing I like to do. I've always had a yen for anthropology. This is the closest I'll ever get to it. Where can I find John O'Brien if I wanted to run into him casually?"

"He's on the Irishtown Road, out past the CIE depot." Mary Delaney looked at her watch. "Oh, Lord! It's late." She got into the car.

If I were thirty years younger! Molloy gazed down at the sleek body behind the wheel.

Saint God of the fucking Protestants!

"Remember! If you're around this area, drop in and we'll psyche ourselves up against the hostilities of the natives."

Delaney glanced up at Molloy. "I have to psyche myself up all over again now. I had reverted to my Irishness on my way here to see Miss Duggan, but it slipped away while we were talking. Keep the faith!" She grinned up at Molloy, and before he could help himself he shot back, "A pox on the faith!"

Without hesitation, Mary Delaney retorted, "You've got that right! A pox on the faith!" and she started the engine.

The blood ran to Frank Molloy's face as he got the sinking feeling that by his comment on the faith he had exposed himself recklessly. Despite his discomfort, he saw the woman was blushing too.

It was with a mixture of relief and desire that he saw Mary Delaney wrap her fingers around the shift lever and slip the car into gear. He stood aside to give her room to turn – this daughter of Mary Tonnery who was allergic to chocolate. She waved as she drove away, Molloy's eyes following the car up the lane, and his mind drifting back forty-eight years.

The yellow buttercups swayed in the summer breeze, and ten-year-old Mary Tonnery was cart-wheeling down the hill in the Beech Tree Field that day after school. Her hand-me-down red dress was caught up at her waist. White and soft, like the pileus of a new mushroom, were the legs that stuck out of the red knitted knickers.

The boy, ten-year-old Frankie Molloy, sat up in the green grass at the top of the hill. He watched the girandole made by the spinning white legs and the wave of long red hair. Before she had climbed back up the hill he had worked out his plan.

As she approached him her red dress was blown back between her legs.

When she reached the top of the hill, Mary Tonnery raised her hands above her head. Frankie ran to her side.

"I'll go with you this time," he croaked, the wicked frog to the princess.

She smiled at him for a moment and then she was a blur of hair, legs and knickers. Frankie ran after her. He fell on top of Mary Tonnery and, as they rolled and tumbled, his inquisitive right hand forced its way into the red underwear. But he was too preoccupied with his falling down the hill to concentrate on what his hand was feeling. Then Mary Tonnery was running away from him.

"I'm going to tell your mother what you did!"

Frankie lay on his stomach in the cool grass. As he watched the racing girl disappearing over the hill he wondered what had come over him. His mother would kill him.

The brake lights on Mary Delaney's car lit up in the distance. Without using her indicator she turned right onto the Davinkill Road.

It was curiosity as much as it was pubescence. But her daughter's knickers are a different matter altogether.

Molloy went back into the house.

You silly old goat! And what would Padrake think?

Chapter 5

Wednesday in the Fifth Week of Lent – 12.30 p.m.

IT WAS OUT of his habit of knocking on other people's doors that Doctor O'Leary rapped his short, imperative knock on Ken Considine's front door. Before his hand had dropped back to his side, he turned the brown knob in the blistered and peeling green door. He used the toe of his shoe to push the rotting bottom inward along the concrete floor.

As always, when he stepped into the porch he felt his skin and hair soaking up the smoke from the turf fire. The sharpness of the smoke made him gasp the way a goldfish gasps when it's dropped back into its bowl after the water has been changed. As he closed the door behind him, he felt the sticky coating of soot on the inside knob. Before entering the kitchen on his left, he rubbed his palm on his blue worsted thigh and spoke loudly.

"It's the doctor!" O'Leary heard boots scraping on the kitchen floor as Ken Considine woke up and called his feet home. The doctor was surprised that his patient was not on his deathbed in his polluted lair.

Puta Keegan being an alarmist again.

The letters of the nickname stood for Poker-up-the-arse.

When O'Leary entered the kitchen, Considine was pulling himself into shape, wiping the drool off his chin with the back of his wrist. Considine performed his hurried preening in the manner of a proudly solitary person caught in the state of unkemptness by an unexpected intruder. In an attempt to reinforce his effort to appear alert and normal, Considine asked in a weak voice, "Is dachew, Con?" And immediately he tried to erase his mistake by saying too loudly in an ingratiatory tone, "Ah, it's yerself, Doctor O'Leary. D'eyesight's gonta hell. Pull over deh chair dare."

As O'Leary swung a battered bentwood chair into the middle of the floor, the patient continued his exhibition of normalcy. But his breathy words were only noise to distract the doctor. "I'd say 'twas Fadder

Keegan sencha. He was here ah a quarter t'ate, crack a dawn. Dare's a clockwork man for yah. I'd say his constachewshun runs like a ningin, too; goes to deh lav, I'd say, ah deh same time every day. Nottin' like been regaler, but din if sumtin' happens an yah can't go whin yah should go, yah geh as hardbound as a hatchin' turkey." The thin chest fell in on top of the deflated lungs, the patient wheezing for air with open mouth.

As Considine continued with his impressions of the sacerdotal scatology, O'Leary's haughty, forty-five-year-old eyes were starting their journey around the kitchen, beginning with the ruptured wickerwork in the seat of the chair he was about to sit on. He had been in this kitchen so many times before, had heard the same stories and the same bullshit so often, that he had devised a game to distract himself; he tried to detect whether there was anything different about the kitchen since the last time he'd been here.

Doctor O'Leary shied away from the shoring up of collapsing psychological structures with the same determination that he avoided conversations with drunks. But he did not discourage his patients from doing a little cerebral venting as long as he had control over its duration, and as long as no empathic grunts were expected of him. The doctor believed cerebral venting was as good in its own way as was the venting of the gastro-intestinal tract. In Considine's case the hearing of the one equalled the smelling of the other. O'Leary used one of the ventings as a diagnostic tool and endured the other, in small doses, in the interests of the patient's mental health.

With his sudden emergence from sleep, Considine's cerebral constipation was blocking his vents. Weakly he pointed to a cabinet backed to the wall on the far side of the kitchen. "Me mudder useta seh a turkey under dem shelfs, and she only leh ed ouh every second mornin'. Deh way deh scuhur ripped ouha her, deh sound of eh, deh pain of eh, ye'd feel relief yerself. All blocked up in hur, bu once she goh eh goin! God! It musta tore d'arse off hur! Every second mornin' ah ate. I tink turkeys have ta shite oftener nor a man."

O'Leary turned his plump, sun-tanned face away from Considine as he continued his boredom-defeating exploration of the hovel, but he had stored Considine's comparison of the avian and human excretory tracts for recall at some future social occasion. O'Leary's eyes glanced off the wide wall above the open fireplace, the wall blacker than coal.

The crane and the hanging kettle were adrip with sooty stalactites which had been polished to glossiness by the drops falling down the chimney when it rained. Above the blackened mantelpiece a framed picture of the Sacred Heart had faded behind the sooty glass. A few books lay where they had been carelessly thrown on the mantel, along with a sock and two small square tin cans. All were coated in grime, and nothing had been moved for the thirteen years O'Leary had been attending Considine. The doctor had wondered once, a long time ago, if Considine left the mantel untouched out of sentiment for his twenty-year-dead wife. Now he wondered if Considine knew there was a mantelpiece in the kitchen at all.

"Deh wife seh a turkey in dare once buh, a course deh luck was so aginst us be den, noh a negg hatched. Noh if she'd a sat on dem hurself would dey a hatched."

O'Leary let his eyes drift to the wall across from the fireplace. An open china cupboard sat atop the cabinet where Considine's mother and his wife had kept their brooding turkeys. The whole thing had fallen out of symmetry from age. The top shelf contained two willow pattern serving dishes, each with as many cracks as creases in a crone's face, each faded beyond redemption, because the sooty smoke had eaten into the potter's glaze. On the middle shelf were pieces of paper, hopes ripped from their envelopes and then, when disappointment was found, thrown with annoyance into a pile beneath the ever descending smoke. There were seven empty beer bottles on the bottom shelf.

To the left of the cabinet was a picture of two yellow-downed chicks, a blue ribbon around one's neck, a pink one around the other. It was only because he had been familiar with the chicks before the smoke got them that O'Leary knew their colours. One day, a long time ago, the picture had been casually slipped into the main narrative of Considine's cerebral venting. But since he had heard his patient's life story so many times, the doctor believed the picture's gradual addition was only another piece of moss added to a tale which had collected a lot of moss since it had first begun its downhill roll. Keeping pace with the ever-fattening story was Considine's own downhill slippage into debilitating self-loathing, his imagination feeding his increasing self-abasement by adding new horrors as his despair demanded.

O'Leary remembered precisely when the chicken picture had been inserted into the story. It was on one of Considine's fearful days, when he knew God's hand would spring out of the clouds, snap him up and dash him against the back wall of hell for all eternity. He had followed the doctor's gaze and the new piece of moss had been attached.

Mrs Considine had taken the picture off its nail and was cleaning the glass when she heard the shouting on the road that last day of her life. What she had heard was a man's voice calling for help, calling for someone to stop his cattle on the road outside the house. Considine's wife rushed out to give assistance, and she ran right onto one of the horns of Saint Willie Gorman's running bull. In paralytic terror, Considine's wife grabbed the other horn and kept herself impaled while the confused bull did his best to dislodge her by tossing his head.

Listening to the story, coated in a patina of self-pity and proud martyrdom, it sounded to O'Leary as if Considine was cleansing his soul by wallowing in horrific details, like a sow cleansing herself by wallowing in the mud.

Saint Willie Gorman's bull, unable to see and unable to get rid of the screaming weight on his horn, broke into an infuriated gallop which came to an end one second later when he fell into the deep ditch beside the road. The horn, ripping up and out of Considine's wife's stomach, was to her viscera what a boy's scooping stick is to frogspawn in weedy water in springtime. After stepping on her face several times, the bull ascended out of the ditch and charged down the road with a purple ribbon flapping from the horn. A day later Considine had discreetly placed the piece of purple guts, wrapped in a piece of butter paper, in the coffin, piously believing that all the corporeal pieces should rot in the same place in order to insure a more perfect body on the day of resurrection. Despite his diligence, Considine was not convinced of the wholeness of his wife's body. Because his luck was so atrocious, he worried that maybe one of her kidneys had not been noticed lying in the bottom of the ditch and that a hungry dog had found a feast which bloomed on its palate with a fine tang of faintly scented urine.

"Wance God took d'luck away dare was nuttin' ta be done. Ih was only natcheral deh bull gotter in d'end. D'only ting surprised me was ih twasn't me ouh dare swingin on deh horn. I deserved ih, buh she never did. Deh worst ting she ever did was fart in deh bed."

O'Leary was still gazing at the chicken picture when he realised

Considine had spoken, was digging up his wife again. But before the doctor could kick the shovel out of his hands, Considine said, "I gave her deh pitcher two weeks before deh chile was borned; blue an pink ribbons, just ta be on deh safe side. 'Twas all she kept when deh chile died. She burned everting else."

Even as Doctor O'Leary heard his own smothering words spraying toward Considine, the last thing which his patient had uttered was registering, and the doctor wondered if this new revelation was just another piece of the bullshit. And as his words splashed onto Considine and quenched his exhumatory enthusiasm, the doctor decided not to follow up on the matter with Considine. He would, instead, ask Puta Keegan about it.

As he fixed Considine with his paralysing professional eye, Doctor O'Leary asked, "Are you feeling bad, Ken?"

The sudden question whacked Considine's train of thought broadside, and it took him a moment to focus; he was still burying his daughter and wife. But before his brain had time to put its filters in place, he blurted out, "I'm in a black hole, Fadder-I-mean-Doctor."

"You've been drinking again, Ken," O'Leary said without accusation, and his head indicated the beer bottles on the cabinet, the only things which had changed position in the kitchen since the last time he'd been here.

"Just a few bohells of ale, Fadder, and I drunk dem whin I was in deh hole already. I mean Doctor." Considine's head rolled around on his shoulders like a ball on a circus-seal's nose. When it stopped lolling, his chin was resting on his chest. With tiredness and with self-induced despair he said, "If I'da gun I'd shoot meself."

O'Leary stirred uneasily on his ruptured rattan seat. He felt put upon, pissed off. But despite his discomfort, a part of his brain was interested in the situation just presented by Considine. He reasoned Considine was saying something other than that he wanted to die. From his visits to the precipices to which Considine had brought him in the past, only to pull back at the last moment when a revelation was about to be made, O'Leary already knew Considine wished he could change something which had happened a long time ago, a long time before Saint Willie Gorman's bull had paunched his wife. O'Leary suspected that they might, at this moment, be standing on one of those precipices again. There was excitement in the prospect of hearing an old secret which had festered for years in another man's chest.

As he looked at Considine, the doctor saw the same grey hair moving back off the forehead in slow, thick waves. It had not been combed in several days. The parchment-like skin of the face was more creased than wrinkled. It was the startling black eyebrows which gave the face any character it had, the black eyebrows and the terrible brown eyes. Considine had not shaved for a week and the grey stubble lent the vague air of a two-day-old cadaver. The once-white collarless shirt was dirty and open to the third button. With his hands in its pockets, Considine had his gabardine overcoat tightly wrapped around himself, one pocketed hand over the other at his crotch. Only a small part of his trousers was visible, and they could have been any colour once upon a time. The accumulation of years of grease, sweat, spit and snot had given them a waterproof, glossy sheen. The wellington boots came to the knees, green rubber smeared with streaks of old mud.

His lips shaped as if he had just kissed someone else's dead dog goodbye, Considine was staring at the knot in O'Leary's tie.

"Do you not think it's better to be alive than dead, Ken?" the doctor asked.

There was no response. Considine continued to stare at the doctor's tie. O'Leary silently cleared his throat in preparation for another question. But Considine saw the Adam's apple ascending behind the knot on the tie, and he said, "I did sumtin' with tree udder min wan time an I swore I'd never tell." He looked at the doctor's eyes. "I'll be dead in a day."

The doctor didn't think he would be able to hear about Considine and his friends fucking a sheep behind a hedge, or whatever the hell it was the four clodhoppers had done. Without flinching, he could scientifically explore every hole in Considine's body, but maintaining his precarious viewing position on the edge of Considine's soul demanded a different objectivity which the doctor wasn't sure he could muster.

For a long time they sat in the silent kitchen, the doctor wondering if he could keep himself from standing up and walking away. His sense of decency told him he was cheating, playing the role of priest, satisfying his own prurient inquisitiveness, gawking with upstretched neck while a long-buried shameful act was dug up.

"If I tell yah sumtin', will yah promise noh ta tell anywan else?"

Doctor O'Leary looked over his shoulder through the window. If he had been asked what he had seen through the dirty glass, he would not have been able to tell. The backward glance was born of a boyhood nervousness that someone would catch him masturbating in the shed behind his parents' house in Dublin. He knew he was playing with Considine.

"Yah muss promise, Fadder-Doctor. Yah muss swear."

The doctor's shining brown shoes moved on the filthy floor. Through his arse on the bentwood chair he felt where the ratten was ripped.

"I swear," he said, and there was something in his throat interfering with the words.

"Say, I swear ta God."

Like a boy being inducted into a secret gang, Peter O'Leary, MD, softly repeated the magic words which would open the locked door.

Immediately, like a suddenly released stream, words flowed out of Considine; about how four of them Guards had drowned Tony Donaghue in a sink in the barracks that night in Duneamon and how Considine had put his hand on Kelly's shoulder and jumped up and swung around and sat on Donaghue's head and Magee had said Donaghue would say he had killed Kit Foley if they half-drowned him and there was Magee and Considine and Kelly and Collins the four of them and Magee was the sergeant and Considine was the youngest Magee down on the ground holding Donaghue with his arms around his ankles and the other two with an arm each twisted up behind Donaghue's back Magee fell off his bike in Sligo two years after and split his skull in two and Kelly got shot in the chest hunting rabbits by himself when the gun went off getting through a gap in a hedge on a mountain in Wicklow and Collins drunk himself blind and then he died in a drain of water in Cork and that's why Considine was dying too they were all cursed cursed by God and they only wanted to make Donaghue say he did it and when he wouldn't and he drowned the four of them said he did Magee told them to and then Kelly, Collins and himself had thrown the body in the river.

When Considine finished he looked at the doctor as fiercely as his age and stamina would allow, defying the doctor not to believe him, defying him to run out and tell anyone what he had just heard. There was a pride in the way he glared at O'Leary, as if he was proud to be the one who had been chosen by God to suffer for his sin. It wasn't that

Donaghue was a victim; no, Considine was a victim-martyr.

Then as if someone had lobbed a bucketful of hot potatoes into his lap O'Leary jumped up. The bentwood chair fell over making an almost musical sound as the light, taut wood hit the concrete floor.

"Why did you tell me that?" O'Leary yelled. "That's something you should tell in confession."

"I told ih in confession," Considine said.

"Then why the hell did you tell me? I don't want to know this shit. What am I supposed to do with it! Why don't you tell the fucking Guards?"

"Fadder Keegan wouldn't leh me confess ih anymore, and I had ta tell sumwan before I die, just in case."

"Just in case what?" O'Leary shouted. He was aware that he was shouting at a dying man, but he didn't care; the bastard deserved to be shouted at.

"Just in case I didn't confess ih right."

"Oh! Fuck you, Considine! What am I supposed to do, now that I know whoever killed Kit Foley is still walking around?"

"Yah can't do anytin', because yah swore noh ta tell."

"But I *know*, you big fucking eejit! I'm a doctor, not a priest!" O'Leary roared. He grabbed his bag off the kitchen table and marched out the door.

Chapter 6

Wednesday in the Fifth Week of Lent – 1.30 a.m.

THE SQUARE chrome-and-glass clock on the marble mantle made a whirring sound, gathering its energy to strike the half hour. Father Keegan had been waiting for the sound since shortly after one. He was not wearing his glasses, and the clock's face, with its Roman numerals and two keyholes, was blurred. He heard the mechanism raising the hammer, and the click before it fell.

The people in the parish in Manchester had presented the clock to him thirty-two years ago. It chimed when the lady with the fat arms presented it to him, and she had said, "Bing! Bing Crosby." Everyone had laughed. They were almost all women; one or two men. It was always women who surrounded the young priest; son for the older ones; uncle for the youngest; safe fantasy for the ones in between.

The chiming of the clock should have wakened Father Keegan, feet on hassock, body spread out in black armchair. But he had not napped at all.

Since Maura Gilligan had made her announcement after the twelve o'clock mass, Frank Molloy had been on the priest's mind. Like mud at the bottom of the lake billowing into the clear water in the wake of a fast-departing pike, Gilligan's gossip had stirred up disturbing memories. Frankie Molloy had developed into a whirling dervish, dancing around the synapses of Keegan's brain.

Frankie, a closer friend than a brother could ever have been, had, once upon a time, left Davinkill as a newly ordained and enthusiastic priest. But he had ripped off his priesthood, had flung it back into the face of the Church. The people of the village had been further scandalised when Frankie moved in with a woman who wasn't even a Catholic, eventually marrying her without reference to the Church, and having children by her – bastards, as far as Davinkill was concerned. He might as well have shouted, "Stick the Church up your arse." Frankie's mother and his younger brother, Gregory, had been mortified.

With a jerk, Father Keegan sat up in the armchair. He joined his hands at his chest and pressed the tips of his fingers against his lips. Frankie's betrayal of the priesthood, Frankie standing there in Keegan's memory with a bunch of rejections hanging from his waist like a string of dripping scalps on the belt of a savage, was focusing a spotlight on Keegan himself.

Keegan knew, as surely as there are dregs in every bottle of wine, that deep in the soul of every priest there is doubt. And the apostatised priest would always be a threat to the one who remained loyal – the light of the apostate's certainties illuminating the hidden doubts of the loyalist. Over the years Father Keegan had kicked his misgivings under a rug of fear and shame, and there they were pressed into flatness by social and ecclesiastical pressure. With the doubts safely stowed away, there had been no reason to make a personal decision.

The priest shuddered in his chair as he recalled what had happened when Frankie decided to eat of the fruit of the tree of knowledge. The personal decision had resulted in a precipitous downward slide. As surely as the ceremony of ordination boosted a young man through many social layers and gave him instant entrée into a privileged world which could be retained with ease by taking a daily shower and giving obeisance where it was politically correct to do so, so could the act of apostasy fling a man out of the orbits which had become familiar – orbits in which he had brilliantly shone – and plunge him into a void that was not only friendless, but genteelly hostile as well.

Oh, Christ. And the way Keegan had turned away from his friend. He had been dumb, stupid and weak for letting Frankie slip away without making any effort to help him get on his financial feet, without a word of encouragement lest through the communication there would be contamination. Keegan had been so self-righteous then, had been the good, orthodox priest.

This kind of thinking was like pulling back a flap of skin and seeing beneath a living mass of white maggots swarming in a pus-filled sore. God!

Father Keegan thrust himself out of the chair and, with the relief of a sleeper waking out of a galloping nightmare, he heard the housekeeper's gentle knock on the door announcing lunch. For a few moments he stood there letting Frank Molloy fade into the background of his brain. He went into the dining-room.

Father Keegan liked the idea of being seen as a vital part of the village. But he maintained a careful distance from the people, a distance he himself had measured off and jealously policed; only two people in Davinkill called him by his first name.

Despite this remoteness, at any time of any day the priest could make a respectable guess as to the whereabouts of most people in the parish. So it wasn't until three o'clock, when he knew dinner would be over and work resumed, that he left the presbytery to go out to Roongarry to visit Gregory and Elisabeth Molloy.

Before leaving by the back door to get his car, he told the plump and widowed Mrs Westman where he was going. He did not know if the housekeeper had heard the Gilligan gossip yet, but even if she had, and saw a connection between the gossip and Father Keegan's visit to Molloy's brother, she did not give any indication by tone of voice or lift of eyebrow. The cleric had long ago trained her not to comment on parish business, either verbally or bodily. But no matter how well she minded her own business, Keegan still feared she might be a peephole into his house. Consequently, he never said anything, never did anything, never left anything lying around which could be the basis of gossip.

By the calendar it was the last day of March, and by the weather it was a March day when Father Keegan stepped into the backyard. The priest loved the blustery weather, when wild wind whacked without warning from any direction. He loved the argumentative cawing of the crows in the dead elm trees on the far side of the orchard wall, their nest-building instincts on full alert after a week of balmy weather. Another blustery day like this might cool their ardour, but there would be no cooling of the blood now that it had started coursing to the imperatives of spring. Down the familiar yard he walked, a defiant and glaring crow hopping ahead of him, its dull beak full of hard twigs and small sticks. From an avian architectural point of view, he thought, the crows are primitives, their nests no more than heaps of sticks.

Father Keegan walked through the doorless archway into the barn where he kept his car. Despite the Irish setter's attention-getting whimpers coming out of the shadows, the priest's eyes skipped from the roof of his car up to the rafters. Even before he saw them, he knew they were back. He could hear them chirping.

Damned sparrows!

Every year they built their nests on what used to be the floor of the hayloft in the days of horses. Now the floor was rotting and full of holes. Until the young birds were kicked out of the nests, the roof of his car would be the sparrows' dung heap. Every time he pulled the plastic sheet off the roof of the French car, Father Keegan fantasised about firing a blast from his shotgun into the floor above. But he knew he would do more damage than good. And there was a pair of shoes up there somewhere among the sparrows' nests. Kit Foley was in his head again; Kit Foley and Tony Donaghue. To divert the unwelcome visitation from what was buried in his conscience, Keegan used more energy than was necessary to throw the sheet of spotted plastic aside. He inspected the paintwork. Although it was clean, he took a rag and rubbed it around the polished metal, his hand and the rag dimly reflected in the blue paint. He wiped the area around the door handle, and when he threw the rag back to its hole in the wall, the dog's whimpering became more urgent. The hopeful tail thumped the side of its wooden-barrel doghouse. Keegan went to his dog and gave it the comfort it sought, scratching it between the ears until its elevated rear leg trembled uncontrollably with pleasure.

As he walked back to the car he heard the contented dog patting down its bed of straw with its paws in the dark.

Around the familiar holes in the backyard the priest drove to the archway in the presbytery wall. At the usual place he took his foot off the accelerator, and without benefit of brakes the car came to a stop at the near side of the footpath. Delicately, he touched the accelerator and the nose inched out, the driver's vision limited to what could be seen straight ahead.

As he slipped out of the archway Father Keegan looked to his right and was slightly startled to see two wide-eyed faces a few feet away from his own. Two of the younger Culliton scallywags, one of them with a dried streak going from his left nostril to his left ear, were gaping at him. Each had a schoolbag strapped to his back. Their outer coats had been pulled on with such roughness that the turned-in collars, the bunched-up armpits and the twisted sleeves gave the priest the itch.

One of the boys blurted out a stream of words that sounded like, "Mister Kelly punched Mister Fayne in the eye and there was blood all over the place this morning Father." The boy had last night's crud stuck to his eyelashes, his hair a nest of bent spikes.

Father Keegan stopped the car. "What did you say?" he asked, not because he hadn't heard the child, but to give himself time to react appropriately to what he had heard. Kelly and Fayne were teachers in the boys' school. Fayne was the principal. By virtue of being the priest, Father Keegan was the manager of both the boys' school and the convent school. As manager he was Fayne's boss.

The boy who had not spoken touched his brother with his elbow. They looked at each other and fled, blurs of legs and feet and flapping coats, their schoolbags jumping up and down on their shoulders. Father Keegan opened his mouth to call after them, but before any words came out he changed his mind.

The stories boys tell are so exaggerated the kernel of truth is often hard to find.

Wondering if it was going to be necessary to face up to Fayne again, the priest took his foot off the clutch and edged out onto Pearse Street. He turned left. Thoughts of Fayne were pinpricks of anxiety in his brain.

The footpaths on either side of the street were dotted with schoolchildren on their way home. After years of growing cynical by constant, intimate exposure to the human condition, the one thing which still diverted Father Keegan was children. Their innocence, no matter how distasteful their behaviour, had an eternal appeal. Their name-calling had a freshness which outweighed the evil intent. And their wild stories had more of their own fears in them than they had facts.

Some of the children recognised his car. They waved to him, the boys bringing their hands to their foreheads in military-type salutes. The nuns in the convent school, from whom all the children of the town received their first religious lessons, interpreted the catechismal exhortation literally where it said that, out of respect, priests should be saluted. The girls who saw him bowed their heads.

Here I am, the privileged one, acknowledging the cheers of my subjects!

When he came to Connor's Corner, where the village's two major roads intersected, he stopped and waited for a straggling line of boys to cross. Connor's Corner was a windy place on the best of days, and the boys were as scraggly looking as the windswept crows in his backyard. A chill swept over the priest and he started to close his window. As the glass slid up he heard a shrill defensive voice: "It was Fayne who was bleeding!"

The priest looked up, but the shouter was part of the crowd. The moving line of children was a clothesline of overcoats and caps.

Maybe there's something to what the cruddy Culliton child said. Damn that stupid Fayne! All meetings with him are confrontations.

A break appeared in the line of boys, and the school manager drove across the intersection onto Downs Road.

Bill Fayne's a fool, and Michael Kelly's a lunatic.

In the priest's mind, the more evident it became that Fayne was a total ass, the more prominent the teacher's buck teeth became, and thicker grew the lenses in his eyeglasses.

How could the Department appoint such a complete donkey to be a principal! On paper he was good. If only someone had bothered to meet him for half a minute before he was appointed.

Fayne had all the social graces of a hungry bullock at a manger. He didn't know how to teach. Just a few weeks ago he had cut the pages out of two geometry textbooks to show that two triangles were identical. Placing one page on top of the other, he had held them up to the window so the students could see how the triangles fit each other perfectly. One of the mutilated text books belonged to the son of Tim Bergin, the bank manager and one of Keegan's golfing partners. Bergin hadn't been nearly as concerned for the mutilation of the textbook, for which he had paid, as he was about Fayne's method of proving the equality of areas hemmed in by lines of the same length. When Father Keegan had approached Fayne with Bergin's complaint, the meeting had quickly degenerated into a contest to see who could show the most contempt for the other without seeming to get personal.

The other teacher, Michael Kelly, was a highly strung man, and Keegan had his own theories as to why Kelly was forever teetering on the edge of a stumble into nervous collapse.

For one thing there was his wife with her heavy make-up and dyed hair. She only spoke to those who were equal to or above her in social standing. The priest suspected that Mrs Kelly spent more money on clothes and make-up than her husband's salary could cover.

Then there were the four daughters with their exotic names: Dympna, Georgina, Griselda, Cynthia. Their beautifully developed teenage bodies were a source of spite to every other female in the village, and their father was suspicious of every male capable of an erection.

Lastly, there was the fact that Kelly had Fayne for a boss.

As Father Keegan's imagination lingered on the bodies of the Kelly girls, his mind created perfection, beauty and mystery which only an inexperienced imagination could conjure up. If he had been told it, he would not have known where the humour was in the story about the blind man tipping his hat as he passed the fish shop and saying, "Good morning, ladies."

Saint Willie Gorman's tractor came roaring over the crest of the small hill at Cullen's shop. Blue smoke screamed out of the tall exhaust pipe, and the sound and the fury surrounding the tractor gave the impression of great speed. Saint Willie Gorman was sitting hunched in the seat, the empty manure spreader behind the tractor so thickly coated with dried dung, it was difficult to tell it had once been red. When he saw the priest's car, Saint Willie Gorman raised his hat and his tractor swayed dangerously across the road. Father Keegan returned the greeting in a rather diluted form by raising two fingers off the steering wheel. And then Saint Willie Gorman was disappearing in his polluting cloud of noise and smoke.

The female Kelly bodies reappeared and drove Saint Willie Gorman out of Father Keegan's head, but they were rudely evicted when a car horn shrieked at him with such ferocity that, for a moment, he thought he was crashing. His feet and sweat glands were reacting simultaneously when he saw the sucker Gilligan's muck-covered car waiting to pull out of the Davinkill Road. It was obvious from her smile and her waving hand that she had only blown the horn to get his attention.

As his heart raced and his pores itched, Father Keegan mildly returned her wave.

You'd swear there was a plenary indulgence awarded for greeting the priest. And she wasn't interested in waving to me. She was just letting me know she has seen me acting on her gossip. She assumes she knows where I'm going. When that woman dies, I'll be as relieved as when the Duggan woman died. But there will be someone waiting to step forward as the most annoying person in the parish.

Is it me or them? I hope to God it's not me. The dirt of her car! Golfing images flickered into the sacerdotal brain as he passed Maybridge Road. The only thing which controlled his passion for golf was his fear of people talking about the amount of time he spent playing the game. A second set of clubs was always in the boot of the car just in case the opportunity for a round arose when he was away from the parish. The furthest extreme to which he had allowed his obsession to push him was the time he had pulled into a golf club when in fact he should have kept going to attend the funeral of an old priest at the far end of the diocese. Despite his efforts to keep her at bay, Kit Foley fled across his mind; she was lying on the golf links' grass, and his feet were weighted in lead boots as he trudged his way to her.

Roongarry Road surprised him with its sudden appearance, and the tyres protested when he made the hasty turn to the left.

The car took up the width of the narrow road. In second gear, the priest drove his car carefully around the bends between the leafless hedges. On the country lanes he was fearful of an animal charging over a hedge into the side of his car, or a tractor careening around a corner. Past the crumbling ruins of a long-deserted cottage he carefully drove, the stumps of yellow mud walls, like rotting teeth, almost obscured by the stalks of last year's nettles.

Gregory Molloy's house was at the end of the lane, the farmyard and the stables surrounded by a ten-foot wall. Father Keegan brought his car to a stop just beyond the solid green gates. The sharp March wind whipped at him when he stepped out onto the lane. He pulled at the collar of his overcoat and tugged his hat down on his forehead.

When Keegan went through the wicket door, Gregory Molloy had just stepped out of his kitchen into the paved yard. He was dressed for town, car keys in his hand. When he looked up at the noise of the closing wicket door, his jaw dropped, and he said, "Eddie! I was just on my way to talk to you. Frankie's home."

Chapter 7

Wednesday in the Fifth Week of Lent – 3.00 p.m.

"FRANKIE'S HOME."

Father Keegan suspected that Gregory's casual tone was a glint of steely sunlight reflected off a tiny disturbance in calm water moments before a barnacle-coated and enraged whale erupts through the surface.

"That's why I came out to see you. Mrs Gilligan spoke to me this morning," Keegan said as he walked toward Gregory.

"I saw her last night, and I never saw her walking her dogs down this way before," Gregory replied. "She loves other people's misfortunes. Come in and have a cup of tea."

Keenly aware of his own limitations in the face of his parishioner's expectations of supportive advice, Father Keegan, without enthusiasm, followed Molloy to the kitchen door. Although the Molloys considered the priest a friend of the family, Keegan, as he did with all the people in Davinkill, kept the Molloys at arm's length. He allowed for the use of his first name by Gregory and Elisabeth only because of his past friendship with Frankie.

Keegan loved the Molloy house; it was a welcome change from the coal-smoke-smelling, dirty-dished, filthy-floored, laundry-strewn, snotty-child-crowded houses of the parish. It was only his guilt at feeling superior which stopped him from naming most of the people of Davinkill as boors.

Even though he had been in the kitchen many times, the priest was once more impressed when he stepped through the door on the heels of his wealthiest parishioner. Maybe it was the fact that there was no other house like it in the parish which impressed the priest; maybe it was that the house bespoke wealth in a country where wealth is never displayed, lest an avalanche of ever-lurking, poorer relatives and voracious, hydra-headed, charitable organisations descend like a swarm of blue-bottles on a piece of decaying meat.

In the kitchen's west and north walls several small-paned windows, set in wide cherry-wood frames, threw sparkling light onto the cherry-wood cabinets. In the synthetic marble counter-top, contoured to the windowed walls, a swan-necked faucet hung over the off-white double sink. Amid the cherry-wood cabinets beneath the counter-top, were the garbage disposer, dishwasher and trash compactor. The six-flamed gas stove was adjacent to the full-sized, double-doored refrigerator with its external ice-dispensing mechanism. Beyond the refrigerator a combined toaster oven and microwave cooker was attached to the wall.

It's Gregory's wealth, his success, that makes him a target. The ridicule his mother had endured when Frankie was withering away in his whirlwind of disgrace in America, she worrying about her child while everyone got their kick in. It was a field day for the ones who hate success in anyone else, themselves still at the same financial and social levels of their own grandparents. The air was thick with the jeer.

Copper-bottomed pots and pans, strainers and colanders, and an array of kitchen utensils hung from beams in the ceiling near the cooking area. A large table with six chairs did not overcrowd the kitchen floor. In the centre of the table an arrangement of dried flowers in a Waterford Crystal basket was reflected in the table top.

The jeer will be on the march again, already is. Maura Gilligan is like an ass with a bunch of stinging nettles stuck under its tail, braying the news of Frankie's return all over the country, digging up a long-buried corpse and throwing it in the street. Everyone will get another kick in, and the gossips will crow like roosters.

Two couches in solid blue upholstery sat snugly against the wall across from the work area. A small-flowered pattern on the light-blue wallpaper gave the kitchen the air of a high-spirited summer day. The lines of brown caulking between the off-white Italian floor-tiles ran to elusional convergence at the far end of the kitchen. There were several hanging plants.

When the two men entered, the Molloys' new au pair, working at the computer in a corner alcove, looked up and smiled. While Molloy introduced the blushing girl as Claudine Duchosal from Charrot in Switzerland, something in her face – the contour of the jaw, the slope of the nose, the shape of the mouth, he didn't know what it was – leaped into Father Keegan's memory and furiously poked around, looking for a match. As the girl spoke to him in sprained English, Keegan examined her face for whatever it was that had set off the search in his head.

While the girl spoke, Gregory Molloy took Father Keegan's coat and hat, and hung them on the free-standing rack near the door.

Claudine Duchosal was wearing a black warm-up suit which hid the shape of her body. Her straight black hair fell to within an inch of her shoulders. The tip of her nose had an upward tilt, and the condition of her teeth allowed her to smile broadly. Because she was Swiss, Keegan supposed it was her exposure to fresh mountain air which had produced her glowing skin. She exuded a maturity beyond her seventeen years.

When Claudine had finished practising her English, Gregory asked her to make tea and bring it to the parlour.

The parlour was as expensively and as warmly appointed as the kitchen. Floor-length green drapes hung at the windows. Horses with over-long necks and sagging, inflated bellies galloped in framed prints around the papered walls. All the horses seemed to be laughing, and their big-bellied, red-coated, red-faced and top-hatted riders were all in danger of falling off. Brass lamps with green glass shades stood on the floor and end tables. There were enough couches and chairs to seat twenty people and yet the room was not over-furnished. Throw rugs spotted the polished floor.

Gregory Molloy led Father Keegan to the end of the room where four upholstered chairs surrounded a round, inlaid cocktail table. In the large room this was the place for intimacy.

Gregory indicated one of the chairs and said, "Elisabeth's gone for the children." He took the seat across the table from the priest.

Gregory Molloy was skinny, the way a long-distance runner is skinny. His black hair had lost its lustre, but there were no signs of a massive grey invasion. The wire-framed glasses, with their small lenses, gave him an intellectual appearance.

Gregory had spent eight years after graduation as a country veterinarian in Tipperary. There, with the help of a keen eye and a lot of luck, he had bought a thoroughbred foal which grew up to become the winner of the Grand National. Suddenly he had become the owner of the most valuable pair of testicles in the steeplechasing world. Now, here he was on the farm where his father had worked all his life, the old man always one step ahead of hunger. If his father came back from the dead he would not recognise the place from which he had extracted a subsistence at the cost of his every waking minute. The fifty acres were now three hundred and fifty acres. There wasn't a cow or a root crop on the farm. The old house and the farmyard were gone. Miles of hedges had been bulldozed and replaced with miles of white wood fences.

A circle of forty-five, state-of-the-art, always occupied box stalls was the source of Gregory's ever-increasing fortune. But as much as his wealth, it was how the people of the community viewed him that was important to Gregory Molloy. His father had judged his every public action against what he imagined the neighbours had thought and, in this respect, Gregory was his father's son. What he imagined the community was saying about him was his superego, more than his own conscience was. Had it not been for his wife, Gregory would still have been living in his parents' damp, low-ceilinged, small-roomed house. As sophisticated as he was in the business arena, parts of Gregory's personality still dwelt, only partially developed, in the dark corners of a childhood never totally relinquished.

Keegan was yanked into Gregory's reality when his host plunged into the subject which had brought the two of them together. "I never thought this day would come, Eddie." Molloy's fingers moved nervously against each other. After a short silence he gratefully invoked the deaths of his parents as their protection against the pain of knowledge.

Father Keegan put his elbows on the arms of the chair, put the tips of his joined index fingers against his lips. He knew the barnacle-maddened whale was about to shoot through the surface.

"I prayed he'd stay away," Gregory continued. "All the crap about Frankie leaving the priesthood is going to be flung around the town again like a load of shit off a dung spreader, and I'm the one the shit's going to hit. You know this town, Eddie. They love to see someone falling on his face. I prayed he'd stay away, let everything stay buried even if it was only buried close to the surface." Gregory sat forward on his chair, dropped his head down between his shoulders, his unseeing eyes staring at a past he futilely wished he could change.

After a long silence Keegan asked, "Don't you think there's a contradiction in there somewhere, Gregory?" But Molloy was worrying the past, biting his nails at it, cursing it. He made no response.

The priest continued. "If you accept the whole Gospel thing, you would be out greeting Frankie with open arms. Even if you'd never heard of the Gospel, don't you think you should be killing the fatted calf?"

Gregory looked away from the past, and gazed balefully at Keegan. "There's a hell of a difference between what I should be thinking and what I'm feeling."

"Frankie is your brother."

"He stopped being my brother a long time ago, Eddie, and you know that as well as I do." Gregory moved his fingers around his face, joined them at his belly, then put them back to his face. He suddenly stood up and blurted out, "Frankie died years ago as far as I'm concerned. That… that person who's come to live in Miss Duggan's house is not my brother. He's nothing but an embarrassment!" Gregory slammed his fist into the back of the chair he'd been sitting in. "Fuck him!" The expletive gnashed its way around the room like the attacking teeth of a trapped rat.

The prospect of dealing with Gregory's intransigence weighed Father Keegan down in his seat. It was only when he began to see himself as a conciliator between the brothers, and not as a priest of whom pious mutterings were required, that the debilitating effects of his worm-eaten faith began to dissipate. Suddenly he was free of the chair and his right hand was on Gregory's shoulder. "Come on, Gregory," he said. "Cut this out and get on with your life."

Gregory roughly shrugged off the priest's hand. When he swung around, anger was bristling on his face. His mouth was ugly, ready to spew bile, but before the first word was out, the sound of knocking came from the door at the far end of the parlour. Then the door swung in and Claudine Duchosal entered carrying a tray. Gregory motioned to Keegan to sit down, and when the priest had sunk back into the chair Gregory sat down too.

Claudine walked the length of the silent room, the colour in her face rising as she neared the two men. When she had placed the tray on the table she picked up the teapot, but Molloy thanked her and told her he would pour it himself. As if she knew she should be walking on eggs, Claudine left the room, her heels not touching the floor.

The kitchen door closed behind Claudine Duchosal before either man spoke, and then they spoke at once. Both stopped and Father Keegan said, "You go first." There was defiance in his voice, as if he were daring Gregory to come up with even the semblance of a reason why

Frankie was an embarrassment.

"I made Frankie promise me a long time ago he would never come back to Ireland."

Chapter 8

Wednesday in the Fifth Week of Lent – 3.30 p.m.

"YOU MADE FRANKIE promise never to come home again!" Father Keegan exclaimed. "You told me Frankie said he never wanted anything to do with Ireland again; that Ireland was Joyce's sow, forever eating her own farrow. And now you're telling me you made him *promise*?"

"I did it to protect my mother!" Gregory said angrily.

"To protect your mother you made her son promise you he'd never see her again?"

The accusation in Keegan's voice fanned the horseman's anger. He jumped to his feet and, from the glaze on his eyes and the mist of spittle at his mouth, it was clear he had lost control.

"Yes! That's why I told him never to come home again!" he shouted, and the ever-discreet Father Keegan knew that Claudine Duchosal could hear Gregory, no matter where she was in the house. "And then I told my mother she would never see him again. I told her that so she could get it over and done with, this grieving for Frankie which had been going on from the day he left the priesthood. What do you think it was like for her to be asked the innocent questions in the village – questions asked only to torment her with the latest dirt on Frankie? How do you think she felt when Maura Gilligan asked her if it was true that poor Frankie had left the priesthood, when all she could hear was the jeering in Gilligan's voice? 'And is it true that poor Frankie has shacked up with some floozy?' That's why I made Frankie promise never to come back. Because then it would be over as much as it could ever be over. Because then he'd be forgotten and she wouldn't have to listen to the likes of Gilligan. Because now his absence would take him out of their minds and they wouldn't gossip about him anymore, make jokes about him in the pubs. Frankie swore he would never come home. Never, he said. Well, now he's back and the whole thing has been reconstituted like a piece of dried horse shit in a shower. It's not Frankie who's going to be jeered at. It's me!" Gregory Molloy pointed to his chest with his thumb. "I'm the laughing-stock again. I'm the successful one they love to pull down. Frankie's my albatross. His failed life is now dragging me down. I am suffering for the sins of my brother, the brother who thought of no one, except himself." Gregory stopped for air. His anger had crested, and he stood there shaking in the wake of its release.

Father Keegan exhaled a long breath as if he had been sustaining himself against Gregory's outburst. He now found himself in a state of indecision, not knowing whether to express his anger at Gregory's titanic audacity or whether to invite a very insecure Gregory to extract himself from the centre of his own attention, so he could see the effect of Frankie's long exile on a lot of other people, including Frankie.

Keegan stepped over to the window on the far side of the room. He put his hand on the top of the lower sash and gazed out across the white-lined fields. The March wind slipped through the scattered, young-budded trees, leaving them motionless. After a few moments of staring he realised he should not pursue a line of attack at all; attacking decisions made in the past was not what was needed now. As well as that, who was he to attack? He was supposed to be the healer. Then he thought of Frankie being here in Davinkill, and he realised he was glad for the return of his one-time best friend.

Through the window he saw a flock of partridge gliding over a white fence to land in a nearby field. They remained motionless when they landed, all on the lookout. Then, as if on a signal, they all started foraging at once. He thought of his shotgun and his dog and the sound of wellington boots in barley stubble.

When Keegan turned away from the window Gregory was cleaning his glasses with a handkerchief. "Gregory," he said, "this is not a time for anger. Look beyond your embarrassment and see what has really happened. Your brother has come home."

"My brother's dead as far as I'm concerned, and that's the way he's going to stay." Still wiping his glasses, the short-sighted Gregory looked over at the priest.

"You can behave that way, Gregory, and you'll be ridiculed all the more. Or you can face the facts now and take the power away from all the Mrs Gilligans."

"Yes, I'll face the facts all right," Gregory replied with force. "Frankie is a self-centred little boy. There was money spent on Frankie when there was no money to spend. It was always Frankie! My father went into the bank to send him to Winter Hill, to keep him there for five years. And in every letter he wrote home, Frankie was looking for something. Send sweets, he'd write, as if we were sitting around at home doing nothing but eating sweets. Meanwhile, I was milking two cows every morning before riding my bike twelve miles to and from the Christian Brothers in Duneamon, and coming home to help on the farm every evening before I got to do my homework. Frankie's education was the only thing my father went into the bank for, and Frankie left the priesthood before the loan was even paid back. That was the great irony of the whole thing – going to the bank to pay off Frankie's loan and knowing he had thrown everything into the wind. It was like paying a doctor for a cure that didn't work while the corpse is rotting in the ground. My father never had two red pennies to rub together because of Frankie."

Father Keegan went back to his chair and sat down. He knew there was no use speaking till Gregory had spoken out his bile. He pushed his hands into the opposite sleeves of his jacket, an old habit from his days in the seminary, where the students were not allowed to put their hands in their pockets.

"He never lifted a finger to help us out. I never heard Frankie mention that loan. He never even said thanks, and we paying it off while he was wandering around America doing God-knows-what. In three years he had over thirty addresses from one side of America to the other. There were times when we didn't hear from him for months, my mother worrying herself to death about him, not knowing whether he was dead or alive, her friends asking how Frankie was doing, and she pretending she had just heard from him and that he was doing great. I saw her crying for him over there." Gregory Molloy waved his hand across the room.

Father Keegan let his eyes come to rest on the rocking chair where Mrs Molloy had spent the last years of her life. He remembered her in the rocker weeping for her lost son, weeping just to see him once before she died, Keegan the solicitous priest holding her hand and feeling self-righteous because he had stuck with the priesthood.

Gregory sat down in the chair he had already abandoned twice in anger. In an exhausted voice he said, "Frankie wrote to me about four months ago. I ignored the letter. Then he wrote a second time, about two months ago, and told me again he was coming home. I ignored that too." He wiped his face with his handkerchief, pushed his glasses up and wiped his eyes as if he'd been crying. "Elisabeth knew about the letters. She told me to take out an ad in *The Duneamon Times* and announce he was coming, take the wind out of their sails, welcome Frankie home. When I said no, she didn't interfere any further."

"Don't you think you should go to Frankie and…"

"No!" Molloy rose out of his exhaustion. "He let us all down, Eddie," he said. "It's too big a hurt, and he has no shame about it at all. It's going to be embarrassing all over again to go into the village, face all the people. It's worse than having an informer in your family. I'm going to put an advertisement in *The Duneamon Times* all right, only this one will say that as far as I'm concerned Frankie is dead." He picked up his cup and drank down its contents as if to fortify himself with a shot of whiskey.

Father Keegan's eyes fell away from Gregory's face. At the bottom of his cup he saw a few escaped tea-leaves leaking their fading colour into a trace of sugar and turning it sepia. Then, as if he were speaking to a small child holding its baby-brother's head under water, he said, "You know you can't do that, Gregory. You'll have to try something different."

"Yes. Someone will have to tell Frankie to go away and, if you don't mind me saying so, I think you're the one to tell him. He's a scandal to the whole town."

Another silence descended between the two men. A blast of March wind blustered against the windows and, despite the coziness of the room, a shiver shot up the priest's back like a cold spear of wind on a pond in summertime. Father Keegan put the cup on the table and pushed his hands into his sleeves again. He stared at the inlaid table without seeing the beauty of the marquetry. "I'm going to talk to Frankie," he said. "I won't tell him to leave. But, if you want me to, I'll tell him what you said."

"Yes, Eddie, tell him I said I wish he had died a long time ago."

"That's something you'll have to tell him yourself, Gregory."

Molloy put his cup on the saucer, and both men heard the door to the kitchen opening. Then there was the sound of children's voices. Father Keegan did not turn to look as footsteps came down the parlour toward him.

"Daddy! Where's Father Keegan? His car's outside and Claudine said he's in here." The girl came to the priest's chair and she only saw him as she finished speaking. She put her fingers to her mouth and blushed, her eyes glistening.

Father Keegan stood up. "Ann Marie! I think I gave you a fright," he said to the twelve-year-old with the long single braid hanging down her back to the waist.

"Yes, Father. I didn't see you, but I'm all right now." She went to her father and kissed him on the cheek.

Father Keegan liked the way the Molloy children spoke to him with the directness which they had learned from their mother. There was no trace of the bowing and scraping to which he was usually treated when approached.

The priest turned to the sound of other footsteps. Martha and Michael. Eight and seven.

The black-haired, bespectacled boy spoke, the words cascading out. "Mr Fayne punched Mr Kelly and there was blood all over the place."

Before anyone could react to this announcement, Elisabeth Molloy entered the room, a bundle of envelopes in her hand. She was eighteen years younger than her husband. In astuteness she was his equal, in common sense she was his superior. She wasn't beautiful, but she was good-looking without the help of any make-up. In comparison to most of the other women of the town, she was clean and healthy looking. Her shoulder-length, blonde hair had the permanent look of just having been shampooed. She was wearing a black trouser suit. Her shoes were low-heeled.

She greeted Father Keegan by shaking his hand, looking him straight in the eye and not blushing. "It's good to see you, Father," she said, using the formality for the children's benefit. Then she turned to her husband and said, "Prepare yourself for an announcement, Greg!"

"Daddy," Martha said, "we have an uncle, and he is home from America. He was a priest and he ran away with a woman. That's what Sisso Casey told Sister Eucharia."

"Why did he run away?" Michael asked.

"Sisso Casey told Sister Eucharia he ran away."

Gregory Molloy stood up, his eyes popping. He looked at Father Keegan. "This is exactly what…" he began, in a clenched-teeth tone of voice. But his wife cut him off. She sank to her knees in front of Martha and Michael.

"You do have an uncle," she said. "His name is Frank. Uncle Frank."

"Elisabeth!" Her husband snapped, but she ignored him.

"Uncle Frank is Daddy's brother, and he has been in America for many years. He was a priest a long time ago but he decided to stop being a priest. He got married and he has two daughters."

"Elisabeth!" Gregory Molloy snapped again.

Elisabeth Molloy continued as if she had not been interrupted. "Uncle Frank has come back to Ireland to live."

"Did he bring us anything from America?" Martha asked. "Brigid's aunt brought her a shirt with a picture of Mickey Mouse."

"Mister Kelly's nose is broken," Michael said. "There was blood all over the place."

"What's our cousins' names?" Ann Marie was smiling.

Elisabeth Molloy got to her feet. "Karen and Jeanne," she said, and she stroked Ann Marie's hair. "But they are much older than you. Now go to the kitchen, children, and we'll talk about this later. Daddy and I have to speak to Father Keegan for a minute. Claudine is making hot chocolate."

As soon as the kitchen door closed behind the children, Gregory Molloy snapped, "I don't think that was the way to handle this, Elisabeth!"

"Elisabeth did the correct thing," Father Keegan said. "The children already knew, Gregory. All Elisabeth did was take the gossip and the mystery out of it for them." Then, realising he had plunged in between husband and wife, he made a hasty retreat. "But I should not be speaking for Elisabeth."

For a moment there was silence. Gregory Molloy looked from the priest to his wife. "I hate the idea of the children thinking of Frankie as their uncle," he growled.

"That's what he is, Greg, their uncle," Elisabeth said. "There's no way to change that. And it looks like the uncle has written you a letter." She stretched her hand toward her husband, a white envelope between her fingers. "The return address is on it, like they do it in America, and there's no stamp. He must have come here to deliver it himself."

Gregory did not take the envelope from his wife. "You read it," he said.

Elisabeth Molloy tore the envelope open and took out a sheet of paper. She read aloud. "I'm back in Ireland, Gregory. I'm living – underlined – in the old Miss Duggan house on Wheat Mill Lane. Frank." The hand with the letter dropped to her side, and she looked at her husband. "That's it, Greg."

"It sounds like the shout of a defiant child," her husband said.

"It sounds like you're going to be angry at Frankie no matter what he does," Elisabeth said.

"Look at the letter as a handshake, Gregory," Father Keegan offered.

"How can I?"

There was silence in the room. Then: "Can you not think at all about how Frankie feels?" Keegan asked. "Do you think Frankie came home just to hurt you? Whatever his reason, do you think it has been easy for him?"

It was a long time before Gregory replied. As the silence dragged on Keegan feared he had blundered into an area of intimacy where he had no right to tread. When Gregory finally spoke the words drifted quietly to the floor like falling autumn leaves on a breathless, frosty morning.

"Eddie, you didn't see how my father and mother suffered on account of Frankie. It would have been easier if they'd stood in the cemetery and watched his coffin being lowered into a grave."

Father Keegan looked back to Elisabeth Molloy. "I'm going to leave now," he said. He started for the kitchen door. Elisabeth began to show him out, but he told her with a movement of his hand to stay with her husband.

When Keegan entered the kitchen the Molloy children were sitting at the table spooning their chocolate drinks out of steaming mugs. Claudine Duchosal from Charrot in Switzerland was standing at the stove. In strangled English she invited the priest to have a cup of hot chocolate. When he turned down her offer, the au pair went to the coat rack at the door. She handed him his coat and hat.

The children called their goodbyes and Claudine smiled in farewell. As he waved to her, Keegan's memory ended the search it had begun an hour ago.

Chapter 9

Wednesday in the Fifth Week of Lent – 4.05 p.m.

IT WAS CLAUDINE'S drooping eyelids in the crack of the closing door that brought the results of the memory-search gate-crashing into Keegan's already preoccupied mind.

As he turned to go to his car he saw himself approaching the almost-covered body lying out there on the flat expanse of the golf links in the white morning sun. In the slow movement of a paralysing dream he moved forward, knowing he would have to see the wound again when he uncovered her head to give the last rites a second time. He was so frightened and so exhausted he thought he would never pull it off, that he would fall apart and tell the sergeant everything. Slowly, laboriously, he raised his eyes from the bare feet sticking out from under the sergeant's overcoat, and under the big leafless tree, across the dew-glistening grass, his eyes came to rest on Miss Duggan's accusing eyes, she with her right hand desperately holding the tuft of handkerchief caught between her clenched teeth, keeping herself from sliding down into the grief which would cripple her mind for the rest of her life. Through the white sunshine and the wet grass he trudged forward, a man waist-deep in treacle, the music teacher's eyes unflinching, unforgiving, despairing. In the barely moving nightmare he knelt on one knee and lifted the black raincoat with the silver buttons at the epaulets, heaved the coat off the pale face in the grass, the half-closed eyes peering at nothing through the long hair which had fallen across them, the mouth partly open, the terrible wound in the side of the neck.

As if slowly coming out of a profound sleep, Father Keegan became aware that his arm was on the roof of his car pillowing his head. With a start, he straightened up and looked back to the wicket door in the wall of Gregory Molloy's yard. He glanced at his watch and then looked around again. But no one had seen him in his distracted state; all the Molloys were in the house and the nearest neighbour was a mile away. He sat into the car.

The remembered feelings of terror at being found out subsided as he drove away. Before he reached the first bend in the lane, he had forced Frankie to the forefront of his mind again. He realised that he grudgingly admired Gregory's success in submerging Frankie beneath the communal consciousness. Keegan had not heard Frankie Molloy's name mentioned in Davinkill in many years. In a small town the impossible had been achieved; even if the scandal had not slipped out of the town's collective memory, the story had slipped out of its consciousness. And then Father Keegan thought of Kevin Bannon.

As he drove back to the village along the narrow lane, the priest shook his head slowly at what he was remembering.

Two weeks after his arrival in Davinkill, Keegan had been told about Kevin Bannon by Kevin Bannon's mother. In one of those tricks of history, the kind of trick which had allowed ancient Egypt to die out of people's memories until Napoleon's engineers rediscovered it, Kevin Bannon had fallen out of the memory of the people of Davinkill. Outside the immediate Bannon family no one was aware of Kevin's existence. And being the expertly protective mother she had evolved into, Mrs Bannon had made Kevin's existence known to Keegan by naming her child as the target of uncharitableness while confessing her sins. Kevin was a confessional secret, and as such only Mrs Bannon could mention him outside the confession box. Before Keegan had slid the little door across the wire mesh, Mrs Bannon had made all the arrangements for the priest to take care of the spiritual needs of her child. A half-hour later, when Keegan stepped out of the confession box, she was waiting for him in the church. She also had a "weak-minded" daughter who never left the house, she told Keegan, and the daughter, too, would be in need of his ministrations.

The first time Keegan knocked on the cottage door, the diminutive Mrs Bannon, without a word of greeting, led the priest across the kitchen to the bedroom door. As he looked around he was surprised at how fresh the air smelled. Usually he found the atmosphere in sick rooms so thick with old breath and historic farts that words could be carved in it. The first thing he saw was the pot of red geraniums in the wide window sill across from the door. But then the hairs on Keegan's body moved as his eyes came to rest on a young woman kneeling near the bed. She was wearing a yellow dress with large red polka dots. She had a thin face – like a ferret, Keegan thought – and her hair was thin, long and damp. The tracks of a wide-toothed comb were visible on her skull.

Near her, a hairy man was kneeling at a backless chair. The man's beard was fierce, black, and defiant. Out of tiny eyes Kevin Bannon looked at the priest the way a cornered rat would watch for a terrier's next move. The hair on his head was black and cut at the shoulders. It, too, had been tamed with a wet comb, the tracks visible from the door where Keegan still stood.

As the shock drained away, the priest felt his anger for Mrs Bannon rising. She hadn't lied, but she had certainly misled him. Keegan swallowed his ire and went through the motions of what he had to do

As he approached them, the girl announced in a startlingly high pitch that they did not need confession. Without uttering a word outside the prescribed ritual, the priest administered the sacrament. He left Kevin and his sister kneeling as he had found them, only now their eyes were closed.

After the priest stepped back into the kitchen, Mrs Bannon pulled the door closed behind him. When she turned around the priest was waiting for her. "Mrs Bannon, I need your permission to speak to you about something which you made a matter of the confessional."

Mrs Bannon folded her arms across her chest. "You don't have my permission to talk about anything I said to you in confession, Father. But to stop you worrying about anyone's welfare I will tell you there was a boy, thirty-seven years ago, whose father was no good. The father took advantage of a woman who didn't want to be his wife. The sisters of the boy's mother threatened the boy when he said Dada for the first time. The child did not speak until he was five, and then the children in the school laughed at him. His mother kept him home from school, and whenever someone came to the house the boy ran into a room and hid under the bed. After a while the child wouldn't come out of the room during the day, and when he did come out at night the first thing he did was lock the front door. The child's mother took good care of him. The father died a few years later, and the mother and her other four children take care of the shy child. Thank you for coming, Father Keegan."

That was that! Once a month for the last thirty-two years Father

Keegan had brought the sacraments to Kevin Bannon, and the people in the village thought he was attending to the needs of Mrs Bannon's weak-minded daughter. Nobody had ever mentioned Kevin Bannon to him. Mrs Bannon was still alive and, by the looks of her, she was going to be alive for another few years. Kevin was bald now, his beard was white, and his sister had a hump. Besides that, nothing had changed, and Mrs Bannon and family had kept their secret in this town of no secrets.

Father Keegan carefully drove around a sharp corner in Roongarry Lane. He let the steering wheel spin itself back to its neutral position, and the car headed for the junction with Downs Road.

His mind went back to Gregory Molloy keeping Frankie at bay until Frankie decided to change the rules. Even under the pressure he must have felt when he saw his mother grieving for the son she would never see again, Gregory had not fallen apart.

Fallen apart! Keegan, too, had endured pressure without falling apart. But the remembrance, thirty years later, of the sergeant coming to the front door of the presbytery to ask him to administer the last rites to Kit Foley still made him sweat.

Again he evicted Kit Foley from his head. He forced himself to think of the silver lining in the cloud of Frankie's return. Keegan would have the opportunity, a second chance, to do the right thing by his old friend.

At the head of Roongarry Lane, Keegan became aware of a horn blowing. A truck sped redly across his eyes on Downs Road and he saw a waving arm at the driver's window.

The knacker!

The priest stirred in the seat of his car.

How long have I been sitting here? He looked at his watch and said, "Gosh!" He remembered he had to call on Bill Fayne to find out what the hell had happened in the school today. He turned right into Downs Road.

Chapter 10

Wednesday in the Fifth Week of Lent – 9.00 p.m.

ALL THE DRINKERS in FitzGibbon's pub had humps, all hunched over whatever their elbows were resting on. Along the bar and at narrow tables, they sat huddled together. Spittle and breath and cigarette ash drifted down to the surfaces of the pints and half-pints between the protective elbows.

All the men were dressed in suits, shirts and ties, each of which had been blue, white and blue in the earlier stages of their existence. Age, dirt and the grease of life now lent a metallic sheen to the clothing. Each man wore a cloth cap, the centre of each peak greasy and worn smooth from years of handling.

The half-dozen women in FitzGibbon's were big-breasted, big-toothed, big-armed, big-voiced and big-arsed. Their flowery dresses were buttoned to the throats. Their head-scarves, covered with palm-treed islands lapped by the white-crested waves of a blue sea, were knotted severely under big chins. Bubbly wine was their drink.

The women were in the pub to keep a grip on their family's purse strings.

Whenever the door opened, every head jerked up, like the heads of old roosting hens jerking at an unexpected sound. When the newcomer was recognised the heads went down again.

In FitzGibbon's pub few distinguishable words could be heard above the steady murmur, which sounded like a distant herd of bison running in a cowboy picture. Distinguishable words were only necessary when something new was being said. The bison herd had been running for several weeks now, as old news was repeated in mumbles and grunts.

Occasionally the body of one of the humped drinkers shook, and his face went from red to purple. While he appeared to be having a heart attack, the drinker was only laughing.

Loud farts, crackling like sharp rifle shots, could be heard frequently, but they evoked as little reaction as a cough. Occasionally an elbow-poke would be used to indicate acknowledgment for the stink level of a particular blow-out.

Belches, no matter their loudness or the size of their bile-smelling clouds, were not noticed at all.

The proprietor of the pub, Matty FitzGibbon, served all drinks and received all receipts. His clothes were old and worn like everyone else's. His face had the look of a child's after its mother has scrubbed it with a rough cloth, the child's squirming face trapped between parental thigh and cleaning hand. The oil in his faded red hair would have glistened had there been sufficient light shining on it. The hair was plastered to the skull, not one strand loose.

While FitzGibbon stood with his arms folded across his chest, waiting for someone to order another drink, his eyes flitted around his customers. In his head, he added up the money he knew would be in the till at closing time. He had been right now for thirty-six days in a row. His streak would have been ten days longer, only Pat Farrell had cut down by one pint a night at the beginning of Lent.

Tonight's tally would be tricky because Paddy Dillon was coming to do his reciting and collecting. It was always a toss-up whether the coins thrown at Dillon's feet would add up to the price of one or one-and-a-half pints. If Dillon was within three pennies of the price of the extra half-pint, then FitzGibbon would throw in the needed coins, but only if it meant keeping his streak going.

In FitzGibbon's pub, Paddy Dillon was permitted only to use proper words for female and male body parts and for the sexual act. FitzGibbon prided himself on being a strict censor. He believed this gave him special standing in the community. When he strutted back down the centre aisle on Sunday mornings after receiving holy communion, he could hold his head high knowing that he was perceived as an upright man who did not allow profanity on his premises. Everyone knew that Matty FitzGibbon had a great devotion to the Sacred Heart; that a picture of the Sacred Heart, with the little red lamp always burning before it, was hanging in his pub. If his patrons wanted an uncensored version of Paddy Dillon's recitation of dirty words, they could go to the more *risqué* pubs, like Lamb's or Dunphy's or Mansfield's. It was in those places they could hear real filth. But it could never be said that anyone enjoyed the dirty Paddy Dillon in FitzGibbon's.

FitzGibbon's fat wife was washing glasses in the sudsy water at the end of the bar. In her bent-over position her dress was pulled up at the back, exposing wads of white flesh at the backs and sides of her knees. The flabby flesh above her elbows shook as she scrubbed and rinsed.

While he sensually gazed at his wife's enormous arse, Matty FitzGibbon heard the pub door opening. Before he raised his eyes, the bison herd broke into a gallop. A few distinguishable words were flung into the air. Before his eyes got to the door, FitzGibbon knew Paddy Dillon had arrived.

But he was wrong.

At first he did not recognise who it was standing under the one bright light near the door. Then, because he was expecting to see a man, his brain could not see the woman. Between the time FitzGibbon recognised Maura Gilligan, and the moment Gilligan spoke, a thought sped through his mind; Gilligan had come to get someone to hump her; she had the knacker, but it was Lent and they weren't doing it. Maybe she'd gone mad for sex.

Like two badly tied sacks of oats sharing one hat, Maura Gilligan stood inside the pub door. As she opened her mouth to speak, she dropped her hands to her sides, and Matty FitzGibbon thought he had been right about her needing a hump; she was going to pull up her dress and expose her cascading hairy belly and beefy thighs. He was in the act of closing his eyes and turning his head aside when he heard her.

"Frankie Molloy is home from America and he's living in the old Duggan-one's house on Wheat Mill Lane."

It was her moment of glory. Before she turned to leave, the glow of triumph could be seen on her face. She had made the scoop of her life, and she knew it by the stunned silence of her audience. All day she had kept her secret to herself, hoping that no one would beat her to the punch. And now she knew she had gambled and won.

With the panache of a self-absorbed superstar grandly pirouetting off the stage, Maura Gilligan spun around to the pub door and crashed into Paddy Dillon, who had just stepped in out of the cold. Neither of them fell, but they staggered around trying to keep their balance while the silent audience gaped at them. In voices loud enough to be heard by everyone in the pub, but heard by no one, Gilligan called Dillon a blind bastard, and Dillon called Maura Gilligan a dried-up cunt. Otherwise, they passed each other like ships in the night.

It was miraculous, one of the drinkers would later tell his wife. One minute Maura Gilligan was there and gone, like an apparition of the Blessed Virgin, and then there was Paddy Dillon in her place, looking like the devil.

Under the bright light near the door Dillon stood, this morning's scabbed razor cuts visible between the swathes of beard missed by the razor. His trademark – the long, narrow tongue – was hanging down over his chin.

Paddy Dillon's greasy, grey, ankle-length gabardine was open, all the buttons long gone. With his arms stretched wide, grasping at the misinterpreted, silent adoration of the patrons, Dillon's hands were lost in the too-long sleeves. The open overcoat exposed the underlying suit, shirt and tie, all of which looked as if they had once belonged to a car mechanic who worked, slept, ate and fornicated in a grease pit. As he smiled broadly at his imagined fans, Paddy Dillon's one, long, front tooth glistened yellowly in the light.

From where FitzGibbon was standing, the tufts of hair sprouting out of Dillon's ears and nose could be seen. The hair on his head had been combed back from the forehead with a water-dripping comb.

Paddy Dillon bowed to what he thought was his breathless audience. As he started straightening, with his parade of vulgar words lined up and ready to tumble off his tongue, he was startled by a loud voice.

"That's your man! What did she call him? Your man that was dead and came back to life. What's his name! Lazarus! Lazarus our brother is not dead but sleepeth! Let me say it! I have it! I have it! Molly Malone!"

"Molloy, you thick fucker, Maguire!"

"Language, FitzGerald," FitzGibbon sharply shouted.

Paddy Dillon was confused by these inexplicable outbursts. He drew in a deep breath so he could float out his string of obscenity and justly claim his price for a drink. But before he got a word out, a question was flung into the air.

"That fellow Father Molloy, as he was then, gave me his first blessing when he was ordained. My question is this: because God knew back then that Father Molloy was going to be an Ascarriot, did God stop that first blessing from being any good? Answer me that, lads? If I was God, I know that's what I'd a did."

"Done!"

"Dunne isn't here tonight. He has a cow calving."

Paddy Dillon gasped for breath, but before he could activate his vocal cords, another question was thrown into the air.

"When his lordship, Lord Gregory Horseman-of-the-Year Molloy, admitted a whole lot of years ago that his brother the priest had thrown in the collar, myself and the wife got Father Keegan to say a mass for him, and I sent a mass card to his lordship because I was drawing six loads of horse shite out of his place every week...

"And no better horseshite is to be had!"

"... and my question is this: What happened to the value of that mass that was offered for a lost priest who has stayed lost, and that cost me ten bob at the time? Is the value of that mass floating around out there in space waiting for Father Molloy to die so that it can be put against the saving of his soul from purgatory? That's what I want to know, lads, or should I go to Father Keegan and ask him to give me back my ten bob?"

Half-way through this question Paddy Dillon drew in another breath and held it. When the question ended he would be ready to jump into the verbal vortex and capture the attention that was rightly his. But the question was so long, that when it was about to end, Dillon, red in the face, had to expel the breath or burst. Quickly he sucked at the air. He was late again.

"When Father Molloy was ordained, myself and the wife gave him a present of two pounds. I had a job then. Now he is not a priest anymore and he must have spent my two pounds, it was so long ago that he got it. My question is this: I gave him the money because he was a priest. Now he's not. Can I go and ask him for my money back, especially because I didn't do a day's work for the last fifteen years? That's my question lads, and it's not that I'm mean or anything."

"With interest, Mick!"

"Aye! With interest, of course!"

FitzGibbon, behind the bar, was beginning to worry that Paddy Dillon wouldn't get the price of a pint. The proprietor's forecast would be wrong, and his streak of correct predictions would be broken, unless the long-tongued entertainer got control of the situation.

Before the proprietor could intervene on behalf of Dillon, another voice soared up out of the bison herd.

"I've heard it on good authority that a fallen priest still has all the power of a priest, but it's all turned around because he's not facing God anymore. Will the fallen priest use his new bad power against us, and will he bring us bad luck by living with us?"

"May the Sacred Heart of Jesus be praised," shouted FitzGibbon to get the attention of his patrons. But at the same moment Paddy Dillon shouted out his effort to recapture the spotlight. No one in the pub understood what the bartender or the entertainer had said.

As another question was flung into the dark ceiling, Paddy Dillon slapped his thigh, and with his yellow tooth getting in the way, he loudly lisped, "Hure's melt!" Trickles of hot alcoholic anxiety itched their way into the dirt-clogged pores of his body.

"Now! Father Molloy was a priest. He got married outside the Church and had two children. My question is this: every time Father Molloy gave his wife a poke of the pole, did he commit a mortal sin? And as well as that, I always thought that when a man was ordained a priest they did something to him so he couldn't use the pole. So when he became an Ascarriot to the Church did he have to go to a doctor to have himself put right again?"

Paddy Dillon was lashing his dry, addicted lips with a not-so-wet tongue, when silence broke out. Not only was his tongue almost dry, his throat was parched from the anxiety-induced rapid breathing which had been shaking his body for the duration of the last question. The picture of the froth-headed pint was beginning to get blurry in his imagination. His arms flapping like a turkey trying to fly, the tails of his overcoat flying through the air, his hair losing its traction with the evaporation of the water which had been holding it in place, Paddy Dillon made a desperate effort to regain his rightful place among the drinkers in the pub.

"Hey! Hey! Hey!" is what he intended to shout. What came out was the sound of dry air rasping across vocal cords as tight as a bull's hole in August: "ee, ee, ee."

A huge voice lifted itself out of the line of men at the bar. When the words came and hung like a dropped ceiling just above the heads of the pub patrons, Paddy Dillon could no longer deal with his anxiety. With his left hand he grabbed the crotch of his trousers and started skipping like a small boy in the direction of the pisswall at the back of the pub.

As he bounced off the sitting patrons, he felt the waters of anxiety beginning to warm his clutching hand. He pushed the pisswall door and disappeared into the urine-saturated darkness, the strong voice of the next questioner whacking him in the small of the back.

"Do you think lads, because his wife is dead, he's come home looking for a new one, or at least for someone to jump up on? Will our own women be safe? That's my question!"

For a few moments the sounds of the bison were heard in the distance as the drinkers expressed concern about their wives, mothers, sisters, granddaughters, daughters and grandmothers. Above the dusty rumble, the beginnings of sentences could be heard, all of which started with the words, "If I ever see that fucker near my..." Gradually the level of talk increased until there was tremendous noise. Mrs FitzGibbon stopped rinsing glasses and straightened her back. She looked at her husband for reassurance and saw him, lips moving, throwing a prayerful glance at the picture of the Sacred Heart. This inspired Mrs FitzGibbon herself to fling an ejaculation in the direction of the picture. Then she glanced at the hatchet handle which her husband kept under the counter. He had told her he could brain a buffalo with one wallop. As Mrs FitzGibbon, reassured by her remembrance, bent over the sink, she saw Paddy Dillon silhouetted in the open door of the pisswall, his gabardine clutched tightly at the front.

Paddy Dillon began the long journey back to the spot where he hoped he would be seen and heard. But he was unable get past the bar. His alcoholic craving got the better of him, and his hand shot in between two humps. The hand came back holding an almost empty half-pint, brown porter suds streaking the inside. Like a trapped spy trying to dispose of secret plans by eating them in a hurry, Dillon two-handedly brought the glass to his mouth, the glass clanking against the one protruding tooth. But before he could tilt the porter into his voracious mouth, the glass was slapped out of his hands onto the floor. As he fell backward from a curse-laden push in the chest, rough hands grabbed him up from behind and sent him stumbling toward the door. And as he stumbled, another voice emerged from the tumult.

"This Father Molloy, and I got his first blessing too, is an Ascarriot because he gave up the faith. He's an atheist like a Russian. Is he going to take our children away from the faith of our fathers? And that's my question!"

As the drinkers called out their opinions on the imagined atheistic influence, they could not hear Paddy Dillon shouting at them.

"You crowd of mean hures!" The yellow tooth shone with invective. "You rotten, fucking farmers." His maledictive spittle sprayed the unlistening drinkers. "May the curse of God fall on the whole fucking lot of you, mean fucking hures that you are." In his anger, Paddy Dillon got personal. "And as for you, FitzGibbon! May your fucking pub burn down with you and your fat fucking wife in it." With his hands in the pockets of his overcoat keeping his wet crotch covered, Paddy Dillon turned on his heel and kicked the pub door open. "Fuck the lot of you," he prayed, as he faded into the darkness, unnoticed by anyone, except FitzGibbon.

"You fucked up my forecasting, you mangey cunt," FitzGibbon silently flung after Dillon. "That you may die of the thirst in the gutter!"

Chapter 11

Thursday in the Fifth Week of Lent – 11.10 a.m.

JOHNNY AND JIMMY Culliton were identical twins down to their dirty noses, except that Johnny was a nervous child and Jimmy wasn't. At the age of twelve they were an ever-moving and threatening entity to the people and property of the village of Davinkill. Their very existence was as nerve-racking as living downstream from a dam with a crack.

They knew Father Keegan played golf every Thursday. They knew sparrows built their nests on the rotting floor of the loft in the old barn where Father Keegan kept his car. They knew about the golf because everyone in the village knew, and they knew about the sparrows because they knew every place where birds built their nests within a half-mile radius of their house.

The Culliton twins liked to cut the heads off young birds, and they continually experimented with different forms of decapitation. When they executed all the chicks in a nest, they divided up the warm, purple-skinned bodies and threw them at each other the way normal children throw snowballs in wintertime. Since the discovery, through deduction, of the nests on the rotting loft floor in the priest's barn, they had driven each other to the edge of hysteria with their fantasies about the big dead-bird-fight which lay ahead. And now the moment had arrived.

They came in over the high wall which separated their weed-infested backyard from the priest's orchard. They came prepared, Jimmy carrying the rope which he had unknotted with great difficulty from the winkers of his father's donkey, the knot sealed in years of donkey saliva. Johnny had a brown bag folded in the pocket of his jacket for the gathering of the booty. In his left hand was a piece of bread.

Through the narrow gate which led from the orchard to the priest's backyard Jimmy brazenly strode, with Johnny, as usual, a few nervous steps behind. They slipped from one hiding place to another, because if Mrs Westman saw them she would tell. She was their mother's cousin, but she was ashamed of her association with anything named Culliton. Having been chosen to be the priest's housekeeper had raised Mrs Westman out of the peasantry, and she zealously guarded herself against contamination by the cousins she had left behind in her former social class.

From their last hiding place the twins dashed into the barn through the doorless archway. When an air-whacking cloud of startled sparrows whirred low over their heads, Jimmy did not even blink. It had been the observation of this sparrow traffic, through a hole in the orchard wall, which led them to deduce the presence of nests.

They were prepared for Father Keegan's Irish setter. When they heard it putting itself on alert in its dark barrel, Johnny, with deadly left-handed accuracy, landed the piece of bread at its feet in the straw. The dog lived in a state of perpetual hunger, so it didn't have a choice between barking the alarm and eating.

They had already decided who would have the first chance to throw the rope across the exposed rafter eighteen feet above their heads. The trick was not only to get the rope over the rafter, but to avoid protrusions as it fell back down on the other side.

Jimmy put the rope on the ground at his feet, spat on his hands, and rubbed them together to make the nerve-endings tingle the way he had seen safe-crackers do it in the pictures. He retrieved the rope, felt the balance of it on his fingertips, and flung it up.

When the rope did exactly as Jimmy wanted it to do, the two boys gaped at each other with the same expressions of disbelief, each one seeing at the image of himself in the other: a galaxy of freckles across the nose; blue eyes too close to bespeak monumental intelligence; eyebrows almost invisible; hair the same hue as an orangutan's fur, looking like it had just been examined for fleas by a who-gives-a-shit fellow orangutan. Both had front teeth growing across each other, already creating sizeable gaps between themselves and their immediate neighbours. Whenever the boys spoke there was a lot of spittle in their words.

By prior agreement, the one who failed to secure the rope would be the first to climb it. So when he had gone up the rope, using the irregularities in the stone wall as footholds, and when he had pulled himself into a standing position on the rafter, a sight met Johnny's eyes which went far beyond his wildest expectations. He had ascended into a sparrow housing project, each nest full of open beaks, each beak quivering and making toneless guttural sounds.

"Jazus, Jimmy!" was all Johnny Culliton could bring himself to say. He peered into the darker edges of the light and when his eyes had adjusted, he said, "Jazus, Jimmy!" again.

"What do you see?" Jimmy called out.

Johnny moved away from the wall to make room for his brother on the rafter, and no sooner had Jimmy landed than he exclaimed, "Jazus, will you look at that!"

"I know, Jimmy! Will you look at them over there, too." Johnny pointed across to a dim corner of the loft.

"I don't mean them. I mean there at your feet," Jimmy pointed. "Don't make a move or you'll step on it."

When Johnny looked down he said, "O Jazus, will you look at that!"

Almost touching his boot was a heap of moss and sparrow dung. The boys did not see the years of accumulated grime and dried droppings. All they saw was a nest, built in the heel of a shoe, and the five bald, squawking heads on the ends of stretched purple necks.

"The lads would never believe us," Johnny said. He took the paper bag out of his pocket and shook it into shape. "I'll put the whole thing in here to show them." He had to use the toe of his boot to pry the shoe loose. When he picked it up he blew into the scalds' open mouths to agitate them.

When the shoeful of nerve-wracked nestlings had been lowered into the bag, Johnny folded over the top. With the bag in his right hand he stepped onto the loft floor, which had been nailed into place more than ninety years before. Even though it was pitted with holes, it never crossed either of the boys' minds that the boards could be rotting.

So it happened that Johnny suddenly sank through the boards and that he was accompanied on his way down with a shower of dust, bird droppings, nests full of begging beaks, and shards of rotting wood. Grunting like a grown man grunts when he is smacked in the testicles, Johnny hit the shed floor and didn't move.

In a blur of activity Jimmy lowered himself on the rope and ran up the priest's yard. He was screaming.

When Mrs Westman came to the back door to see what was going on, he shouted that his brother had been killed.

"Me brudder's kilt. Me brudder's kilt."

The priest's slightly deaf housekeeper looked at him in disgust, and asked him what had he said.

"Whawja say?"

Chapter 12

Thursday in the Fifth Week of Lent – 11.10 a.m.

THE COW WAS black, and her belly was like a mountain between her dead rump and her dead head. The dead teats were like four deflated fingers attached to a white, thinly-haired balloon from which the air had slowly escaped.

John O'Brien, all elbows and knees, was sitting on the black mountain in the March wind that was still blowing on the first day of April. From a distance he could have been a thin vulture contemplating a meal.

One half of O'Brien's sandwich was still on the piece of brown wrapping beside him, the cow's dead hairs stirring in the breeze at the edge of the oft-used paper. Tiny waves rippled across the milky tea in the plastic cup beside the sandwich.

Everything about John O'Brien was long and thin. He needed his large feet to keep his high body anchored to the ground. From close up, he could have just stepped out of an El Greco painting. The flame had gone out of his straight red hair, but his eyebrows and the backs of his hands still flashed reminders of what had been. His sixty-six-year-old face was elongated enough to accommodate the nose, out of whose cavernous nostrils cascaded a faded, bushy mustache. The head was sufficiently twisted to one side to situate his left eye in a direct line with his navel. This twist had developed after he lost his right eye to a chip of limestone when he was twenty-four. The piece of glass which now filled his eye socket stared bluely and blindly and unmoving at nothing. As if to give validity to the old saw about closing the barn door after the horse has bolted, O'Brien was wearing a pair of imitation World War II aviator goggles. The black elastic band holding them in place made a track in the faded red hair, adding a touch of the macabre to his appearance; the top of the head, above the elastic, could have been been attached by a surgeon with a poor sense of proportion.

As he brought the sandwich to his hairy mouth, O'Brien saw a man approaching the gate in the high, wire-mesh fence. The man was wheeling a light motorbike

O'Brien took a bite from his sandwich, and the shadow of a scudding cloud sped across the enclosure. The wind was instantly colder.

The intruder, an apprehensive Frank Molloy on his first outing to dip his social toes, stopped at the wire-mesh fence and looked up at the five signs.

"John O'Brien – Knacker". The red letters were on a white background.

"Trespassers Will Be Prosecuted". A guideline in pencil was still visible under the row of letters.

"All Kinds of Dead Animals Removed Day or Night". There had been other words on this sign. Molloy moved closer and narrowed his eyes. The painted-over words had been written in black: "You Fucking Vulture".

"Meat on These Premises Not Fit for Human Consumption (Dept. of Health)". The graffitist had struck here, too, and the coat of white paint had obscured, but not erased, his message: "Knacker eats dead cows you fucking hyena".

"Greyhound Meat Packed on the Premises".

Frank Molloy looked in at the premises through the open gate.

The shadow of the scudding cloud swept across the ground with the movements of a speedy, vast and flat caterpillar. Fifty feet away, in the sudden sunshine, Molloy saw the silhouette of John O'Brien sitting on a stretched-out dead animal, and the remembrance of an exhausted Don Quixote fled across his mind. It looked like the Don was eating a sandwich.

Maybe he won't recognise me, who I was. Coming back into people's lives is going to be a pain in the ass. Dealing with the questions will be like fencing a small army. But I have to get my feet wet and this is as good a place as any to practice.

Behind the jaded knight and his dead Rozinante loomed the facade of a large corrugated-iron shed, the high double-doors wide open, sunshine caught up in the dirt in the narrow windows of the back wall. Beyond the shed the lone, level and heather-covered land stretched far away. Clumps of dwarf birches, waterlogged and poorly nourished, spotted the landscape, their leaves like silver pennies furiously dancing in the sun.

Salvador Dali must have been here.

Sitting on the cow, John O'Brien rubbed the sleeve of his brown suitcoat across his lips. He picked the teacup out of the fretful dead hairs beside him.

"Are you coming in or what?" he called.

Molloy looked up at one of the signs he had just read. "Will I be trespassing?" he shouted.

"I'm here, amn't I!" O'Brien called back. "I'm O'Brien. What is it you want?"

"I was only passing," Frank shouted back.

O'Brien shook his head as if to shake distortions out of his one-eyed view. "Are you looking for something?" he asked.

"Did you ever hear of Salvador Dali?" Molloy called. *That's a great opening line, Molloy! Salvador Dali! Who are you impressing?*

O'Brien snorted the snort of contempt he kept in reserve for people who imagine they are better than they actually are.

"It's Daly around here, not Dowlee, and you're on the wrong road altogether. Mister Daly lives on the road to Duneamon. Are you a relative of his?"

"No." Molloy continued looking at the landscape. *Daly!* "It's a lonely place out here," he called into the wind.

"What did you say?" O'Brien asked, without raising his voice. He shifted his finger in the handle of his cup and bent his wrist.

"It's very quiet out here," Frank shouted.

O'Brien flicked his wrist and, before the spear of tea pierced the soft earth beside the dead cow's wrinkled nostril, he leaned forward and stood up. He turned his back on the entrance to his premises.

Frank Molloy looked at the enclosed, brown circle of dust sitting in an otherwise green and purple landscape. *It's like a prison! I wonder is he a little mad all by himself out here in the middle of nowhere, sitting on a dead cow. Maybe he didn't hear me.* "I said it's very quiet out here," he shouted, and at the same time he walked forward, a hand on each handlebar of the motorbike. But the Don did not seem to have heard.

With his back still to Molloy, O'Brien had picked up his flask and was screwing the cup onto its top. When he turned around, he was so surprised to see Molloy so close that he blurted out: "Are you an inspector or what?"

Frank Molloy was wearing blue jeans with the cuffs turned up. His shirt was green and the anorack was blue and red; canvas shoes; the same goggles as O'Brien's. "What would I be inspecting?" he asked.

"I don't know what you'd be inspecting," O'Brien said.

"Do you get inspectors often?" *God! The the stink of him.*

"Are you from the department?" O'Brien enquired, looking straight into Molloy's eyes.

"No, I'm not. I was just passing."

"Well, if you are from the department I have nothing to hide." On the leg of his trousers O'Brien rubbed the dirt off the bottom of the Thermos. He stepped around the dead head of the cow and headed toward the shed.

"What happened to the cow?" Molloy called after him.

Over his shoulder O'Brien flung the words out of his long lips: "She died." He continued to the doorway in the shed and turned left.

"You don't say! I thought she was just pretending!" Molloy flung back, but he didn't know if he had not been heard, or was being ignored.

When O'Brien reappeared in five seconds, he had an apron and a short piece of rope in his hands. Frank Molloy was standing at the cow's head, a slight stoop on his back as he peered do`wn at the dead eye. He had moved his goggles up above the peak of his cap.

O'Brien dropped the rope on the cow's belly. He shook out the apron with such vigour and noise that Molloy suspected the knacker was telling him to get lost. The knacker put the loop around his neck and was tying the string at his belly, with obvious annoyance in his long, bony fingers, when Molloy said, "It's a grand looking animal. I'd say whoever owned her is kicking himself." He looked up at the knacker.

"He'd rather be kicking me," O'Brien said.

"Why is that?" *The stink of him! I'll have to stay on his windy side.*

"What's your name?" O'Brien asked.

"Frank Molloy! Why would the owner be angry at you?"

"Because I'm the knacker – the one all the farmers hate. Nobody calls me John. I'm Knacker to everyone. Are you related to the Molloys of Roongarry?" By the tone of his voice O'Brien did not like his nickname.

"I am! I gathered from the graffiti that someone didn't like you," Molloy said, and he shook his head in the direction of the signs near the gate. "But why shouldn't they like you?"

O'Brien looked over toward the gate in his fence as if he'd been told that he'd missed something on the way in. He looked back at Frank. "Well, Mr Molloy, I'm the one who comes to take away their dead animals."

But Frank Molloy still did not understand why the farmers didn't like O'Brien. "They'd have to dig holes to bury the animals if you didn't take them," Frank Molloy said. "Aren't you doing them a favour?"

"It's a favour they have to pay for," O'Brien retorted testily. "Where do you think the petrol for the lorry and the jacker comes from, and the insurance and the money to keep them running, and tyres? The farmers think I should be paying them for the dead animal. It takes money to run this place."

"And that's why they get angry at you?"

"That's why they'd rather be kicking me than kicking themselves when an animal dies. I'm the lousy shagger who comes in his lorry, as welcome as a hearse at a wedding, and charges them for hauling away the carcasses the vet couldn't save, and they have just paid the vet before they pay me. So the farmer thinks he's lost three times in a row: the animal, the vet's charge and my charge." O'Brien pulled at his apron. The apron had narrow blue and white stripes running from top to bottom. Despite the vigorous shaking-out it was still coated with animal hairs fretting in the wind.

Frank Molloy looked away from O'Brien, his eyes moving around the enclosure. "So that's why you built your place off out here away from everyone," he said.

"What do you mean?"

"To get away from them, you built your place off out here," Frank Molloy explained.

"No! No! I built this place out here because of the smell. But besides the smell I'm glad I did, because it's better to be out here where the shaggers can't jeer at me. At least out here all they can do is write something lousy on the signs out there."

"The graffiti!" Frank said. "Yes, I saw the stuff on the way in."

Once more O'Brien glanced at the gates as if expecting to see something. Then he picked the piece of rope off the cow's belly. The two ends were knotted together. He went to the rear end of the cow, put the doubled rope around the legs just above the dung-covered hoofs, put one loop through the other and gave a sharp jerk. "Do you go to the pubs?"he asked, as he rubbed his hands down the front of his apron.

Molloy stepped back from the cow when he saw O'Brien was getting ready to do something to the carcass.

"What pubs?" he asked. "Are you going to start cutting up the cow?"

"The pubs! Any of the pubs around." O'Brien moved his hand to include every pub in the country from Waterford to Donegal. He grabbed the cow's tail and casually pulled it up. The wind blew the dust out of his hair. O'Brien looked at Molloy shuffling back from the exposed and swelling anus.

"No! I don't like pubs," Frank said, and he pushed the motorbike further back when O'Brien put his huge boot on the cow's belly.

"Where do you live?" O'Brien asked. He pushed down on the cow's stomach. Escaping gas made a spluttering sound at the cow's tail.

Frrank Molloy pulled his left hand out of his pocket and shook out a white, folded handkerchief. He put it over his mouth and nose. *Jesus! The stink! It makes O'Brien smell good.* "I'm not good with this kind of thing," he said, his voice distorted through the handkerchief. "I've never seen an animal getting cut up." He took another step back. "Are you going to start cutting?"

"I have to jack her first. The jacker's in there." The knacker threw his eye over his shoulder in the direction of the shed. "Where did you say you live?"

"On Wheat Mill Lane on the far side of Davinkill. I suppose it's like everything else. You get used to it," Frank said.

"What's to get used to on Wheat Mill Lane? Maura Gilligan's beagles?" O'Brien laughed like an unthinking father laughing off a frightened child's nightmare. He took his big wellington boot off the cow.

"I didn't mean getting used to Wheat Mill Lane. I meant cutting up an animal. It must take a long time to get used to it." Molloy put his hand back on his motorbike, but he kept the handkerchief in his fingers. *God! This is becoming a huge effort.*

O'Brien said, "I know everyone on Wheat Mill Lane, unless you've moved into Miss Duggan's house. It's the only empty house on the lane that I know of."

"Yes, Miss Duggan used to live there."

John O'Brien stepped away from the cow's rear. He took two hard, paper-wrapped sweets out of his apron pocket. Short hairs were stuck to the wrapping, In the hand which had lifted the cow's tail, he held one of the sweets out to Molloy, who waved a negative and said, "Thanks."

"That's a cosy little house," the knacker said, as he dropped one of the sweets back into the pocket. With his long fingers he started to worry the wrapping of the other one. "Poor old Miss Duggan was never the same after the Foley girl was killed. They were like a mother and daughter, only Miss Duggan was a spinster and Kit Foley's mother was dead. So was her father, for that matter. At the end she went sort of mad, Miss Duggan, and frightened children with her wild stories. For the last few years before she died people tried not to run into her, with her mad talk. She was dead in the house a few days before Maura found her, or her dogs did, from the smell. Did you buy it?"

"I did," Molloy said. And to head off what he thought would be the next question he continued, "It's the yew hedge wrapped around the three sides that makes it cosy."

"How did you say you're related to the Molloys of Roongarry?"

"I didn't say. But I'm Frank, Gregory's brother," Molloy responded.

At first it seemed O'Brien was going to skip on to another question, his mouth muscles already in motion to shape the lips. But his face suddenly fell apart. He sucked in a deep breath through lemon-juiced lips, while his one eye fell down to the area of Frank's navel. His fingers stopped wrestling with the wrapping on the hard sweet.

"Father Frank." The sound floated out on his exhaling breath, a sigh, a remembrance. Then words fell out of him like the first trickle of water coming off winter's melting snow. "I got your first blessing the day you said your first mass." The one eye came back up to Molloy's face. "Do you remember? There was an awful lot of people. Everyone in the church queued up because we all knew you from the time you were a child, Peter's son." Molloy, taken unaware by this outpouring, was unable to deal with O'Brien's steady gaze, and his eyes skipped from the knacker's boots to the knot on his tie to the trembling hairs on the apron. "The missus had gone to the earlier mass and was home with the child. I don't know if you'd remember how she was delicate, the child. I rode home to Ballafalia on the bike, and told her to go back to the church for your blessing. He'll be gone by the time I get there, she said. Then I told her how many people were waiting for you to put your hands on them. She went in on her bike, with the child in the carrier behind her. I always remember it, how I thought the three of us would be safe because we got your first blessing, you being one of ourselves, and a new priest with no sins, as it were. But the child died before she was three: hole in the heart. And the missus only lasted a few months after that. She lost the will, and a dose of pneumonia got her."

In the silence that followed O'Brien's outpouring, Molloy saw himself that day, moving along the line of believers, calling down the blessing of God on them while he laid his newly oiled hands on their heads. Bitterly, too, he saw himself in the first flush of the priesthood, a delicate, unsuspecting flower about to be yanked out of the ground, indelicately chewed and consigned to the first stomach of the great dumb cow, the institutional Church. As the silence lengthened between the two men standing on the open ground in the wind, Molloy's mind was flooded with images of places he had been, of spaces and states he had visited, of relationships he had been through, of pains and joys, and all the time, unbeknownst to him, he had been woven into O'Brien's sad memories, had probably been thought of kindly at times when he would have been glad of a little gentleness and kindness. For too many years he had looked for kindness within the priestly brotherhood. By the time he realised his search had been futile from the start, he himself had become a spiritual wasteland, his soul a stretch of barren moonscape strewn with mountainous isolates of anger and bitterness.

When Molloy glanced up at O'Brien, a ripple of warmth, emanating from a dim awareness of solidarity, slipped into his chest, and he knew that if he had found even this much connectedness with his fellow churchmen, he would probably still be a priest.

His eyes dropped down to the twisting sweet in O'Brien's fingers. "My mother probably told me in a letter about your wife and child," he said. "When you're away it's hard, after a few years, to remember who has died. Someone's death in a letter is just a few words on a page. You don't see the sorrow in the faces at the graveside to help you remember."

"It's all right," O'Brien said. "I never told anyone else that story. The minute you told me who you are, it sort of jumped out of me."

"I'm glad you told me," Molloy responded. "And I still have priest's ears."

As O'Brien nodded his thanks, his lips compressed into a shape that bespoke the uselessness of trying to come to terms with the shit that comes hurtling down the turnpike of life. "Anyway!" he finally exclaimed. With a great shudder as if shaking off his sadness, he asked, "When did you buy it – the Duggan house?" Without giving Molloy an opportunity to respond, he galloped on, trying to expunge a quaver from his voice. "Maura Gilligan was in here a week ago and she never said anything. She comes in every Wednesday for a head – should be here anytime now. She always comes around twelve. Maybe I'll give her this one." O'Brien pointed with his chin at the other end of the cow. "She lives on the next lane past you, Sommers Lane; in the last house. You must have seen her with the dogs on the golf links. Nothing but beagles since Seamus died! She rears them for the fox hunters on the horses. The golfers are always complaining about the dog shites on the greens." O'Brien smiled, and again he fidgeted with the sweet wrapper. He held the sweet at arms length and squinted his eye. "They hate getting dog shite on their nice shoes, the doctors and bank men and priests." He moved his arms as he tried to bring the sweet into focus. "The eye is shot to hell, and the bloody goggles make it worse," he said. "Do you play golf?"

"No." *I don't want to be here when Gilligan comes.* Molloy leaned the motorbike's saddle against his hip and pulled up the sleeve of his anorack. He looked at his watch. It was two minutes to noon. "I should be off." He turned his feet in the soft earth so he could keep the gate in view. "I've seen Mrs Gilligan walking the dogs." *Riddling me with questions the minute she saw me.* To take the abruptness out of his intended departure, he asked, "What's this about the head?"

The knacker put one end of the wrapper to his lips and blew.

"There it is!" he said. He pulled the paper off the candy. "I'll never figure out how the hairs get through the paper. But shag them! They haven't killed me yet." He popped the sweet into his mouth. "She boils the head for the dogs. Where'd you live before now?"

Boils the head! Eyes and all! Hair and all! A boiled head! How does she take it out of the pot, the lips and ears falling off? The grinning teeth! The terrible eyes! Boiled! "In New York. I'm going to take off." Without moving his feet Molloy put his body in motion to give weight to his words. "Maybe I'll call in again when I'm passing." He moved his goggles back to his eyes.

"Sure, if you hold on for a few minutes you'll meet Maura."

Molloy shuffled away from the dead cow, away from the possibility of an encounter with that woman with the beagles, loud and coarse. The spurts of dust soaring around his white sneakers were whisked away in the wind. "I've met Mrs Gilligan." He glanced towards the gate. "Well, Mr O'Brien, I must be off. I'll see you again." He pushed the motorbike and took a determined step forward.

"The Guards asked me to help with Miss Duggan," John O'Brien threw out, as if felling a tree across the road to slow down Frank's flight. "Just because I dig graves and cut up dead animals they thought I'd handle a rotten old woman."

Molloy stopped walking, kept his body turned towards his escape route and twisted his head back over his shoulder. "What did you tell them – the Guards?" he asked.

O'Brien moved the candy from one cheek to the other. He stuck out the tip of his tongue and picked off a hair between the nails of his thumb and finger, wiped his hand on the side of his trousers. Unfaded hairs in his thick mane reflected coloured sunlight. "I said I'd not do them a favour, but that I'd do it. They knew what I meant." He winked his good eye and, with a quick move of his head, indicated he had gained an advantage over the Guards.

"That was clever of you," Molloy said. "It does no harm to have the law on your side." He turned his head and walked forward, and O'Brien quickly threw down another tree.

"She nearly fell apart on me. But I got her in the box without letting her burst. I was glad, because I always thought she was a nice old lady. Mad, but nice."

Frank kept pushing the motorbike. He twisted his head back to O'Brien. "I'd say they were glad of your help." He turned his head to the gate, and a car, so dirty it was impossible to tell its colour, was slowly bounding over the uneven ground through the opening in the high wire fence.

"Shit!" Molloy said through clenched teeth.

Chapter 13

Thursday in the Fifth Week of Lent – 11.35 a.m.

TIM BERGIN WAS a sore loser, and when he played golf with Father Keegan the soreness began to fester before the first ball was teed off. He knew he would never win against the priest.

On the outside, Bergin, the manager of the Bank of Ireland in Davinkill, was a pleasant golfing partner, but inside he seethed with jealousy and golfing bitterness. Every time Father Keegan stood over a ball, Bergin directed a continuous mental flow of golfing maledictions against him.

And so it was as Father Keegan was addressing the ball on the tenth tee, Bergin was standing opposite him wishing that the fucking ball would slice off the fucking club at right fucking angles, and get lost in the fucking furze bushes and never be found again. As the number two wood made a perfect arc and whacked the ball dead centre, Bergin's secret cavern became a primeval swamp of invective. While he followed the flight of the ball, and weighed it down with a flight of silent expletives, Bergin saw movement in the corner of his eye. But he kept Keegan's ball in sight and cursed it all the way to the green.

"That was a nice shot, Father," Bergin said pleasantly, as the white speck rolled to a stop ten feet from the pin. Then he looked around to see what had moved while Keegan's ball had been in flight.

It was a golf cart, and Anthony Furlong, the keeper of the greens, was heading toward them. With all the wishfulness his soul was capable of mustering, Bergin prayed that something was about to happen which would interfere with the priest scoring an eagle at this hole.

"The best I've ever had at this hole, Tim," Keegan responded to Bergin's sugar-coated words of congratulations. A trace of a singular achievement flickered around the priest's lips in the shape of a smile. Then, because the golf cart had worked itself into the corner of his eye too, Keegan said, "I hope Anthony isn't coming to get me!"

Anthony Furlong brought the cart to a careful stop on the grass and touched the peak of his cap.

"Men!" he greeted, and without waiting for a response he said, "You're wanted, Father."

Before he asked what he was needed for, Father Keegan shot a glance down the fairway at the ball, sitting, waiting to be tapped into the hole. He looked back to Furlong, and the grounds-keeper was already answering the unasked question. "It's one of the Culliton twins, Father. Mrs Westman said he fell through the loft in your barn where you keep the car. She says he might be kilt."

At the words "loft in your barn" Father Keegan's gorge rose with such suddenness that he became dizzy, and he had to fight down the vomit in his throat; he became weak at the knees, and a layer of greasy sweat burst onto his forehead. But despite his physical reactions, his well-drilled defense system wobbled onto terrified and bristling alert. Before Furlong had finished his message, Keegan, on the outside, was a man who had fully recovered from a grenade blast which had exploded ten feet from his face. Even though his mind was reeling and his stomach was dealing with an inrush of unneeded juices, he had the presence of mind to direct all his strength to his knees to keep them from collapsing.

As Anthony Furlong finished his message, Tim Bergin saw Keegan glancing back at his ball on the distant green. It was a jewel on emerald velvet that would never be worn in triumph.

But Bergin was wrong. Keegan wasn't even thinking about the golf ball; he was avoiding eyes; he was sucking on his salivary glands, trying to get some liquid into his mouth so he could lubricate his vocal chords; he was striving to maintain an outward appearance without appearing to do so. In his lifetime, the priest had seen many drunk people trying to project an air of sobriety, but trying so hard it was the trying which gave them away. Keegan was grasping for an appropriate response to the precise message the grounds-keeper had delivered, and he had to be extremely careful that nothing else leaked out.

Satisfied that his vocal cords would not crack if he used them, Keegan said, "He was probably after the birds' nests. Sparrows have been building there for the last thirty years." As soon as he said thirty years Keegan winced inside. He had just done the very thing he had wanted to avoid; he had made a connection between the loft floor and thirty years ago. It wasn't that the whole village had thirty years ago on its collective brain; it was just that the whole village had taken a deep breath thirty years ago, and was still listening for one small clue which would uncover the true identity of a murderer. Even though Tony Donaghue was the official killer, everyone knew in their hearts that he had been innocent, that someone was living among them who had killed one of their own.

Tim Bergin made some tragedy-related noises as he and Keegan threw their golf bags onto the back of the cart. Then, as if words would hinder their progress, the two of them, in silence, crowded onto the cart seat beside Anthony Furlong.

As the golf car turned back to the clubhouse, Tim Bergin secretly exulted in the way things had turned out; Keegan would never be able to rejoice over the eagle at the eighth hole, an occurrence as rare as a hole-in-one at the short sixteenth. Suddenly aware that his exultation might be registering on his face, he glanced quickly at Keegan.

From the look of Keegan, it was obvious the priest was in the state of mind which Bergin hoped he was in. But, again, Bergin was wrong.

The Culliton twins were being subjected to a raging gale of anger in Keegan's head. He was raging, too, at their mother, who had substituted Jesus for her husband, to the point where she was as ineffectual a parent as was the children's drunkard-father. Father Keegan was also being battered by a storm of anxiety as intense as the one he had felt thirty years ago, when he had hidden a pair of shoes on the same floor the Culliton child had fallen through; shoes which would have destroyed him, had they been associated with him. When he'd found them on the floor of his car, between the front and back seats, panic had overwhelmed him. Thirteen underhand throws it had taken to get them through the small hole at an angle, so they would land on the floor and not come crashing back down on his head. God, the panic! Everyone in the village out looking for the shoes for two days on the golf links, and they in his car the whole time. Every time he'd missed the hole and hit the loft floor instead, a shower of dust had floated down, blinding him, covering him with dust. When the second shoe had finally plonked onto the floor, he was crying, shaking, and the front of his trousers was wet.

When the golf car bumped as it drove up and across the Davinkill Road, Father Keegan was shaken back into the present. He tried to get a bearing on his whereabouts; how long was it since he'd spoken? If he spoke again would it betray anxiety? He was unable to keep silent.

"I hope he's all right, the child," he said, and he twisted to look at Furlong. "Did Mrs Westman say… What did she say?"

"He might be kilt, is what she said. I asked her what she meant. She said she only saw him from the distance and there wasn't a move out of him. Face down. I told her to call Doctor O'Leary, and she asked me did I think she was an eejit or what!"

After a pause Tim Bergin said, "It had to happen to one or the other of them sooner or later." He was going to remark on how the twins were like a nervous twitch roaming the village, when he felt pressure on his thigh. He looked down and he saw Father Keegan withdrawing his pinkie finger.

The priest, grateful for the opportunity to appear rational, asked, "How are they related to you, Anthony? Isn't Mrs Culliton your first cousin?"

"Right you are, Father. First cousins once removed as the catechism would say, the twins are," Anthony Furlong said, and Tim Bergin knew Furlong was doing his bit to impress the priest, as every peasant in this fucking village did. Tim Bergin also knew he himself should be grateful to Father Keegan for having saved him some mouth damage from his own foot. It was one of the many disadvantages of being an outsider in any village, that he was not aware of who was related to whom.

"You have a good memory, Anthony," Father Keegan said, and to the priest the words were a sigh of relief that no one had picked up on his "thirty-years-ago" gaffe.

"And it was way beyond thirty years and Kit Foley that I learned my catechism," Furlong responded, and Father Keegan's small intestine snapped like the slack being whipped out of a fishing line by an outraged pike. But Furlong careened onward. "I remember, too, the way my mother taught me how to spell catechism: Catty Atty Told Eena Conroy How I Sell Matches. It's a terrible word to spell, and Mr Goodwin was a hure with the stick, if you'll excuse the word, Father."

Tim Bergin was not one to over-indulge the murmurings of swains. He rudely waded in and brought the conversation back to a middle-class level. "Would you have got an eagle on that one, Father?" he asked, knowing he was not only whacking Furlong, but the priest, too.

Only too glad to relieve the tension, Father Keegan responded. But he brought the subject back to the Culliton child, lest his talk of golf in these particular circumstances be seen as callousness.

"I'll never know, Tim… I wouldn't be surprised if Doctor O'Leary is up at the Blackwater Bridge seeing Ken Considine. Mrs Westman will have a job trying to get him. Ken wasn't too well again this morning." Father Keegan was an experienced pitcher of empathising noises, and so he had no difficulty expressing words of concern even though they were forced out between raging anger and high anxiety.

Anthony Furlong brought the golf cart to a rolling halt at the players' entrance to the clubhouse. Before the wheels had come to a stop Father Keegan eased himself off the seat, and he ran to the clubhouse door. But it was not the Culliton boy he was thinking about. The only thing on his mind was the pair of shoes. What if they had come down when that… that… that little fucker had fallen.

Father Keegan ran to his locker and fumbled with the lock. Under no circumstances would he appear in his parish in his yellow trousers.

Chapter 14

Thursday in the Fifth Week of Lent – 11.36 a.m.

MAURA GILLIGAN'S CAR came slowly bounding across the knacker's yard like an aged greyhound remembering the glory days of youth. It looked as if someone had sprayed the car with muck, the pie-quarters made by the windshield wipers the only clean spots. The encrusted headlights were the blind eyes of old Romans in marble busts.

In the clean spot on the driver's side was Gilligan's enthusiastic face. The ruins of her last perm hung around the sides of her head like the stretched-out springs of a destroyed machine rusting under a hedge. Her dentures were the long yellow teeth of an old mare. She had the nose of a boxer who has taken too many punches between the eyes. Her hands grasped the steering wheel like a clawing bird on a branch in a storm.

As the car came loping across the rough surface, gusts of wind whipped the dust off the balding tyres. Frank Molloy, pushing his motorbike towards the gate in the high, wire fence, quickened his pace, trying to give the appearance of a man in a hurry.

But the car stopped ten feet in front of him.

Shit.

The dirty window was half open on the driver's side. Mrs Gilligan's head was hanging in the open space. She led with her teeth.

"If it isn't Frank Molloy, goggles and all!" she shot at him. "What the hell are you doing in a place like this? I saw Father Keegan on his way down to Roongarry yesterday." Twisting her eyes to John O'Brien at the dead cow she shouted, "You clever bugger, O'Brien! You never told me you knew Frank Molloy was home." When Gilligan spoke she employed every movable part of her face in the manufacture of words: cheeks, lips, eyes, eyebrows, forehead, jowls and wattles, all shunted back and forth like the parts on a clacking, highly strung machine. When she ran out of breath she continued to make sounds on the indraught. "The two of you look like beetles with your goggles. Two big beetles." She neighed at her own witticism.

Molloy looked on helplessly as John O'Brien set himself in motion, grinning like the cat in the tree, his seven-league wellington boots bringing him to the car in a few giant steps. But he wasn't moving fast enough for Mrs Gilligan.

"Get a move on, John," she called. "I'm in a dangerous hurry! The dogs are barking with the hunger, and that jumped-up whore down the road will be complaining to the sergeant again. May God deliver me from that braying bitch! Such notions she has! Now she has a woman coming into the house once a week to clean – to clean, mind you! Mag Dempsey from Rathnafir, two pounds an hour and feeds her. I hope you have a head ready for me."

Frank Molloy got the feeling he was Mrs Gilligan's audience, and that the identity of the braying bitch was about to be revealed in her dramatic brushwork.

But John O'Brien effortlessly fell into the role of chorus.

"You mean Pat Farrell's wife?" he asked, while he ran his one eye over the muck-covered car. O'Brien's speech was faster than before, as if Gilligan's careening verbal style was contagious and he had caught it; as if O'Brien had abandoned Molloy and joined Gilligan on her stage.

"Herself!" Maura retorted, and she winked and nodded her head at Molloy.

"You can have that one there." O'Brien threw his eye over his shoulder at the dead cow-corpse.

"Grand! A fresh one. Whose is it?"

"Saint Willie Gorman's. Died calving. She was too old, but one of his young bulls got her."

"How about the calf?"

"Died too. It's in the lorry."

"If Saint Willie Gorman spent as much time working as he spends on his knees praying, he'd be a better farmer. If he'd taken care of his fences years ago his bull wouldn't have got out and killed Ken Considine's wife," Mrs Gilligan declared *ex cathedra.* "I never saw anyone working so hard at sainthood at everyone else's expense. That cow would have brought in four-fifty. His wife will be going to the shops again with her apple cakes trying to make a few bob."

Frank Molloy looked away from the car, and was surprised to see O'Brien's one-eyed face was beaming. The thought sped across his mind that this pair might have an interest in each other which went beyond meat for Gilligan's dogs. His determination to get away suddenly weakened. He was discovering an amusing side to Gilligan, and she certainly did not seem as fierce as when she was a solitary gossip reaper. He would simply parry her thrusts as best he could.

The former priest was moving his goggles back over the peak of the cap when the car door creaked open. Arthritically, Mrs Gilligan emerged, palm of right hand planted above hip as it slowly pushed her groaning body into shape; the left hand taking care of the perpendicular by clutching the roof of the car above the open door.

Her wellington boots were splattered with dry cow dung and the hem of her colourless dress covered the tops of the boots. She was wearing a once-maroon cardigan, as shapeless on her shoulders and breasts as a blanket on a thorny bush in a storm. Her hands were dirty and her nails broken.

The knacker lifted his left foot onto the bumper. He put an elbow on the bent knee, and humped his back. He reverted to his own speaking pace.

"If you keep washing your jalopy like this, Maura," he said, "you'll have no paint left on it at all." He laughed at his own joke, and his laughter had a pleasant sound to it.

"Wash my arse, John!" Mrs Gilligan replied with a grin. "And when were you going to tell me that you knew Frank Molloy was home?"

"We just met," Frank Molloy cut in, forcing his way out of the wings. But he was elbowed off the stage at once.

"He's retired, John. At least I got that much out of him yesterday." She threw her eyes at O'Brien, but swung them back immediately to keep Molloy in his place. "He's been home since Monday, home to live like a lord on his American money, and I didn't know it till yesterday."

O'Brien tried to get his penny's worth in. "He lives in the old Duggan one's house on…"

"Oh! I know that." Mrs Gilligan whacked him with the words as if they were karate chops. Then, like a mistress of the loquacious arts taking on all comers, she swung back to Frank Molloy and immobilised him with her eyes. "I told him already how you scraped Duggan off the floor. I never liked that one, with her ghost stories and frightening the daylights out of Marion and Ned since they were children. They're still afraid to go near that blasted garden of no-flowers and rocks, and he's twenty-five and she's twenty-four. Did you find out anything else, John?" Mrs Gilligan pulled the flaps of the cardigan together at her neck, her dirty-nailed hand keeping it closed against the wind.

Molloy, feeling as if he were listening at a keyhole to a conversation about himself, tried to change the subject. "What were Mrs Duggan's stories about? You mentioned them too," he said, and he nodded to John O'Brien.

But O'Brien ignored Frank's question. "Did Gregory kill the fatted calf when he saw you?" he asked.

Molloy's defences were all pointing toward Gilligan, and here was O'Brien waltzing in from the rear. For a moment he was nonplussed, but he quickly recovered.

"I haven't gone to see Gregory yet, and I'd rather have a fatted chicken. Red meat isn't good for the arteries," he said with a smile, hoping the answer might act like a handful of dust in the eyes. "Tell me what Mrs Duggan's ghost stories were about."

"They were about Kit Foley," O'Brien responded, and the sound of his voice was gasoline to Maura Gilligan's smouldering voice. So instantaneous was her verbal combustion that Frank wondered if her labile mouth was merely a true reflection of a labile mind.

"Mrs Duggan! She was Miss Duggan," Gilligan announced. "And she was a proper miss, too. She missed everything, including a man. She talked to everyone as if they were a child of six. I loved to swear in front of her. She hated bad language, but she thought nothing of frightening children with the story about the Foley girl. There was only one story and it was hard to understand; she used words they used ages ago. It was as bad as the *Confiteor* when the mass was in Latin."

As Mrs Gilligan stopped for a breath, John O'Brien jumped in.

"The Foley girl's little garden is fifty yards from your house, out on the golf links. You wouldn't see it for the briars and nettles unless you knew where to look. She was murdered there."

"No she wasn't, John." Mrs Gilligan snatched the narrative back from O'Brien. "Her body was found there."

"That's what I meant," John O'Brien assented.

"Them two brothers of hers aren't worth a pig's fart," Gilligan declared. "They let the weeds and bushes take over the garden and no one else would dare clear them away. Old Bessie Duggan told the children that Kit's ghost keened on Tuesday nights at eleven. Bessie was a bit mad, living by herself all those years with her cats, and going to mass every day of her life, with nothing only the piano and the few children who came to learn to play. I'd swear to God I used to hear the sounds of that piano coming across the links in the middle of the night when I'd be up with a bitch pupping or Seamus dying. I'll tell you, lads, those sounds floating around the links in the dark used to send the shivers up and down my spine."

"Maybe it was the keening of the ghost you were hearing." In comparison to the high-powered noise which had been shooting up the landscape, John O'Brien's voice was a lark ascending after a shower. He took his foot off the bumper of the car, stood up straight and bent backward, hands on hips, thumbs pointing forward.

"Ghost my arse, John!" Gilligan chopped. "Nobody believes in ghosts anymore, and who believed d'oul Duggan one except the children? She's a good riddance, if you ask me." Gilligan snapped her eyes off Molloy's face. "Will you cut off that head for me, John?" She flung a dirty hand in the direction of the dead cow. "I don't want that bloody sergeant knocking on the door and telling me that a certain person has complained about the dogs barking. The last time he told me about the certain person I said to him, 'Certain person, my arse, sergeant! You mean that jumped-up bitch who had nothing but a pair of wellingtons with holes in them before she married Farrell…' What's America like, Frank?" The unexpected switch from narrative to question was like a chop to the back of the neck. It took a moment for Molloy to recover.

"That's like me asking you what Ireland is like," he responded. "You tell me what Ireland is like and I'll tell you what America is like."

"But you were born and bred here," Gilligan said. "You know what Ireland's like."

"I've been out of it for thirty-four years."

For a moment Mrs Gilligan was speechless, and this amused John O'Brien. "Hah! Maura," he said. "You're stuck!"

"Stuck my arse, John! I was adding numbers in my head," Gilligan replied. "Show him how unstuck you are and you tell him what Ireland is like."

"It's the island of saints and scholars," O'Brien recited without hesitation. "That's what the teacher used to say when I was young. All I could think of was everyone in school learning or in the church praying, and I didn't think such a place was so great."

"That was a long time ago, John," Gilligan pointed out, "and I'd say there were a few whores and thicks around then, too, the same as there's a good few hard-working and sober people around today, even though some say Ireland is the island of drones and drunks."

"Drones and drunks!" Frank Molloy said. "Isn't that a little hard?"

But it was O'Brien's question which diverted her. "What's a drone, Maura?"

"It's a fellow who's been on the dole for the last fifteen years, and has no more right to it than I do, because he has a job or could have one. He's a drone!" Mrs Gilligan said, and it seemed she had stumbled across one of her favourite targets. There was super-animation in her voice. "When I see them lads queuing up at the barracks every Tuesday morning in Duneamon for the sergeant to sign their dole papers, I feel like kicking the whole bloody lot of them. The sergeant well knows they're not entitled to any dole. One day I said as much to him, and do you know what the eejit said to me; ah sure, says he, it's only pub money and it's not as if they're depriving the wife and children. I never yet met a Guard who wasn't as thick as a double ditch. I could have whacked the sergeant across the mickey, if I could have found it. God! And the country broke, and the rest of us paying taxes out the armpits." She pulled the cardigan back to her throat. "John! Cut that head off for me so I won't have to see that thick's fat arse tonight. This wind would cut you in two."

"I'll be going," Frank Molloy said. He pulled the goggles down over his eyes.

But Maura Gilligan was not in the habit of letting her prey escape. "How come you took so long to come home? Was it the brother didn't want you, or what?" she asked.

A gust of wind whipped the dust off the ground near the gate and swept it into the three talkers. Maura Gilligan twisted away from the blast and put her hands to her eyes. John O'Brien turned away and spat the dust out of his mouth. Frank Molloy took out his handkerchief and rubbed it across his goggles.

"Oh, I suppose we all take different paths when we grow up," Molloy said. "It just took me this long to get home again." His response caused a momentary silence. *Maybe even Gilligan recognises territory where angels fear to tread.*

But Maura Gilligan was no fearful angel. "Were you never invited home by Gregory?"

"It wasn't that. Some people go away and never come back again. They get taken up with living their own lives."

Maura Gilligan never gave her victims any advantage. She waded in with her next question as Molloy's last answer was falling off his lips. "How were you living your life in America?"

"The way I wanted to," Molloy replied. He took hold of the motorbike's handlebars.

"But was there something wrong with the way you were living it as far as you brother was concerned?"

John O'Brien suddenly developed a minor case of Saint Vitus Dance. His agitated movements only became obvious to Maura Gilligan when he elbowed her in the side. For less than a second she unhooked her eyes from Molloy's face and glanced at O'Brien. No sooner had her eyes snapped back onto Molloy than she was poked again.

"For Christ's sake, O'Brien!" she snapped. "What the hell's wrong with you?"

O'Brien jerked his thumb in Molloy's direction.

"Are you having a fit or what?" Gilligan demanded.

Then, like a stammerer suddenly uncorking a word from his throat, O'Brien blurted out, "You're embarrassing him!"

Molloy saw his escape route. "She may be embarrassing you, Mr O'Brien, but she's not embarrassing me. If I don't want to answer a question, I don't. And I am definitely going to leave now." Molloy pushed his bike forward. "I'll see you again!" he called. He turned around and waved at the couple standing near the dead cow.

"Oh, have no fear of that, Frank!" Mrs Gilligan said. "After all, we are neighbours."

As the former priest threw his leg over the saddle of the bike, Maura Gilligan demanded: "Why the hell did you interfere, John?"

"Because you… You were cutting into him." O'Brien was angry. "It was like I was standing here watching someone getting hacked to bits. The things you were asking him! Sometimes you go too far. All that stuff is his."

"No it's not!" Mrs Gilligan pulled the cardigan tightly across her bosom. "If he's going to live here, then we're going to know something about him."

"If you gave him time he would tell you everything. You don't have to chop him up."

"Chop my arse, John! There are things he doesn't want anyone to know because he's ashamed of them."

"Now, how the hell could you know that, except that everyone has something he's ashamed of."

"Because he's too careful with his answers," Mrs Gilligan declared, and there was no more anger in her words. "He's being too cagey. Now get the jacker out and cut off this head for me."

O'Brien put his hand to his chin. "You know, I think I said fuck a few times before I knew who he was."

"You big eejit! Do you think he never heard the word fuck before?" Gilligan prodded John O'Brien in the stomach with her elbow.

He grunted and said, "Lower and not so hard." He touched her arm.

"I'll make you hard when Lent is over, you old bull," Gilligan said, and she backed her rear end into his crotch.

"Oh, shag, woman!" John O'Brien said in mock dismay. "What would Father Keegan say if he saw you!"

"A good roll in the hay wouldn't do that man any harm."

"Come on now, Maura!" O'Brien said, and the mock dismay was gone out of his voice. "Don't be disrespectful."

"Disrespect my arse!" Maura said. "Maybe if that man had a good ride once in his life he'd stop dancing around in the pulpit. A good hump never hurt anyone."

John O'Brien's respect for the clergyman was overwhelmed by Gilligan's sexual posturing. He reached out with the intention of pressing Maura Gilligan into his crotch to show her the effect of her words. But the woman pulled away. "Get that head for me, John, and I'll give you all the head you can handle on Easter Sunday." When she laughed at her own witticism her laughter sounded like the crowing of a pheasant in wintertime when all the ash trees are naked.

As Frank Molloy was about to start his bike, he heard the sound of an engine. Through the knacker's fence he saw a tractor coming out of John O'Brien's shed. A long arm was attached between the back wheels. The dust at the tractor wheels was blowing away like turf smoke whipped from a chimney in a storm.

John O'Brien backed the tractor over to the cow. When he stopped, Mrs Gilligan stepped under the long arm and pulled down the heavy metal hook. She slipped it into the loop of the rope around the cow's back legs. Above the noise of the tractor Molloy heard her voice: "Pull her up!" Gilligan stepped aside and the back legs of the cow rose from the ground, her tail falling and bending over her back, the mountain between her rump and her head moving as the jacker lifted the body higher. Finally the head moved, lifted, and the ears fell down, covering the eyes. A puff of wind lifted the dust out of the cow's hair and blew it like a disappearing ghost across the heather.

The tractor moved forward and, with every bounce of the wheels, the cow's nose touched the soft soil and left a mark. With Mrs Gilligan walking slowly behind, the tractor and cow became a silhouette in the door of the sunlit shed.

The gloves Frank Molloy took out of his anorak pockets were black; black leather with white wool inside, a gift from Padrake the Christmas before she died, bought from a street vendor in Manhattan. "They probably fell off the back of a truck," she had laughed. As he pulled on the gloves, he shook the memory out of his head and ruminated about his decision to respond truthfully to any question he would be asked on his return to Ireland. Back in New York he had not allowed for grand inquisitors like Maura Gilligan.

Molloy started the motorbike. He pulled the cap firmly down on his head and thought of Walter Cotswold.

Chapter 15

Thursday in the Fifth Week of Lent – 11.55 a.m.

AFTER THIRTY YEARS, any dispassionate man or woman knows that a pair of neglected leather shoes will have disintegrated, turned into dust and had their shape blown away by the wind. But Father Keegan was not dispassionate when it came to leather, and he had read of archeaologists who had dug up Egyptian leather in a good state of preservation thirty-three hundred years after it was tanned.

If the artisans of Egypt, so sophisticated yet so unscientific, could make leather that withstood thirty-three centuries of time, surely modern-day leather-makers, so sophisticated and so scientific, could make a pair of leather shoes which would withstand at least thirty years of time.

Time was all the shoes had to withstand up there on the rotting floor of the loft in his barn.

Father Keegan felt lightheaded. He also felt like throwing up.

Leather! He knew the history of leather, because he had studied it, looking for a glimmer of relief. He knew the presence of a particular enzyme in dog dung was the reason it had been used in the manufacture of leather until the nineteenth century.

Every time he heard the word leather was like being reminded he had an irremovable bullet sitting half an inch from his heart.

Father Keegan knew the pair of leather shoes ensconced on the floor of the loft must not be discovered; else he would die, and the dying would be far worse than physical death. He would be dealt with as severely as was Hester Prynne, although he had never heard of her; a scarlet letter for Hester the close-mouthed; a public pillorying for the equally close-mouthed cleric, the gleeful celebration of the fall of the falsely virtuous man replacing the missiles directed at the entrapped head.

As he drove from the golf links to the presbytery, Father Keegan was speeding, not so much in order to attend to the Culliton boy, but to discover if the shoes had been found, if they had been brought to the ground by the little shit when he fell. He was already imagining himself surreptitiously kicking the mouldy shoes into a dark corner.

As he sped along the narrow road, Keegan felt weak in the bowels.

Thirty years ago, within half an hour of tossing the shoes onto the loft floor, the priest had realised the stupidity of hiding them there. Someone, at some time, would find them. But there was no way he himself could recover them. He did not own a ladder. If he had asked for the loan of a ladder, or bought one, everyone in the village would have known about it. As surely as the subjects in a kingdom would know that their king, wearing his crown and his ermine, was seen returning to his castle with a long ladder over his shoulder, the people of Davinkill would have known about Father Keegan's ladder. And what would the king be doing with a ladder? What Father Keegan was doing with a ladder would give rise to such curiosity, there would have been keen competition among the villagers to be the first to find the answer, or invent one.

The tyres of the car screeched as it rounded the corner where Maybridge Road swung into Downs Road. Nobody was within ear-shot to put the priest-car and the screeching tyres together, else the event, at some future time, would have been used as a date-stone on a par with the Culliton boy's fall:

"That was two years before the Culliton boy fell and Father Keegan came from the golf links, the tyres of his car screeching like a sow with her tits caught in barbed wire."

The loft was eighteen feet from the ground. How many times had he looked up and tried to figure out how to get up there? He never did find a solution, even though he had once thought of building a platform on the roof of his car. He could not hire an outsider to come with his ladder under the pretext of checking out the safety of the loft floor. The first and only thing the tradesman would see was shoes.

So, for thirty years Father Keegan had lived with the bullet lodged near his heart. And the bullet had shifted when the grounds-keeper of the golf links had driven up with the news of the Culliton boy's fall. Now, with his frightened system hyperventilating, his throat as dry as the Gobi desert, he drove into the village with his mouth open. The steering wheel was a lifebelt, and his grasping hands kept him from sinking beneath the tidal wave of anxiety pounding him down. Everything in his stomach had turned to liquid, was slopping around out of control.

He was not aware of the people on the footpaths turning to look when they heard the car speeding up Downs Road. By their mere seeing of the car, the onlookers were becoming bit-part narrators of the drama which would be put together over the next few days. But to Keegan the people were cut-outs of darkness on an otherwise sun-bright pavement. Then he was aware that a curious feeling had fallen over him, as if the water in a cold shower had unexpectedly turned hot. He felt he was inside a man-sized glass jar, moving laboriously in clear, viscous, pleasantly warm liquid. His grip on the steering wheel loosened dangerously and it appeared the car was hurtling along the main street with all the velocity of a three-toed sloth.

Finally, he saw the entrance to the presbytery, and he knew, when the moment came for him to step out of the car, he would not be able to appear normal.

As he turned into the entrance, one of the front wheels missed the slope and jarred over the curbing of the footpath. He was jolted out of his bottled fear and, in the space of time it took to drive into the yard, he managed to take in a deep breath. As he slowly released it, his bottom lip trembled and, for a brief moment, he saw himself as a child, hysterically telling his mother the pup had died during the night, the wounded words falling out between shivering lips.

He could only drive half-way down the yard because Doctor O'Leary's car was in the way, the electronic screeching of a microchip with a Japanese accent telling the world that the doctor had left his door open.

Short-stepping his way on rubbery knees to the barn entrance where O'Leary was kneeling over the boy, Keegan swallowed repeatedly, while his eyes swept the ground around the doorway. As he moved closer he scanned the area beyond the doctor's bent shoulders.

Keegan could hardly contain his bowels, and the Japanese microchip was now assailing his eardrums like sharp icicles in the hands of a torturer. There were clumps of things in there in the dark barn. Some of the heaps were large enough to be a shoe covered with birdshit. There was a brown paper bag.

His momentum was carrying him toward the largest clump, until he realised there were other people present besides Doctor O'Leary. They were moving aside for him like they were the waters of the Red Sea and he was Moses' command to part.

When the priest came to a stop just inside the door, the boy and the doctor below him swayed as if they were in a hammock and he were up in a tree about to fall on them. He felt vomit rising in his throat. Then, as far as the onlookers were concerned, the distressed priest fell to his knees directly opposite Doctor O'Leary, the Culliton boy between them. The onlookers saw the bowed priestly head and the clasped hands between the thighs praying for the recovery, maybe the resurrection, of the victim. But in fact Keegan was making a powerful effort to back out of a brown-out which was threatening to suck him into a full-scale black-out. As he bore down on his rising stomach with every available muscle, he grabbed a wad of inner thigh-flesh in each hand, squeezing until all his attention was focused on the pain he was inflicting on himself.

He felt the blinding ache, like a too-tight turban, unwrapping itself from around his head. The brown-out gave way to light, and he began to salivate like a hyena smelling its first meal in a week. Swallowing rapidly to accommodate the sudden influx, he wiped the escaping excess off his dripping chin with the palm of his hand.

As the self-inflicted pain in Keegan's thighs began the stirrings of a non-sexual erection, the boy on the ground between himself and the doctor moved and snorted. Keegan looked up and saw the doctor snatching the stethoscope out of his ears and flinging it aside. O'Leary put one hand on the boy's buttocks and the other on his neck.

"Don't move!" he commanded. Then he turned to the onlookers. "Which one is this?" he demanded.

"Johnny!" several people answered at the same time, each longing to have his name engraved in the future narration of the drama unfolding before them.

Before the doctor could speak again he felt a weak struggle in his palms. "You're all right, Johnny. You fell through Father Keegan's loft floor and knocked yourself out." Like a trussed duck on its way to the knife, the Culliton boy squirmed under whatever was pinning him to the ground. "I'm Doctor O'Leary, and I'm holding you down so you won't move. You might have hurt your back or something else. I'm going to take my hands away and examine you. Relax, and if I touch anything that's sore, tell me." As O'Leary cautiously removed his weight, Johnny Culliton moved his head and squinted up out of one eye, the other closed against the gravel under his face. What the boy saw was Father Keegan's face. With a squeal the boy jumped to his feet, ran and disappeared through the gate into Father Keegan's orchard. A gasp went up from the small group of people, and a woman and a boy ran after Johnny Culliton.

The priest and the doctor gaped at each other, the space between them empty, each of them kneeling on the barn floor. From where the onlookers stood, the doctor and the priest looked like two grown men kneeling in the dirt, about to play marbles.

Keegan was unaffected by the recovery of the boy. He was still in deathly danger, and he was being extremely careful. With nerves stretched to the breaking point, he knew that at any moment they could snap, that he would collapse, a slobbering mass, beneath a heap of his own broken and twisted nervous conduits, blabbing out the truth about the shoes because he could not bear it all anymore.

Without making any noise, Keegan took a deep, relaxing breath and decided he would not speak until the doctor spoke to him. Holding the breath he sat back on his heels and looked over at O'Leary. The doctor, still on his knees, was gathering up his stethoscope. He glanced at the priest. "You'd better do something about that loft, Father." Still looking the priest in the eye, the doctor silently called Keegan by the derisive nickname he had for him. Puta, Puta, Puta, Puta.

Instead of taking umbrage at the gratuitous advice about his loft, Keegan saw a whole string of Christmas lights flashing inside his head. But the lights had been flashing for a few seconds before he even saw them. Then suddenly they flared brighter and he caught up with the realisation which was already in his brain – he could now bring a long ladder into the presbytery yard on his shoulder in broad daylight and, instead of being curious, the villagers would be sympathetically cheering him on. But the lights dimmed when he remembered that the shoes might not be up there anymore, that they might be on the ground in full view of the gawking spectators. He wished they would all go away so he could look around, so he could dig himself out of this pit of anxiety.

Doctor O'Leary was getting ready to stand up, the retrieved stethoscope hanging out of his jacket pocket. "I think that lad's going to be in bed for a few days," he said. "If it's not the shock, it'll be his paining muscles and bones that'll keep him there." Without putting a hand to the ground, the doctor rolled backward off his knees onto his bent toes. He stood up without grunting. His knees didn't even creak.

If he had not been weak with fear, the priest might have been able to get up by putting only one hand on the ground. As it was, he barely made it with two hands pushing, his rear end trying to find the centre of gravity. And while he felt as awkward as a sea lion on hot sand, he was aware that he had yet to say something to the doctor, something which would fit into the immediate circumstance. As he rubbed the dirt off his hands with his gleaming handkerchief, he said, "That loft will be down tomorrow, Doctor." Then he went back over the words in his head to examine them, to make sure there was nothing incriminating in them.

O'Leary swiped at the dirt on the knees of his trousers. When he straightened up he looked around at the bits and pieces of nests among the bits and pieces of rotting wood. "Boys and birds' nests!" he said. And then, changing the subject so quickly it took Keegan several moments to catch up with him, the doctor asked, "Your man, Considine. Did his wife ever give birth to a child?"

Inside his head, Keegan said the word Considine several times. O'Leary was pulling him into a minefield that was every bit as treacherous as the one he was standing in. Keegan wondered if Considine had finally told the whole story to the doctor; he wondered if O'Leary was laying a trap for him. When he answered, he sounded like a disoriented old man. "Yes... Considine... Yes... Ken. His wife had a baby girl. She lived for about a month."

"What happened?" The doctor took another swipe at his trousers.

"Something the mother passed to her in her milk."

The doctor made a final adjustment to his jacket. "I was just wondering, from something he said. I have to go. Goodbye, Father Keegan."

Even though they were two of the few professionals in the village, the priest and the doctor treated each other formally. When he had arrived in the village to take over the practice, the doctor had introduced himself to the priest as Peter O'Leary, and the priest had reciprocated by introducing himself as Father Keegan. Since then O'Leary had maintained the formality.

It was when the doctor closed his car door, and in the process silenced the screeching microchip, that the intensity of Keegan's anxiety lessened by a hair. Considine! What had Considine…? But as he looked after the departing car, he knew he had to get rid of the small group of parishioners. Then, without thinking, he had fallen into his old authoritative role and was walking toward the gawkers, saying, "Well, that was a fortunate child." He held his hands out as if he were shooing a flock of turkeys before him.

For the first time since he'd driven into the yard, he was able to see the people as individuals, and the first one he saw was Paddy Dillon. Keegan knew then that an exaggerated and cruelly humorous version of what had happened in his barn would be heard in all the pubs in the village before closing time.

As he herded the onlookers from the yard, Keegan boldly turned aside requests to see the nests which had fallen from the loft. Picking up on what O'Leary had said, Keegan made small talk about boys and birds' nests as he ushered the herd out into the footpath. Then he closed the archway's two large double doors and checked to be sure the wicket door was deadlocked.

For a second he rested his back against the door, but using his shoulder blades he propelled himself forward and quickly returned to the barn. There he examined every clump on the ground, turning most of them over with his toe. There were no shoes on the ground, nothing but nests. Some had broken eggs; one had a dead chick, hairy and bug-eyed beneath purple-skinned lids. Several chicks were shivering their way to death among the debris. Finally, Keegan stood against the end wall. It was almost dark where he was standing. Leaning back he put his hands to his face, his fingers on his eyes under his glasses. He wept.

It was the sound of his whimpering dog that penetrated his self-centredness, assuring him that things had returned to normal. The dog's whimperings turned into music, and as he listened to it, the priest took in sobbing lungs of air. He pulled the handkerchief from his pocket and dried off his face. He blew his nose loudly.

Another sob shook him unexpectedly as he walked across the arched and doorless doorway. He continued into the dimness to where he could hear the dog's tail thumping in expectation. The dog came forward to meet him, the links of the long chain making the same noise against the side of the metal barrel as a child's stick playing over the bars of an iron railing. Father Keegan took the dog's head in his two hands. If he had been less inhibited he would have kissed the dog on the forehead. As it was, the dog whimpered painfully under the onslaught of the fierce one-sided, physical affection. Rising off its front paws, it tried to extricate itself by pulling backward. Keegan, unaware of the pain he was inflicting, followed the dog through the straw. He stepped on something which moved beneath his foot, and his ankle twisted painfully. The dog slipped out of his grasp.

The priest bent down and groped around in the semi-darkness for the thing he had stepped on. Whatever it was, it did not feel good; it was covered with little lumps which were ravelling away beneath his grasp. As he walked to the door to examine his find, he stumbled over the paper bag. There was something in it. He bent and picked that up too, and then he walked into the light of the doorway.

Chapter 16

Thursday in the Fifth Week of Lent – 12.00 noon

IT USED TO be that when he thought of Walter Cotswold his stomach went to war with itself.

Even though it was over thirty years since Frank had last seen him, Molloy knew that, once upon a time, Cotswold had held power over him to such a degree that his first religious superior had become a permanent resident in his psyche; that he would never be entirely rid of the bad memory. Somewhere along the line, the memory had festered all the more when Frank had learned that power is given away, not taken.

"Rat-faced bastard!" he heard himself saying, above the putt-putt of the motor bike.

Ahead of him, the early-spring hedges on each side of the narrow road converged in the distance. Dandelions were sprinkled in the grassy verges, their sunny faces warning of the impending onslaught of spring. He thought he detected a promise of green in the bushes. Neither man nor animal was in view. But Cotswold came back.

The Very Reverend Canon Walter Cotswold was the personification of the underside of the Church, and Frank Molloy, as a newly ordained priest, had discovered him in the presbytery in Falworth.

When he stepped through the door of that presbytery, he walked into the dark tunnels which had been formed over decades of solitary isolation under the rock of the Church. Molloy's innocence, enthusiasm and freshness had cast an illuminating light into the passageways of horror. Slimy, toothless creatures with big mouths slithered around him until he was in a constant state of withdrawal, in a constant state of jumping aside to avoid the long, sticky, foul-smelling bodies oozing past him in the narrow passageways. It took him one week to recognise and give names to the horrible things: cynicism; laziness; xenophobia; pomposity; self-conceit; immaturity. There was no religion under this rock, no humanity, no love. Cotswold spent his life panting outside the bishop's door hoping to be noticed, hoping for a position in the administration of the diocese from where he could prod his fellow priests, forcing them to acknowledge his privileged position. Cotswold was the epitome of the old priest stuck in the mind-set of the clerical student; a psychological monster who had gone to seed before growth was achieved, bloated on his own notion of the privileged position of the priest in the community. To Cotswold, all people who were not priests were inferior. They were also fools.

From the moment he stepped through the door of that presbytery, Frank Molloy spent seven years trying to disentangle himself from the priesthood. And for five years his anxiety level was close to that of a hysterical woman clawing at a squealing bat in her hair on a dark night.

On his motorbike, on the road home to his new house in Davinkill, Frank Molloy shuddered.

It was my fear of Maura Gilligan's probing scalpel that reminded me of Cotswold. It's my determination to keep him out of view that makes him pop up, like trying too hard to keep an inflated balloon under water. Maybe some day I'll be able to burst the balloon and let it float away. Maybe some day soon I'll finally convince myself that Cotswold was just an affection-starved child, and that his behaviour flowed from some angry place. But even if I do, will I be able to let him go, bury the fucker once and for all, forgive the shit?

Another shudder swept Molloy's body, and he felt Walter Cotswold slipping away like the hard tip of the probe slipping out at the end of an colonoscopic examination.

The road began to rise and, as he got closer to the village of Davinkill, the hedges on either side gave way to barbed-wire fencing, wisps of wool trembling on the barbs closest to the ground. Clumps of off-white sheep spotted the landscape. Some of the closer ones looked up at the approaching motorbike, appearing to frown when they twisted their black ears to Molloy's intrusive sounds.

Joyce said a nun invented barbed wire. Having his little joke at the expense of the nun's guarded virginity. Joyce was a mocker. But can anyone leave home for a long time, and not feel impatient with those who stay, the homebody constrained by brittle social pressures every bit as naturally as a turtle locked in its shell. I was intolerant of Maura Gilligan and John O'Brien; he sitting on a dead cow, picking his lunch out of the hair; she dirty, and as feminine as the back end of a camel. I'll have to be wary of my impatience. I didn't take a shower every day until I went to New York, and I'd never even heard of dry cleaning or deodorant. I'll have to be careful, too, of revealing my liberation from ecclesiastical manacles and unforgiving social pressure.

The strip of asphalt began to slope down to its junction with the Limerick Road. Molloy sat up straight in the saddle and switched off the engine. As he sailed down the slight incline the rushing wind was loud in his ears.

Right now I know I was right to come back. I'll have to remember these moments if the going gets tough, when I have to face Gregory.

When he came free-wheeling around the sharp corner at the bottom of the hill, he put on his back brake. Ten yards ahead, a green bus flashed by, its roaring exhaust pipe tearing the air apart.

At the stop sign Molloy put his feet to the ground, and the sound of a car horn screeched beside him.

"Jesus Christ!" Molloy glared at the car, his skin crawling from the fright the raucous klaxon had given him.

He recognised it immediately. Even before the window beside him started to open, Molloy's defence mechanisms went on alert.

Maura Gilligan was leaning across the front seat when she spoke, her eyes turned up in their sockets looking at him. "I told you we'd run into each other," she shouted above the noise of the engine.

In a streak of red, a motorbike without a muffler shattered the environs of the Limerick Road, nailing its metallic noise onto the countryside with the grace of a riveter working in a small room.

When the assault on his ears had abated, Frank drew back as the smell from Gilligan's car sprang out at him. He put his hand to his mouth, the flesh of his face pinching his pores closed.

God! She must have shit in her drawers. How the hell can she stay in there!

Molloy, unable to respond to Maura Gilligan's greeting, coughed into his hand.

"I told O'Brien I'd catch up with you before you made it to the main road, and as well as that I wanted to ask you something without O'Brien listening. He gets embarrassed. So, tell me! What was wrong with the way you were living your life in America?"

Frank recoiled further from the car. While one part of his brain told him he was pulling away from the question as much as he was retreating from the foul odour, another part was scrambling around looking for an appropriate answer. Even though the unexpected encounter with Maura Gilligan had the effect of a bushwhacking, Molloy was surprised at the defence his mind threw up.

"You didn't wait to get the head after all!" he shouted.

With an almost unnoticeable backward flick of her eyes Maura Gilligan shouted back, "I got the head all right. That only took as long as it took to cut off and put in the car. I said to O'Brien, I'll bet the story we heard about him getting married outside the Church is true, and he said no, he doesn't have the look of a man who wasn't married in the Church." The car rolled back a few feet, and when Gilligan jammed her foot on the brake her collapsed perm shook.

That must be the stink! The head's in the trunk and the smell's escaping into the car.

"The look of a man married outside the Church." Molloy said. "When we were small we used to think we could tell a Protestant by his looks. We thought they were all red-faced and a bit fatter than Catholics. They were a different breed."

Through the open window Molloy saw the condition of the inside of the car. A plastic statue of Saint Christopher on the dashboard, the folds of its plastic clothes filled with dirt, was almost overwhelmed by torn envelopes and small pieces of paper. Dogs' collars and leashes were pressed in a tangled heap against the glass.

Gilligan was still leaning across the front seat with her eyes twisted up at her quarry. "I could pick out a Protestant in the dark," she yelled, and her false teeth were uncovered for a moment. "They smell different than Catholics; it's their scented soap. I can even pick out a Catholic who has Protestant blood in him from years ago. It's in the eyes."

I wonder can she pick out an atheist who was once a Catholic?

Molloy heard the sound of a tractor. He glanced back. "Someone's coming," he yelled. "Maybe you'd better move out of the way."

Maura Gilligan sat up and rolled the driver's window down as far as it would go. She waved at the tractor to pass. With the window down there was an increase of light and Molloy could see into the rear of the car.

Lying on its side on the seat was the head of the cow – horns, ears, eyes, nostrils. The jaw was slightly out of line and several green-smeared teeth were visible along the edge of the sneering lip. The whole thing looked huge, monstrous. Frank took another step away. To detach his eyes from the head, he had to swing his head away.

Saint God! With the back of his hand he wiped the saliva off his lips. *This woman is a savage.*

The clacking noise of the oncoming diesel tractor overwhelmed the sound of the dog woman's idling engine. For an instant the sounds and the smell threatened to overcome Molloy. He tightened his grip on his handlebars.

But the tractor did not pass by. When it drew level, the driver jammed his feet down on the clutch and brake pedals. He did not push back on the accelerator lever. The engine roared and the tractor vibrated as its exhaust stack spewed screaming black smoke into the sky. The driver, a man of about seventy wearing a fedora, was grinning. He raised his hat to Maura Gilligan.

Maybe he's an idiot!

The tractor driver's lips began to move.

Above the roar Frank heard Gilligan's screaming voice, saw her gesticulating hand waving in the air above the car. *Screw this!* Molloy started his engine. Without looking back he edged up to the side of the Limerick Road. He waited for a car to pass and then he slowly putt-putted across the highway.

No wonder Joyce was a mocker. Frigging assholes!

Chapter 17

Thursday in the Fifth Week of Lent – 12.20 p.m.

THE COMMONS WAS a low plateau of about five square miles. The Davinkill Road on the west and the Maybridge Road on the east separated it from the surrounding farms. Two minor roads off the Davinkill Road dissected the Commons, but they ended before they reached the Maybridge Road. Maura Gilligan lived in the last house on Sommers Lane, and the old music teacher, Bessie Duggan, had lived in the last cottage on Wheat Mill Lane. Although there were about twenty homes scattered around the Commons, this was public land. The farmers who grazed their sheep here paid the local county council by the head. The Commons Golf Links, partly situated between Sommers and Wheat Mill Lanes, paid a yearly rent.

There were few trees on the plateau, and what hedges there were did not serve as demarcation boundaries. The hedges were clumps of random bushes, resulting from seeds dumped indiscriminately on the blind commands of avian excretory systems.

As Frank Molloy glided uphill he could hear the sound of dogs barking.

Gilligan's hungry beagles! I hope to God I get past the entrance to Sommers Lane before she catches up again. I could take her in small doses – almost enjoy fencing with her. But she doesn't know when to back away. I can't afford to tell her to mind her own goddamn business. There's nothing as awkward as an alienated neighbour, especially one you have to run into every day. What was wrong with how I lived my life in America!

Across the stretch of green land to his left Molloy could see Maura Gilligan's house, two slim, van Gogh trees dwarfing it from behind. The other cottage, this side of Gilligan's, belonged to the Farrells; Bridie Farrell, she of the proprietary rights to a pair of leaky wellingtons, now the wife of Patrick Farrell, and the complainer to the sergeant of Gilligan's noisy dogs.

Bridie Farrell is forever pigeonholed by Gilligan's venom. The leaking boots transform Farrell into poor trash, and at the same time gives Gilligan social elevation.

Molloy was within fifty yards of Sommers Lane when the sound of an approaching vehicle caught up with him. Before he had time to wish it was not Gilligan again, the sound of the horn blasted him.

Shit! It's her.

The car drew level with the motorbike and the horn blew again.

God! What a loud woman!

Gilligan came to a stop ahead of him. When he drew level, Molloy kept his distance from the window. Gilligan's body was stretched across the seat, her eyes on Molloy. Twists of grey-black hair hung on her forehead.

Maybe that's how she drives – lying across the seat, always ready to talk.

"That was Saint Willie Gorman on the tractor. He's as deaf as a post, but he never turns on his hearing aid, and he answers all the questions he imagines you're asking him. It's like talking to someone with brain damage. He only wears the hearing aid because of his wife. He thinks that because God made him deaf he should stay deaf. If I was married to him he'd have been a martyr a long time ago, as well as a saint. He talked for five minutes with the tractor roaring under him like a volcano. You never answered my question – is it true you were married and got divorced and got married again?"

"No! That's not true. I think I heard the beagles barking when I was back there a bit."

"They'll bark for another while till I get this thing boiled. The Missus Farrell will have a canary. So you were never divorced?"

"No."

"But you got married outside the Church?"

"Yes."

"What happened to the wife. Is she still in America?"

"She died."

"My Seamus died, too, five years ago. To tell the truth I got a new lease on life. It was time for him to die. We moved here about a year before, and I gave the farm to Ned. Marion's training to be an accountant in Scotland. She wanted to do nursing but I told her nurses are so plentiful they thatch pighouses with them in England."

Maura Gilligan's head disappeared, and suddenly she was standing at the other side of the car, her folded arms resting on the dirty roof.

Shit! I'm stuck.

"Two of the dogs belong to O'Brien. All Seamus ever did was moan and gripe about the cost of feeding them. Well, it costs nothing now. I take care of O'Brien's dogs and he gives me heads." Maura Gilligan suddenly and furiously rubbed her nose with the back of her hand. She continued to speak as the tip moved around her face.

"O'Brien's all right, even though the farmers don't like him. You'd think he was the cause of the cattle dying. He hates being called the knacker. A good few call him 'that bollicks from Gannonbeg'. He came into the village about forty years ago, and you'd think he'd come from China! You know what this country's like. Unless you were born in a place, you'll always be an outsider, and sure Gannonbeg is only a couple of miles up the road. We're two outsiders, O'Brien and myself. I married into Seamus's place just after you were ordained, and some of the old ones around here still treat me like a stranger. When I walk into a place they all shut up and look at me like I was a disease. O'Brien's the same. They all hate him because they think he's an outsider making money off them. They hate the smell of death from his lorry when he comes to pick up the dead animals. The farmers say O'Brien's so mean that he'd package the animals' holes and sell them if only he knew how. But O'Brien's all right. He says the only time he would turn his back on a farmer is at Sunday mass. As far as he knows no one in Ireland has ever been murdered during mass. I told him there's always a first time." Maura Gilligan cackled at her own joke.

"There's the dogs again!" Molloy said and, for emphasis, he held his head in a listening pose. But Mrs Gilligan chose not to notice.

"He's a real outcast, but he knows more about everyone than anyone else in the town. It's like he gathers all this stuff just to spite them. I'm about the only friend he has who was once a farmer. The smell of the dead animals is like everything else; you get used to it. Had your wife any children?"

"Two."

"You'll never give away too much about yourself, will you, now, Frank? First a priest, then married, then two children. In a month I'll find out everything. What do you bet, Frank?"

"There's nothing to find out," Molloy said.

"Oh! I think there's a lot to know, Frank. You can't just move in among us unless we know all about you. It wouldn't be fair. Everyone here knows everything about everyone else. Do you hear those dogs! The Missus Farrell will be on the phone, la dee da, to the sergeant if I don't get home with this head. Why don't you drop over for a sup of tea sometime?"

"I'll do that!" Frank Molloy lied.

"You're the first person that I ever met who married outside the Church, and a priest one time as well, and you're not so bad. I thought you'd be real hard and cranky." Maura Gilligan disappeared and the car moved on its springs when she sat into it. She switched on the engine and, as she pulled away, she shouted through the open window, "One month, Frank!"

Frank Molloy looked after the car. Once again he started the engine and slipped the bike into gear.

Walter Cotswold's head popped up like a target in a shooting gallery, and Molloy shot it down immediately with a mouthful of invective.

I never thought I'd be scrutinised like this. I'm too used to the anonymity of the sprawling suburbs. Anonymity was the first dividend of leaving the priesthood, and it's going to be a real pisser to give it up. But I'll be ignored if I refuse to be integrated. And the only way I'll be integrated is to spill my guts. Maybe I should be more generous with the mundane stuff. But Maura Gilligan with a piece of gossip is like a child swinging a heavy chain in a crowded schoolyard.

Molloy looked down Sommers Lane as he passed by. Gilligan's car was bouncing its way out of sight at the head of a cloud of wind-whipped dust.

Does the cow's head slip around on the back seat, blood and secretions all over the place? Does she ever clean out the car? Maybe she lets the dogs in to lick up the mess. Saint God!

The road intersecting the golf course under Molloy's motorbike became a piece of black ribbon dropped on the landscape by a passing giant child. The short, sheep-grazed grass came up to the edge of the narrow road on either side. One hundred yards to his left the flag of the twelfth hole fluttered in the same breeze that shook the brown leaves of the huge beech tree standing close by.

No golfers were in sight.

Bare, flowerless stalks of ragwort stuck out of the ground like miniature dead tree trunks, but the colours of spring were waiting just below the ground to follow the dandelions.

Snowdrop. Anemone. Daughter of the wind. They're gone already. But next spring I'll see the snowdrops here in Ireland. Yeats and his sister in Holland Park wishing to feel the earth of Sligo! How often have I longed to see the white snowdrops, to smell the primroses, to feel a dodgeball of cowslips pressed into my face. Dodgeball, dodgeball, tell me the truth – how many more years have I to go to school? – a piece of twine stretched between the backs of two kitchen chairs and the two of us stringing the cowslips.

The sound of another vehicle broke over Frank Molloy's thoughts with the harshness of a winter wave breaking on a cold beach. Even as he guided the motorbike to the edge of the road, the horn blared at him and sent a shiver of fright up his back.

Them and their fucking horns! The motorbike wobbled and, to keep his balance, he had to steer onto the grass. *Shit!*

As soon as the small red lorry drew level with him, Frank Molloy gasped. The smell of rotting flesh. Putrefaction.

The vehicle swerved onto the grass ahead of him as Molloy brought the motorbike to a stop. When he got his feet on the ground he pulled out his handkerchief. The vapours of death sank into his lungs before he could cover his mouth and nose.

It can only be the knacker. No wonder people hate him!

"We meet again," John O'Brien called out as he appeared at the back of his meat wagon. Without the goggles, his face looked longer, and the glass eye looked smaller than the real one. While he walked back to Molloy, he continued talking. "As Maura said, we'll keep running into each other." O'Brien's long, stork-like legs carried him quickly to where Molloy was trying to keep his stomach contained. A fainter version of the lorry's odour wafted off O'Brien's person.

Molloy wiped his eyes and returned the handkerchief to his face.

"Are you all right?" O'Brien asked. "You don't look so well."

"I'm not used to the smell. I'm afraid it caught me by surprise."

O'Brien slapped Frank Molloy on the shoulder. "As Maura says, you can get used to anything."

Even though Molloy could still taste the corruption in his mouth, the nausea which had shaken his stomach was abating. He took the handkerchief away from his mouth. "Yes, I suppose you can," he said.

O'Brien rested his frying-pan hand on the centre of the handlebars.

"Now let me show you something. Do you remember Maura and me telling you about the Foley girl? She was found murdered right over there."

O'Brien pointed past the lorry to the pile of long grass and leafless briars near the edge of the road. It was the same spot which Mary Delaney, the day before, had pointed out to him from the front door of his house. "There's a little garden in the bushes with stones around it. I haven't seen it myself since about a month after the flowers were planted. People came from all over the place to see it then. Come on!" O'Brien took his hand off the handlebars and started walking.

"I'll meet you over there," Molloy replied. "I want to keep on the windy side of the truck."

When the two men came together again, O'Brien said, "They never found where Donaghue jumped in, but it only took him one day to wash up on Scattery. They say he was a very big man, nearly six foot six. I didn't know him, only to see. He had come here a few months before. He worked for CIE."

Frank Molloy stayed on upwind of O'Brien. "Could *you* drown yourself?" he asked.

"If I had to face a wife and four children at home after doing it to a young girl, and then sticking a pipe in her neck, I could." O'Brien put his hand inside his jacket and scratched at his armpit with the abandon of a dog tearing at an itch with its back leg.

"What do you mean, *doing it*?" Molloy asked.

John O'Brien yanked his hand out of his armpit and swung it around in the air. "Oh... you know... You were a married man yourself. He gave her a rub of the relic. Then he had to kill her in case she told about it."

Frank Molloy glanced at the knacker and saw he was blushing. "Rub of the relic?" he said with a question mark in his tone. "A relic of the true cross?"

They had reached the clump of briars and grass. Stems of dead nettles and brittle, black, dead leaves shivered in the breeze.

John O'Brien poked his long leg into the wild growth. "You're being funny, Frank. Here. Put the bike down and stand near me so I can balance myself."

Molloy pulled the bike up on its stand and, when he stepped over to the weeds, O'Brien clasped his shoulder with long talons. He swung his wellingtoned foot from side to side. "I kissed a relic of the true cross one time. It was in Knock."

"I read that if all the relics of the true cross were put together, there would be enough lumber for railroad ties from Jerusalem to Jericho," Molloy responded.

O'Brien's body swayed in the opposite direction of his swinging leg, and Molloy braced himself against each transmitted burst of energy.

"Protestants say things like that about Catholics," O'Brien said, and he hopped forward on his left foot to get at more grass and briars. "One time in the North, when the Catholics had a parade, the Protestants hung a side of bacon in a butcher's window and wrote 'Cured at Lourdes' under it. Wasn't that a terrible thing to do! Terrible blasphemy. It's a wonder God didn't strike them dead. And you're a Catholic!" O'Brien halted his ground-clearing activity and looked at Frank Molloy.

"I'm not a Catholic now."

O'Brien stopped beating the dead weeds. "You're not a Catholic? And you after being a priest!" he said with accusation in his voice. But then, as if to erase what he had blurted out, he immediately took a step forward and, with the pressure of his fingers, pulled Molloy after him. "You shouldn't talk about the true cross like that, no matter what you are, in case God would strike you dead."

"I was only telling you about something I read," Molloy said.

"Even so! You have to be careful with them kind of things. Ah! I just felt a stone with my toe. Look! There it is! A few rocks in a ring. The family hadn't a pot to piss in. Excuse me." John O'Brien released Molloy's shoulder and stepped forward. He flattened the remaining weeds with his big boots.

Besides the circle of field stones, there was no evidence that a sad garden had been planted here once by a grieving family.

John O'Brien sank down onto his hunkers. He looked up at Frank Molloy. "Donaghue was like Maura and myself, an outsider, even though I'm only a two-miler. He was from County Donegal, away off at the back of beyond." John O'Brien stood up and energetically rubbed the backs of his legs. He turned away from the garden of stones. "That's Donaghue for you, now. His nuts got the better of him for a minute and look what happened. The girl got murdered, he killed himself, his wife was left a widow and the children were made orphans. All because of a pair of nuts."

Frank Molloy pulled the motorbike off its stand. "Is she still alive, the widow?" He started walking toward the road. O'Brien fell in beside him on the wrong side. Molloy put his handkerchief to his face.

"She's alive. I saw her at mass this morning. A great looking woman," O'Brien said. "They say she's real nice and she did a great job with the children. All of them went to the university. One of the daughters even went to a school in France. She is terrible brainy. They say the widow has a well-off brother in America who paid for everything. Maybe it was better off she was with the old lad killing himself."

I wanted to kill myself once. At least I wanted to die very badly.

They came to the edge of the road, and Molloy moved into the wind. "Well, I'll be off," he said. *I've had enough socialising for one day.*

"So long, Frank!" O'Brien called after the bike. "I'll tell Maura I ran into you again."

Two hundred yards to the head of the lane... Will I make it before I'm waylaid again?

As he neared Wheat Mill Lane, Molloy heard the knacker's lorry coming up behind him. He braced himself for the screech of the horn. But the noise increased until the sound of the motorbike was overwhelmed.

When he wheeled into the lane, he glanced back over his shoulder to see what machine was threatening his eardrums. A tractor was roaring along in a low gear, its engine one revolution ahead of the flooding diesel fuel that was trying to drown it. Saint Willie Gorman, his hat at a rakish angle, was sitting in the seat in the middle of the noise, an idiotic smile on his face, one hand waving with enthusiasm.

Molloy returned the greeting with an anaemic gesture and kept going.

Chapter 18

Thursday in the Fifth Week of Lent – 9.06 p.m.

THE AIR WAS turgid with the sounds of Vivaldi's *Dixit Dominus.* The Red Priest had lived at a time when the people of Venice knew God was on their side, when it had been their city's turn to rule the waves. The self-righteous and triumphant feelings, which had once swelled Venetian breasts, had been trapped by Vivaldi nearly three hundred years ago. The several choir lofts in Saint Mark's had been used to great stereophonic effect by the composer, but Frank Molloy wondered if Vivaldi had heard his own composition as clearly or as powerfully as he was hearing it in a small room, lying on his couch.

Molloy closed his eyes to the sparsely furnished front room and the plastic-shaded bulb in the ceiling. As the music and voices rose he contracted all his muscles and held the tension until the choir began to slide out of the crescendo. Pleasure swept through him, a shiver almost. He drew the multi-coloured blanket closer to himself, and luxuriated in the warmth of the cover, as if he were in a hot bathtub on a winter's night, the wind howling outside.

Frank found himself thinking about the Athabasca glacier in Alberta. He and Padrake were holding hands as they walked on the dirty ice, holding onto each other because it was slippery underfoot. The small crevasses, like giant knife cuts, gave the glacier the look of a tightly bunched herd of white-backed animals. They turned from the tourist-spotted mountain of ice. Ten feet away was the toe of the glacier where the ice melted and ran away in fast, narrow rivulets.

Frank spoke. "Can you imagine being a drop of water and wondering if you would ever be free: trapped for a thousand years and thinking of the times you floated in a cloud, or rushed down the side of a mountain in a stream, or watered a daffodil."

"Oh, you great big poetic Mick!" Padrake smiled. "You're so romantic."

"I wasn't trying to be romantic. I was thinking of myself when I saw the water: the priesthood – being trapped in it: trying to find a painless way out: melting out of it as unnoticed as the water melting out of the ice."

They gazed down at the fleeing water, rushing away from the monster which had held it prisoner for so long.

Vivaldi swelled into his ears again, and he knew why his memory had pulled the glacier out of its storage banks.

Venetian emotions, glacial waters and himself. All trapped once upon a time. All free now.

Frank shuddered at the memory of the chains which had bound him. But to look back was to get trapped all over again, like Lot's wife. No forward movement was possible if the two eyes were kept firmly on the past. Never again! Like the post-war Jews – never again.

The instant the room emptied of the music a loud banging took over.

Molloy jumped up, his knees protesting the hurried movement, and he stiffly strode to the door, the blanket over his left arm.

Whoever it is must have been knocking for ages. God! Maybe it's my brother.

He threw the blanket over his shoulder and pulled back the crude sliding bolt near the floor. He turned the old-fashioned key and pulled the door in, his heart pounding.

It was a man in a hat. Black overcoat. Glasses. Tall. Shoes shining.

Molloy said, "Hi," and the man outside said, "Hello, Frankie."

Frank's heart leaped, and he peered at the face, barely lit from the ceiling light behind him. "Gregory?"

"Eddie Keegan."

Eddie Kee… Feelings of disappointment and relief washed over him. "Eddie! Jesus! Eddie, come in!" Molloy stretched his greeting hand to the priest. As Father Keegan stepped forward he took off his hat.

They shook hands, examined each other, both grinning, Molloy barefooted, casual shirt open at the neck, coloured blanket a vague North-American-Indian prop.

The priest was in his official uniform: black suit, black shoes, black hat, white collar. If clothes maketh the man, then Keegan had it over Molloy in intimidation.

As they shook hands they blushed. After so many years Molloy was shocked to see how age had changed the features, the stance, the hair, and he knew he was looking at himself in Keegan.

"You wore well, Eddie!" Molloy finally said. *He's the cleanest person I've seen since I came back.*

"I think I wore better than you, Frankie!"

"You did, Eddie, at least on the outside." Molloy rubbed his hand across his bald head. "Give me your coat."

They were both smiling when Molloy turned around from hanging the coat on the back of the door. He pointed to the couch. "Sit, Eddie!"

In a flushed flurry of questions and answers, they each established the other's present circumstances. Keegan did some breast-beating about the abandoning of his friend when Frankie needed him most. But Molloy reminded Keegan that thirty years ago when a priest left the service of the Church there was an immediate closing of the ranks behind him. The departed priest was a threat to the ones who stayed, and the only way to deal with him was to ostracise him.

"You were a child of the times, Eddie."

Then, awkwardly, they stumbled around, nervous, as if they were naked, afraid of bumping into each other, Molloy not knowing Keegan's agenda, Keegan in the presence of one who had thrown out everything he himself had held onto, even if it was so long ago.

"How long were you knocking?"

"Four or five minutes. I thought you were either dead or deaf."

"And I'm neither. I like some music loud."

"That wasn't *Galway Bay* you were playing."

"Vivaldi. *Dixit Dominus.*"

Eddie Keegan, who had been sitting on the edge of the couch, now sat back comfortably. "It can't ever be got out of the system, they say."

"What do you mean?" Molloy asked, as he, too, relaxed into the far corner of the couch.

Keegan waved his hand at the speakers on the shelves. "The Church, the sacred music."

"It's not because it's sacred that I listen to it. I'm not sure if Vivaldi thought of it as sacred. He was more of a musician than he was a priest."

Keegan moved his position on the couch. "Oh, I didn't even know he was a priest. Anyhow, I didn't mean to…" He smiled broadly with his mouth, the eyes not joining in. "How the hell are you, Frankie? Wouldn't it be nice if we could transmit in a few seconds all the things that happened since the last time saw each other?"

"I'd have to do some editing before I transmitted," Molloy said. "I imagine you would, too, Eddie."

The priest hesitated. "Sure I would. I don't think anyone likes to put himself on display without some protection."

Silence descended on them, as if they were cataloguing what to hide from each other.

"Before we go any further, Eddie, can you tell me why you've come? I think that would put us on a more equal footing."

Holding out his hands as if to show he wasn't concealing anything, Keegan smiled over at Frankie. "Gregory asked me to visit you, but I was coming to see you anyhow."

"What's the message from Gregory?" Wariness rang off Molloy's tone.

"Come on, Frankie!" Father Keegan moved on the couch again. To an observer the movement would not have been a writhing, but to Father Keegan it was the closest he'd come to feeling discomfort at the hands of another. A long breath sighed through his nose. "I went out to see Gregory yesterday because I heard you had come home." Again Keegan moved, and it looked like he was firmly caught in the tentacles of a squirm. "I'm afraid the Molloys became the subject of vicious gossip after you left the priesthood. Gregory's success with the horses made him an obvious target. You know what it's like here. When you succeed anywhere else in the world, everyone shouts three cheers. In Ireland they shout three jeers. Your perceived failures were used to batter Gregory because there was nothing else to batter him with. But eventually the gossip dried up. Now your unexpected homecoming is the talk of the village, and of course when I saw Gregory today he was in a state of great anxiety."

"In a state of great anxiety!" Frankie echoed Keegan with such sarcasm and suddenness that the priest was startled. "And are you sure anxiety is the proper word? Is it anxious or angry he is, Eddie? Angry because he thinks his image is being pulled out of shape?"

Keegan's composure was jolted. "As a matter of fact he is angry, Frankie, because, according to Gregory, you promised you'd never come home again. Your turning up like this is very upsetting for him. Gregory had a real bad time when you left the priesthood and…"

"And what do you think I had, Eddie? A fucking honeymoon?" Molloy stood up and, even though he knew he was not being fair, he continued to spew his anger all over the priest. "His own brother comes home and the only thing he can feel is anger! Well, fuck Gregory!"

Keegan seemed to flounder like a sailing ship hit by an unexpected squall. "Come on, Frankie!" There was an appeal for the use of common sense in his voice. "Put yourself in Gregory's shoes. By coming back you've opened an old sore. I think his reaction is fairly normal."

"Is that your reaction, too, Eddie? Are you normal like Gregory? Are you pissed off because I came home?" Molloy went over to the disc player and switched off the power. A red light on the console faded into darkness. When he turned around Eddie Keegan was standing.

"Frankie," the priest pleaded. "I'm not saying Gregory is right. Maybe you've been away from Ireland too long to appreciate Gregory's reaction." When he saw that Frank was going to shoot off another salvo, he held up his hand, and with the raising of the hand, his voice changed; there was a metallic edge to the words. "I don't know why you're angry, Frankie, but whatever it is, you're not going to take it out on me. Will you…"

Frank was close to shouting when he interrupted. "I don't want to hear this shit about what I've done to him." Molloy clenched his fists and waved them in the air close to his face. "I'll take responsibility for what I've done," he jammed his thumb into his chest, "but I will not take responsibility for how my brother feels about it."

"You promised him you'd never come home," Keegan said. "If you broke the promise, don't you have to bear the consequences?"

"Yes, Father Keegan! But don't assume for one second, Eddie, you can play the priest with me. Fuck you and your tight-assed, abstract morality. In the first place, Gregory never had the right to pry that promise out of me." Molloy's voice went up an octave for the delivery of the next announcement. "He squeezed that promise out by telling me I was killing our mother, that it would be better if I never came home to Davinkill again."

The two men looked at each other across the room. At the same instant they looked away from each other. Frank went over to the front window and stared out onto the dark golf links. Keegan went to the bookshelf and looked blindly at the row of compact discs. He ran his finger along the smooth edges of the square, plastic cases. Finally he turned to where Frank was standing. When he spoke, his voice was calm. “Gregory asked me to tell you to go away because you are a scandal to the whole town. I told him I would deliver his message, but that I wouldn’t ask you to leave.”

Frank Molloy did not react. His hands were joined behind his back.

“That’s all there is about Gregory,” Keegan continued. “I don’t see why your brother, and what he thinks, should come between us.”

Molloy turned and looked at the priest. “What do you think, Eddie? Do you think I should leave? Do you think I’m a scandal to the people of the town?” By his tone, Molloy gave notice that an unacceptable response would be jumped on and beaten to death.

Keegan replied, “I have wondered why you didn’t find a place in another town, if only to spare your brother the discomfort of having the family dynamics played out on a stage for all the locals to see. As far as scandal goes, Frankie, I think you’ll be circumspect.”

Frank Molloy said nothing. It looked as if Keegan’s response had taken the wind out of his angry sails. But, even though his anger was waning there was still enough left in him to make his sails flutter. “By expecting me to be circumspect, you’re saying I’m a source of scandal,” he said as he turned around.”It’s all right with me, Eddie, if that’s how you see me. Of course I won’t go out of my way to give scandal, whatever that scandal could be, but I will always answer a question as truthfully as I can, no matter who asks it. And you’re right about not letting Gregory come between us.” He paused for a moment as if to let his brother fade into the woodwork. Then he asked, “Would you like a cup of tea?”

Like a tightly inflated balloon suddenly losing its helium, Keegan’s body shrank out of its defensive posture. His shoulders sagged. “Sweet Jesus!” he sighed, “I’d love a cup.”

As the tea was prepared, Frank Molloy discovered that Keegan’s parents had died six years ago within two weeks of each other. His three brothers and two sisters were all married, and the priest had twenty-four nieces and nephews. Every week, on his day off, he visited a different sibling. They were all living in Westmeath and Dublin.

Because Molloy, during the summer holidays of his fourth year in Winter Hill, had successfully got his right hand under her blouse, he asked in particular about Keegan’s sister Deirdre. She was a doctor now and had two children. The remembrance of that first feel of a girl’s breast was tucked away in Molloy’s memory and, by association of experiences, the memory had often been recovered and looked at fondly, but with fading prurient delectation in these latter years. The nipple had been rougher than he'd expected.

By the time they sat at the kitchen table with the tea, they had wandered into silence again. Frank knew they were back to themselves, that if they were to communicate at all, each other's walls would have to be scaled. To lower a rope, and thus invite intrusion, would be too embarrassing. After the silence had gone on too long for comfort, he half-heartedly slapped a ladder against Keegan's defences. "How come you were never transferred out of Davinkill?"

The priest put down his cup with such deliberation that Molloy suspected he had placed his scaling ladder against a sensitive point.

"I have this theory about peepholes in the houses of small Irish towns, Frankie. The peepholes are peoples' mouths. The peephole into my house is my mouth. A priest in a small town can't afford to let anyone near his peephole, so I never discuss anything about myself." Keegan locked his hands around his cup as if to warm them, as if to show he had firmly closed a door and would not tolerate any further knocking on it.

Frank Molloy looked at him in astonishment. He stumbled over his own feelings of rejection before he asked, "Not even with your own fellow priests?"

"Especially not my fellow priests!" Keegan replied without hesitation.

"You don't talk to anyone about yourself?" Molloy asked, disbelief dripping off his inflections.

"You're putting me in a position where I have to defend myself, Frankie."

"You've put yourself in a position where I can't even begin to approach you, Eddie."

"Of course you can approach me. I'm not an ogre. I don't think people in the parish have difficulty approaching me."

"They may approach you as their priest, but not as their friend. Don't you trust anyone at all? Your brothers? Your sisters?"

"The way you're asking the questions, Frankie, I feel very defensive. As a matter of fact I feel uncomfortable. I think you're prying."

Molloy put his elbows on the table and rested his chin on his fingers. Amazement was in his eyes and in the way his lips were parted. "Eddie,

I'm not your parishioner. You're not my priest. I don't give a shit why you've never been transferred out of this town. You came to my house without invitation. You said you were here because I was your friend once. The implication was that we could be friends again, at least that was the implication I heard. Now you sit here and shut me out as if I'm the local yenta. If you were hoping to renew an old friendship, then the attempt is dead in the water."

Father Keegan's eyes fell off Molloy's face. His hands were flat on the table, the fingers splayed. For a long time he seemed to be staring, not seeing. Then, without raising his eyes, he said, "I don't have any friends, Frankie."

Molloy was still smarting from Keegan's rejection and he could not let the opportunity pass. "I wonder why, Eddie!"

Keegan, still without looking in Molloy's direction, held up his hand. "All right, Frankie. I hear the sarcasm. I haven't had a friend since I was ordained. You can't be a priest and have a friend."

"Is that another one of your theories?"

Keegan abruptly pulled himself together, his stretched-out feet scraping the floor. The movement and the noise seemed to be his version of sabre rattling. He looked Molloy in the eye. "You're very blunt, Frank."

"Life is short, Eddie."

"You were never like this."

"Neither were you, Eddie."

"Tit for tat, Frankie!"

"Not at all, Eddie. You stated a fact. I stated a fact. We are different from what we were in our twenties. I'd like to renew the friendship. I trust you, Eddie. Obviously you don't trust me, so what's the point? Let's say goodbye and call it quits."

To Molloy's surprise Keegan snapped, "No, I'm not going to call it quits."

Again they sat in silence for a long time. Neither of them drank from the cups, as if the movement might be be equated with a blink.

"Why did you come home, Frankie?"

"Screw you, Eddie!" Molloy stood up, chair scraping floor like nail on blackboard. He switched on the plate under the kettle. "Would you like more tea?"

"Yes, please." Keegan moved his chair so he could look to the stove without twisting his neck. "Two years after I came here a girl was murdered," he said. "A man by the name of Donaghue was asked to go to the barracks in Duneamon for questioning. The Guards finished with him at one in the morning. A day later his body was washed up on Scattery Island. His wife was left with four young children. The people gave her the cold shoulder and the children in the town started calling names. I let myself be seen at the house and with her children in the street. One thing led to another, and I became a kind of remote surrogate father to the children. As time went by I imagined my role in the Donaghue family was so important that, every time the bishop transferred me, I asked to be left for another few years. The last child finished school about six years ago. I haven't been asked to move since then. The bishop hasn't been functioning for a long time, but when he dies I expect the new man will move me out of here."

When the story ended, Keegan turned his palms up, raised his eyebrows and lifted his shoulders.

During the story Frank had been leaning against the stove with his arms folded. Now he pushed himself upright. He said, "If the father died thirty years ago and the last child finished school only six years ago, that last child must have been at least…"

"She was twenty-five," Keegan said. "She was one when the father died."

"What kind of school was she in? Is she retarded?"

Eddie Keegan laughed. "No, she isn't retarded. As a matter of fact she's the opposite. She got a doctorate in philosophy from the Sorbonne. Her name is Peggy."

"The Sorbonne!" Frank Molloy was impressed. He narrowed his eyes and turned his head slightly to one side. "Are you telling me you paid her way, Eddie?"

When Eddie Keegan moved, he reminded Molloy of a turtle about to retrieve its vulnerable parts. But before Keegan could retreat into his discretionary shell, Molloy grabbed him by the neck and held on.

"For God's sake, Eddie. Stop editing. Do you think I'm going to run out and gossip?" he paused. Then, "For Christ's sake!" He swung around to the boiling kettle and snatched it off the stove. The piping hot water sputtered into the tea cups. He replaced the kettle and turned back to Keegan. "Eddie, I don't want to know the secrets of your soul. But if you're going to weigh how much you can trust me every time you speak, then don't tell me anything. I don't want to know you through your fearful filters. I don't want to see you mistrusting me." Molloy slapped his hands against his thighs. In frustration he put his hands to the sides of his face and closed his eyes. "I'm sorry," he said. "It's none of my business what you do or did. I haven't had a friend in a long time myself, not since Padrake died, and I'm probably grasping desperately." Molloy sat down at the table. He squeezed his tea bag against the spoon and watched the drops falling into the cup.

"It wasn't easy to come home," he said in a subdued voice. "It was scary, emotionally and financially, but the finances were not the worst part." Molloy put his elbows on the table. "There are a couple of reasons why I came back. One is that I had to convince myself I was at ease with the person I had become. The second one is that I want to be my unbelieving self in this place, so soaked in Catholicism, where I was brainwashed as a child." Molloy paused and, with a wan smile on his face, looked over at Keegan. "I came home to exorcise myself of the Church, Eddie. I have exorcised God. But I still haven't exorcised the Church which infiltrated my defenceless psyche when I was a child; I now know that the Church was a fungus, and that it sank into something delicate and made it rot."

Keegan stared at his cup. The table and all its contents were reflected in his sparkling, rimless glasses.

"From where I'm sitting that's disturbing stuff, Frankie. My immediate reaction is that I must save you from…"

Molloy put his hand on Keegan's arm and looked his old friend in the eye. "Eddie, don't save me. No hell could be worse than the one I lived in when I…"

The priest pulled away his arm and took back possession of the conversation. "You didn't let me finish. I was saying that my knee-jerk response is to save you. But it's not you I have to save, Frankie. It's me. That's why I said this is disturbing stuff. Years ago, just knowing that you had left the priesthood put a strain on my own anchor chains. But you were far away and I didn't know why you left, so the strain eased off quickly. When I heard you had come back home, the first thing I felt was anxiety. I knew I would find out why you left, that I'd have to look at my own reasons for staying in. The currents that pulled you away are going to start tugging at me. The links of the anchor chains are starting to snap at each other again."

In the silence that followed, Molloy saw the two of them as a pair of small boats bobbing on a breeze-whipped pond, one straining at the end of a rope, the other blowing across the water, now sideways, now sternwise, now bowwise.

The sounds of the house settling for the night went unnoticed. Maura Gilligan's distant beagles, barking in the night, did not penetrate their consciousness. The contracting sounds of the cooling stove were not heard.

Then Eddie Keegan made a noise as if he were calling for attention. "I paid for Peggy Donaghue's education," he said. "I paid for the other children as well."

"John O'Brien, told me Mrs Donaghue had a rich brother in America."

"I've heard that many times myself," Keegan smiled.

Then Frank Molloy asked, "Did you ever sleep with Mrs Donaghue, Eddie?"

Eddie Keegan jumped up from the table and his chair fell over with a loud clatter. Molloy's heart took off at a fast gallop. "Jesus, Eddie!" he exclaimed.

"Jesus, yourself, Frankie!" Keegan shouted.

Frank Molloy came slowly to his feet. He put his hand to his thudding chest. "Are you protesting too loudly, Eddie?" he asked, his tone giving his words a cynical lining.

"No, I'm not protesting too loudly, Frankie!" Keegan replied in a voice which tried to replicate Molloy's. "I'm not protesting my innocence at all. But I am protesting your rudeness."

"If you think my question was rude, then you have been living a remote life for too long."

"How many women have *you* slept with, Frankie?" Keegan asked with a sneer in his voice that made his question rhetorical.

"Eighteen or nineteen," Molloy answered.

For a moment Keegan's mouth fell open. A blush soared violently over his face. "That's disgusting!" he said.

"What's disgusting about it? They were all nice women."

They stood at the kitchen table glaring at each other. Molloy could see the ceiling light shining off his bald head in the reflection in Keegan's glasses.

It looked like Father Keegan wanted to leave, run to the front door and escape. But Frank guessed Eddie Keegan was too titillated to leave, and it wasn't Frank's admission that was causing the titillation; it was the naked honesty Keegan had just tasted which was making him stay.

At the same moment each man saw the quiver in the other's lips, saw the creases at the corners of the mouth making way for the smiles that finally spread across their faces.

Keegan beamed until he was wearing the face of a magician after a spectacular magic trick. "No, I didn't sleep with Dervla Donaghue, Frankie," he said.

And immediately Molloy asked, "But you did fantasise about it?"

Molloy saw fleeting cracks in Keegan's smile, but the priest gallantly replied, "I did fantasise about sleeping with Dervla Donaghue many times."

Five minutes later the forgotten kettle boiled again and Frank turned off the stove. Eddie Keegan said, "One time a fellow went to confession and made several efforts to tell the priest he'd had sex with a woman. But he had a difficult time putting the deed into acceptable language. In the end the priest growled at him, 'Did you sleep with the woman or what?' And your man answered, 'That's what I'm trying to tell you, Father! I never slept a wink.'"

Chapter 19

Thursday in the Fifth Week of Lent – 9.55 p.m.

BESIDES A SHORT weekly visit from one townie, Paulie Lamb's customers were all farmers. The farmers felt comfortable in his pub. They didn't have to worry about the smart alecs from Davinkill or Duneamon coming in to comment on their boots and clothes. They knew they were not as sweet-smelling as the people who lived in towns but, even so, they didn't want some bollicks of a townie coming in to make insulting remarks.

There were two reasons why the one townie who came to Lamb's pub once a week was acceptable; he was harmless, which meant he wasn't all there, and his dirty talk was the poor man's equivalent of a girlie magazine. The townie could recite a list of twenty-six words which named the male and female sexual organs and which described the sexual act between men and women. He also had a collection of common scatological expressions which might, or might not, have made a nun blush.

Everyone knew Paddy Dillon was too poor to support a louse and that the purpose of his weekly visit to Lamb's was to beg the price of a pint. The farmers allowed him his pride by laughing at his stammerings before they threw coins on the counter to show their appreciation.

While they endured Dillon as much as they enjoyed him, they did not rely on him like the patrons of the non-farmer pubs. The farmers were never without interesting conversation. They spoke about animal prices, milk prices, milk quotas and about all the paperwork required to get a few pounds out of those fucking functionaries in Brussels. Religion was never discussed because they were all devout Catholics, seeing the hand of God behind the downpour as the hay baler was hauled into the meadow, or in the deaths of calves from the scour. Even when a child died, they said, "Welcome be the holy will of God," instead of beating the shit out of the doctor who had been too drunk to save the child.

But on the night of the day the Culliton boy fell through Father Keegan's loft, they talked about the boy's brush with death and his miraculous recovery. With every new arrival in the pub, another detail of the story was patched in. And then was brought the breathless news of the fight in the school between Fayne and Kelly. Before the teachers had been boned and boiled to insipidity, another arrival announced the return home of Father Frank Molloy. As this latest news was sweeping Fayne, Kelly and the Culliton boy out the back door, Paddy Dillon was entering through the front door of the pub, already feeling the pull of the outer reaches of delirium tremens.

Paulie Lamb was the only one to notice Dillon's arrival. Despite the turmoil among the farmers, he had easily heard Dillon banging the door behind him, as he usually did, to get everyone's attention.

As Dillon glared at his distracted audience out of watery and bloodshot eyes, a voice rose up and the general clatter fell away like the supportive gantries falling away from an ascending moon rocket.

"... and I know for a fact that the former Father Molloy isn't even a Catholic anymore, because that's what he told the knacker..."

"That bollicks from Gannonbeg!"

"... when they were looking at the garden on the golf links."

Standing at the wall inside the door, Paddy Dillon muttered under his breath. "Fucken farmers!" Again, to let the fuckers know he had arrived to amuse them, Dillon turned toward the door and slapped the top panel with the palm of his hand. He saw a few faces glancing in his direction, but there was no noticeable change in the vocal chaff. "Fuck yiz!"

Another voice pulled away and soared for part of a sentence: "... and that Mary Delaney from Gannonbeg brought a box of french letters from Miami to Father Molloy on..."

This announcement brought all conversation to a stunned and scandalised halt. As it was, none of the farmers was comfortable with the sound of "french letters", but with the presence of the other two ingredients, Father Frank Molloy and that slip of a girl, Mary Delaney, an explosive piece of gossip had been hurled into their midst. There was an eruption of strong and scandal-tinted statements. Ejaculations were hurled at various saints in heaven, along with the directing of a shower of maledictions at the malefactors. Eventually there was a collective pause for breath. The instant silence caught Paddy Dillon off guard, and he only got out one word before he was overwhelmed by a voice of judgement.

"That young Delaney one from Gannonbeg with all the paint on her face and nails and rings on her fingers and in her ears and bracelets and necklaces who plays music on a ship was in the former Father Molloy's..."

"That Ascarriot!"

"... house yesterday for a long time. She couldn't even wait to go home to see her mother. Now, Father Molloy had his own wife..."

"Whore, if you ask me!"

"... in America, and no doubt he used to give her a swipe of the sausage. His wife..."

"Whore, if you ask me!"

"... being the woman..."

"Whore!"

"... whore, then, if you like..."

"That's what I like!"

"Will you stop interrupting, Hughes, you hure!"

"... this Father Molloy, when he was in America, gave his hure a poke of the parsnip and she wasn't even his wife because they got married outside the Church. Where the fuck was I, Hughes, you hure? When Mary Delaney from Gannonbeg with all the paint on her face was in his house, did he bury the white puddin' in her, too, seeing that the two of them are from America and she uses paint and he jumps on anything that doesn't move? Will our own women be safe? is what I'm trying to say, you fucker, Hughes."

Near the door of the pub, Paddy Dillon shuffled his shoulders and did a little alcohol-withdrawal dance. Using his hands in his pockets, he pulled the gabardine coat closer to his shivering flesh. As the farmers talked about the sexual security of their womenfolk, another voice pulled away from earth and declared, "Father Molloy has been asking a lot of questions about Kit Foley. The knacker..."

"That bollicks from Gannonbeg!"

"... said that Father Molloy..."

"Ascarriot!"

"... has already examined the garden..."

"The ring of rocks!"

"... and that he pulled the briars off the stones when we all thought it was forgotten about, dead and buried. Do you think Father Molloy could have been hired by the Guards in Dublin to try to find out what happened to Kit Foley? And if he was, what is he going to dig up to destroy this town with, like it was nearly destroyed years ago when every man was guilty until Donaghue ups and drowns himself? Are we all going to be guilty again?"

Amidst the loud talk which followed this alcohol-inspired observation, Paddy Dillon shuffled his way to the bar. He put one filthy claw in the air to attract Paulie Lamb who was purposely ignoring him. "Ya fucker, ya see me, ya shite fucker," Paddy Dillon breathed. Then, as loud as he could he called, "Gimme a drink, Mr Lamb."

Not by the smallest twitch of muscle did Paulie Lamb react.

Paddy Dillon was no longer in control of his alcoholic want. He banged the counter with the side of his fist and pain shot up his thin arm. "Mr Lamb, gimme a fucken drink, shite dung ploppens droppens."

When Paulie Lamb turned he saw the saliva on Dillon's stubbled chin. Then, the pub-owner was suddenly inches away from Paddy's eyes, the unconscious recitation still oozing over his bottom lip and slithering down, "jow crap scutter".

In a whisper as fierce as the finger of God carving an unamused message onto a hard rock, Paulie Lamb told Dillon if he ever touched his bar again with his filthy fucking fingers he, Lamb, would tear his fucking throat out and shove it up his arse sideways.

In stunned silence Dillon backed away from the bar, and of all the words said behind him, he only heard two.

"... that Father Molloy said blasphemous things about the true cross when he was up at the knacker's place. He said that if all the relics of the true cross were gathered together there would be enough stakes to fence in the Curragh. Do you know what the knacker said about him? He said Father Molloy was worse than the Protestants in the North who hung up a side of bacon in a shop window and wrote 'Curates' Hures' under it. Isn't that awful, saying priests do it with pigs?"

Dillon dragged himself to the door and without taking his hand out of his pocket, he pressed the latch. With the gabardine pulled as tight as a bandage around his throbbing body he fell out into the darkness, noticed by nobody, except Paulie Lamb who always kept an ear on the door of his pub.

Chapter 20

Monday in Holy Week – 2.05 p.m.

ELISABETH MOLLOY SELDOM rejected her husband's advances, and she never used her body as a bargaining chip. She enjoyed the ways her husband led her to gasping orgasms, before finally burying the relic in her quaking reliquary.

But Elisabeth Molloy knew that the minutes immediately after sex were different from other times. It was as if the physical entrée lowered the obstacles which were strewn around her husband's best-defended areas. And so it was as she lay entwined in Gregory's limbs after an energetic encounter on a wet afternoon, she suggested, as her opening gambit, that Gregory should visit his brother Frank. When Gregory sleepily turned aside her suggestion, she slipped back into silence. Then, as if the idea had just occurred to her, she announced that she herself was going to drop in to see her brother-in-law.

Knowing that an unchallenging response would be rewarded with a few minutes of endorphined sleep, Gregory grunted his acknowledgment of her intent and, within a few seconds, gave one snorty snore.

Elisabeth could hear the rain on the roof as they lay together until Gregory abruptly moved to look at the clock.

"Hell!" he muttered, as he replaced his arm across his wife's hot body. "The inspector's coming in half an hour." As he pushed himself against her, they both straightened their legs and, belly to belly, they lay for a few moments. Then, without a word, Gregory swung out of the bed and went to take a shower.

Elisabeth pulled the bedclothes onto herself, and snuggled in the warmth her husband had left behind. Gregory's loud return from the bathroom hauled Elisabeth back out of sleep's sinuous tendrils. As Gregory dressed at the side of the bed, he half-heartedly rounded up, and gave voice to all the reasons why he could not be reconciled with his brother.

In silence, Elisabeth listened as he sloshed around in the jading quagmire. She turned on her back, put her hands under her head. Before Gregory could get around to attacking openly her resolve to visit Frankie, she distracted him by asking if he thought Claudine Duchosal suspected her employers of romping away an afternoon in bed.

"Is that what we were doing, romping?" Gregory asked, and he touched her foot beneath the bedclothes.

"I meant to tell you! Claudine asked me yesterday, how long does it take tea to paint, as in draw. I laughed out loud. I think I discouraged her."

"Maybe it'll all happen suddenly for her – the language – like a born-again Christian."

Elisabeth went to the bathroom door. "When I get back with the children I'll go to Frankie's. Maybe I'll bring one of Claudine's latest cakes. It will help break the ice." Elisabeth had intended getting into the bathroom before Gregory responded. She wasn't successful.

"I didn't think you were going today. The inspector will be here in a few minutes." Gregory put a foot on the edge of the radiator and tied his shoelace.

"Oh, Gregory. You can get on without me. It doesn't take a genius to fill in a few columns in a book. Barry has done it before. I should strike while the iron is hot. As well as that, it's so rainy I'm sure to find Frankie at home."

"What's the iron that's hot?" Gregory put his other foot on the radiator.

"My determination to go." But then she held up her hand. "No, that's not it. It's your not objecting to my going – that's the hot iron."

Whenever he saw his wife attempting to be obsessively honest with him, remembrances of Gregory's initial in-loveness with Elisabeth floated to the surface of Gregory's blood near his heart. The memories whacked his remaining stubbornness. However, his pride demanded that he not give in too easily. "Why are you pushing so hard on this, Lizzybeth?" He slipped his arms into his jacket sleeves.

The use of the pet name betrayed him immediately, and Elisabeth knew the argument was over. But she still pursued her determination to liberate her husband from his stubbornness. "He's my brother-in-law, he's our children's uncle, his girls are the only cousins our children have, and they are our nieces. Frank is a part of this family, and I like the idea of an extended family." She did not say, "He is your brother."

"He changed his relationship with his family when he did the things he did, puked over everyone and never once said he was sorry."

Elisabeth had heard this line before, word for word. And of late, during Gregory's recitation of the plaintive motif, she had found herself wondering if Gregory was angry at his brother only out of habit; if this whole thing would suddenly evaporate if Frankie simply asked forgiveness of his brother. But forgiveness for what? Maybe it was only out of loyalty to his mother and father that Gregory had a need to keep alive his feelings of hostility.

Before Gregory was half-way through his repetitious lament, Elisabeth knew it was time to change the subject again. She pulled her bathrobe apart and flashed her husband. "I hope we have another wet day soon," she said. Then, as she closed the door she asked, "Will you wait for me? I don't want to face a suspicious Claudine by myself. I'll be ready in a minute."

"Gosh! If you were as bashful before sex as you are after it, I'd never get you to the bed." For a moment Gregory smiled to himself, but, the moment the bathroom door closed, other thoughts immediately flooded into his head.

It was becoming apparent that Elisabeth was growing uninterested in his rantings about Frankie. He sensed that, of late, she was indulging him more than empathising with him. Did she already sense what he himself was beginning to suspect? Stuff was pushing up inside his awareness, buried stuff which was distasteful to deal with. As he leaned forward to look at the knot in his tie, he imagined himself naked in a patch of briars, his head, body and limbs entwined by the thorny vines. Energy and patience would be needed to disentangle himself without ripping himself apart. As he adjusted his tie and collar so that his yardman, Barry Curry, would not suspect he had been in and out of his clothes since lunchtime, Gregory tried picking at some of the briars.

There had been the battle with Eddie Keegan a few days ago, during which it dawned on Gregory that the underpinning emotions which had supported his anger were long gone.

Then there was the face-saving angle – was he only keeping his anger for Frankie in place because he didn't know how to let it go?

And now that he was home, Frankie was a person again – no longer an object, no longer a monkey on Gregory's back. To let go of the monkey would be to lose "look-at-me" martyrdom: look at poor me, look at the special burden I have to carry – the shame of a Judas in the family – look at my Judas brother, look at him and pity my shame.

Gregory closed his eyes and ground his teeth. He knew the shedding of the habituated shame would affect a change in his very self – the monkey on his back would have to be excised.

He looked at himself in the mirror and told himself that it had been his own loud mouth which had painted him into the corner he was standing in. Now a fight was expected of him. He was a little bully boy in the schoolyard who couldn't back down when face to face with the enemy he has been bad-mouthing in public.

"I have been so fucking self-righteous!" He was startled at the sound of his own voice. He glanced at the bathroom door. The shower was still running. If only Elisabeth had been around when the whole Frankie thing was erupting! He knew she would not have let him make the ridiculous moves he had made then. He knew how fortunate he was to have a wife like Elisabeth, and he wasn't even thinking about her rambunctiousness between the bed-sheets. There were times when she had interjected a warning when he was in danger of lumbering head-on into a bad business deal. He had never resented her interference. Many times he had told her how comforting it was to know she was near by. This was why he wanted her to go to Frankie. His expressed reluctance was his childish way of trying to wriggle out of his prideful and stupid position. But now, even though her common sense had navigated him between many a Scylla and Charybdis in the past, he did not believe she was capable of resolving the present impasse without someone, particularly himself, being shown up as a total fool. The people in the village would surely have a field day looking at him plunging around in his own pile of briars, glowering, red and thorny scars all over his eyelids, ears, lips, nostrils, cheeks, chin, neck, forehead.

Gregory reined in his galloping brain. He listened for the sound of shower water and heard silence. Elisabeth was already drying herself, and he didn't want her to see the funk into which he had sunk. Through the bathroom door he told her he would be late for the horse inspector unless he left now. She would have to face Claudine Duchosal by herself.

He took one more look at himself in the mirror to make sure he was ready for Barry Curry's scrutiny. But no matter what he did about his appearance, Gregory knew that a remark would be dropped to indicate the yardman was aware that conjugal delights had been enjoyed after lunch.

Chapter 21

Monday in Holy Week – 2.05 p.m.

WITHOUT A BREATH of air to disturb it, the rain fell straight down as if it had been falling forever, as if it would never stop. Without the distraction of the wind in the trees and bushes, the sound of the falling rain permeated the world and hypnotised living things.

Mesmerised cows stood silently in fields, the steady downpour massaging their backs and haunches. The water ran down their sides and poured off wispy hairs at their bellies, looking like liquid icicles binding them to the earth. The cows gazed into the distance as far as their short-sightedness allowed them, and they only blinked when a raindrop fell directly onto their hooded eyes.

Sparrows and starlings huddled with their own kind on the bare branches of bushes, and chattered their annoyance when the insulation of their feathers was threatened by the touch of a neighbour. On grasping claws they shuttled nervously back and forth to maintain their distances.

Without perceptible variation in its steadiness, the rain fell out of the low, grey sky onto the soggy ground. So enclosed was the earth in wet clouds, it was difficult to imagine the sun shining on warm beaches and browning bodies in other parts of the world.

Frank Molloy had forgotten what a wet day in Ireland was like. He gazed through the streaked glass of the sitting-room window, and it was sound rather than sight that played on his senses. The steady downpour on the roof slates was like the purring of a large cat. Without encouragement, his memory had found matching images for what he was seeing, and the pictures which floated across his memory screen were all of snugness.

One picture would have flitted by unchecked had it not been embroidered with stitches of danger. On wet days, when he and Gregory were small, their father brought them to school. In the car shed, the children climbed the spokes of the unsteady wheels as Mr

Molloy, already ensconced on the wooden seat of the cart, used the reins to fight for control with the high-strung red pony. Under the galvanised iron roof, soaked in the rain's deafening tattoo, the pony was a trembling machine of pent-up energy.

The children made themselves comfortable in the golden straw on the floor of the cart, their backs against the driver's seat and their feet braced against the tailboard. They snuggled together under the waterproof cape while their mother inspected to make sure they were covered.

When she was satisfied, Mrs Molloy said, "Be careful, John." Mr Molloy let the reins drop onto the pony's back, and she took off at high speed amid the jangle of chains and the rattling of iron-shod wheels. As they sped up the yard to the gate, Frankie stuck his hand through the opening in the cape and waved to his mother. The remembrance of her walking to the kitchen door, an old overcoat over her head and shoulders, was chiselled into his memory. She always saw Frankie's hand and she always waved back.

Up the lane the pony galloped. For the children the illusion of great speed was created by their facing the back of the cart, the hedges and fields and trees whizzing past. It was as if a giant artist at their backs was throwing painted shapes onto a giant canvas, magically creating an ever-shrinking picture.

Through deep potholes and over unpaved road, the red pony effortlessly hauled the cart, water and stones shooting aside, tacklings jangling, wooden cart groaning, wheels protesting. The ever-present fear of crashing was fuelled by the speed and the noise.

More than half a century later, as the rain ran down the glass in front of him, Frank Molloy was remembering. It was only when he heard the knocking that he saw the front end of a car in Wheat Mill Lane outside his watery window.

"Gregory!" It felt as if twenty pounds of blood suddenly dropped into the pit of his stomach. As he went to answer the knock, he did not hear one of the Brandenburg Concertos fluttering around the room.

He didn't know if he remembered who owned the car before he saw Mary Delaney, or whether it was when he saw her that he remembered immediately. Gregory fell out of his head. Delaney was wearing a Red Riding Hood coat, only it was black. There was something in her arms. A box, maybe.

Lust.

His throat closed. His body quivered with lust. He knew they were going to be sexual with each other. How did she send the signal? What antenna of his picked up the signal and caused the instant thickening of his blood? Did he leave her standing there in the rain while his superego fought for a say in the matter? Or did the sensations and argumentations simply wash over him so fast that she never even noticed his hesitation? Was it the mingling and crackling of their respective signals which made the air between them thin and unbreathable?

Without speaking he invited her into the sheltering warmth of his house.

Come into my parlour.

When she silently handed him the box her shining eyes and wide smile were loquacious and less than subtle, and he clearly heard what they were saying.

With the world outside so wet, it was with amazement he saw her dry hair falling into place around her face. When he held up his hands she turned and let the Red Riding Hood coat slip down.

She was wearing a black pants suit with brass hardware. No make-up or jewellery was visible to Molloy, although Delaney had stopped on the way and, using the car mirror, had made her eyes bluer and her cheeks pinker.

Afterwards Molloy would recall that every word they had spoken, every gesture they had made until she finally came to him on the couch, had been part of foreplay which was all the more exciting because they both knew what was going to happen. What should have been the final barriers had crumbled when they saw each other in the doorway. As they had talked on the couch, each used the conversation to reach the point where the physical coming together was inevitable, logical and breathlessly lustful.

After hanging her glistening coat on the hook behind the door, Molloy indicated the couch with his hand. He knew that when he would speak she would hear the excitement in his voice. Even his vocal chords were turgid.

No sooner had Mary Delaney graced his couch with her body than she, still blushing, asked, "So, former priest Frank Molloy, how did you get to the point where you can say 'a pox on the faith' without blinking?"

"Ha!" laughed Molloy, "I can also say I don't believe in God without fearing a lightning strike. But I have to be careful who I'm with. Some people look around nervously. Usually they glance up at the sky... So, you must have mentioned me to your mother."

"Of course I did. The minute I got home I told her about calling here looking for Miss Duggan and finding you."

"Did she remember me?"

"Yes. She said you were a curious youngster. Those are her words, curious youngster."

"I'm sure she meant intellectually curious," Molloy smiled.

"I don't know what she meant, but I don't think my mother would know what intellectual curiosity means. She said you were in the same class in school for a while. Are you going to answer my question?"

"Which one?" Molloy asked, and he wondered if she felt his eyes feeling her face, sliding down her neck.

"How did you get from priest to blasphemer, is the little question."

He swept his eyes across her breasts and he knew she saw him looking. "The little question has a very big answer, as big as about thirty years of history."

"Give me the the chapter headings or the titles of the volumes – whichever is suitable." Mary Delaney flung her arm onto the back of the couch and left her body unprotected. Her hand drooped on the upholstery like Adam's hand waiting to receive life from God in the Sistine Chapel. "Tell me in one sentence why you left the priesthood, got married, what happened to your wife and why you came home, leaving your children behind and knowing you would cause your brother a lot of grief because you are a great embarrassment to him." She pulled in a loud breath and laughed. "See! If I can ask all the questions in one sentence you can answer them in one sentence."

"You seem to know a lot about me already."

"From what my mother tells me, you have been a one-man *Peyton Place* in these parts for many years." She uncrossed her legs and, with heels against toes, she slipped out of her shoes.

"Gossip is like a snowball on a hill," Molloy said. "It picks up more than snow when it's rolling. I was the good man off in a foreign country who succumbed to the temptations of the world. My fall was embellished with the fantasies of people who never left home. I'm afraid my

Peyton Place was rather dull."

Mary Delaney pulled her trouser legs half-way up her calves and sat on her feet. She returned her Michelangelo hand to the back of the couch.

Molloy waited until she had settled herself before he continued. "I joined a priesthood that existed only in my head and in the imaginations of the priests who came to the schools to recruit. The real thing was like something you find under a rock that hasn't been moved in a hundred years. I spent my priesthood trying to grope my way out of the underside of the Church.... And now stand back while I take a deep breath for the history answer."

Molloy's chest expanded and, as he started speaking, he felt her fingers touching his on the back of the couch – Adam giving life to God. "When I left the priesthood I got married and we had two daughters – my wife died suddenly some years ago and I came back here to prove to myself that I'm a whole person or maybe out of loneliness – my two daughters are married and they can visit me here or I can visit them – and whatever grief my brother has to endure because I came home is his problem – how's that? and I still have some breath left." Molloy blew out air until his chest collapsed.

Mary Delaney's fingers stopped moving. After a few seconds she asked, "What do you mean by the underside of the Church?"

As Molloy spoke he brushed her skin with the pads of his fingers. "I suppose the top side of the Church is the image that is projected – the polished public relations picture – the hard working, concerned, committed and pious nuns, priests and bishops who live in sisterly and brotherly love with each other. The reality is very different. The low, slimy life found under a rock has its counterpart behind the scenes in the Church." Molloy rested his fingers in the valleys formed by her metacarpi.

"Is that as specific as you're going to get? What exactly are you talking about?"

Molloy started running his fingers up along the valleys. The tips of his fingers touched the strap of her watch. "Why are people so inquisitive about priests and what they do?" he asked. He moved his arm on the back of the couch and in the same movement encircled her wrist loosely with his fingers. "Why are you curious?" he asked.

Delaney moved. She didn't move toward him, but she positioned herself so that she could move toward him with grace. She didn't want to look like a beached seal when the time came.

"It's like the Mafia," she said. "Because they're so secretive, people are interested in them. For instance, did Father Frank Molloy ever have sex with a woman?" Her eyes and tone of voice pasted an oestral patina onto the question.

Molloy knew his blood was going to rise into his face but, instead of fighting it, he accepted his spreading rubicundity as part of the sex play crackling between them; it was a part of becoming naked.

"Yes, I had sex with several women when I was a priest. But don't you think a more important question is, how long did I stay in the priesthood after I lost my belief in it. I have known priests who lost the faith two or three years after ordination, but they grew old in the Church because they were afraid or too comfortable to get out." Molloy moved the circle of his thumb and forefinger along her wrist.

"How many women?" Mary Delaney's blush deepened.

Molloy recognised Mary's effort to keep the conversation focused on what was going to happen between them. He knew this was not the time for a discussion on priests with no belief in what they were doing, nor was it a time for a lecture on the underside of the Church. "When I was still a priest, I probably had sex with a dozen women."

"Where did you do it?" Mary moved on the couch again, and Molloy's thumb and finger slipped farther up her arm.

"Various places. In rectories mainly. Once I did it in the ruins of a castle. I did it in an abandoned garage, in a hayloft, on the bog..." Molloy slid his hand along her arm as far as he could reach. He locked the thumb and forefinger. "I'm not saying this by way of excuse, only as an observation; most times it was the woman who made the first move. Of course I gave off signals that I was willing and able." With almost imperceptible pressure his finger and thumb became a handcuff on Mary's wrist. With the slightest pressure he pulled her towards him. With grace, without the slightest suggestion of a seal-like movement, Mary Delaney slid across the couch. She put her head on his shoulder and her right arm around his middle. His left arm was around her shoulder and her left hand was in his right. When the rustle of movement had ceased Molloy spoke again, the smell of her playing hell with his olfactory and other nerve endings.

"We had a spiritual director in the seminary who was famous for warning the students, and I was one of them, that there is a certain kind of woman who will go after any man in a uniform, even if he's as ugly as sin. That's the part he's remembered for: even if he's as ugly as sin. At the time, we all categorised the statement as just one more of his inanities. But he was right. It was only when I had sex for the first time that I realised how often I had been propositioned before."

"How old were you when you first had sex?" She didn't move as she spoke.

"About twenty-seven. How about you?" Molloy moved the arm around her shoulders and he stroked her hair.

"Seventeen."

"Where? When? With whom? It's your turn to talk for a while." He put his hand under her hair, touched her neck. She shivered.

"With whom! If you had never left Ireland you would have said, who was it wid?" Mary Delaney took her head off his shoulder. She sat up straight and moved closer, thigh to thigh. "I did it with… Well, the first time I tried was with a boy named Seamus Reagan. He was only fourteen. I suppose I seduced him, or tried to." She entwined her fingers in Molloy's. "He got so excited he came before I even touched him. He was one of the Reagans from Tubbermore." She looked at Molloy, held her face up, and he brushed his lips across her mouth. "Christ!" Mary Delaney said. She swallowed and moved on the couch. "The first time I succeeded was with a twenty-year-old who had learned all he knew about sex from watching horses doing it. He was as subtle as a stallion. While my bruises were healing I began to wonder about sex as a pleasurable thing. Then I met an older man – well, he was older than I was, about fifty – I met him about two hours out of Saint Thomas. By the time the ship anchored he had renewed my interest in sex."

Molloy disentwined their fingers and his hand glided over her left breast, barely touching her clothing. Delaney made a noise.

"Where was the most daring place you did it?" Molloy stroked her face with the hand which had brushed her breast. He ran his middle finger across her lips. He touched her forehead with his lips.

Delaney breathed noisily before she replied. "I did it on a crowded beach in San Croix. The guy was the bursar off the ship. God! He was a middle-aged Adonis. He was wearing jeans and a tee shirt. I was wearing a short skirt. The instant he dared me to do it I told him to stop walking. I kicked off my sandals, put my hand on his shoulder for balance, stuck my other hand under my skirt and pulled off my drawers. I can still see the grin on his face."

Molloy ran his mouth across her lips.

"Shit!" Delaney blew her breath out through barely opened lips. "We walked on another bit and I told him to undo his zipper and get his thang ready."

"Thang!"

"It's a thing when it's small. When it gets big its a thang."

"I have a thang."

"God!" She sailed her open hand across the front of his trousers.

"Jesus!"

As if to catch their breaths, they sat motionless.

"He lay on the sand and I plonked down on him, a knee each side. My skirt covered what needed covering. I raised myself and he placed his thang in the proper place. God! I went to the moon and back a zillion times. I can't remember his name."

Molloy used his right hand to tip up her face. They kissed before they groped in a gentle way. They groped for a long time before they stood up and became naked in front of the two-barred electric fire. They squeezed through the bedroom door and over to the edge of the bed, floated onto the covers.

Not long after she roared like an animal in pain, her face buried in the pillow. When she had recovered he moaned like a bear in pain while she, with arms and legs, tried to meld their bodies into one. Silently they lay until they felt their bodies parting, until the chill in the air sent them under the bedclothes.

Chapter 22

Monday in Holy Week – 2.48 p.m.

NOT LONG AFTER her post-coital shower, Elisabeth Molloy was waiting in her car for her children outside the convent school. The windows were fogged up, and the rain pounded the roof. As she looked at her watch and discovered she had more than ten minutes to kill, the passenger door was yanked open and Doctor O'Leary, uninvited, sat in beside her, water dripping off all his surfaces.

After greeting Elisabeth, and not once referring to the weather, he conveyed the latest gossip.

"All gossip finds its way to the good doctor's ear, and I am good." He beamed a brief, self-applauding smile. "When Frankie Molloy's wife died, he had an affair in New York with the Delaney girl from Gannonbeg, the musical one who works on the cruise ships. She *happened* to come home a few days after Frankie arrived, and they are at it again in Wheat Mill Lane. To put it bluntly, they are screwing their brains out."

Elisabeth was not amused at the doctor's blunt words.

With every new word O'Leary spoke, it sounded as if he were about to break into Gregorian chant. "I have to be less than couth. Supposedly, Delaney brought Frankie a box of french letters when she called to see him on her way home to Mama. How does anyone know that?" O'Leary shrugged his shoulders. "Rumour has it she was so much in heat – excuse me again – that she couldn't even get home to see her mother – had to get laid first, but that sounds like the fantasies of a man who hasn't had his… Excuse me!" O'Leary then turned to Elisabeth, drops of rain on his plump, brown cheeks. No matter what time of year it was, the doctor looked as if he had just come back from a Mediterranean holiday.

Elisabeth was not sure if her temporary speechlessness was caused by the doctor's forwardness or by his remarks. Besides wondering what had actually occurred to give rise to such stories, she was weighing the wisdom of letting the only doctor in the village know what a boor he was.

O'Leary leaned forward and rubbed the fog off the windshield with the back of his fingers. "So, how is Gregory doing?" he asked, with a familiarity which only his self-conceit allowed him. "Is he still denying the existence of the prodigal brother? He should admit he made an ass of himself and get on with it." Again O'Leary glanced at Elisabeth. She was looking at him with her mouth ajar. The doctor had never seen her at a loss for words before. He asked if she was feeling all right and when she nodded he patted her hand and said, "If you ever do see Frankie, tell him to keep away from my wife and daughters. Rumour has it he will copulate with anything that doesn't move." He smiled.

Elisabeth swallowed hard and she felt her face flushing.

"Well, I must be on my way," he said, but then he continued speaking. "Ken Considine is thinking of dying again. I left a message with Mrs Westman this morning that he is definitely on his way out this time, and that he should get the final, very last, last rites. This will be the fifth time. I gave him an aspirin and I hope he chokes on it. Even though every doctor's battle is a losing one in the long run, a high profile case like Considine's is bad for business. With Considine it's a no-win situation. The former policeman is determined to destroy my practice before he dies. Don't bother to thank me for the latest gossip, Elisabeth!" O'Leary gave her a wry smile and stepped out of the car into the lashing rain.

Despite what she'd just heard about Frankie, Elisabeth wondered if, once again, O'Leary had propositioned her with his florid, sexual language, or if he'd simply made one more rash effort to wriggle into the Molloys' circle of friends. She sat bemused in her car until the children ran screeching out of the schoolyard, their school bags on their heads.

Chapter 23

Monday in Holy Week – 2.48 p.m.

FRANK MOLLOY LAY on his back and Mary Delaney lay on her side facing him, his left arm under her neck, her left arm across his middle. After their noisy copulation, the sound of the rain on the roof had soaked back into the house.

"The rain," he said. "I'd forgotten the rain."

After a while Mary Delaney said, "Well, O former priest Frank Molloy, why did my mother say you were a curious child?"

Molloy lay there wondering if it was proper to tell the daughter about his exploits with the mother. But, he decided, they had only been children then. "When I was ten I wanted to find out how girls were shaped between the legs. A young girl named Mary Tonnery was doing cartwheels down a hill, and I had some sort of pre-pubescent attack. My curiosity overcame any discretion I had."

"Did you find what you were looking for?"

"No. It's difficult to concentrate on anything when you're falling down a hill and someone is whacking you in the face at the same time." Molloy slipped his hand down her belly and let it rest in her hair.

Mary Delaney ran her nails over his ribs. "She said you sat together for a year in school."

"We did, in the convent school. Which means I'm as old as your mother. Which means I'm old enough to be your father."

"Is there a judgement in there somewhere?"

"Not a judgement. A question."

"I'll marry a man closer to my own age, but older men are better with female bodies. Older men are not selfish. Also, there's something about doing it with a priest, even though he's not a priest anymore."

"And all along I thought it was my charm. It's a good thing I wasn't wearing my Roman collar!"

"Uniforms don't do anything for me."

Molloy suddenly dipped beneath the surface of the sleep which had been tugging at him. Then, in the mazes of his brain he heard Mary calling to him.

"What happened to your wife?"

On his way back to Delaney's voice he saw blue and red lights flashing out of harmony with each other, the people's faces made all the more panicky by the colours' incessant flickering. Even though Frank was still beneath sleep's surface, he knew he was talking and saying something he didn't want to say. "I was waiting at the next station, waiting for her and ..." He made an apnoeal gasp as he surfaced. "Padrake," he said. "Padrake was her name." He paused to establish his mental whereabouts.

"Your wife's?"

"What did I say about a station? I was having a dream."

"You were waiting for her at the station, you said."

"Yes. I met her every day at the railroad station. What did you ask me?"

"What happened to your wife?"

Molloy took a deep breath. "She died suddenly. It was a bad time. When we met..."

"It's all right," Mary Delaney said. "I didn't realise her death is still..."

"Thanks, it still is." They listened for a long time to the steady downpour. Molloy's mind was in a Greek restaurant in Mineola, and he was telling Padrake a story about goats' eyes and Robert Kennedy on a visit to Turkey with Robert McNamara.

"Are you a grandfather?"

"I'm not one yet, but I will be in July."

"Then you're the first grandfather-to-be I did it with."

"A grandfatherly rub of the relic."

"A what?"

"That's what the locals call it – a rub of the relic."

"Yours is no relic!"

"Well, whether it is or isn't, it certainly enjoyed its pilgrimage to your shrine." They giggled through their noses. "It's funny how many names we have for the various parts. Sylvia Plath called them turkey gizzards."

"Called what?" Delaney asked.

"The male genitalia in their benign state."

"Turkey gizzards! Dorothy Parker called the vagina the bearded clam." Molloy barked a short laugh. He pushed his hand down between

Delaney's legs until it came to rest against her buttocks.

An orgasm later, Copland's *Billy the Kid Ballet Suite* had vanquished the rain on the roof, the hoe-down fiddles high-stepping through the kitchen door.

Across the formica-topped table Mary Delaney's face, framed in her dark hair, was glowing. She and Molloy were having tea in the kitchen. Molloy asked, "What route have you travelled to arrive at the point where you can totally disregard the faith of our fathers?"

"That's what I asked you," Delaney said through the fruitcake in her mouth. The cake had been one of the items in the package she had brought with her.

"Well, I'm asking you the same thing."

She took a sip from her cup and returned it to the saucer. "I didn't realise until I left the country that the Catholic faith, as I was taught it, was more repressive than it was liberating. I decided that any religion which represses is a heap of crap. That's all. It took a while to recover from the repression."

"If your enthusiasm in the bed is any indicator, I would say you have fully recovered from the sexual repression, at least."

Delaney touched Molloy's hand. She smiled. "There are still times when I realise I am under the influence of some repressive teaching, and I have to do more housecleaning."

"I'm not free yet, either." Molloy declared. "I doubt if I ever will be, but I keep doing my best."

They heard Billy the Kid getting shot in the sitting-room, and between the shots they heard the rain on the roof. They shuddered at the same moment.

"I'm very glad you came over here today," Molloy said.

"So am I. But I had a few other reasons for coming. First," Delaney leaned over and put her hand into the box beside her on the floor, "here is a different kind of relic from Miss Duggan, *The Scarlet Letter.* Remember! I told you she gave it to me the last time I was home." She handed the book to Molloy. "I'll never read it, and it belongs to this house."

Molloy let the pages ripple through his fingers and he saw a speeding blur of notes in the margins. "Thank you," he said. "It will be part of the house's history. Do you remember you were going to write out the…"

Mary Delaney held up her hand. "Never let it be said that my mother raised a jibber," she said, and she leaned down into the box again. She returned with a picture frame. As she hand it to him she sang, "Da, dee, da!"

A typewritten sheet of paper was mounted on a black background, a white skull and crossbones in the centre above the heading, "Miss Duggan's Ghost Story".

"Jeez," Molloy exclaimed, "you didn't have to go to this trouble."

"Don't get too excited. I used a word processor in the office in Duneamon where my sister works, I reduced it on the office copier to fit it on one page, and I found the frame behind a wardrobe in my mother's house."

Molloy's eyes fell down through the reduced type and knew he would have to take off his glasses to read the tiny letters. But the handwriting at the bottom was much larger: "As told many times to Mary Delaney".

"Miss Duggan never mentioned Kit Foley in the story," Delaney said, "so I put in a few dates and facts on the back."

Turning the frame over, Molloy read aloud, "Kit Foley, 17 years old, was found murdered on the Davinkill golf links by Miss B. Duggan. It is believed that Tony Donaghue, who subsequently drowned himself, killed her. Kit Foley had been raped. She was five weeks pregnant at the time of her death. Miss Duggan was her music teacher for eleven years." Frank Molloy looked up at Mary Delaney. "The poor girl," he said.

"Yes, the poor girl," Mary Delaney repeated.

"I didn't know she came here for music lessons."

"Her mother died when Kit was two. Her father died when she was young, too, and she lived with her two older brothers. When she was six, the nuns in the school asked Miss Duggan to take her on as a student. According to my mother, Kit Foley became very attached to Miss Duggan – she almost lived here."

Molloy put the picture frame down on the table. "I was in Duneamon last Friday, and I went into *The Times* office to get a copy of the murder story. As it turned out, anything over five years old is in the National Library. Now I'm glad it wasn't there. I was getting it for fun. I was going to show it off, build up some kind of mystique. But these were real people: a young girl without a mother, an old woman without a daughter; a young girl – pregnant, raped and murdered. God,

I feel stupid that I even thought of hanging the ghost story on the wall. All the sadness there must have been when it happened!"

They heard the rain purring on the roof.

"I'm sorry you went to all this trouble, but now I know I can't hang it up. It's more than just a piece of history. It's a record of sorrow, and there's people still around who remember the grief. Maybe in a hundred years, when the pain is no longer around, someone can hang up the story as a curiosity."

"You're right," Mary Delaney said. "I hadn't thought of it that way. It is a sad story. It was sad, too, for the Donaghue family. They must still feel the pain of it all, and Kit's brothers, too."

The rain drummed on the roof, the steady downpour showing no signs of abating. On wet days, when he was a child, Frank Molloy had imagined it had been like this when God sent the Deluge, when all the people began to realize the rain was not going to stop, that the water was not flowing away anymore. The rain kept falling and the water kept rising and people got tired holding their children on their shoulders. His father would have had to let him drown with Gregory. The terror of it when your feet could not touch the ground anymore.

Molloy sighed loudly.

Delaney asked, "Did you ever find John O'Brien?"

"I found him, but I didn't get a chance to get any history of the house out of him. There was a woman in the way."

"Oh?"

"Maura Gilligan."

"She's a piece of work, isn't she? She and O'Brien have a thing going."

"A thing going?"

"They fuck."

Molloy burst out laughing at Delaney's succinctness."That's the only way to describe the relationship," Mary Delaney said. "O'Brien stank when I was a child. Did you happen to get a whiff of him?"

"I did. He smells like a bad dose of gangrene."

Mary Delaney held up her hand, and her body took on the air of a setter pin-pointing a pheasant."There's someone at the door," she said. Molloy listened, but all he heard was the rain on the roof and Aaron Copland prancing around in the Wild West.

He stood up. "Any time I hear a knock I hope it's my brother

Gregory." As he passed her chair, Molloy bent down and sank his lips into Delaney's hair.

When he came to the disc player he lowered the volume and the sound of the rain went up. He was anxious as he pulled the door open. Eddie Keegan was standing there, the hard rain slapping into the puddles at his feet. Despite the umbrella, the brim of his hat was drooping and water was dripping in fat drops onto his shoulders. The priest was smiling.

"Come in, Eddie!"

Keegan stepped into the doorway. He turned around and shook out his umbrella. "Welcome back to Hibernia, Frankie," he said. "The land of winter. If Saint Patrick got anything right it was the name of this place, where you can have winter weather any time of the year." Keegan folded the wet umbrella and snapped the buttons of its tie together. He stepped into the sitting-room.

Molloy took the priest's coat, hat and umbrella, and hung them on the hooks at the back of the door.

"I hope you don't mind me dropping in like this, Frankie. I was just over at Maura Gilligan's and I've taken a beating. Did you buy a car?"

Molloy pointed his thumb over his shoulder and said quietly, "I've got a visitor, Eddie." And, as if on cue, Mary Delaney appeared in the kitchen doorway.

Molloy did the introductions. But they were not necessary because, not only did the priest and the woman know each other, the priest had married her parents and baptised Mary when she was born.

While Mary, acting as hostess at her own suggestion, prepared more tea in the kitchen, Father Keegan wiped the raindrops off his glasses and talked about the weather. By the time he and Frank were seated on the couch, Delaney appeared with the tea and a slice of fruitcake, using a dinner plate as a tray. Molloy stood up and brought the chair from the window. Father Keegan said, "I'm glad to see you're still going to mass, Mary. I saw you with your mother yesterday."

Mary straightened up after putting the tray on the seat of the chair. "I only go to mass when I'm home, Father," she said. "It keeps my mother happy. Otherwise I don't relate to the Catholic religion in any way, besides reflecting the personal decency it incidentally encouraged."

"At least that's something – the decency part. A lot of people who emigrate lose the faith."

Frank Molloy gestured at Mary to sit at the other end of the couch, but she had something to say before the moment passed. "Oh, I didn't lose my faith, Father. I flung it away as far as I could."

Frank Molloy noticed the emotion which had crept into her voice. Mary turned to Molloy. "I'm going to leave, Frank," she said. "I told my mother I'd do the cooking for her – the first cheeseburgers in Gannonbeg."

Frank Molloy went to the door to get her raincoat.

Father Keegan put the steaming cup back on the saucer. "Are you angry at the Church, Mary?" he asked.

"No, Father, I'm not. If I spent my time being angry at it I wouldn't be free of it."

Molloy stood behind her and held her coat. As she slipped her arms into the sleeves, Keegan asked, "Are you really free of the Church?"

"Oh, yes, Father, joyfully so." With a touch of her fingers she flipped her hair free of the coat collar. "It's like when someone comes out of a prison cell after spending twenty years in the dark and the damp." She continued to speak as she looked down at her fingers fastening the buttons on her coat. "When I think about it, I want to do a little dance."

Father Keegan stood up. "Well, Mary, I'm not going to defend myself or the Church. I'm glad you're at peace with yourself. You certainly look happy." He held out his hand. Mary Delaney took it.

"Thank you, Father."

Frank walked her to the door. For a moment they stood in the open doorway. Molloy asked, "Will I see you again?"

"Damn right, you'll see me again," Mary Delaney said quietly. "You've got one hell of a schwanstukker, former priest Frank Molloy."

"A what?" Frank Molloy asked, but she had stepped out into the downpour. "Drive carefully!" he called after her.

He waited until she had turned the car on the narrow, sloshing lane. As she drove away she was smiling like a disappearing cat in a tree.

Chapter 24

Monday in Holy Week – 3.35 p.m.

WITH THE FLAT of his index finger Eddie Keegan rounded up the crumbs of the fruitcake, while Molloy, smiling at Delaney's word for his thang, returned to the couch.

"Would you like another slice of that, Eddie?" he asked.

"No, thank you. That's enough at my age." From the tone of his voice, Frankie decided that Keegan's disposition, which had been warm and fraternal when Mary was present, had taken a nosedive. The priest pulled in his chin and looked down his front for crumbs. Even though he saw none, he still brushed the black clothing with his fingers.

"You were very accepting of Mary's position. I was surprised you didn't do a little arm twisting to get her back in the fold." Molloy sat down at the other end of the couch.

As if he were using water, Keegan washed imaginary crumbs off his hands, holding them away from himself so the imaginary water would not splash him. "A few years ago I might have. Now I envy her."

For a moment, Frankie was speechless. Then he said, "Are you telling me you're in the dark cave that Mary mentioned?"

Father Keegan sipped from his teacup before he responded.

"The enthusiasm is gone, Frankie, and when that went most of the peripheral things seemed to make little sense, and even some of the central..." Keegan's voice trailed off as if he had lost sight of his thoughts, or had purposefully let them go.

"Few people can keep their enthusiasm at boiling point for a lifetime, Eddie," Molloy said. "Christ escaped at thirty-three, and he probably would have been fed up with the whole thing if he'd lived into old age. As it was, he was pissed off at the Apostles sniping at each other, and for not knowing what he was talking about; Mary Magdalene was hanging around his neck, and Martha and Mary were bitching at him to come over for a visit every day."

A wan smile came over Keegan's face. With an almost imperceptible shrug of his shoulders, he moved out of the delicate area into which he had unintentionally wandered. "Anyway," he said, "I let the busy work keep me distracted – like going to ask Maura Gilligan not to walk her beagles on the golf links. That was one thing I didn't want to do. No one on the golf committee would volunteer to go, so we drew lots."

The sudden lashing of a sheet of rain against the side of the house meant that the wind was at last on the move; the clouds would be stirring and moving away. The two men shivered.

"You were brave to go to her at all," Molloy laughed.

"It's the kind of thing I hate doing. Years ago an American did a study in County Clare, an anthropological study. I memorised a sentence from it that made a big impression on me: 'The community can invade the family and regulate its members through gossip, verbal censure and direct intervention in the person of the priest.' There's nothing I can do about the gossip or the verbal censure, but I never have been that kind of priest, even though a lot of people have tried to cast me in that role. I don't want to invade any family on behalf of some gossipy women, or gossipy men, for that matter."

"I'm surprised to hear you talking this way, " Molloy said.

"Oh, I'm not an enlightened sociologist, Frankie. I just don't like jumping into people's houses to tell them how to live their lives. It's too easy to get sucked into every little family dispute. I know too much about everyone in this parish. It will be good to get out of here. Thirty-two years! The bishop is very sick and he'll be dead in a week, according to the grapevine. I'll be out of here the minute a new man's appointed."

Molloy stood up. "You *hope* to be out of here, but you're depending on a man to die and on Rome to move fast. Maybe the guy Rome appoints will take his time making changes. You could be here for a couple of years yet, Eddie." Molloy took the priest's cup off the chair. "I'm going to put on some potatoes for dinner. Come into the kitchen."

Father Keegan followed Molloy down the sitting-room, naming the priests who were likely to be made bishop and the ones who hoped to be nominated. Molloy recognised some of the names from his days in Winter Hill and the seminary.

While Frank filled a small pot with tap water, the priest pulled out a chair and sat at the table. When Molloy turned off the water Keegan said, "I never thought I'd look forward so much to leaving this town.

It's like there's been a weight around my neck for years. I know all parishes are basically the same – the same people, the same problems. But everything will be fresh for a while. For one thing, I'll be away from the principal of the boys' school. I had to talk to him last week about a fist-fight he had with another teacher in a classroom. The only thing important to him was that the other man had started it. God, what a relief it's going to be."

Frank took Miss Duggan's copy of *The Scarlet Letter* off the table. "I know what you're talking about, Eddie," he said. "But yours won't be like the relief I felt when I left the priesthood. The most wonderful thing was the instant anonymity. I was not owned anymore. No more black suit and white collar attracting the needy and beggars like flies to a shit. The way people would jump up to give me their seat, as if I were an old woman! And all the bowing and scraping! You'd think I was the messiah." Molloy put three potatoes on the table and, with his free hand, picked up Mary Delaney's framed ghost story. But Keegan touched his hand to the frame and delayed its removal while he twisted his head sideways to see the words. "Miss Duggan's what?" he asked.

Molloy let the priest take the frame. "Miss Duggan's Ghost Story," he said, and as he turned to get the potato peeler he did not see Keegan's momentary collapse. "Mary Delaney gave it to me. It's the story Miss Duggan used to tell her music students. She wrote it out from memory." Molloy poked in a drawer for the peeler while, behind his back, Keegan pulled himself together, forced swallowings drawing saliva into his mouth.

The wind made shrill noises in the yew hedge around the house, and fat raindrops flattened themselves against the window glass.

Keegan let his squinting eyes fall down through the small print, and he saw that Mary Delaney had transcribed Miss Duggan's story word for word. He put the ghost story down on the table and said, "If I'd listened every time she told me the story I could have written it from memory, too. Why is it framed like this?" He took a deep breath and held it, as he struggled to bring his composure back under control.

Molloy sat down, peeler in hand. "I was going to hang it up inside the front door, but I changed my mind. How often did she tell the story?"

"Many times. It was in very obscure language, like Old English, and she'd mutter it with her head down on her chest. God! The crap we have to listen to just because of the way we dress – like you said, flies to a shit. There were many times I wanted to tell her to fuck off with her story, but how could I?" Father Keegan asked, and Molloy's left eyebrow arched at Keegan's use of the coarse word.

"Do you know what it's about – the ghost story?"

"Everyone knew it was about Kit Foley, the girl who was murdered out here on the golf links. She and Miss Duggan had a kind of mother and daughter relationship, and Duggan went queer in the head when Kit was killed. She told the story to anyone who'd listen."

"Why did she tell it?"

"Because she was insane."

"Maybe she was just broken-hearted. One time I was so grief-stricken, some people tried to tell me I was mentally ill."

It appeared Keegan was momentarily silenced at being exposed to such an intimacy. "Maybe you're right. Maybe she was broken-hearted. Something happened to the whole village when Kit was killed and Tony Donaghue committed suicide. It's like a wound that won't heal, because there's still something beneath the skin. Nobody was satisfied with the explanations the Guards gave." With his head propped up with his left hand, Keegan slowly stirred his tea. "Some people think Tony Donaghue didn't do it at all, and that someone got away with murder."

"But why would Donaghue have killed himself?" Frank asked.

"The Guards accused him of killing Kit. They told him it was only a matter of time before they had the evidence. Maybe Donaghue believed he was already condemned simply because he'd been accused. You know what small town life is like. But then again, maybe he did kill her."

"What do you think, Eddie?"

"I don't believe Tony Donaghue did it," Keegan said. "Why were you going to hang the story on the wall?"

"It's a piece of the history of the house, a little piece of Miss Duggan," Molloy responded, pointing at the picture frame. "I changed my mind because it's too new. The sadness is still in it."

"It is sad. It was terrible," Keegan said. "She was lying out there on the grass, a young girl, with an overcoat covering the top part of her body, covering the dreadful wound in her neck. She'd been stabbed with a blunt piece of metal, like a cold chisel. I remember walking toward her, thinking how cold her feet must be because she had no shoes on. I had to uncover her head to anoint her, and that's how I saw the gash in her neck."

It occurred to Frank that maybe this was the first time Keegan had talked to anyone about a huge trauma in his life.

"I never have seen anything as ugly, and pieces of her long hair were caught in the dried blood and jagged flesh. It was more a gouge than a clean wound. Some of the hair had been pushed into the wound in front of the weapon."

Keegan hesitated, as if he were pulling his eyes away from the gash. "You should have seen her face! It was a mask of total terror, like she had not only known she was going to be killed, but how painful it was going to be." In Keegan's pause the wind rattled the window and he shuddered.

"I had to anoint Tony Donaghue a few days later. The Guards had turned him over and left him with the back of his head lying in the water. There were four Guards and one of them kept whispering to someone to get a hold of himself. It seemed, all the time I was there, I could hear a loud whisper, so fierce that I kept seeing in my imagination the shape of the whispering mouth: all tight lips and angry teeth." Keegan paused, as if listening and waiting for the fierce whispering to die away.

"Tony Donaghue was a big man, but he looked like a fallen giant, like something out of a fairy tale. I remember sliding down to the riverbank, afraid I was going to pitch forward and fall face first into the water, and not be able to push myself up." Again Keegan paused.

"There was a dark bruise on the side of his forehead, the face dreadful to look at. It was a hard thing to do – give him the last rites. Donaghue had come to see me the night before with his youngest child in his arms – she's the girl who just graduated from the Sorbonne – Peggy. He told me he'd been summoned to go to the Guards' barracks in Duneamon for questioning about the death of Kit Foley. He was a mechanic. On the night before Kit Foley was found he had worked late because a bus had broken down off out on the Glin Road." Molloy watched as Keegan looked at the big man who lay sprawled on his belly above a big engine, a flashlight and a wrench in his hands.

"What a nice man he was! Big and gentle. You'd see him at holy communion holding the child, and the child would be as light as a feather on his arm. It wasn't to go to confession that he came to see me. He wanted me, not only me Eddie Keegan but me the priest, to know that he did not kill Kit Foley. He had a peculiar lilt, an accent from Donegal, and it was nice to listen to him talking. When I answered the door he wouldn't come in. He was too anxious to sit down, full of anxiety because he had been associated with the killing. The Guards only wanted to know if he'd seen anything on his way home the night before, but he was very nervous.

"You know the odd relationship we have with the law and the Guards in this country, Frankie; a hangover from the time of the English, when an Irishman wouldn't be caught dead talking to a policeman. The old informer thing! Donaghue said he was as innocent as the child in his arms. But there was no way to calm him down. I told him I'd go with him, but he wouldn't hear of it, that it would only make him look like a frightened boy with me by his side.

"He went home, said goodbye to his wife and children, and drove over to Duneamon on his motorbike to the Guards." Molloy saw Keegan listening to the putt-putt of the low-powered motorbike as it carried Donaghue out of Keegan's life forever.

"When I saw him there, lying on his back, I could only see a Hollywood prop made of plastic and paint. A few hours earlier he'd been in my hands and I'd let him slip through. If only I'd spoken up, gone to the Guards with him, he'd have been at home with his family instead of dead in a river. But here he was, the back of his head in the water, the eyes half closed, the big hands by his side with scabs on the knuckles where he'd skinned them working on machinery." Father Keegan pushed his fingers under his glasses, rubbed his eyes. When he took his hands from his face, his glasses remained at his forehead and Molloy could see red marks on either side of his nose.

"Of course, when his wife opened her front door and saw me, she knew right away that something was wrong, only she thought the Guards had arrested Donaghue and charged him with the murder. Telling Dervla Donaghue that her husband was dead, and how he had died..." Keegan shook his head. "Even though she stayed on her feet I could see her collapsing in on herself. She asked me to stay while she told the children." Keegan listened again to the mother's whispers and the wailing responses of the older children in the narrow hallway of the council cottage.

"I felt responsible, and I still do feel responsible for Tony Donaghue's death." Keegan took in a deep breath, and when he released it, his shoulders sagged. He looked across the table at Frank Molloy. "So, in answer to your question – no, I don't think Tony Donaghue killed Kit Foley."

The wind was still rising. Boisterous gusts rattled the windows and sent spears of chill into the house through hairline cracks and pinhead holes. The rain on the roof sounded now like sheets of water slapping on the slates.

The moment Frank Molloy scraped his chair on the floor, as he stood up to lower the heat under the boiling pot, Keegan said, "I bring communion once a month to the Guard who arrived on the scene first after Tony Donaghue's body was discovered. Ken Considine's his name. He's old beyond his years. His wife was killed years ago by Willie Gorman's bull. Considine's dying, and Doctor O'Leary says there's no reason why he should be dying. Every time I see Considine I'm reminded of that day on Scattery. He was the one being whispered at. He was having a hard time dealing with the corpse, and one of the other Guards kept yelling at him in fierce whispers."

Molloy brought a sharp knife back to the table and started slicing the peeled potatoes. "So, Miss Duggan was not the only one affected by Kit Foley's death," he said, and he went to the light switch at the door.

"Everyone was affected," Keegan said. "Some of the older women are still cautious about where they go and where their daughters go. You see, the Guards never came out and said Tony Donaghue killed Kit. The case was closed. And because the whole thing was left vague, every man in the area was tainted with suspicion. And the smell of that suspicion, no matter how vague, has never completely blown away."

"You're right about that," Frank Molloy said. "It seems the Kit Foley story is the main tourist attraction around here. I've been running up against it since I came home. John O'Brien showed me the garden out on the golf links. After what you've just told me, I see why it was allowed to get covered with weeds. Everyone's trying to forget about it."

"It wasn't enough that the brothers put a big gaudy headstone over her grave in the cemetery, they had to plant that garden where she was found, too," Keegan said. "They were a terrible thick bunch, still are. Eddie Keegan pulled his glasses off his forehead, and looked at his watch. He immediately stood up. "I had no idea it was so late. I have someone coming to see me at half five. I know she's going to spend half an hour talking about her drunk husband and will you come up to the house and talk to him, Father, as if that would make any difference." Keegan followed Molloy out to the sitting-room where Mozart's *Clarinet Concerto* was blowing itself around the sparse furniture, unlistened to. "I hate dealing with drunks," Keegan said.

Molloy took the priest's overcoat off the hook at the back of the front door. Keegan turned his back and as he pushed his hands down into the sleeve holes, he said, "The latest rumour about you, Frankie, is that Mary Delaney brought you a box of french letters on her way home from America." He shrugged the coat up onto his shoulders, and before he turned around he continued. "The story in the pubs is that you and she were having an affair in America before your wife died and..." Keegan turned around to face Frankie, and was taken aback when Molloy burst out laughing.

As Molloy continued to laugh, Keegan tried to hide his blushing by bending forward to button up his coat. Molloy put a hand on Keegan's shoulder.

"You know, Eddie," he said, "the best kind of sex for some people is the kind they imagine other people are having. Maura Gilligan must have binoculars or a telescope, but she is interpreting her data incorrectly. French letters!" Molloy laughed again. "Did Maura say the condoms were chocolate-covered?"

Keegan, a smile twitching at his mouth, waited for Molloy to stop laughing. "It wasn't Maura Gilligan who told me. It came from the pubs. There's talk, too, about the men being worried that you are a womaniser on account of..."

"Jeezus, Eddie, listen to yourself. They'll soon start blaming me for killing Kit Foley, and they'll come out here in a mob and lynch me from the nearest tree."

"I'm only telling you what the rumour is, Frankie." Keegan took his umbrella off the hook.

"Well, thanks for telling me, Eddie. I'd better get curtains for my windows or I'll have voyeurs lining up outside."

"It's a small town, Frankie. Now I'm sorry I told you. If you'd prefer I won't…"

"Oh, always tell me, Eddie. It's good to know what the neighbours think about you." Molloy handed the wet hat to Keegan. "I won't walk you to the car, Eddie. Tell me when you're ready and I'll open the door."

As Keegan adjusted the collar of his overcoat he asked, "Have you heard from Gregory?"

"No. Should I have?"

"Well I was hoping he might make some effort to talk to you."

"Well, he hasn't," Molloy said, and then he asked, "Was it to tell me not to screw around with Mary Delaney that you came over here, Eddie?"

"No, Frankie. That wasn't the reason. But I did come over to tell you what people are saying."

"When you arrived you said you came over to recuperate after visiting Maura Gilligan."

"I was trying to be diplomatic."

"I'd rather you were truthful with me, and from where I'm standing you're applying subtle pressure to make me conform. What was that line you quoted about the intervention of the local priest?"

Keegan looked as if he'd received a low blow. His eyes changed. "That's not why I came, Frankie. I don't care what you do in your own house. I told you as a friend what people are saying."

"But why are you telling me if you're not trying to change my conduct?" There was annoyance in Molloy's voice.

"Frankie! I don't care what you do. I told you what people are saying because some people take these rumours seriously, as if they were fact. You may be confronted about your behaviour when you least expect it."

"What does confronted mean, Eddie?" Molloy asked, with exaggerated inquisitiveness in his inflections.

For a moment Keegan said nothing. He looked down at his feet. Before he lifted his head he began speaking. "Frankie, you are like a long-lost brother to me," he said quietly. "Don't fight with me." He lifted his head and looked Molloy in the eye. "As your friend I told you what the people are saying about you. The reason why I told you was to let you know you should be circumspect."

Molloy took a deep breath as if it were part of a relaxation exercise.

"What can I do if a box of chocolate-covered macademia nuts is mistakenly identified as a box of condoms?"

"Nothing."

"Then why tell me the rumour?"

"Because when I came here today Mary Delaney was here."

"So what?" Molloy asked in exasperation.

"If people know there is a woman visiting you, Frankie, they don't think you're fornicating, they know it," Keegan said with equal exasperation.

"Fuck them!" Molloy said.

Except for the wind and the rain there was silence for a moment. Then Keegan laughed at Molloy's directness. "I'm glad you came home, Frankie. I would like you to stay. Be careful."

Molloy put his hand on the latch. "I am going to stay, Eddie. Come again. You'll be very welcome." He lifted the latch with his thumb. "If I'm in bed with someone when you arrive, cough once and knock three times. That way I won't answer the door wearing nothing but a condom." Molloy laughed. Then he pulled the door open and said with imperativeness, "Hurry up, Eddie, before the rain blows in."

As Keegan went past him, Molloy slapped him on the shoulder and encouraged him out into the howling rain.

Chapter 25

Monday in Holy Week – 4.05 p.m.

As Elisabeth Molloy brought the car to a stop at the head of Roongarry Lane, she realised that the rumours which Doctor O'Leary had passed along had already become a part of the Frankie phenomenon in her head. All the negatives she had heard about her brother-in-law had coalesced and produced in her the expectation of a man bitter and twisted. A remembrance of Quasimodo was giving shape to what she imagined she would see when she met him.

A few weeks ago Frankie was someone lost in America; he was a photograph – a young man in a white shirt and a green pullover, one of several young men with shotguns over their shoulders, the trap for launching clay pigeons at their feet in the spring grass, spring leaves on the bushes behind them, handfuls of cotton thrown against the pale blue sky above them.

As she slipped the car into first gear she heard a loud mechanical noise. The fear that part of the car engine had come free of its mountings flashed across her mind. But a second later she sighed with relief as Saint Willie Gorman's tractor roared past on Downs Road, Saint Willie sitting between two Catherine wheels of dirty spray spinning off the tires of his tractor, and he looking so wet and dirty he could have lately crawled out of a slurry pit or a primeval swamp. As he aquaplaned by, he raised his collapsed hat and beamed his beatific grin at Elisabeth's car.

Elisabeth laughed aloud as the tail of the dung-caked manure spreader wobbled out of sight like the rear end of a running duck.

She was still smiling when she turned right, wondering if her laughter was a symptom of nervousness.

After half a mile she turned right again onto the Davinkill Road and there, waiting to join Downs Road was Eddie Keegan's car. Elisabeth stopped quickly and rolled down her window. The priest opened his window at the same time, and two of the four cleanest people in the county faced each other across a one-foot, rain-filled space.

"Eddie," Elisabeth said, "you'll never guess where I'm going." Water blew into her face as she spoke. "To see Frankie, the prodigal brother-in-law."

"Are you bringing a hatchet to bury?" the priest asked.

"The next best thing. A cake made by Claudine."

"I hope it'll be accepted as a peace offering. I was just up there with him." Keegan wagged his head in the direction of Frank's house. "He's in good form." A sheet of rain blew into his face. He rolled up the glass until there were only two inches of window left. He raised his voice. "I'm in a bit of a hurry. I hope all goes well, Elisabeth." He waved. The priest's car moved away and Elisabeth put her car in gear.

Shaped like the vast sails of vast sailing ships, sheets of rain swept down the fairways of the golf links. Elisabeth drove slowly on the ribbon of road between the deserted greens. Miss Duggan's famous tree sighed against the grey sky, the long thin branches clashing against each other in the windy rain like the bones of a forgotten skeleton swinging from the yard-arm of an abandoned ship. In the warm, fogged-up car a shiver ran up Elisabeth's spine.

A murdered girl on the moors, a horrible gash in her neck. It could have been taken straight out of Conan Doyle. But Holmes would have unmasked the murderer.

Down the unpaved Wheat Mill Lane her car gently sloshed, splashes of water jumping from under the wheels and falling onto the grass beside the road like jagged, bent panes of dirty glass.

Before she reached the house, Elisabeth stopped the car so she would not be observed from a window. When the engine stopped on the turn of her key, she dropped her head to the backs of her hands on the steering wheel.

I hope he's not mean and bitter. God! I hope I say the right things.

Elisabeth sat up straight, took a deep breath and pulled the hood of her coat over her hair. She released the breath as she unnecessarily felt the sides of her face for stray hairs. Leaning over, and briefly catching her reflection in the rear-view mirror, she satisfied herself that everything was in place.

When she stepped out into the rain with the cake box in her left hand, the front door of the house opened. Before she dropped her eyes to negotiate her way around the puddles, the shape of a man filled the space between the door-jambs like the life-sized painting of a dynasty founder hanging above a fireplace. The yellow glow of electric light behind him threw his features into shadow. Elisabeth picked her way around the holes of water, her shoulders hunched against the rain, her head bent into the wind. When she raised her face again, she saw surprise on the man's face. He stepped back to let her come in. There was music, something familiar by Tchaikovsky, but she was too distracted to put a name on it.

They looked at each other, he with his mouth open, she with her hand to her hood about to flip it off, looking for and seeing no resemblance to her husband in the face of the gaping man.

"Frankie Molloy, I presume," she said, with an edge to her voice, because uncertainty had suddenly flooded over her. The music was filling the room with trumpets and dance, leaving little space for her words.

He smiled. "And I am going to guess that your name is Elisabeth Molloy."

"I'm your sister-in-law." *God! I'm gushing.*

"For a minute, as you were stepping through the rain, I thought you were someone else – Mary Delaney from Gannonbeg. I'm sorry if I unnerved you. Mary was here earlier and both of you have the same raingear. And she had a box in her arms, too."

Elisabeth Molloy blushed, and because of what she'd heard from Peter O'Leary only an hour ago, a warning, a fear, a thrill – she couldn't pigeonhole it – sped down the front of her body, and affected the stability of her knees.

"Let me have your coat," Frank said.

As she slipped out of the rain gear she passed the cake box from one hand to the other. With a tiny move of her head, the blonde hair fell into place around her face.

There wasn't even the trace of a Quasimodo about her brother-in-law. He didn't look like a man who had abandoned the priesthood, nor like a man who had been married and widowed. *What is a once-priest supposed to look like? In a corner of my mind I expected him to have a mark on his forehead like Cain, or at least to be disfigured in some way. What a fool I am.* She felt like a Peeping Tom caught in the act, when she realised that Frank was looking at her, was speaking.

"You look disappointed. I have the feeling I'm not living up to some expectation."

Elisabeth put a hand to each side of her face. "I'm sorry," she said. "I was staring, wasn't I?"

"Yes, you were." Still smiling. "Would you like to sit down." Molloy waved a hand at the couch. "And would you like some tea?"

Elisabeth had difficulty hearing him above the whirling music. "No thanks, at least not yet. I brought you this." She held the cake-box out to him.

Frank took the box in his hands and weighed it. "Thank you! What's in it?" he asked.

"A cake. Our au pair from Switzerland made it."

"A Swiss roll?" Frank smiled. "This is the second cake I got today. Mary Delaney brought me one, too. If I have any more visitors I'll be able to open a cake shop. I'll put this in the kitchen. Sit down."

As Molloy walked away, carrying the cake like a waiter with a tray, Elisabeth hastily looked around the room. Her ricocheting eyes saw all the gaping places which sighed for a woman's touch. Without bidding it to do so, her brain rearranged, added and took away. For the most part it added. Then, in the corner of her eye she saw Frank stepping out of the kitchen door, and she knew she would use the word "monastic" when her husband asked her about Frankie's house. Maybe Frankie would like to use some of the furniture they had stored in one of the out-offices.

The music paused to catch its breath and then, in what sounded like a torrent of circus music, poured forth again, as if assisting a herd of bull elephants to swing their trunks in unison at the edge of a sawdust-covered ring. Without seeming to be conscious of doing it, Frank touched a button on the console as he returned. Before the sound of rain and wind replaced the music, he spoke as if defending a point. "Tchaikovsky's *Capriccio Italien.* Some people say he's a terrible composer. But I don't know enough about music not to like him." Then, "I don't know if I was expecting you, as much as I was hoping you'd come." Suddenly, he seemed to be embarrassed by his little speech. He gestured with the small box in his hand and added, "One way or the other, I'm glad you're here."

Elisabeth said, "Thank you," and by the time her brother-in-law had taken his place at the other end of the couch, she felt she had finally shuffled her disoriented parts back into place. She crossed her legs and brushed at nothing on the knee of her brown slacks.

"Why were you expecting me?" she asked.

Molloy dropped his eyes to the box in his hand. As he pulled the lid open he said, "Eddie Keegan told me he'd spoken to Gregory. When he told me the kind of person you are, the way you spoke when the three of you were discussing me, I thought you'd come." Molloy put the opened box on the couch between them. "Those are macadamia nuts, chocolate-covered. Mary Delaney was bringing them to Miss Duggan when she came home a few days ago. Of course, she discovered Miss Duggan had died, and I inherited the nuts. They're from Hawaii."

Elisabeth leaned over and looked at the chunks of chocolate. As she spoke she blushed. "I'll try one later. They look like a mouthful." She knew the colour rising in her face was obvious to Frank and as she brought her hands up to cover her cheeks, she said, "You must think I'm a blushing schoolgirl."

"I've heard of people being allergic to chocolate," Frank said, "but this beats the band. I'll take them away." As he spoke he put out his hand to the box.

At the same time Elisabeth put her hand out to stop him, and their hands touched. She withdrew as if she'd touched a hot surface. "No," she said. "I'm not allergic…" She looked directly at Frank and found herself speechless. His face looked as if it were suddenly caught in the first rays of a rising sun. Then his mouth fell open, and Elisabeth did not know what was going to be expressed on his face next. She was surprised when he laughed, his mouth wide open and his front teeth showing, pieces of dental metal glistening in the weak light. Frank lifted his left hand and slapped it down on the cushion beside him. As he laughed Elisabeth saw him as a dog just out of water, shaking a sunlit spray out of its hair.

"You heard the rumour!" Frank said, when he regained control. He knew from Elisabeth's face he had hit the nail squarely on the head. "And did you hear, too, that Mary Delaney and I had an affair in New York?"

With her hands still at her hot cheeks, Elisabeth nodded. "Yes. I heard the rumours."

Frank picked up the macadamia nuts. "Behold the box of condoms," he said. "I hope you didn't believe what you heard."

"I don't know if I believed the stories, but once I heard them they were in my head. Knowing them affected my perception of you."

"But did you believe them?"

"I don't know. All I can say is that I didn't want to believe them."

"Why not?" Molloy dropped the nut box back on the couch.

"When Gregory told me you were coming home I was delighted. I think it's wonderful that you're here. You're a new member of our family, a whole new area of our lives, you and your daughters. I didn't want you to be what the rumours said you were." The redness was gone from Elisabeth's face. She put her laced fingers around her knee.

"What about Gregory?"

"What about Gregory?" Elisabeth echoed. "I'm not here to talk for Gregory. The two of you have to work out your own differences. And I'm not going to be an intermediary."

There was silence for a moment. They heard the gusting wind whacking the side of the house with a watery blast. Then Frank said, "I think you're telling me that you're accepting me warts and all."

Elisabeth smiled and held out her hand, fingers extended. "Yes, warts and all, as Cromwell said." Frank put out his hand, and when he touched Elisabeth, she said, "Welcome home, Frankie." Each squeezed the other's hand and looked in silence at each other, both of them with tight smiles on their lips.

When Frank released her hand, she said, "I'd like that cup of tea now."

"I'll get it." Frank stood up, the box of macadamia nuts in his hand. Elisabeth got off the couch and said she would go with him.

When she was seated at the table Frank told her she was the third person he'd had in his kitchen since noon.

"I met Eddie on my way here," Elisabeth said. "He told me he'd been here to see you."

"Did he tell you Mary Delaney was here when he came?" Molloy asked from the stove.

"Are you kidding?" she responded. "Eddie is so secretive there's times I wonder does he reveal anything about himself to himself. I was surprised he even told me he'd been here. He said you were in good form."

"In good form, like a racehorse." Frank turned on the hot water tap and rinsed mugs in the sink. "And talking of horses and the horse business, tell me how you and Gregory got together. You don't appear to be a likely pair."

"There is an age difference."

"I can see that, but there's more."

"Like what?"

"Gregory can't get around the bullshit as… Excuse me. You don't have the hang-ups Gregory has, or which I imagine he has."

"We are all children of our times and places, and I can handle the word bullshit," Elisabeth said. She put her elbows on the table and, after trying different positions, she felt most comfortable with her folded arms on the table across the front of her body.

Frank glanced at her and as he turned back to the soapy mugs in the sink he said, "So, tell me. How did you get together – you and Gregory?"

Then, as Frank dried the mugs and prepared the tea, she told him the same story Gregory had told her many times; had told the story in the way old lovers like to dwell on a defining moment; the same story which she had asked Gregory to tell many times – like a child requesting a favourite fairy tale. But she told the story flatly, without the tones and nuances and giggling which made the story part of the play which inevitably led to sex.

Gregory had seen her face for the first time among a thousand other blurred faces at the Dublin Horse Show. With her back to a chestnut filly, she had been running her hand down its flank. Gregory Molloy had stood and stared. He became flustered when she looked at him, had blushed and walked away.

Gregory had seen her again at lunchtime, eating by herself in the shed-like and immense cafeteria. From a safe distance he had watched her nibbling at a sandwich while reading the spread-out paper on the table. Hurriedly, he finished his lunch and walked up behind her. In his own mind he became intimate with her by way of a close-up look at her hair and hands as he passed.

It was she who had unwittingly brought about their first meeting. In the late afternoon Gregory had returned to his own area after taking a look at what other breeders were offering. She had been talking to Barry Curry, Gregory's stableman, the two of them standing beside Timahoe

Two, a lazy mare lacking motivation of any kind. Gregory had stood there looking at her until Barry Curry noticed him.

Elisabeth Delacy was her name, and Barry Curry was in the process of not telling her the truth about Timahoe Two. But Gregory Molloy had not been interested in the sale. He was finding it difficult to speak properly. He made such an awkward attempt to get rid of Barry Curry, that Elisabeth had divined before Curry had what Gregory was up to. The stableman had taken so long to take the hint that when he finally did go, Gregory and Elisabeth could not help but smile at each other. Then Gregory had told her why she would not like Timahoe Two. To his own amazement he had then invited her to dinner and, to his further amazement, she had accepted.

Two years later, besides making an observation about the age difference to their daughter, Elisabeth's parents had greeted their nuptial announcement with encouragement.

That was thirteen years ago, their marriage, when Elisabeth was twenty-three and Gregory was forty-one. He'd had to endure the usual spears from the gossip-chuckers in the village, this time about robbing the cradle.

When Elisabeth finished her story, Frank asked, "Are you happy?" He put the mugs on the table.

"Yes, I'm happy," Elisabeth answered. "I suppose I live with the same anxieties the average person has, but basically I'm happy."

"What do you get anxious about?"

"Oh, the usual stuff – fears that something will happen to the children, or that Gregory will fall off a horse or get kicked."

Then they told each other about their children; compared memories about colic, teething, chicken pox, the terrible twos and bones broken. They laughed at all the details of child rearing they had in common, as if their distance apart and their different cultures should have made a bigger difference in their experiences. And while they laughed, Elisabeth realised that Frank was prolonging the talk about children, that it was soon going to be his turn to talk about himself.

When he had poured the water, Frank pulled out his chair and sat down. Then he remembered the gift Elisabeth had brought. "Would you like a piece of cake?" he asked.

"No, but I'd like to try a macadamia nut," and as she spoke, Elisabeth knew that Frank knew she was going to ask him questions. Since her arrival she had noticed how he had managed to keep the conversation away from himself. Now she watched him twisting around in his chair, taking the nuts off the draining board, exclaiming that the nuggets were too large for one bite, standing up to get a small plate from the cupboard, closing the cupboard doors and then remembering the paper napkins. By the time he sat down again she saw his face had changed, was set against the questions she was about to ask. But she was going to ask them, because she was determined that this relationship would be solidly grounded.

Molloy put his elbows on the table and folded his forearms, building a redoubt across the front of his body.

Elisabeth did not immediately take one of the nuts. With her elbows on the table she used the steaming cup as a prop, the same way a lip-syncopator would use a dead microphone. When she blew gently on the tea, the vapour bent and turned itself invisible as it floated over the far rim, mist disappearing into sunshine. "Why did you come back?" she asked.

"If Padrake were still alive I would not have come back," Frank said. "Any roots I had put down in America withered up quickly when she died."

"How about the girls?"

"Karen and Jeanne! When Karen and Jeanne were young like yours, I never imagined they'd grow up, not need me any more. But once they married, I had nothing left to hold me in America. I can visit the girls almost as easily from here in Ireland. Jeanne lives in Maine and Karen in New Mexico. Next year they could be in Alaska and Hawaii. Americans move around with a fluidity that makes Europeans look as immobile as Clocowen Castle."

Elisabeth sipped at her cup, and circled closer. "Where did the name Padrake come from?"

"It was a pet name. When we met we were doing our best to impress each other, the way people do when putting their best foot forward. She knew some of Padraic Colum's poetry, only she pronounced his name Padrake, the way it looks on paper. Her name was Patricia. At first I teased her by calling her Padrake, and after a while it became a nice name for her." Frank took a drink from his mug, and before he had lowered it, Elisabeth had asked him the question he had learned to answer without falling apart. He played with his mug as he answered. "Several years ago, a man shot some people on a train just outside New York City. Padrake was one of them." He looked over at Elisabeth. She had an elbow on the table, a hand covering the lower part of her face like a mask, her thumb making a white indent on her right cheek. With shining eyes, she looked like she might lose the battle with her tears. But she blinked herself to victory.

"Some day we'll talk more about it. Most of the time I can keep the pain at bay. But, sometimes, when I least expect it, it shoots through the surface, mostly when I'm in a food store. We always did the food shopping together."

Knowing the uselessness of trying to say something that would give comfort, Elisabeth said, "That shooting was in the papers here. Imagine, I read about it and I never even… The senselessness of it…"

"The senselessness of it is what feeds the anger. Why did the asshole have to do it?" The way Frank spoke the words, the lack of tones, bespoke the uselessness of the question and the fatigue of having asked it a million times. "He was killed within a month of going to prison; stabbed thirty-seven times in the face and neck with the handle of a spoon that had been honed to a point on the floor of a cell. Fuck him."

After they sat in silence for a while, both of them doing something with their mugs, Elisabeth tried to lead him away from what he was looking at.

"So that's why you came back. Because there was nothing there to hold you anymore."

"There was more to it," Molloy said. He appeared to shrug his shoulders. "I guess I'll never be clear in my mind why I came home. Came home! Came back! Does everyone, who leaves home, look back with longing at what was, once upon a time, and in some hopeful way imagine the opportunity will eventually come to go back into what was, once upon a time." He looked up at Elisabeth. "I knew I wouldn't find paradise lost when I returned. But I know I'll find something. Just being here where my father and mother lived, where all our neighbours lived, gives me a feeling of some kind. They are all dead, but they're not totally dead yet. They're still here in the memories of the people who knew them, lingering. I like going to the cemetery. All the families I knew when I was young have someone buried up there." He paused and she waited. "Maybe I just want to be in the place where the old times happened. That in itself, being where the old times happened, gives me a feeling I can't explain. Maybe it's easier to die in a place where there's continuity around you all the time; dying becomes an easier part of the process. You drift into it. It just becomes your turn."

Frank had been glancing at Elisabeth as he spoke, and she had been looking at him, hearing him and trying to figure out what he was, who he was. She was comparing him to Gregory, because her husband was the only point of reference against which she could measure this newly dug-up brother-in-law.

"Does it really matter why I came back," Frank said, rather than asked.

Elisabeth started to speak, but it was so long since she had used her vocal cords, she had to jump-start them with a cough. "I'm glad you're here, Frankie – home, even if you're not in Roongarry. And, yes, I think eventually, for Gregory, the reason why you came home will matter."

Frank interrupted her. "Why eventually?"

"When he finally wades through all the embarrassment he brought on himself and comes out at the other end, he'll be rational enough to see this is you with no strings attached, that you didn't come home out of brazenness."

"That's what he thinks now?" Frank said, with a touch of wonder in his tone. "I can't believe he would even think that way."

Even though Elisabeth agreed with Frankie, she would never say anything negative about her husband. "I said when I came in that I'm not going to be an intermediary in this. But..." She put down her mug and rested her cheeks on the backs of her fisted fingers. With pursed lips she looked at the tabletop. Finally she raised her head, her hair falling into place with ease and grace, like a field of wheat moving in waves before an August breeze. "If I put in a 'but' I'm breaking my own rule." She gazed across at Frank and met his eyes head on. She saw no appeal in his eyes, no plea for help. "Is Gregory important to you?" she asked.

"Of course he is," Frank replied. "I know he wishes I had stayed away. And it seems too much to hope that he'll accept me for who I am, which is all I want from him. I'm not a bad person, and what difference does it make to him...?"

Elisabeth put out her hand and brought Frank's verbal traffic to a halt. "You're building up an argument for your own case, Frankie. That's something you'll have to tell Gregory yourself, and it's certainly not something I'm going to get dragged into. I accept you for who you are. Whatever transpires between you and your brother is not going to be the point of a wedge in my marriage. There are no sides for me in this. I have already chosen Gregory *and* you."

They looked at each other across the table. The rain had stopped and the wind had already begun the task of drying out the water-logged earth. The sound of the rushing air filled the house and exaggerated the feelings of warmth. From its elbow on the table, Frank's arm slowly fell down and across. His hand came to rest on Elisabeth's arm, and as she felt his fingers through her sleeve, he said, "Thank you."

When they broke contact, Frank said, "Even though you're not going to be an intermediary, I know you are going to influence Gregory, even if he is not aware of it. But you must know that if there is something I can do or say which will..."

Elisabeth shook her head slowly. "This is going to take a while, Frankie. Gregory is only at the stage where he thinks you should ask forgiveness for the way you have spent your life."

Frank attempted humour. "Maybe he should rename Roongarry, call it Canossa!"

Elisabeth raised her eyebrows.

"You've never studied Church history the way seminarians do. Sometime in the ten hundreds, one of the Holy Roman emperors spent three winter days waiting for forgiveness outside the castle where the pope was holed up. The castle was at Canossa," a broad smile swept into Frank's face, "and as far as I remember the pope was one of the Gregorys. Ha!" He laughed.

Elisabeth smiled. "The big difference is, there's no reason why you have to ask forgiveness."

They looked at each other. They heard the hard wind slamming into the house, and as much as the kitchen chairs would allow her, Elisabeth relaxed as she would relax with an old friend.

"Tell me about your family, your brothers and sisters," Frank said.

Elisabeth drew him in and wrapped her family around him, introduced him to the saints and the sinners, the oddballs and the drunks, the whiners and the winners, the suicides and the succourers, the hangers-on and the adventurers which make up the fabric of all families.

When she came to the end of her saga, Frank came as close to making a speech as he had since the last time he had given a sermon.

"You have set me into a context, and I love it the same way I love having come from this place; I love it the way I love the idea of being buried in the cemetery among my immediate family, my extended family and the families of the children I went to school with. I'm going to bring home Padrake and bury her here."

Chapter 26

Monday in Holy Week – 9.35 p.m.

NOBODY IN DAVINKILL ever asked Paddy Dillon, "How are you, Paddy?" People who passed him on the streets averted their eyes until the last moment. Then they grunted something which could not be interpreted as an invitation to conversation. The Christian precept of love thy neighbour having been fulfilled, the reluctant Samaritans accelerated their pedestrian pace, and hoped the drooling, dirty Dillon hadn't even seen them.

Nobody in Davinkill, not even Father Keegan or Doctor O'Leary, knew anything about Dillon beyond the odd, and sometimes criminal, behaviour he exhibited. Nobody ever extrapolated the probable activity of his brain waves from his external self. And nobody saw anything but humour in the latest silly thing he had said or done.

"Did you hear what Dillon did last night? Ran out on the street and shouted, 'Fire, fire!' When everyone came out and asked him where the fire was he said, 'In everyone's house bar mine.' Isn't that a good one?"

Like the air-borne seed of a weed, Dillon had blown unnoticed into town, his cross-eyed self, his cross-eyed wife and three cross-eyed children.

The children were demented because they had been malnourished from an early age, had even known hunger *in utero.* But their cerebral and physical weaknesses were not entirely due to malnutrition. Dillon and his wife were half-brother and half-sister. They had their father, whose name was not Dillon, in common. Their mothers, named Dillon, were sisters and they, in turn, were first cousins of the man who had impregnated them on the same day. The three of them had become aroused on a mountainy road while looking through a hedge at a bull mounting a cow. The bull's activity had served as their only foreplay.

When they discovered his penis was not limited to passing yellow water, Paddy Dillon and his wife-sister started fucking in the bed they had shared all their lives in their mothers' house.

They moved down from the mountains into Davinkill to be near the post office. Their marital relationship was never questioned, since they came dragging three children behind them, underfed, undersized, and underwashed.

When Paddy Dillon ran out of his attached council house and shouted 'Fire, fire!', the people who heard about it didn't hear Paddy Dillon shouting that he was cold, his wife and children, too; not that Dillon had much time to dwell on their misery, since he was drowning in his own. When he shouted 'Fire, fire!', the people did not know enough about him to know his children were behaving like a small litter of pigs in a corner of his kitchen, fighting for the warm spot, continually displacing each other and then beginning the piling process over again. The people didn't stop to think that Dillon might have been shivering in his own house, wrapped in his greasy gabardine, sitting on the floor of the kitchen like a demented ape; peeping out through the crack where the lapels met in front of his face; in the dim light looking at his equally demented wife-sister wrapped in her threadbare overcoat, as she hugged herself near the candle stuck on the floor in front of the dead fireplace, her hands pulled up into the sleeves, rocking back and forth, the top of her head visible in the hole made by the buttoned collar of the coat; the four thin children in the corner opposite their father, always moving, eternally squealing with hunger and cold, forever glancing at the warm flame of the votive candle which they were forbidden to approach.

The electricity in the house had been cut off shortly after their arrival in their new home. Every month the Saint Vincent de Paul Society paid the Dillons' rent directly into the county council's office.

Besides two mattresses and some blankets there was no furniture in the house. Even the banister's newel and supports were gone. There were no chairs, no table.

The reason why Paddy Dillon went to early morning mass during Lent, during the winter, was to get warm and to steal candles from the votive stand in the Lady Chapel, just two at a time so they wouldn't be missed. Everyone in Davinkill knew about the votive candles, but no one was willing to make the theft a public matter and run the risk of being branded a mean whore in the pubs. Mane hure.

On wet days, when the schoolyard emptied quickly, Dillon slipped into the classrooms to steal sticks of chalk, before Mrs O'Meara came to sweep the floors. The chalk was hard on the gums, but once it got soft it didn't taste bad. The chalk dried out Dillon's system and he would shit bullets for several days afterwards.

The back door of the convent was a reliable place for food, but Paddy had been told he could only come twice a week. On the bottom of an empty chocolate-bar box, the kitchen nun would have arranged all the little pieces of food she had saved after meals; half a breakfast sausage; sliver of orange; quarter of peeled apple; spoonful of cabbage; half-full shell of boiled egg; rind of a bacon slice; big spoonful of turnip; small potatoes; many potato skins; bread crusts; crumbs of sweet cake; peas.

Most times Dillon, unable to contain his own screaming hunger, unable any more to sustain in his brain the picture of his starving children and wife, would eat everything as he left the convent grounds, tear the cardboard apart to lick it, drop the chocolate-bar box on the ground. When he ate a piece of boiled egg, he ate it in the shell, his gums bleeding afterwards and he wondering why his spit was red.

And all the time his metabolism ached for alcohol. Money existed only for the purchase of alcohol. All food for himself and his family was either stolen or begged. Money was liquor in a different form. The money he begged for, the money he picked off the floors of the pubs, was instantaneously converted into liquor. When his wife arrived at the post office every fourth Monday, ten minutes before the pubs opened, Dillon was waiting for her; went in through the peeling green doors to the scarred high counter with her; stood beside her as her Children's Allowance book was stamped; held out his hand for the postmistress to count the money into it, the postmistress trying not to touch the filthy paw, her face scrunched up against the dirt and the ugliness and the smell. With his wife trailing him like a turkey chasing another turkey with food hanging from its beak, Dillon headed for the nearest pub, the flaps of his coat floating on the breeze he was creating.

They stayed in the pub until the money was gone. Drunk, they supported each other on the way home, vomiting into the gutter, vomiting on each other. Like two things out of a swamp, they went into their dark house, fell on their bed, pushing their children away like a sitting man would unthinkingly push aside a dog's annoying, poking nose. When the children finally came to terms with the absence of food, they sought out heat by sleeping around, between and on their drunken parents.

Dillon and his wife had not had sex since the conception of their second to last child. Paddy was so far gone in drink and malnutrition that he did not think about sex anymore.

Paddy did not know he was not the father of his youngest child. Someone had impregnated his drunk wife when he'd lost her on the way home one night, the Children's Allowance playing havoc with their brains. She had lain down in the archway to Father Keegan's back yard, and had never known that a virgin, middle-aged farmer, passing by on his bicycle, had seen the opportunity of a lifetime in the brightness of the street light; the farmer, not being very choosy about the condition of the orifice he was fucking through the unbuttoned fly of his trousers, had ever since recalled that moment to facilitate his masturbating in his cow shed. Dillon's wife-sister didn't know that Dillon was not the father of her youngest child.

Paddy had lived so long with physical pain that he didn't know his body was absorbing pain every moment of his waking life. Although there was only one tooth visible in his mouth, there were also several stumps rotting their way to oblivion in his gums. It was only when the nerves of one of these took a direct hit from an apple seed or something else small and hard that the pain shot its way into his consciousness. He had never been in a dentist's chair. Whenever he cut himself his flesh took a long time to recover. The backs of his hands were never free of scabs. During his lifetime he had broken three toes, a bone in his right ankle, and a bone in his right wrist. The bones had mended in their own ways. Whenever the weather was right, and it almost always was, rheumatism took up its painful residence in the ill-mended fractures. His persistent, hacking cough would have led a doctor to check immediately for tuberculosis, and the doctor would have found dense clouding in the picture of his patient's lungs.

Dillon did not know much about the world he lived in. In fact he didn't know he lived in a world; he simply lived in a house in a row of houses near the post office and near the pubs. But he knew where Miss Duggan used to live on Wheat Mill Lane because, when she was alive, she would bring him into her house for a mug of tea and a thick slice of bread, which he ate at the kitchen table while she told him a story in words he pretended to understand, but didn't. When he was young, someone had told him the moon was the back of the sun and he had never given the matter any more thought, had not thought about the moon or the sun again. He had not seen the stars since he was a child, and now he had forgotten they existed.

On the afternoon of Monday of Holy Week, Paddy Dillon had gone to the priest's orchard, searching the long brown grass for an apple that could have been, but hadn't been, missed in the autumn. Without a system, he crossed and recrossed the space beneath the trees, expecting at any moment to feel a round apple slipping out from under his boot. This was the eighth time he had searched the grass since apple-stealing time. It was when the hunger was felt in the marrow of his bones that he came back to Father Keegan's garden. Now, as he walked under a low-hanging branch, his cap was swept off his head. He cursed out loud at the branch and he cursed his cap. As he bent to pick it up, one of the two Culliton children, who had been looking at him through the hedge for a long time, said loudly, "You dirty hure!"

Paddy Dillon did not hear the voice because, when he bent to pick up the cap, the blood rushed to his head and blocked up his ears. As he slapped the retrieved cap onto his head, the other Culliton boy said, "You terrible shite!" This time Dillon heard the sound and he walked over to the hedge to investigate, his hands buried in the pockets of the gabardine, keeping it closed against the cold which he could never keep out. He saw the two shapes through the leafless privet. "Wa cha say?" he asked.

One of the shapes said, "He said you're a terrible shite." The other voice said, "He said, you're a dirty hure."

"Fuck yiz!" Dillon said without emotion. "Fuck yiz and yer mother's cunt has teeth." He walked away from the hedge. Then, from somewhere in the depths of his memory, something floated to the surface. He stopped but did not turn around, even though in his mind he was addressing the shapes on the far side of the hedge, his intestines trying to eat themselves. "Yer mother is yer father's sister. Fuck yiz, ye cunts with teeth." He turned and walked out of the orchard into Father Keegan's backyard. He was too hungry to be aware of his intrusive self, but from somewhere in his memory a feeling of safety was sent up to Dillon's brain, the memory having originated in Dillon's once-upon-a-time knowledge that Father Keegan played golf on most afternoons. From the hedge behind him came words which made no sense about hures and cunts and madness and cockeyed children. Letting the words fall on him like scattered raindrops, Paddy Dillon made his way up the priest's yard. His brain sparked and he suddenly veered to the right, went over to the priest's back door. He banged it with the side of his fist, but didn't wait for someone to answer because he knew no one would, no one ever did.

He walked out through the archway, shuffled across the very spot where his unconscious wife had been impregnated without knowing it, and stood on the footpath. If it hadn't been for his knowledge of his wife-sister and his children, his name and the clothes he was wearing at that moment, Dillon was as possessionless as a crow in a winter's tree. It would not have mattered if he had gone right or left. He was coming from nowhere and he had nowhere to go. He was very hungry, he knew that much. He didn't know his teeth stumps were throbbing deeply, that his old bone-breaks were aching. But these pains were seeping into his being, abrading the little bit of sanity which still attached him to his humanness.

He turned left, and, audibly, he cursed the two fuckers on the far side of Father Keegan's hedge; he cursed the fucking cold weather, and he cursed Father Keegan's fucking housekeeper who always hid when she knew he was coming, "you old cunt may you rot in shite with teeth!" He cursed Father Keegan's orchard that never had a fucking apple in it; he cursed FitzGibbon and the fuckers who went to his pub to drink, all too busy talking to remember to give him the price of a pint, "the whole fucking lot of yiz so busy talking about that fucker who came home from America!" He cursed the farmers in Lamb's pub who pretended not to see him, "them with their fucking bulls and bales of hay not one of them would give ya the steam off his fucking piss."

And as he walked along, hugging the pockets of his coat to his crotch, he remembered the two great fires he had lit and, for a fleeting moment, so fleeting he only got a whiff of the feeling, he felt the joy of burning a fucking farmer's hay barn to the ground, the colours of the great flames dancing in the dark, the wonderful heat making the front of his body hot, and then nothing left for the fucking farmer but the twisted stanchions standing against the night sky like burned bones.

"Fucking farmers," Paddy Dillon said aloud, and schoolchildren on their way home pressed their frightened selves against the front of a house to let him pass. But the children knew they were being made special because they would be able to repeat to adults the forbidden words they heard Dillon using. "It's Mansfield's pub tonight and I'll burn ye all down in the middle of the fucking night to make me warm ye cunts with teeth."

Shivering on his kitchen floor, wrapped in his overcoat like a demented ape, Paddy Dillon peeped out through the crack where the opposite sides of the coat met in front of his face; in the fluttering flame of the dying votive candle he looked at his wife hugging herself on the floor near the dead fireplace, her hands pulled up into her sleeves, rocking back and forth. The four thin children in the corner were almost quiet, sleepy squeals whimpering into the dying light.

The votive flame flared, stood on its toes for a few seconds, and died.

For a long time no one stirred in the black darkness, and Dillon continued to stare at the spot where the flame had been. Like the body of a lately-hatched bird screaming for food, every nerve-ending in Dillon's body screamed for alcohol, and it was more from alcohol withdrawal than the cold that he was shivering. Again he thought of yellow and red flames leaping out of haysheds, but the flames gave no comfort. He thought about a big black glass of porter with the priest's collar of froth on top. But the fuckers wouldn't give him one, all talking and talking and not seeing him, and Lamb telling him to fuck off when he begged for a drink. In semi-consciousness, until he heard the children stumbling in the dark on their way to the mattresses, Paddy Dillon held his hand out for the elusive pint of porter and all he could hear was talk about the American.

It was time to lie on the mattress and Dillon leaned forward until he fell onto his hands. As he pushed himself off the floor, someone in the dark stepped on his fingers. He snarled in pain and squealed, "You fucker. I'll drive the nuns' fork through ya."

Chapter 27

Tuesday in Holy Week – 2.35 p.m.

ONCE AGAIN, FRANK MOLLOY found himself standing in the open gateway of the knacker's place of business.

The clouds, like low-slung rolls of dirty wool, had changed everything's perspective and, in comparison to the first time he had seen the place, the premises looked grim, forbidding. The dirty, hulking clouds had squeezed the vivacity out of the whole world. Things with colour had suffered excessively, as if they had been pressed between the pages of a thick book for a thousand years.

Molloy's mood matched the greyness of the day, and he didn't know why. Yesterday's wet day had kept him housebound, but he'd had the three unexpected visitors; one he'd had sex with, one he'd broken down old walls with, and one had welcomed him home. Yet he was feeling down.

His gloomy gaze fell across the five signs on the knacker's fence. It took a moment for the writing to register on his torpid brain.

Knacker. Trespassers Prosecuted. Dead Animals Removed. Dept. of Health. Greyhound Meat.

Molloy closed his eyes and he recognised the depression into which he was slipping as a familiar narrow cave, the same one he had discovered for the first time in Falworth many years ago. He quickly opened his eyes and took practised steps to keep himself from slipping further down. Again he heard Nina Borruso drilling through his layers of depression, after Padrake had died, repeating over and over the ploys which would help him to force his way out of the deep, black hole which the cave had become.

With a conscious effort he made himself look for a distraction. *The Knackery! That's what he should call this place. The Rookery. The Hatchery. The Rectory. The Bakery. The Presbytery. The Knackery. On a shingle, swinging from a gibbet, he should have* THE KNACKERY, *with pieces of animal bodies – kidneys, livers, hearts, stomachs – melting down over the letters like the watches in* Persistence of Memory. *The Persistence of Decay, it could be called – the painted shingle.*

The rolls of clouds above the Knackery did not move. Wisps, which had become detached from the main body, twisted slowly like fantastic fish caught on barbed and barbarous hooks.

The Persistence of Decay! Everything's in a state of decay: things, people, ideas. He who is not busy being born is busy dying. Where did that come from? A song of years ago.

Molloy saw a human shape, O'Brien, he surmised, striding across the space made by the open doors of the big shed. O'Brien disappeared, but reappeared almost instantly with what looked like a bow saw in his hand. He vanished into the area he had emerged from in the first place.

You spend your life bogged down in someone else's decomposing mess, unless you step smartly. Like me bogging down in decay when I joined the priesthood, trying to run but sinking deeper in the rottenness with every step taken. I was drowning in liquid putrefaction.

As he stood in the gateway to the Knackery, the saddle of his motorbike resting against his thigh, his eyes took on the twelve mile stare, and his jaw fell ajar as his mind slipped away from him into the cave, back to his room in the presbytery in Falworth, the room which, in his mind, had become the symbol of rejection and bitterness.

The many details of his life in that room had long been compressed in his memory, like many drops of resin from an ancient tree compressed and hardened into a solid. But the feeling that paralysed him whenever he thought of that room, sprung from the presence of those details contained in the cerebral compression, even though he wasn't aware of all of them individually anymore.

On a late summer's day he had arrived from London at the presbytery in Falworth with the bishop's assignment papers in his pocket, and assurances, backed by fat smiles in a creased episcopal face, that he would find his first ecclesiastical boss to be a kind and fatherly man. In response to Frank's trepidatious knocking, the Reverend Canon Walter Cotswold had answered the door. Replying to the new priest's introduction of himself, Cotswold, from his point of vantage three steps above the pavement, had sent down the seminal words, "I wasn't expecting you, Father. Frankly, I don't need you."

Like the caustic soda his father had used to burn the horns off newborn calves, the pastor's words had seared themselves across Frank's soul.

Then, after a long silence created by Molloy's inability to respond, the pastor spoke again from the third step. "The vicar general of the diocese is spending his holidays here with me. He is in the guest room. If you wish, you can take the spare room in the attic. We have a continuous flow of priests staying with us during the summer and autumn. They come to take the sea air, so I'll see if I can use you when the holidays are over. In the meantime, I'm sure we'll have enough food for you."

It was in the isolation of the attic room that the seeds of bitterness sent out their first tentative roots – tentative because the bitterness was directed against the very thing he had loved and fantasised about since he was a child; tentative, because the bitterness was there in his breast only three months after his ordination to a priesthood for which he had prepared all his life. Cotswold never asked him to do anything, never involved him in the parish in any way, never took him into the conversation at the dinner table.

Canon Cotswold seldom left his demesne, where he reigned over his own little world, ruling with magisterial gravity on the amount of hot water to be used in the bath tub or the installation of hundreds of locks in the presbytery and church.

On Sundays, when he finished his breakfast, he went to his room with the collection money, and there he played with the coins until late at night, fondling the brown piles of pennies. He counted and piled and bagged and emptied the bags of pennies again to make sure he had counted correctly. He made up forms with columns to accommodate the number of halfpennies, pennies, threepenny bits, sixpenny pieces, shillings, two shilling pieces, half crowns, ten shilling notes and one pound notes which were taken in at the two collections during the seven Sunday masses; fourteen piles of coins to be played with, to be stroked lovingly. He moved columns of stacked coins around his counting table, positioning them to the best advantage, so they looked larger than they really were.

At bedtime he bagged the coins for the final time, and threw his columned forms in the trash can, every box filled in. On Monday mornings he swung open the front door of the presbytery to the armed men who came in an armoured truck to take his treasure to the vaults of the Bank of England.

Cotswold spent his life sequestered in his rooms, in the morning working on his account books which held the records of pennies saved and pennies spent. He rang his small hand-bell and called the housekeeper to bring him fresh water and his pipe, to tune the radio when it was time for his favourite music programme. His lunch was brought to his busy room, and as he ate he looked down on the traffic on Tanner Street below his bay window. During the afternoons he read Agatha Christie and napped and read again. When he swept into the dining-room for dinner, wearing the frills of his canonical rank, he expounded on what he had seen on Tanner Street during lunchtime.

It was at the dining-room table where Cotswold performed for the current clerical visitor. Grasping for the most outrageous racial slurs, the most scatological jokes, the most pontificating positions, he strove to captivate, and he did not hear the sycophancy and loud insincerity in the laughter of his guest.

Every Thursday afternoon Cotswold went on his only weekly outing. He visited the convent to hear the nuns' confessions, then, in solitary splendour, he ate the high tea they served him. When he departed, he was cheered off the convent steps by the nuns, the old ones, the blind ones, the ones on canes, crutches and walkers.

Meanwhile, Frank Molloy was trying to live up to his oath of obedience to the bishop and his delegates. For three months, like a caged and outraged animal, he paced his room, tried to read, looked out at the roofs down the hill from the presbytery and went for night walks near the stony beach. And it was on a Thursday afternoon in November, when he was furiously gazing through one of the dormer windows, and trying to hold at bay the thoughts he didn't want to have, that he heard a knock. The door opened before he had time to back out of the dormer.

"May I come in, Father Molloy?"

"Yes, of course."

Cotswold closed the door and surveyed the room, eyes darting like agitated wrens in a holly bush. "I had forgotten how charming is this room. It must be years since I was in here. I'm glad to see you have spared the walls any more nails." He stepped over to one of the windows facing the sea. "I love these slanting ceilings and the way one has to bend over to see out."

As Cotswold went back to the centre of the room, Molloy could see the tracks of the comb's teeth disappearing over the sharp hill of his head.

"Won't you offer an old man a seat, Father?"

Molloy pulled a blanket-covered armchair away from the bed. By motion of head or hand he indicated the chair to his pastor.

"The blanket, Father!"

"It keeps the stuffing in the chair."

"I'd prefer it without the blanket. One must be content with the furnishings provided, Father."

Frank removed the blanket and pieces of foam rubber fell on the floor.

"We mustn't let a little thing like stuffing upset us, must we, Father?" Cotswold crossed his legs and Frank saw the silver-buckled shoes and the red socks.

"Do sit down, Father. There are a few things I have to say to you." Cotswold waved the back of his left hand toward the bed.

As Molloy went to sit, he hit the leg of the bed with his foot and almost fell onto the mattress.

"Careful there!" Cotswold exclaimed, and he flung out a supporting hand.

Molloy recoiled from the outstretched claw, and at that moment, when he saw Cotswold's hand as a claw he realised that no matter what Cotswold had to offer now, it could never undo what had been done to his soul since his arrival in this presbytery. It was too late. Close to the surface of Frank's consciousness, the knowledge was already brewing like magma beneath the top of a mountain, that he was finished with the Church. But like the stewing magma, it would take time for all the forces to assemble themselves in his chest before the moment was ripe to blow the top off the mountain, before the lava would cascade in burning anger down the slopes.

"Is the bed comfortable, Father?"

"Yes."

"Good. At least one piece of furniture is to your liking."

The pastor looked up at the corner of the ceiling, took a deep and loud breath, held it, and said, "What I want to speak about, Father, is your happiness." He loudly blew out his lungs and the wrenish eyes skewered Frank in their deathly gaze. "When you came here three months ago, you were bushy-tailed and bright-eyed. You were excited about being a priest. You visited the church and said your prayers. You never went out at night." He paused. "But you have changed. All that has changed." Cotswold used his arms to show how big the change was. "You never smile. You never join in the table conversation in the dining-room. I had to ask you if I could sit down when I came in just now. What has happened to the smiling, courteous Irish lad who appeared on my doorstep a few months ago?" Canon Cotswold pushed his small eyes forward in their sockets, forming the dots of two question marks under his thin eyebrows. He cocked his head to one side, moved his hands in his lap when he realised he was not going to be answered, moved his red-stockinged feet.

"You have nothing to say!" There was a trace of umbrage in the challenge. "You don't say your prayers anymore. That's dangerous, Father. I must remind you that not only am I your pastor, I am your spiritual director, and I must warn you about the danger of missing one's prayers." He emphasised the gravity of the danger by moving his right hand up and down. "I want you to be happy in my house, Father Molloy. I want you to see the housekeeper as your sister. I want you to see me as your father."

Frank pulled his eyes away from the pale and puffy face; away from the dead flesh that to Molloy was only an extension of the inner corruption of this man who had lived too long beneath the rock of the Church. Cotswold followed Molloy's departing eyes with his emphatic voice, a nagger staying close to his victim.

"Don't cut yourself away from us. Come to me with your problems."

Frank only heard empty, lifeless words floating around the room and he felt trapped, straight-jacketed. He could think of nothing to say. His anger was too pent-up for him to speak, and he knew if it was unleashed, the eruption of the expletive-laden diatribe would be used to punish him.

Cotswold continued. "I have been in this business for many years, and I know what you're going through. Go back to your prayers and don't go out at night." The red sock and the buckled shoe moved back and forth. "I know you will take your oath of obedience to heart and do as I say. My prayer is that God will give you the grace to succeed."

A shroud of cold embarrassment fell on Frank when he heard Cotswold speaking of God and grace.

The pastor stood up. "I will leave you to meditate on what I said."

Without speaking, Molloy followed Cotswold to the door, and he saw pieces of white stuffing clinging to the back of his soutane. Kath, the sisterly housekeeper, would brush them off. Frank opened the door, and as Cotswold passed out of the room he said, "May God give you strength."

When he closed it, Frank stood with his back to the door. He gazed at the window across the room and he saw thick, grey clouds rolling in from the sea. They tumbled forward like billowing smoke rising from the heaps of burning bushes in the fields of Ireland in the springtime, the breastings of hedges.

Inching his feet away from the door, he slowly slipped to the floor. His chin fell onto his chest and he did not try to hold back as he slid into the small cave which he had recently discovered.

Propelled by an anger which he did not know how to express any other way, he slapped an outraged fist into his left palm. The noise of the slap was like a squawking bird flapping around inside his brain.

He smashed his fist into the cave wall and the sound was a terrified bird screaming past his face in the dark.

Spiritual father! Pompous arse!

Mad birds wheeled and shrilled in confusion in his head.

In the dark cave, he ripped off his collar and flung it to the ground. His fingers opened the top buttons of his cassock and then with impatient hands tore it open, buttons scattering. Birds screamed, called at Cotswold. Before one finished six started. Before six finished twenty started, and Cotswold was thrown around his skull in little pieces.

Again he slammed his steel fists into the black wall. As it collapsed, the distraught birds threw the sounds of the falling rocks at each other. He scampered up the rock pile and flung his ragged cassock behind him.

He took iron-shod steps down the red-black rock pile and he saw Cotswold sitting in his pink armchair reading *The ABC Murders.* The birds were gone.

"You could have used the door, Father," Cotswold said, without raising his eyes from the book.

Frank was Samson at Gaza, pulling the pastor's door and its frame out of the wall. The ragged birds swooped and screamed when he flung the door onto the floor in front of Cotswold's chair.

"Now you can plainly see who goes by. Plainly see. See me going out at night. No more peeping."

Without losing his stride Frank went to Cotswold and kicked Agatha Christie into the ceiling. A thousand screaming beaks devoured the book. A new copy of *The ABC Murders* appeared in Cotswold's hands. Frank jerked back the pastor's head by its thin hair until the mouth was gaping. To the depth of his own elbow he stuffed the book down Cotswold's throat. A new book appeared and the reader read.

The hassock splintered when Frank kicked it from under the pastor's feet. He yanked the phone out of the wall and, as he smashed it against the fireplace, the flocks of crazed birds in his brain screeched cacophonously.

"Now you won't hear who calls him up. You won't hear. But you can plainly see who goes by. Who calls him up."

Frank saw his own half-naked, steaming body, glistening rivulets of sweat spating between the conflictive muscles.

He leaped across the room at the money-counting desk and tore it asunder, ripping out its twelve locks. He shredded the account books. He smashed all the windows as he hacked the locks out of the sashes, the sound of the glass shattering below. The mad birds broke lose of the sharded glass and they clawed the seventy-three locks out of the doors and closets in the church. They pulled the five locks off the front door of the presbytery. They dumped sixty-seven locks from the remaining doors and windows of the house at Cotswold's feet.

Frank saw the powerful muscles on his own adamantine arms, the purple-thonged veins binding the muscles to the bones. His fingers were prongs of steel squashing the locks the door the phone the accounting books the counting desk; kneading them until they were a soft dough. And as he kneaded, the squawking, blindly-fluttering birds in his head scratched out a raucous *O Salutaris Hostia.* The kneaded metal and wood in his hands took on the shape of the dead man with gaping holes in his hands and feet. The ugly, pain-twisted face stared wherever the head lolled. The corpse turned green as it decomposed and the birds screamed, "We worship the corrupt body of the dead Christ. *Adoremus.* The dead Christ. The rotting Christ. *Adoremur cernui.*"

Frank lunged at Cotswold, caught and lifted him by the throat and genitals, slammed him into the decomposing body – pieces of the rotting flesh splatting onto Frank's legs.

The birds descended and covered the living and the dead in a gluttonous orgy.

"This is not it!" Frank screamed, scalding tears of rage leaving glowing tracks in their wake. He put his torn hands to his face and pulled his bloody fingers down his cheeks. As he fell to his knees the birds cackled in the darkness.

"It should be warm like the priest's house. The priest's house. There is no warmth."

He covered his ears so he would not hear his own words of realisation. "I was given a scorpion when I expected bread."

He bent over and banged the floor with his fists. The birds fled soundlessly into the graying distance. Tears, boiling up out of enraged and outraged ducts, fell off his chin, and he saw his own white hands pounding on the cracked linoleum of his bedroom floor. He took a deep breath and leaned his head back against the door.

"O Jesus Christ," he breathed, not in prayer. He rolled his head from side to side. "O goddam Jesus Christ, what have I let myself in for?" He wiped the tears from his face with the back of his hand. "What have I walked into?"

From where he sat he could see his suitcases where he had stored them under the bed. Five weeks after ordination he had packed them with enthusiasm and expectation.

"O goddam Jesus Christ! With enthusiasm and expectation."

He stood up and shuddered in embarrassment at the remembrance of the naivete of a few months ago. From under the bed he pulled the smallest case, stuffed in socks and underwear. The trains left every hour on the hour for London, and if he hurried he would catch one at four o'clock.

When he opened the presbytery's front door, teeming rain was raising bubbles on the water in the street's gutters. He stepped out and bent his head against the downpour, dismissing the urge to go back for an umbrella. He might meet Cotswold.

On the suitcase, the airline tag of three months ago flopped in the wind like a dying fish until it was waterlogged. It stuck to the suitcase – LON in bright green letters.

Without seeing them, he heard the swish of cars sloshing through the wet street beside him. When they sent sheets of water in his direction he did nothing to avoid them.

The brown water in the gutter flowed with him, his eyes, his sere mind attracted to the things floating on the surface.

He turned a corner and the rain was slanted and slashing. The water ran down the back of his neck, his shoes sloshed with every step: the soft calf-leather shoes – his mother's ordination present. He saw his father's face, too, wearing the pride of having a priest in the family. He saw Gregory.

Avoiding the puddles was of no avail now. The suitcase glistened wetly and the luggage tag had melted away from its anchors.

Before he even saw the railway station he turned back because he knew he was going nowhere. He did not know anyone in London. He didn't even have the price of the train ticket.

He changed the suitcase to his other hand and slowed his pace to a stroll. The wind whistled in the telephone wires and the rainwater flowed down his head, ran down his back and chest until he was enclosed in a cold wetness which he would feel for the next seven years. It would take that long for the pressure to grow which would enable him to overcome his feelings of betrayal of his father and mother and brother and all the people who had sent him forth to conquer the world. By the end of those seven years he would have performed rituals with an ever-decreasing belief in their worth; he would have acted out a delayed adolescence, a monstrous adolescence because of his age, an obnoxious adolescence for those around him; he would have moved to three different presbyteries and found a variation of Cotswold in each one; he would have become more embittered and more difficult to live with; he would have slept with numerous women; he would have left England and moved to the United States in one last desperate effort to salvage his priesthood. And he knew it all went back to that moment when Cotswold had looked down and rejected him.

Frank Molloy became aware of the pain in his side. The twelve-mile stare fell out of his eyes and the knacker's premises came back into focus. He moved the saddle of the motorbike out of his hip.

I wasn't expecting you, Father. Frankly, I don't need you! Molloy rubbed his hip. *I'll go to the grave with the fucker's words still ringing in the recesses of my brain. I have turned around from Padrake's death… no I haven't. But Cotswold was thirty years ago, and I still haven't turned around, looked away, walked away completely.*

His eyes fell on the knacker standing in the doorway of his cutting-up shed, hands on hips, legs apart – a postered Hollywood star advertising his latest movie.

I will never be rid of his words. Their resonance has faded, but they still resonate, an ever-present source of nutrition for hate. Love and hate! We can be as much in-hate as in-love.

Across the enclosed space of the knackery a sound came floating from John O'Brien. It was a wordless sound, but there was a challenge wrapped up in it. Frank waved in response and wondered should he just turn around and go home.

He always felt jaded whenever he visited with the Falworth troglodyte; drained, depressed. But he heard again Nina Borruso's voice, reciting her second rule for fighting depression. "It's like any game that's played with a ball. Never back away; always attack the ball. The same with depression. Go out and meet it head-on. Whack it. Make yourself meet people. Make yourself talk to people."

With an effort of will he pushed the motorbike toward the disemboweler, the beheader, the dismemberer, toward the packager of animals in their entirety except for their holes.

The Persistence of Decay! Maybe Cotswold, in some perverse way, saved me from spending my life plunging around in the whole decomposing mess, from sinking deeper in the rottenness with every step I took. After him it was easier to see the decay in the others, to see through all the disguises priests employed to cover up the uselessness, the emptiness of their lives.

He pushed his motorbike toward the knacker, toward that disposer of corpses, toward the man who had the last chance to make a living out of dead meat before it slithered back into the earth as rancid liquid.

He has to be nifty on his feet to keep ahead of the decay, other peoples' rottenness.

By the way the long body relaxed, Frank knew the knacker had only recognized him when he was twenty feet away from the shed door.

"I thought by the bike it had to be you, but I wasn't expecting to see you so soon again. The shagging eye is gone to hell." He was dressed the same as he had been two days ago, the elastic of the aviator goggles making the same track in the same place around the red-faded, hairy head.

When the smell from the shed touched him, Frank came to a stop.

"Hello, John," he said. "How's business?"

"Good for me, bad for the farmers," O'Brien said without a smile. "I have a big bullock on the hooks and two cows in there on the lorry." Without knowing it he pointed to the lorry with the left front quadrant of his skull. "Would you like to see them? Two big cows from Sweeney down in The Derries. They drank oil he drained from the tractor. The cows were stupid for drinking it, and Sweeney more stupid for leaving it where they could get it. I'll have to be careful not to let the guts burst. I'd get oil all over me, not to mention fucking up the meat. Excuse me. Come on and I'll show you."

Frank leaned his bike against the door. He followed the knacker into his shed. O'Brien put his hand into the pocket of the blue and white apron. He took out two wrapped sweets and, without looking at Frank, held out one of the candies. Without losing his stride Frank took the hairy thing and began unwrapping it.

He knew Nina Borruso would have applauded.

Chapter 28

Tuesday in Holy Week – 8.44 p.m.

SIX DAYS AGO, when the Culliton boy fell through the floor of his loft, Father Keegan had believed a connection between himself and the death of Kit Foley was about to be established. He was still aware of the waves of anxiety he'd had to ride before being put down, by blind chance, on high ground. But while the evidence was now scattered ashes, the close encounter with exposure had also reconstituted his guilt about Tony Donaghue as effectively as if it had been a raisin in hot water. However, on the same day his remorse loomed large again, he had discovered the conduit through which he could release the guilt. Slyly, he had been on the look-out for such a conduit for thirty years, and it was only when he had been exposed to naked honesty in Frank Molloy's kitchen, that he realised he had at last found the person to whom he could entrust his secret.

Although it was with anxious relief that he looked forward to finally baring his soul, Keegan had to be sure that Frankie would understand exactly why he had done what he had done. That was why the priest had spent the last five days preparing the presentation of his confession. Frank Molloy would be invited to gaze through Keegan's peephole, but it was Keegan who would be in charge of the peephole's focusing mechanism.

The priest changed down to second gear as he turned onto Wheat Mill Lane. Once the car was on the muddy, unpaved road his eyes travelled out to the end of the headlights' beam and lost their focus. It wasn't until the car bumped its way across the shallow potholes to a complete stop, that he remembered to lift his foot off the depressed clutch. With eyes still trapped in the stare, he slipped the car into first gear and resumed his journey.

As he watched the bouncing headlights exaggerating the condition of the road's surface, the priest realised that he had known all along he would make this journey some day. But he hadn't thought it would be like this – along Wheat Mill Lane to the house of an atheistic former priest. Many times he had dimly seen himself as a speck on a tree-lined avenue, moving with the gait of an old man toward the vague outline of a distant monastery. But since Frank Molloy's display of honesty last Thursday, the likes of which Keegan had never seen before, the dim and vague outline of a monastery, which housed anonymous monks who would not know who he was, had been replaced by the sharp outlines of Frank Molloy's house, wherein resided the one person in the world who knew anything about him. It had been during that first meeting, when Molloy had asked him if he had ever slept with Dervla Donaghue, that Keegan knew for certain where the confessional pilgrimage would lead. And it was yesterday's encounter with Mary Delaney's unangered honesty in Frankie's house which had hastened this moment.

"I didn't lose my faith, Father. I flung it away as far as I could."

And now that the moment when he was about to expose himself to another human being was here, the priest's synapses were lighting up in ways they had never lit up before. It was the fear that he might not be able to keep his resolve which had distracted him to the point where he had allowed his car to come to a stop in the middle of the journey.

If Father Keegan only had the remembrance of the first tryst of a liaison stored away in an oft-visited tabernacle of his memory, he would have had an experience to which he could compare his present feelings of excitement. As it was, he did not understand why the blood was pounding with such sharp throbbing in his temples; he did not know why his breath was jerking in and out in short, hot gasps. His heart was thumping so violently it was sending shock waves into his upper body, and his anus seemed to have geared itself up for any eventuality, to say nothing about the peculiar sensations which were storming through his male parts.

Keegan moved his rear on the car seat in an effort to ease this visitation of alien sensations. He broke his stare off the headlights' beam, coughed, rubbed nose, massaged dry lips with wet tongue, took deep breaths.

Jesus! Will I ever be able to do it!

For the hundredth time he went over the approach he would take, easing himself into the story so he would be seen as much a victim as Kit had been. He knew his approach had a major flaw once the whole story could be seen from its end: Kit Foley and Tony Donaghue were dead. Maybe there wasn't anything he could have done to save Kit, but Donaghue was a different story.

The nearer he got to Frankie's house the more anxious he became. But he had to tell. Not only that, he had to ask Frankie to give him Miss Duggan's ghost story.

It felt as if a million microbes were skate-boarding on the surface of his colon, and again Keegan moved his cheeks on the plush seat of his car. Then, suddenly, he was at the end of Wheat Mill Lane, outside Frank Molloy's house.

Glancing at Frankie's door as he stepped out of the car, he pulled out his handkerchief, shook it out of its folds and dried his moist palms.

Keep the attention on the brothers. They're the blackguards.

And as he thought the thought, Keegan unwillingly heard the gasp of the girl as Martin Foley yanked his erection out from between his own sister's legs; unwillingly Keegan saw the fallen trousers around socked ankles; saw bony knees, hairless thin legs, bobbing penis at bottom of hairy belly. Out of the Rembrandtesque lighting, Kit Foley's body emerged, bent on her back across four bales of straw – two on two, her dress pulled up to her chin. It took an extra moment for the other brother, Mick, to emerge from the gloom, he kneeling on the floor holding Kit's wrists. Martin's rough and dirty hand slowly moved off the girl's right, unrounded breast. "Who's dat?" he huskily asked, as he squinted into the darkness outside the lamp's nimbus.

God! And Mick springing out of the straw like a leopard with something in his hand, the fear running down Keegan's body like the glowing red and yellow sweat running down the body of a half-naked foundry worker, the fear nailing his feet to the floor.

Unthinkingly, Keegan moved his hat and touched the parietal bone where the weapon wielded by Mick Foley had whacked him thirty years ago.

When he raised his hand to knock on Frank Molloy's door for a second time, he heard music, a piano, and he was annoyed at Molloy for not having heard him.

Bloody music! Can't he bear silence?

He knocked louder and the door swung open before his knuckles were finished.

"Eddie!" Frank Molloy's cheery salutation grated across Keegan's nervous frame of mind. Some part of his brain had expected Frankie to be as anxious as himself. His train of thought screeched across vast yards of track as he sought a smooth line of response. He forced a semblance of cheerfulness onto his face and into his voice he forced a lightness.

To Keegan's ears, as he shed his hat and coat into Frank's hands, the loud piano was the screeching whistle of a boiling kettle. To Frank, as he hung the sacerdotal garb on the hook behind the door, the fingers on the keyboard were the wisps of hay in a whirling fairy-wind in a summer's meadow, the released sounds of Beethoven's *Emperor Concerto* as joyous as a lampful of escaping genies. When Frank turned around from the door he said, "I'm glad to see you, Eddie."

Keegan knew his agitated state of mind was interfering with the exchange of pleasantries. What he wanted to tell Frankie about Tony Donaghue was already oozing through the pores in his face and forehead. To get Molloy to turn off the music, Keegan pretended not to have heard Frankie's words of welcome. "I didn't hear you," he lied. And it was at that lying moment that he lost his resolve to confess his part in the death of Tony Donaghue.

In a raised voice, Molloy repeated himself and, as he strode over to the amplifier, the piano player rode the genius of Beethoven around the room on the crest of an air-wave. When he cut off the sound Frank silently apologised to the pianist and the composer.

With his collapsed resolve at his ankles like a fallen pyjama bottom, Keegan was left with a psyche full of pent-up energy. As he groped around for an emergency release valve, a disclosure of his inner self unintentionally got snagged on the head of escaping tension. To his dismay, the parts of the inner self which he started laying out at Frankie's feet had never been explored before, not even by himself.

Frank was in the middle of seating himself on the couch when Keegan erupted with such force that it seemed the priest was in an expostulatory speed wobble, veering almost out of control.

For the best part of an hour, raw, unedited revelations flowed out on the energy which was supposed to have powered the confession of his involvement in the Foley and Donaghue deaths. It was as if Keegan had grabbed Frankie by the wrist and taken him on a galloping tour of his unexplored psyche, at times Keegan himself as amazed as Frankie at what had been buried many years ago. He couldn't stop himself once he got going, the compressed tension flowing out of him as he strode around Molloy's room, sometimes speaking quietly, sometimes roaring with raised fists beside his face, most of the time skipping, without obvious logical connection, from one subject to another.

"The bishop's dead. He died yesterday at two, and when a new bishop is named, I'll be shifted out of here, sent someplace where nobody knows me, where I can start all over again. It's like that fellow in America in the sixties said – the one who spoke like a prophet. Free at last, free at last, thank God almighty we're free at last."

Then, in a voice bristling with bitterness, Keegan went on. "There's three or four lads in the diocese wetting their beds tonight with anxiety, wanting to be the next bishop. If they're not picked, someone else will be, and that's worse than not being picked. The jealousy among them is as bad as sexual jealousy among cats. It's hard to stomach the juvenile pandering, the jockeying that goes on. And it all boils down to affection, love. There are lads out there so deficient in affection, they'd do anything to get it from a superior. They're so hungry for recognition that they'd lie in a bishop's urinal and let themselves get pissed on. From the time they were thirteen they have suffered from a deficiency of love, the same way someone would suffer from a vitamin deficiency. They have emotional scurvy. Affection only comes from the top in the Church. You saw the aberrant behavior in the seminary yourself: the lads like parched prisoners in a deep pit, arms stretched up, calling out to be noticed. 'Look at me. Look at how good I am. Give me a position. I don't care what it is. Put me in charge. Just notice me above these others. Make me the prefect in charge of chamber pots. I don't care. Do anything you want to me, but notice me. Beat the shit out of me, but notice me. Take me out of the ranks of all these lads dressed the same in black soutanes and white collars. Make me special. I'll lick your arse, I'll be your whore, your whipping boy.'" Keegan stopped for a moment to take deep breaths, the exhaled air seething with wisps of red anger.

"All those lads cried out for affection from the day they landed in Winter Hill when they were thirteen. You and me, too, Frankie. You remember how it was. The shock of it, like a cold chisel of steel up the rectum without warning. You remember it all as well as I do. the starvation of the emotions. No love, no intimacy, and the age of us all. The emotional barrenness. The deluge of hormones. All of this, and no way to channel it. It was supposed to be drained off in manly games of football played on cold, muddy fields, when we should have been wrapped in the warmth of someone who loved us, even though we were unlovable adolescents, arseholes; when we should have been experimenting with sex only it was all twisted into sin, twisted into something terribly wrong and sick, because Augustine of Hippo got a venereal disease in a whorehouse in Cairo and then found Jesus. It's Augustine's warped view of sex that the Church has sanctified – someone who said what he had to say about sex when maggots were dripping out of his diseased penis. And do you remember the rutting season in Winter Hill every year?Right at the time the opera was put on. Gilbert and Sullivan. The opera! The young boys would play the parts of the girls, all rouged and powdered in dresses. 'Twenty love sick maidens, we-ee.' And during the performance for the student body, the bigger boys with their hands in their trouser pockets holding their erections in the dark. And when the performance was over the older boys' memories of the younger boys dressed up as girls drove them to push the girl-boys into corners and dry hump them, their memories serving the same purpose as the smell of a mare to a stallion. The Winter Hill great annual rut. Getting pushed into a dark corner by a big boy and having him rub up against you until he had an orgasm was to feel loved, to feel affection.

"Getting punished in Winter Hill was better than being ignored. At least there was some contact when the bastards brought the leather strap down on our hands and arses. All the priests of this diocese went through Winter Hill before they went into the seminary. Well, they are all still the same. They are still the little boys craving for someone to rub up against them. I see them every Sunday night at the poker games. It's all there in the affected cynicism, it's in the abundance of whiskey, in the greasy and sweated suits that have not been cleaned since the day they were bought; it's in the loud dramatic talk everyone makes and no one listens to. It's in the dirty, unbathed bodies, in the dirty stories, in the cruelty to each other. They call me Putrid Feet, *the fuckers*!"

Keegan spat out his pain and his bitterness. He was a sobbing child running home to tell his mother about the bullies who had beaten him up, running home to be enveloped between her affectionate arms and warm breasts. But beneath the seething flow was his relief that he had pulled back at the last moment from telling Frank about the other thing.

As if he were a cold-blooded empiricist studying the sudden collapse of reinforced psychological walls, Frank Molloy sat in his corner of the couch. He did not seem to be in the least apprehensive about what might be exhumed next from his friend's cerebral burial ground. Keegan plunged on, telling his mother why the other boys started calling him Putrid Feet.

Over the years, like the creeping tendrils of the last agent of decay, a fungal barrenness had insinuated itself into Keegan's soul. When he allowed himself to think about it, this spiritual state manifested itself in a physical feeling which he could only compare to having his head enveloped in the foul-smelling fumes of burning anthracite.

The priest had never given thought to why his disturbing feelings should take on the form of this horrid odour until one morning, about twelve years ago, he was opening his mail at the breakfast table. The moment he ran his thumb across the embossed emblem on one of the envelopes, the smell of burning anthracite assailed his nostrils.

Winter Hill!

The envelope contained a begging letter from a former seminary classmate, Patrick O'Loughlin, now the priest-principal of Eddie Keegan's boarding high school. Until he touched the raised logo that morning, Keegan had remembered Winter Hill with indifferent neutrality. But as he sliced open the envelope with the back of his breakfast knife, a surge of bile swept up from his liver. Gazing blindly at the white tablecloth, he saw the four long rows of iron-framed beds in the open dormitory.

The cavernous bedroom was on the third floor at the head of the wide stairs. From the basement furnace, the fumes of the burning anthracite drifted up the wide stairwell, and through the dormitory door, the irritating fumes wafted their odorous way.

In a bed near the door, thirteen-year-old Eddie Keegan lay shivering in the wintery morning air, the edge of the white, thin quilt pulled around the back of his head like a monk's cowl. The hot water produced by the burning coal never came cascading through the pipe at the base of the dormitory wall. It was only the furnace fumes which got this far, and when they assailed his nostrils, Eddie Keegan's tears were already running silently into his pillow. Not only was he cold; he was hungry for food; he was starved of his mother's love. His self-esteem had been battered the day before when Father Ryan, the principal, had kicked him for bouncing a ping-pong ball in the corridor; had silently walked up behind him, kicked him in the anus with the point of his shoe, squashed the ball with his thumb and walked on without uttering a word. If he had known then what he knew now, he would have realised he was in the Church's version of the old English workhouse, only the Church called its institution the Diocesan Minor Seminary.

Eddie Keegan cried for the feel of his mother's warm arms around him. He cried for his own warm bed and he cried for fried eggs and sausages and his mother's homemade bread.

The acrid anthracitic fumes went down into his lungs and from there his blood carried them to every part of his body. He felt and tasted and smelled the gritty particles which made up the smoke. In the dark byways of his soul burning anthracite had become synonymous with despairing loneliness and rejection. It was his thumb on the embossed emblem which had shone the light on those dark byways.

Until he felt the raised logo, Father Keegan's appreciation for his parents' efforts to give him a secondary education had kept the horrors of Winter Hill buried deep in his soul. He wondered if it was more than coincidence that these horrors surfaced at the same time that squalls of doubt were making their appearances, rushing at him and buzzing around his head like irritating swarms of summer-evening gnats, before he swatted them away, unlooked at, unexamined.

Keegan had crushed the embossed envelope. He had squashed the letter begging for money to pay for the renovation of Winter Hill. It wasn't until he was squeezing the paper into a hard ball that he realised the depth of his anger. He had left the dining-room table and had written a very short and very indiscreet letter.

"Dear Patrick: *Putrefiat.* Eddie Keegan."

Putrefiat. Let it rot.

Clerical gossip, being the most vicious and fastest moving in the world, had the story of his reply at the poker table on the following Sunday evening. Ever since then he had had to endure the nickname Putrid Feet among the priests of the diocese.

"*The fuckers!*" With rage, in Frank Molloy's front room, Keegan hurled his worst word at his tormentors.

His anger blinded him to the recklessness of jumping headlong into territory which, out of fear, he had never even scouted before. Lifting his head he blindly looked at Frank. "I don't believe in what I'm doing anymore." He paused so he could hear his own words, words which, once spoken aloud to another person, wrought a change as irreducible as the words of a marriage partner announcing unfaithfulness to a spouse. As the momentous sounds lingered between the two men, Keegan suddenly lunged headlong into another thicket of unexplored self, recklessly hacking, jerkily exposing. "I hate what I'm doing. I hate being a priest." He went down on the word hate with all the weight of his being. "I hate the word priest! I hate pretending. I hate... God! What am I saying?" Realising he had hacked his way onto a perilous ledge, and afraid to look over the edge at the truth, Keegan turned to Frank for assistance, for words of assurance.

But there was no assistance forthcoming from Frank. He had nothing to offer. The stuff which Keegan was drowning in would give no buoyancy to another man's life-preserver. Only his own life-preservers, if he had forged any in the smithy of his own soul for an emergency like this, would be of use. Frank looked steadily back at Keegan, and he made not the slightest gesture of hope or support.

Keegan sank his face into his hands, his fingers pushing the rimless glasses onto his forehead. He stood motionless for a long time, one elbow touching a shelf, his anchor. In silence he hung in agony on the cross of his own making.

Frank heard a crow arking as it flew over the house, making a late journey to the rookery in Cloncroghan Woods. His memory instantly presented him with a picture of his father plowing on the hill of the Hollow Field with a pair of horses, the crows hopping in the fresh earth arking to each other about the first red worms of spring.

After what seemed like a long time, shadows began to gather in the room, little pieces of dimness attracting each other, building each other into areas of darkness. And out of the deepening shadows Keegan spoke. "The peripheral stuff makes no sense anymore, and even the central doctrines..." With awe in his voice, the priest was hearing himself speaking of himself as an empty shell. From the isolated world of the seminary, where the human condition was studied in the abstract, he had been launched into the strange world of reality. In the early years of his priesthood he had accepted the people's imposition of the role which was expected of him. It had given him belief in himself. Their expectations had kept him strong, had kept him going without his ever questioning his own motives. That was the time when he had doled out solutions to his parishioners' problems with the same ease as he dealt out playing cards to his fellow priests on Sunday nights. The answers slipped out of his mouth as effortlessly as the satin-finished cards slipped out of his fingers onto the green cloth. He didn't even have to think. His mouth and his fingers went into automatic gear and, whether it was pious words or playing cards, they always fell in the right spot.

But the demands of the people had been losing their potency, had been losing their ability to motivate. For a long time now there was that numbness of soul, that smell of anthracite. The doubts, not taken care of, had eroded his own belief in himself, had eroded his confidence in the very way he was spending his life. The wisdom he was dispensing was nothing but the parroting of vague, hopeful phrases about the role of God in the affairs of men. He was as wise and as vague as an astrologer. The point had been reached where he was comforting people with words in which he himself found no solace. Now, for the first time, it became clear to him that when it came to comforting people with a few well-placed, God-filled phrases, he felt as emasculated as the deluded party hack dispensing the tired party line. He knew that for many years he had been delivering the usual pious phrases to the less educated people in the parish, and his worst fear was that some day, even an uneducated person, after receiving a delivery of trite formulas, would say to him, "Do you really believe that shite, Father?"

"There is no need to believe in anything. All you have to do is conform. There is no way to take the temperature of a person's faith."

Over the last several years Keegan had been rejecting more of the ready answers offered by his automatic response system. On top of everything there had been the stress of the... Keegan almost said "shoes" but at the last moment, he said, "the education of the Donaghue children". In shock at his near-betrayal by his own words Keegan fell headlong into silence.

As the silence deepened he broke out in a cold sweat as he realised how much of himself he had revealed. He was astounded at the collapse of his own security system. Frank Molloy hadn't looked through the priest's peephole. Keegan had pulled his own front door off its hinges, had taken Frank by the scruff of the neck and rubbed Frank's nose in Keegan's own hidden shit. It couldn't have been worse if he had told Molloy that he was directly responsible for Tony Donaghue's death. As the cold sweat grew clammy on his back and face, his body sagged from loss of energy.

Like a man realising that the neighbour's attractive wife, with whom he has impulsively expended his lust, is swaddled in attached strings, Keegan looked in horror at what he had just done.

Like the same man disconnecting from the illicit woman and realising that the sexual act has attached her to him as fatally as a dozen harpoon ropes attached a whale to a longboat, Keegan turned slowly and looked away from Frank, and he loathed himself.

Like the trapped man feeling the juices of spent lust cloyingly cooling at his pubic area, and blaming the woman for having been too willing to spread her legs, Keegan blamed Frankie for having created the atmosphere which had made it easy for him to spill his guts.

Since the day he was ordained, Keegan had not been related to, nor had he related to anyone, in a normal human way, and he did not know what to say or do next. He wanted the ground to open up and swallow him.

After what seemed to him an interminable time of waiting for Frankie to say something, of looking at Molloy sitting there on the couch as comfortable as a fly on a shit, Keegan blurted out, "Well, say something, Frankie."

"What is there to say, Eddie?" Molloy answered calmly.

"Goddam it, Frankie!" the priest snapped. He turned to the bookcase and slapped his hand down on an empty shelf. It was totally dark in the room by now. All the pieces of darkness had combined to kill the light. There were no sounds from outside the house, no sounds of settling down for the night from the house itself. Neither man could hear the breathing of the other.

"I have made a terrible fool of myself," Keegan said quietly. Then he roared and Frankie jumped. "For Christ's sake say something!"

"I have nothing to say!"

"You have something to ask, goddamit!"

"No, I don't!"

"Yes, you do!"

"Tell me what I want to ask, Eddie?"

"Don't be paternalistic, Frankie. You want to ask me why I stayed on being a priest. That's what you want to ask me."

"Why did you not leave, Eddie?"

"Fuck you, Frankie, sitting there like you're some kind of shrink and I'm your mad patient."

"Why are you so angry at me, Eddie?"

"Because you made it seem so easy to..."

Then out of the darkness Keegan spoke quietly. "I'm going home. Please don't get up."

Sliding his feet along the floor he groped his way to the front door. He felt around for his coat and hat, rattled the latch when he lifted it, and started to slip out into the darkness without turning on the light.

Then he heard a strong and distinct voice. "I'll be here for you, Eddie."

Keegan did not respond. He closed the door quietly behind him.

Chapter 29

Spy Wednesday – 1.15 p.m.

When he opened the door and saw Mary Delaney, Frank Molloy became as sexually overwrought as a teenage boy unzipping his pants to a naked girl for the first time.

All the blood dropped out of Molloy's brain into his ascending turgidity, and he was rendered comatose. The only message getting across from his brain to his consciousness was that he was old enough to be the woman's father. But, since an erect penis knows no conscience, knows little caution and is an eternal opportunist, and since Frank Molloy knew it was unlikely he would ever in his life be in this situation again, he allowed himself to be led by his erection as co-operatively as a bull allows itself to be led by the ring in its nose.

While Mary Delaney stood there smiling, proffering her body in the doorway, Molloy's mind threw up a nugget of compressed memory which contained the women who, he believed, had invited him to puncture the pudding. It was only after he had come to learn the ways of women that he realised, with regret, the opportunities he had missed. His behaviour, while in the company of some of the occupants of this particular piece of memory, caused him to feel embarrassed. Jesus! One of them had even brought him up to her bedroom, told him her parents were away for the evening, and sat him on the edge of her bed and he still hadn't understood what she had been telling him. That had been in London and her name was Jackie. The scene with Jackie dissolved as she inexplicably ate a large piece of yellow cheese. Her hair was yellow, too.

Somewhere during his Catholic upbringing, Molloy had been taught that women are unable to initiate a sexual overture; only men could do that, and that the man who made a sexual overture outside of marriage was guilty of a mortal sin. Since Molloy had no significant experience with women until he was twenty-seven, he had no reason to disbelieve what he had been told. He had been dumb enough to follow the learned instructions and, in order to judge the gravity of the offence, had asked every woman who confessed a sexual sin, "Did you take pleasure in it?"

Jesus! If anyone knew how stupid I once was!

But at the time he had never heard a woman giving voice to an orgasm with her mouth in his ear.

And now, Mary Delaney was standing in his doorway. Even though she was wearing an overcoat, he knew the hard-nippled breasts were thrusting at him, that her thighs were offering him a gift already in the state of graceful, sanctifying lubrication.

Molloy hoped to God he wouldn't die before he could get his hands on her and her clothes off her, feel his hand sliding up and over a firm, smooth breast to the nipple; feel his other hand sliding down her back until his finger-tips came to rest in the shallow top of the valley which divided her cheeks.

Why did God make two pairs of cheeks? Because he made an arse of the first pair.

When Frank had been a student in Winter Hill the spiritual director, a small man supporting a host of nervous twitches and tics, had told the boys it was a venial sin to look at the upper arms of a woman – the *pars inhoneste*, he had called them: the parts with dishonour. Molloy's mind was already fondling Delaney's most dishonourable part.

The same juggler of nervous twitches and tics had also said, "It is a sin to touch your member, even if you think it is going to explode like a bomb. And the genitals should never be washed in isolation, *id est*, never stand in front of a sink and just wash yourself 'there' – the chances of arousal are too great; better to wash the John Thomas when having a bath."

"Will you come in out of there," Frank said, "before Maura Gilligan sees you in her telescope and has a stroke."

Delaney stepped in, and by the time he had closed the door she had slipped out of her shoes, put her back to the wall, placed her arms at her sides and raised herself up on her toes.

When Molloy turned and saw her, he was afraid he might suffer a coronary thrombosis. He was also afraid that his one-eyed trouser-mouse was going to come, head first, through the steel zipper in his fly. He pushed it to one side with his fingers. The feel of what he felt always reminded him of rabbit hunting when he was a child; a ferret in a burlap sack on the ground, forever moving and standing inside its prison while the feral smell of the rabbits drove it mad with excitement.

At the wall Mary was not smiling. She was in heat.

His heart thumping like a dynamo with one of its four anchors loose, Molloy approached her, his arms at his sides. He was in rut.

He touched his lips to hers and lightly pinned her to the wall as if she were a specimen of rare butterfly and he the pin holding her in place. When she opened her lips to him he was reminded of the exposed flesh of a peach. With their bodies not touching at any other place they stood there, pulling each other deeper into the most pleasurable, genetically inherited, and Catholically most sinful of their animal appetites. He felt her arms moving and he knew she was undoing the buttons of her overcoat. When she returned her arms to her sides he raised his right hand. He let it fall slowly forward and his hand touched flesh.

Amazing Grace I love your face, I love you in your nightie; and when the moonlight flits across your tits – O Jesus Christ Almighty!

She was wearing the skimpiest of bras – just enough to fool a close observer, a mother who'd once been felt up by the same person her daughter was going to visit. Molloy let his hand slip down Mary's side and he did not touch clothing till he felt a string at her hip.

This state of affairs became a momentary distraction for the two of them. The nerve-endings in their lips lost their concupiscence, Molloy's trouser-mouse lost its ferocity and Mary Delaney's body shook as she tried to control her amusement. Molloy unpinned the butterfly and stood back to look at her. The brassiere was not much more than a narrow ribbon, most of both nipples showing; the underpants were a miniature wedge of pink bunting. The sexual delectation on which he had been gorging was, for a second, diluted with admiration for Delaney's audacity, and delight at her sense of humour. As his eyes lingered on the bunting he noticed a small area of the pink was red. He thought of her leaving her house, almost naked under her overcoat, under the critical eye of her mother; of running the risk of accidentally finding herself in the emergency ward of Duneamon County Hospital, the nurses' amazement at the overcoat and shoes, a ribbon and a piece of miniature bunting with a string attached to each of its three points. But Molloy was in such a high state of excitement that he lost interest in the distractions and, with an animal sound of acknowledgment of her humour, he pinned her to the wall again. His two hands slipped up her back and felt out the engineering of the bra's fastener. But it was a simple bow, and when he pulled a loose end he felt the tension snapping out of the ribbon. His fingers fell slowly down her back and, when he pulled another hanging string, he felt it sliding through its loops. With the fall of the bunting he began to close the distance between their basic differences. But her hands were in the way.

While she opened his trousers and disentangled his masthead from his underpants, his fingertips lecherously explored the hills and valleys of her arse. When she held his testicles in the cup of her hand, as if she were holding a delicate egg, he remembered that the closest he had come to a sexual encounter before his late twenties, besides the furtive feel of Keegan's sister's breast, was in fourth grade when the county health inspector had pushed her hand down inside the front of his trousers and felt for two descended testicles. Unlike Eddie Keegan, Molloy had never been dry-humped during the great operatic rut in Winter Hill. Frank's breaking voice had spared him.

While he stroked the inside of her lips with his tongue, his hands came up slowly, and when they slid forward and over her breasts, she gasped as if a dentist had hit a nerve with his drill. With soft-padded thumbs he skied her nipples until her thighs began to writhe. With his trousers on the floor at his ankles, he moved forward and she opened her legs to his nudging knee. He felt her heat and wetness on his leg. She leaned into him, squashing his thumbs between their bodies. He kept agitating the trapped nipples.

A man used a barometer instead of a thermometer to take his wife's temperature and discovered she was wet and windy.

Delaney moved her arse off the wall and slipped forward on his leg. With his left arm around her waist, his fingers moved around the deepest valley between her buttocks, the fingertips brushing the lentils of her other opening. Mary Delaney groaned and pulled her mouth away from his. She slammed her face into the angle formed by his neck and shoulder and she rode his thigh to a boisterous orgasm, Christing and Jesusing and ohfucking and feralling and aahing and oohing and all the while clinging to his leg as if she were in danger of falling off the world. Slowly at first, and then abruptly, she became quiet and when Molloy began to lower his aching leg she whispered, "Don't move." Then she laughed and breathfully said, "I'll die if you move."

Molloy held his hands steady where they were, aware himself of how pleasure and pain sometimes came close to crossing paths when an orgasm hit its zenith.

Slowly he lowered his leg because he could not hold it up any longer and she made a sound as they wetly came asunder. While he waited for her to recover, his knowledge of what was to come gave renewed life to his erection. It had faded slightly while he was boosting Delaney into orbit around her clitoris.

Stand back, said Adam to Eve, I don't know how long this thing gets.

As if she had come to the end of a long swim, Mary Delaney took some deep breaths and laughed some more short laughs. "Christ!" she said. "I thought I was going to die."

Molloy was too far gone in lust to reply. He put his hand down between their bodies, and as he bent his erection toward the bottom of her belly she opened her legs and grasped it between her legs. "You'll have to wait a minute."

With the overcoat still on, she began to turn him toward the couch, her thighs still holding his penis captive. In short, trouser-hobbled steps he followed her. But she had only been looking for floor space. Before they got near the couch she gripped his penis with her hand and gently tugged him down on top of her on the floor.

The man said to his wife on their honeymoon, I don't know much about sex, but hold onto that for a minute and we'll see what happens.

Somehow, Delaney managed to get her limbs out of the arms of the overcoat, and she lay completely naked, her legs apart, her arms spread out as if she were waiting to be crucified. "Fuck me, Molloy!" she said and she was smiling. "But first let me dress Richard for his visit." Like a magician producing a coin out of the air, Delaney displayed a condom in her left hand. While she tore off the cover, Molloy stood up and removed his shoes and clothes. Then he straddled her, his knees on the floor each side of her belly button. Leaning forward he put his hands of the floor near her head and brought his erection to her hands. She slipped on the condom, held his scrotum in one hand and ran a finger back between his legs following the ridge of his disappearing penis.

Afraid he was getting too excited, Molloy moved his knees back between Delaney's legs. He lowered himself and overshadowed Mary. He lowered his belly onto hers, moved and adjusted until he could feel he was poised on her point of entry. He didn't slip in as he thought he would have. She was tight and it took four or five gentle pushes before the tunnel opened up in front of him.

Delaney threw exclamation points out into the room as Molloy sank to the hilt as slowly as the Titanic slipping beneath the waves. When he was fully in, he stopped moving.

While the clowns clowned all the men were looking at the female aerialist's cunning stunt.

On his elbows, and looking into her eyes, Molloy, to Delaney's surprise, began to speak. "Little Miss Muffet sat on her tuffet, eating her curds and whey; when down came a spider and sat down beside her and said, 'Whatcha eating, bitch?'" He stopped.

"What's that?" Delaney asked. "An incantation to heighten your orgasm?"

"It's a nursery rhyme, you deprived child. Where were you when nanny was reading aloud in the nursery?"

"Nursery, my ass," Delaney said. "Why are you saying it now?"

"So I won't come too fast, you eejit!" Frank said. "You're going back on Saturday and we'll never do this again. I want it to last."

"So you recite."

"You're right, Delaney. You now know my most hidden secret. I'm reciting something to distract myself." He suddenly pulled and pushed out and in and Delaney's eyes swam. "I heard of a man who learned the Gettysburg Address from reciting it after his wife while she tried to keep him from coming too soon." He pulled out again until he was back at the portals of her holy place and then he slowly slid in again. "But one has to keep old dicky from falling asleep by moving him around now and then," he said.

"Does one?" Delaney asked as she moved her body against his intrusion.

"One do!" Molloy said, and he thrust himself against her move.

"One doesn't believe one be having this conver…"

Before she could finish, Molloy pulled out and jammed back in. A noise came out of Delaney. With his legs together he raised himself on his toes and elbows and hovered over her, drew out until only the top of his erection was left inside. Using the tip of his penis he went in and out in short thrusts and retreats.

"Don't stop!" she said.

"One must lest one go blam blam."

"I'm on the very edge of an orgasm."

"Orgasm. Orgasm. We are committing a fucking mortal sin."

"We are committing a mortal sin by fucking. CHRIST!" She slammed into him, brought her non-crucified hands to the cheeks of his arse and tried to stuff him, head belly hips and all into her vagina. "Jesus! Don't move!" Motionless, she held herself against him, and she made noises that bespoke the state of orgasm. Finally she let out her breath and made a tittering sound. Then she panted out some words. "Don't move yet. Let me relax or I'll shatter like stained glass."

Molloy suspected he would have sore elbows in the morning. He put his palms on the floor and pushed himself up, their bellies still stuck together in lust.

I don't know if they were being intimate, your honour, but they were so close together in the doorway I couldn't figure out who the balls was hanging out of.

"One has been fucked," Delaney said, and she was smiling the smile of a woman who has been satisfactorily fucked. "You're one hell of a fucker, Molloy."

"Excuse me, madam, did we start having sex yet?" Molloy asked Englishly.

"What does an Englishwoman say to her husband after sex?"

"Tell me."

"Feeling betta?" Delaney laughed.

"Don't laugh," Molloy said, "or you'll eject the visitor." He pulled and pushed in and out again. "Are you getting sore?" he asked.

"Not at all. I can take another few lunges."

Molloy lunged and Delaney brought up her knees, brought up her legs and presented him with unobstructed entry. She entwined Molloy at the hips. He continued to move until he feared he had reached the point of no return. But he had stopped in time. "Don't move," he said, and he began immediately to distract himself. Delaney lowered her legs.

"What's the Church's most dreaded word?" he asked.

"Vagina."

"Second most dreaded word?"

"Condom."

"Third?"

"Orgasm."

"I disagree. Orgasm should be first."

"Wrong. If the pope saw a vagina he'd die."

"Wrong. He'd have an orgasm, stand there in his robes shuddering like a frog laying eggs."

Delaney laughed.

"Don't laugh. You'll evict the tenant." Molloy pushed and pulled the tenant.

"How long can you go without coming?" she asked.

"Is that an oxymoron?"

"No. It's an orgasm that's going to come."

"If I distract myself I might go for another few minutes, provided I don't shrink from the distraction."

"Don't shrink. The condom will come off. Give me a speech about condoms."

Molloy stoked his fire and then ordered Delaney to change places with him. They tried to do it without coming apart, but just as she swung onto his belly, they separated. When he went over on his back, Delaney raised herself on her knees and reinserted the pleasure stick. Molloy put his left hand on her right breast, ran his right hand up against her vagina until he found her clitoris with the pad of his thumb. Delaney leaned back, a jockey leaning back as the horse beneath her lands after clearing a hedge. She made noises through her teeth. "Easy on the clit," she said, and she grasped his hand with hers and held him in place.

"Condoms!" Molloy said, and he launched into speech. "The Church's attitude toward sex has caused more damage to people than did the Spanish Inquisition. It has impaled millions of consciences on the upright pricks of horny husbands. It has manufactured chastity belts out of terror and locked them onto married women by the million. Can you imagine all the mental stress this has caused, all the psychotic sex?" Molloy suddenly brought his hips off the floor and the rider leaned forward. Delaney gasped. "Pay attention to my speech," Molloy said, and his arse rose and fell several times.

"You have a captive audience," Delaney said. "I'm impaled on your dick, just in case you haven't…" But Molloy launched into her as far as he could go and her breath was taken away.

When Molloy spoke again his voice sounded thick, as if he were trying to talk and endure a great pain at the same time. But he was only trying to hold back the arrival of the orgasm. "The Church gives lectures on sex and marriage, sex and having children, responsible sex, irresponsible sex, controlled sex, all kinds of sex but never the pleasures of sex. *Plaisir d'amour.* The Church should loosen up its own chastity belt, and a good way to start would be to write a new blessing for condoms. May the Lord protect and defend you. Jeez. Don't move." Delaney had been sliding up and down Molloy's shaft of joy as he was speaking. She lowered herself slowly and her clitoris came to rest on his thumb. Without moving the thumb he caressed her with his fleshy pad, slid his other hand down across her belly-button and into her hair. He caressed the pubes with his fingertips. Leaning back, stretching the flesh of her thighs, Delaney hung her head back until she was facing the ceiling, her neck taut. She Jesused a few times and then threw her head forward onto her chest. Through clenching teeth she Ohfucked several times and Christed twice. Grasping his wrist she snapped his thumbing hand away and breathed like a horse after it has taken a long drink of water, made whewing sounds as her breath jumped out of her.

"I have a wonderful view of your tits from here," Molloy said. "And now if I may continue without further interruption!" He touched her thighs with the taut palms of his hands. "At every marriage ceremony, there should be a place for the blessing of the condoms. O Blessed Condom, we praise thine inventor for leading our people out of the bondage of spiritual castration into the freedom of entry without fear. *Sancta Condomanus, laudate.* Now, Delaney, let go of my balls, get off me and assume the missionary position for the final coming of your lord and master."

Again, they tried to change positions without separating, but there was too much slipperiness around. Without assistance from Delaney's hand the penis slipped back into the vagina and as Molloy went in, Delaney raised her legs, presented her wonderful opening to the most advantage. He only pulled and pushed three times before the juices of delight and procreation began to flow through the connecting hose. Molloy made unabashed noises of orgasmic stress, his inherited genetics causing him to lunge forward with each wave of juice delivered. Just after the orgasmic cresting, he remained jammed into her, her arms and legs binding the two of them.

When the last drop of delight dripped off the tip of his penis, Molloy said, "Don't move. It'll break off."

In their respective baths of endorphins, their brains stretched out and relaxed. With their cheeks touching, she looking at the ceiling, he at the floor, they created a bisexual Janus. She saw the deep gold of the ceiling boards and was reminded of Spanish guitars. Less than an inch from his face he saw the floor and he smelled the age of the house.

As the first tentacle of sleep started wafting toward him, Molloy, without speaking, rocked gently from side to side and she incrementally lowered her moist thighs away from his sweated body. He leaned to one side, put his hand between their bodies, grasped the rim of the condom in his fingers and withdrew the sheathed and increasingly flaccid penis. As it left her vagina, Delaney moaned.

Propping himself up on one elbow, Molloy one-handedly slipped the condom off. "There was this girl," he said, "and one night after screwing in the back seat of a car, she was feeling all lovey dovey and she says to her boyfriend, 'If it's a girl we'll call her Melissa, and if it's a boy we'll call him Augustine.' The fella held up a condom and said, 'If he gets out of this we'll call him Harry Houdini.'" Delaney made soft laughing noises and Molloy bent back and put the condom on the floor behind him. When he returned to her side he put his arm under her head. She ran her left hand over his belly, and rested it on his breast.

For a long time they looked into the air above their eyes, neither of them seeing anything. Delaney asked, "Any word from Gregory?"

"No."

After another long while Molloy said, "My first year in Winter Hill, when I was fourteen, we had this priest who was called the spiritual director. He always spoke as if he were afraid someone was going to jump up and laugh at him. He told us a story one time about a teenage boy who was a model of perfection. But the boy got sick and died. When his parents went to visit his grave, the coffin was out of the ground with its lid off. The parents were very distressed by the vandalism and went through all the shit of burying him again. But the next day it was the same story and the day after that. I don't remember how they got the coffin to stay down, but the important part was that the local priest knew from confession that the boy was a masturbator and had probably died with the mortal sin on his soul, and that was why the coffin came out of the ground."

When Molloy finished speaking Delaney said, "What a crock of shit!"

"Only it wasn't a crock of shit to a fourteen-year-old, whose dick was the centre around which the Milky Way revolved. God! We used to pray for wet dreams so we could get some relief."

Delaney said, "We were warned about leading boys into sin, causing them to masturbate, I suppose. The Church should never have gone into the sex business. An institution that's top heavy with crusty old bachelors should keep its mouth shut when it comes to sex. They pronounce on imagined sex, not on the real thing."

Molloy raised himself on an elbow and looked down her body. He put his fingers on her pubic area, leaned down and nuzzled her breast. "I'm going to wash off. Will I bring you a warm cloth?"

"You're a gentleman, Molloy."

"Comes with the service," Frank said, and he stood up.

"And what service it was!"

"You bring out the best in me, Delaney." He picked his trousers and underpants off the floor.

"Maybe we can get together again before I leave. But I'm going to Dublin with the ma in the morning."

"What are you doing on Friday?"

"Good Friday. I have to see an uncle and aunt in the afternoon. But maybe I could pretend that I have to get something in the village and then drop in here around ten."

"I'll be here. I'll be anticipating it so much, that if you don't come I'll have to commit a mortal sin and it'll be your fault."

"You coffin will pop out of the ground."

Smiling, Molloy turned his bare arse on Delaney and walked out of the room.

Chapter 30

Spy Wednesday – 3.20 p.m.

NAKED AS A JAY-BIRD, Mary Delaney was standing in the middle of the floor when Molloy emerged from the bedroom. She had clothes in her hand, but Molloy did not see them. He was looking at her body, his eyes moving from face to breasts to thighs.

"Is everything in the same place as you remember it?" Delaney asked.

"Yes. You are put together perfectly."

"Thanks."

Frank walked over and kissed her on the mouth, his right hand on her left breast, his left on her buttocks. "God," he said, when they separated. He touched his crotch. "Richard is moving in his sleep."

"Just make sure he's awake and up on Friday."

Molloy finally saw the clothes in Mary's hand. "Where did you get those?" he asked.

"You were so concerned with your own bulge when I arrived that you didn't see the bulge in my pockets."

As she went to the bedroom to dress, Molloy watched the moves of the first set of cheeks God had given her. Then he went to the kitchen, but just as he lifted the kettle he heard the sounds of wheels grinding the gravel outside the house. By the time Molloy got to the window a man was already walking past Mary Delaney's car. Frank strode back through the kitchen to the front room and, as he passed the bedroom, he said, "Hey, Delaney! We have a visitor." As he continued to the front door he said, "Don't walk out in your knickers." But Delaney was in the bathroom sitting on the bowl, sanitising herself with a post-coital urination of generous flow.

When Molloy opened the front door, the man – suntanned, Frank noticed immediately – was in mid-stride with his hand already raised to knock.

"Mr Molloy?" the man asked.

"Who's asking?" Molloy had lived in New York too long to have, so soon, discarded old defensive habits.

"Doctor O'Leary," the man said, and he held out his hand.

Molloy began lifting his own hand in response but, before he touched O'Leary, a whole debate about control flashed through his mind, which concluded with his asking, "A doctor of what?" And he kept the reins on his hand until O'Leary replied, "Medicine."

Their eyes wrestled as they shook hands, and then Molloy asked, "Can I do something for you?"

"There's a man dying and he needs you to hear his confession," O'Leary said.

While O'Leary waited for a response he checked the visible symptoms which could tell him about the internal condition of Gregory Molloy's famed brother. From the eyes and their immediate environs he thought he detected a weakness of the kidneys. As he continued his scrutiny the doctor was distracted by a movement over Molloy's left shoulder. There was a woman in there and her head was bent to the task of adjusting her skirt.

The former priest said, "Go fuck yourself." Then he stepped back into his house.

Frank leaned against the closed door, his head flung back, the palm of his left hand on top of his head, his mouth open. His heart was thumping. Again, because he was used to the anonymity of New York, he was raging against the fact that someone would intrude into such a private area of his life; not only intrude, but drag a whole sackful of presumptions with him. His hot-headed, irrational self was yelling at him to pull the door open again, run out and scream at the doctor, tell him he had stepped over boundaries he had no right even to approach.

Mary Delaney, her face and her tone of voice bespeaking confusion, asked, "What's going on, Frank?"

Molloy looked at Delaney. "Some guy in a suit, who said he's a doctor, just asked me to hear someone's confession."

Mary Delaney came over to Molloy. He took his hand off his head when she touched him. He leaned away from the door and was about to touch her, when there was another knock on the door. Molloy's body jerked as if a weak pulse of electricity had shocked him.

"Jesus, Frank!" Delaney said quietly, "You look like you've seen a ghost. Who's out there?"

She stepped around Frank and pulled the door open.

O'Leary was not expecting to see a woman when the door opened inward. It was as if he was suddenly faced with an optical *non sequitur*.

"Doctor O'Leary!" Mary Delaney said, and she tilted her face, half-closed one eye and looked at O'Leary as if she had discovered a new species of slime.

The doctor's view of Mary Delaney in Molloy's doorway was distorted through the prism of the colourful rumours he had heard about the promiscuity of Delaney and Molloy. Despite his education, despite his travels, despite his mistrust of small-town rumours, O'Leary's Irish-Catholic eyes could only see Mary Delaney in Molloy's doorway as a whore. He quickly removed Mary Delaney's clothes with his inward eye, saw the whore naked, felt her pudendum with his lascivious eyes. But he swallowed, gulped away his imaginings, cleared his throat and said, "Hello Mary," as his rambunctious libido left traces of her vagina wavering into invisibility before his jealous eyes.

Mary Delaney did not respond to the doctor's greeting. In delicate situations she was capable of maintaining a calm objectivity which allowed her to see clearly in whose court the ball was, and she possessed the patience to await indefinitely the return of the ball. Even though O'Leary had been her doctor for most of her life, she was not intimidated by him at all. She had always found him to have a condescending air, as if he had no need of an income and was saving the bog-dwelling natives from the ravages of the tsetse fly purely out of philanthropic devotion; the only things missing were an English accent and a pith helmet.

Eyeball to eyeball with the doctor, with one hand on the jamb and the other holding the door, Mary Delaney defiantly defended Frank Molloy's house against O'Leary's presumption.

"I came to speak to Mister Molloy," O'Leary said.

"You've upset him."

"I don't think he heard me correctly."

"He said you asked him to hear someone's confession."

"I did, but I should have told him I was only asking him as a last resort. Ken Considine is dying and every priest in the diocese is at the bishop's funeral."

"Considine has been dying for years. He'll hold on till Father Keegan gets home."

Frank Molloy's voice soared out over Delaney's shoulders, the exaggerated loudness clearly suggesting his words were for the doctor's benefit. "And tell him, too, that I don't believe in that shit anymore."

With deadpan face, Mary Delaney said, "Frank says he doesn't believe in that shit anymore."

O'Leary was about to speak, but Mary Delaney moved and the door swung open.

When Molloy glared out at the doctor, ready to blast him with a barrellful of piercing invective powered with injured dignity, the remembrance of himself standing outside Cotswold's rectory in Falworth burped itself into his consciousness. He was momentarily staggered in the cerebrum. Slowly, his right hand went to Delaney's shoulder and he gently pressured her to move aside. He invited the doctor to come in.

Before he moved, O'Leary said, "I'm sorry if I didn't make myself clear at first – about there being no priest available."

As the doctor stepped into the house, Molloy said, "Even if you had, I would still have reacted in the same way." After closing the door, he continued, "I find it presumptuous of you to expect I'd hear someone's confession. Won't you sit down." Molloy indicated the couch.

O'Leary, his arrogance having banished the issue of control on the day he graduated from medical school, suddenly found himself face to face with someone who didn't know the place of the doctor in the community.

"I won't sit, thank you."

"Suit yourself," Frank said, and he remained standing too, his back to the door. Mary Delaney was standing to one side between the two men, the three of them forming an equilateral triangle.

O'Leary said, "I didn't think it would cause such a commotion just to ask you to administer a sacrament in a case of necessity."

"You didn't ask me anything. You made a statement and expected me to jump through your hoop. Religion means nothing to me anymore."

"When you dumped your religion, did you dump your concern for your fellow man, too?" O'Leary lent a tonal quality to the word "dump" which was not lost on Frank.

"Yes, dumped is the right word because that's what one does with shit," he said. "And no, I didn't lose my compassion for my fellow man."

"Then why won't you hear Considine's confession?"

"I just told you that..."

"You must have heard of *ecclesia supplet*?"

Ecclesia supplet. *Jesus! Thirty years ago and it was all hypothetical then.* Ecclesia supplet. *Still, it's just more of the same horseshit.*

"I don't believe in *ecclesia supplet* either," he said, and he already knew he didn't have to believe in it, but his anger at O'Leary was getting in the way.

"You don't have to," the doctor said.

"That's what makes it so much horseshit," Molloy said, only because it was something nasty to say.

Mary Delaney asked, "What's *ecclesia supplet*?"

Without hesitation, without looking at her, the doctor spoke the answer as if he were answering a catechism question to a nun. "The believing Church will supply the faith which is lacking in a priest who must administer a sacrament."

Despite his atheistic protestations, Molloy's pride and his vestigial adolescence would not allow him to stand by and listen to O'Leary elucidate on matters theological. He made a point of turning to Mary Delaney before addressing her. "It means, Mary, that even though I am an unbelieving priest I can still administer a sacrament in an emergency."

The doctor was unable to contain himself. "That's right," he said, a little boy showing off to the nun at someone else's expense. "Thou art a priest forever according to the order of Melchizedek."

Molloy remained facing Delaney, and he closed his eyes as he listened to O'Leary's quotation from the rite of ordination. He allowed for a pause before he continued. "As I was saying, the faith of the people who make up the Church supplies the belief which I don't have. *Ecclesia supplet*, the Church supplies. It's more mumbo jumbo."

"As far as Considine is concerned it's not mumbo jumbo," O'Leary said. And before he looked away from Mary Delaney, Molloy saw her eyes asking him to give in, to hear the dying man's confession.

While he was caught between Mary's appeal and his own need to blast the doctor, Nina Borruso dashed across Molloy's consciousness. She was laughing at Molloy's description of Irish anger: "Adamantine emotional constipation that dynamite wouldn't move."

Frank turned to Doctor O'Leary. "I have been rude," he said. "But

I will say I found your forwardness abrasive, to say the least." He heard Nina Borruso applauding wildly, heard her laughing, saw her bending backward, her face to the ceiling laughing; then falling forward, her joined hands descending between her knees into the folds of her long skirt.

"I'm sorry if I offended you," O'Leary said, and when he held out his hand Molloy grasped it firmly.

"Of course I'll hear the man's confession."

"I'll drive you there," the doctor said. "Considine is going to die this time and I don't think he has much time left."

Delaney followed them out to the doctor's car. She told Frank she would wait till he got home, and she watched the car turning on the narrow lane, watched until it joined the road at the end of Wheat Mill Lane.

Chapter 31

Spy Wednesday – 3.25 p.m.

THE FIRST FEW minutes of the drive were endured in awkward silence by both men. Frank's anger was still ebbing. Eventually he asked the doctor, "What makes you so certain he's going to die today – Considine?"

It seemed the doctor had been waiting for the tension in the car to break, had been waiting, Frank thought, for the enemy to blink. O'Leary responded immediately. "He opened the median antebrachial vein in his left arm, which is a medical way of saying he cut his left wrist, which is another way of saying he tried to commit suicide. He did it with a safety pin some time this morning, and kept poking at the wound to keep the blood flowing. It wasn't much of a flow, but when I happened to look in on him a while ago he was close to delirium. He had caught every drop in his white enamel milk bucket."

"Shouldn't he be in hospital?"

"Of course he should, but he wants to die."

Molloy opened his mouth, but Saint Willie Gorman's tractor came bellowing around the long bend in the road, the front of the wobbling dung-spreader swinging in and out behind the big rear wheel. Nervously, Molloy waited until the smoke-blowing monster had passed, Saint Willie grinning on the driver's seat like a circus clown, his hat held in the air four inches above his head.

"Are you going to let him die?" Molloy asked.

"I'm not going to force him to stay alive. He's been trying to die for thirty years."

"But if you bandage him up, won't he survive?"

"I did bandage him. He said he'd take it off when I left."

"What about an autopsy? Won't it show how he died."

"I'm the one who decides if an autopsy should be done. The cause of death is going to be alcoholism, which will be the truth. The small wound won't be seen and, anyhow, the sleeve of the shroud will hide it."

The tyres hummed against the surface of the road. Then Frank asked, "Aren't you afraid I'll tell someone what you just told me?"

"I was confessing before the fact."

"If you know so much about *ecclesia supplet* you must know you can't do that – confess a sin before you commit it."

"But I have made it a confessional matter."

"I doubt that," Frank said, "but I will consider what you just said as guarded by the seal of confession."

"Thank you, and I imagine what you see in Considine's house will also be protected by the seal."

"The slit wrist. Why is he trying to die?"

"He has a guilty conscience."

"That means I'm going to hear a story that's been told many times before in confession."

O'Leary said, "It's a good one. It's a pity you won't be able to do anything with it, no more than myself. I heard it after being sworn to secrecy."

For the first few minutes of their talking, Frank had thought that perhaps the doctor was a nice guy after all, that maybe he wasn't the self-righteous prick he had seemed to be at the front door. But now, detecting O'Leary's vacuous pride as easily as noticing a foul smell after someone has farted, he went back to his original opinion. However, it was his own inclination to tweak the doctor's nose which made him respond the way he did. "Don't you think the oath of secrecy would extend to having heard the story at all in the first place."

The car closed in on Ken Considine's house, bearing one man to help him lose his life, another to help him save his soul. As they came to a stop outside the low garden wall surrounding the house, O'Leary said, "The fact that I know Considine's secret is under the seal of confession."

"Is there confession without absolution?"

"Give me absolution, then."

"You're making a mockery of the whole thing."

"You don't even believe in it."

"I'd rather not believe in it than believe in it and abuse it."

Frank wasn't sure how serious the doctor was about demanding the sacrament of him. He was quickly enlightened.

"Well?" O'Leary asked.

"Well what?"

"Have you forgotten the words?"

"No, I haven't."

"Then bless me, Father, for I have sinned."

Frank's head dropped into his hand. After a moment he said, "For your penance try not to behave like an asshole." As he launched into the words of absolution he saw the doctor's body moving in anger.

On the far side of the low garden wall an eight-foot high boxwood hedge had gone wild years ago. It was as unkempt as the hair of a homeless person who didn't care anymore. The weeds in the gravel between the wall and the road were a tangled mass of the rotten and the new. Tall spring grass was growing all across the opening in the wall, and the doctor had to lift the gate to open it, its bottom hinge rusted away.

Frank followed the doctor to the door. Despite the decay he could see that an artful gardener had once lived in the house. A dwarf variety of boxwood still outlined the geometrically laid-out flower beds. Last season's weeds had left their clustered stalks in the abandoned plots. With surprise he saw there had been a fish pond, now rimmed with drooping bushes.

Along the short, weedy walk between the unshorn hedges, Frank followed O'Leary, and he saw where the paint had been weathered off the window-frames, once proud display cases for home-sewn, flowered curtains, he imagined. The leafless, spindly briars of neglected rose-bushes had collapsed at the wall between the dirt-stained windows.

Without knocking, Doctor O'Leary lifted the front door by its brown knob and pushed it scrapingly along the concrete floor of the porch. The door on their left was open and across the kitchen, half-lying, half-sitting in a broken-down armchair, Frank saw Ken Considine, his left arm hanging down, his hand hidden in the enamel bucket on the floor beside the chair, the bucket's enamel pocked with scars of rust.

From where the two men were standing it was difficult to determine if Ken Considine was dead or alive. The doctor entered the kitchen and Frank remained where he was, waiting to hear whether he was going to be called upon to perform one of his old magic tricks.

Chapter 32

Holy Thursday – 10.12 a.m.

A WHOLE ARRAY OF cellos was dragging the sun up out of Franz von Suppé's *Morning, Noon and Night.* But only if the cellos had dragged the April sun under the door and into the dead Miss Duggan's front room would Frank Molloy have noticed von Suppé at all. It wasn't so much that his mind was all astir with what he had learned in the past twelve hours: rather, his brain was lost in the maze of options which his new, unsought information had suddenly built up around him.

"Shit!" Molloy turned over on the couch, faced the back, whacked the upholstery with the side of his fist. He was exhausted. The fire in his skull had kept him awake all night.

After the doctor had brought him back from Considine's, he had read Miss Duggan's ghost story. Then he had sat at the table near the front window in the dark, staring at a yellow window in the back of Maura Gilligan's house, trying to recall what Eddie Keegan had said about Tony Donoghue. Numb in the brain from making, re-examining and rejecting decisions, he had stared at the blackness of the golf links after Maura Gilligan had switched off her last light. The cold in his bones had finally driven him to the warmth of the bedclothes.

When Doctor O'Leary had gently slapped Ken Considine back into consciousness, he had walked out of the tumble-down kitchen to give Molloy and the penitent privacy. And the penitent had wobbled in and out of his delirium, dragging behind him his story of the drowning of Tony Donaghue, and his own involvement in it. When Frank had administered the sacrament he had gone outside, waited while the doctor rebandaged the punctured wrist.

During the confession Frank had drawn back in horror as Considine had told him about sitting on Donaghue's head, keeping the face in the few inches of water, the other policemen holding the body up for a long time after it collapsed to keep the head submerged, to make sure he was dead.

In the April sunlight Molloy's body took in deep breaths as he imagined Donaghue not able to hold his breath any more; how he must have struggled against the helplessness of it, like a fully grown and bound bull feeling the cold knife slitting its scrotum so the testicles could be removed. At the end Donaghue must have vomited into the water that was drowning him, must have shit and pissed when the realisation was final that there was no escaping. Even if he'd wanted to tell the Guards that he had killed Kit Foley, he wouldn't have been able. In the last moments did he think of his family or was he completely taken up with what was going to happen once he emptied his lungs, once he would breathe in water?

When the doctor finally came out of the house he said that Considine would be dead in a matter of hours, that he would come back and be with him.

You mean to keep anyone else out of the house.

Without any other exchange they had got into the car and travelled back to Frank's house. When they had turned onto Wheat Mill Lane, Molloy had noticed immediately that Mary Delaney's car was gone. He was glad.

As they approached the end of the lane, O'Leary broke the silence.

"Well, what did I tell you? Isn't that some story?" he asked.

"What are you talking about?"

"Considine's confession! The story about drowning Donaghue in the sink and throwing the body in the river."

Frank looked at the doctor as if he were confronting a con-artist who had presented a flawed spiel. "You *are* an asshole, O'Leary," he said, and he turned his face to the window.

But O'Leary could not tolerate being spoken to this way and, as the car came to a stop outside Molloy's house, he said, "I'd just like to tell you something, Mister Molloy. I am not in the habit..." But Frank opened the door, got out and strode away.

When he had shut his front door, he went to the table at the window, knowing there would be a note. She had used the same paper he had used to write to Gregory. "Had to go. Ten in the aa em. That should give you time to recharge, old man! Delaney, M." Molloy didn't smile.

He went to the couch and flopped down, but as he was toeing off his left shoe, he stood up again, knowing for certain, and not knowing how his brain knew it, that if he read Miss Duggan's ghost story he was going to find out something about Kit Foley and Tony Donaghue.

With one shoe on and one shoe off he went to the kitchen. Before he got to the end of the first line he had to remove his glasses and hold the picture frame close to his eyes. When Mary Delaney had presented it to him he had only read her notes on the back of the frame. Now as his eyes fled down the page he was too distracted to see how undisguised the story was; he was too disturbed to realize that had he even glanced at the story on Monday he would have penetrated the thin camouflage.

It was only later, in the middle of the sleepless night, that he would know it was his familiarity with Nathaniel Hawthorne's *The Scarlet Letter* which had allowed him to see through Miss Duggan's words as clearly as if he were looking at Eddie Keegan dressed in the clothes of the guilty Reverend Arthur Dimmesdale. And later still, in his tossing and turning, he would think: *And that's why she gave the book to Mary Delaney. Mary was supposed to make the connection with the ghost story, which she knew by heart, only Mary never read the book. I wonder what she would have done with her knowledge if she had. What am I supposed to do with it?* A night full of twistings, turnings and expletives had not produced an answer.

And now a thin beam of the morning sun was cutting into the room as Franz von Suppé's sun set for the night. The disc player's laser beam cut into a Haydn symphony, and the music goose-stepped around the room in the key of G major. But with his face to the back of the couch Molloy wasn't hearing it. He had finally dropped off to sleep.

The soles of his socked feet were dirty, the legs of the socks collapsed in wrinkles around his ankles. The calf of one leg was visible, the hair worn down to stubble by the action of his trouser leg. His hands were crossed in front of his chest and pulled close to his body to accommodate the narrowness of the couch. The strip of white hair above his ears and at the back of his head was in need of combing.

Out of his back pocket was sticking a sheet of paper which had not been folded with care. At one point during the night he had pulled the frame apart and stuffed Mary Delaney's page in his pocket, all with the idea of going to Eddie Keegan's house, banging on the door with his fist, the other hand ready to wave the ghost story in the priest's face. But before he reached his own front door he had changed his mind. For one thing it was almost four o'clock in the morning, and for another thing he had begun to wonder about the anger that was driving him. Why was he angry at all? This was none of his business. The whole mess had been here while he was living in New York. It would have remained the mess it was if he had never come home. All he had to do was forget Considine's confession, forget Miss Duggan's story and forget about Kit Foley and Tony Donaghue. Then he could go to bed and sleep soundly.

That's what he had tried to do and that's what he had failed to do, because according to the Duggan story, Eddie Keegan had been seen with the body of the dead girl in his arms.

• • •

An unvaried pall of cloud muffled the whole expanse of sky from zenith to horizon, the moon a celestial ship, sailing in blinding flashes across the wind-torn vault.

In sad-coloured garments and grey, the woman stood beneath the tree, aged, black, and solemn. For an instant the moon gleamed far and wide over all the muffled sky. So powerful was its radiance, that it showed the familiar scene with the distinctness of mid-day, and there, close at hand, stood Arthur Dimmesdale. Until the ethereal barque had gleamed through a fissure in the clouds, Mr Dimmesdale had been in no peril of discovery.

They stood in the noon of that strange and solemn lunar splendour, and when the sad woman spoke, Dimmesdale threw his eyes anxiously in the direction of her voice. He distinctly beheld a form under the tree, clad in garments so sombre that he knew not whether it were a woman or a shadow.

Suddenly the land was obscure around them, and the tree tossed heavily above their heads, while one solemn bough groaned dolefully to another, as if telling the sad story of the pair that stood beneath.

Again the golden brig cast its light through the fractured clouds, and the sad woman fixed her wild eyes on the girl in Dimmesdale's arms, her daughter, whose innocent life had sprung a lovely and immortal flower; her beauty shining out, making a halo of the misfortune and ignominy in which she was enveloped.

Arthur Dimmesdale looked around, and the woman knew he hath done a wild thing in the hot passion of his heart. He laid the child on the sere grass of winter, cold. He offered his book and an iron pen to the woman. She wrote her name with her own blood, and then he set his mark on her bosom.

However, his power over her did not hobble her speech. "Thou mayst cover up thy secret from the prying multitude, even as thou didst now. Thou hast enticed me into a bond that will prove the ruin of my soul, because I will tell it even though I be sworn. At some inevitable moment, will the soul of this sufferer be dissolved, and flow forth in a dark, but transparent stream, bringing all its mysteries into the daylight, dragging all iniquity out into the sunshine, and send its own throb of pain through a thousand other hearts, in gushes of sad, persuasive eloquence."

Arthur Dimmesdale turned from the girl, and there was a listlessness in his gait. With his departure, the dell was left a solitude beneath its dark, old tree, which, with its multitudinous tongues of bough, would whisper long of what had passed there, and no mortal be the wiser.

• • •

As Molloy's chest lifted and fell with his breathing the protruding ghost story did not move. It was without life, a piece of paper sticking out of someone's back pocket.

The Haydn symphony had stepped aside, had given way to Morricone's music for *The Mission.* The meditative oboe seeped into Molloy's head and conjured up a nightmare of undiluted anxiety laced with glimpses of flashing lights; of a black opening in a silver train; of a body bag being handled without the tenderness he would have given it; with silent people in front of him leaning their heads into his line of vision; the lights, the fucking flashing lights, why does there always have to be so many flashing lights; and with the knowledge ineluctably marching toward him, like an ever-louder drum, that it was Padrake who was in the body bag.

Molloy's chest began to lift faster until it was heaving, until it looked like it was trying to keep pace with a drum that was beating faster and faster. Finally, his body moved as if making a gargantuan effort to push itself up out of drowning water. A strained cry left him as he struggled to escape back into consciousness. And finally he was lying awake on his back, eyes wide open, believing he had just emerged from an apnoeal episode.

As his breathing found its normal rhythm he heard the last strains of the oboe, and he remembered Padrake's house that first night they had gone to bed together, "Gabriel's Oboe" piping through the stereo speakers. She had been very loud during that first encounter, and the next day he had written her a letter from an anonymous neighbour complaining about the noises, threatening to organise a demonstration with placards demanding quieter orgasms in the neighbourhood. But his warm memories fell apart when he remembered what he knew.

"Fuck and a half!" he said aloud, because he had been thinking about Padrake, and that was her expression.

Fuck and a half! He swung his feet onto the floor, and before they touched the old, oiled wood there was a knock at the door. He glanced at his watch. Through the window he saw a car. *Is that what wakened me? God! I must look like a shit.*

As he went to the door he stretched the pains out of his back, combed his fingers through his hair. Before he moved the dead bolt, he ran his hands down his front in the vain hope he was ironing the wrinkles out of his rumpled clothing. He pulled up his socks. When he opened the door he was so surprised that he took a step backward.

Chapter 33

Holy Thursday – 10.52 a.m.

"EDDIE!" MOLLOY GASPED, and his mouth remained open. It wasn't that Eddie Keegan loomed large and menacing outside the door. It was just that the last person in the world Frank wanted to deal with was Eddie Keegan, because he knew the dealing would be like shovelling shit too slushy to stay on a shovel, and he knew that his relationship with his old friend, the little they had re-established, would never be the same again.

So absorbed was Molloy in his own self that he failed to read Keegan's body language, and so he was further staggered when he heard the harsh flatness in the priest's voice.

"I have to talk to you, Frankie," Keegan declared in a tone suited to calling an altar boy to heel.

They looked at each other, Keegan expecting a response, Frank unable to say anything. Along with the shock of seeing Keegan, his mind was still fogged up with wisps of the indecision in which he had floundered all night.

However, last night's detritus was quickly cleared by his recognition of the self-delusional air of authority which Keegan had used. During his time in the priesthood Frank had developed a sharp allergic reaction to such tones. But he was able to temper his response.

"Is there a dog around here that I can't see, Eddie?" he asked.

Keegan, in his priest's best black, with matching hat, gloves and overcoat, snapped back, "A what?" The light sparkled angrily in his spectacles.

Frank could feel the anger creeping into his chest. "A dog, Eddie! Are you talking to some fucking dog out there that I can't see?"

"No, I'm not talking to a dog, Frankie."

"Well stop sounding as if you are!" Molloy snapped, and then his voice changed to that of an overbearing, pedantic old teacher. "For starters, Eddie: 'Good morning, Frankie, and how are we doing today,

Frankie?'" Without giving Keegan a chance to respond he continued in his normal voice. "Would you like to come in Eddie, or do you want to get back in your car and start all over again?"

The priest's body was instantly seized in a cramp of unbendable, celibate rigidity. "Why are you always such a… a…"

"Prick," Frank offered. "Is that the word you're looking for?"

Keegan almost stamped his foot. "I have to talk to you, Frankie. I don't give a damn how I sound. Why are you making such a fuss? I just have to talk to you."

"Come in," Frank said, and he pulled the door open.

"I'd prefer you came for a drive with me. I'd rather not talk in your house."

With raised eyebrows and blank expression, Frank looked at Keegan. *So you can control the situation?* "Do you think I have the place bugged?"

"No, it's not that at all." Keegan held his two hands out as if he were going to catch a ball against his stomach. "Could you just come for a drive with me? Please."

The plea reminded Frank that, as Keegan had slunk out into the dark on Tuesday night, he himself had called words of reassurance after him. And seeing at last that Keegan was in a state of high anxiety, Frank quickly returned to his normal, civil self. "Would you like to come in for a minute while I get ready?"

"No, I'll wait in the car for you."

Four minutes later, his wet beard feeling the cold air, Frank came out of the house and saw that Keegan had already turned the car. The priest was rigidly sitting up, staring straight ahead, with his hands grasping the steering wheel. Frank went to the far side and sat in. Before he reached for the seat belt the car moved forward.

For the length of Wheat Mill Lane neither one spoke. At the end Keegan turned right, away from Davinkill. The narrow road wound around the boundaries of ancient but dismantled English demesnes. Frank remembered this route from his childhood days when his father would bring the family out for Sunday drives in the pony and trap. From those childish trips there was stored in his brain the remembrance that the road sank down into the earth, but now as he drove along with Eddie Keegan he saw the error in his stored memory. It wasn't that the road sank. Instead it was the land around that rose, leaving the road winding along the little valleys created by a series of ever-rising hills. He remembered there was a turn-off somewhere ahead which led to Clocowen Castle.

Twice since they had left his house Frank thought Keegan was about to speak, but each time the effort ended in nervous movings on the car seat. He decided to ram a small hole in Keegan's dam, to shatter the silence which was threatening to encapsulate the palpably vibrant climate.

"Eddie..." The one word acted like a well-placed charge of explosives. Keegan's verbal cascade flooded into the car.

"I never allowed anyone to know anything about myself until the other night." If the flow of words was like water rushing through a broken dam, the anger in the voice was the hard pebbles in the water. "I don't know how it... You seduced me into telling you things..."

"Stop, Eddie."

"No. You stop, Frankie. I told you a priest can have no friends and you laughed at me. Well, I was right and you were wrong. You seduced me into telling you things that could destroy me." The speed of the car was increasing noticeably as Keegan's flow of anger built up. "I can never go on being the priest people think I am if you are around looking at me with those accusing eyes of yours. You think you're right and everyone else is wrong. Why did you have to come home at all?" Keegan suddenly brought the car to a tyre-squealing stop. When he twisted around and flung his right arm back over the seat to facilitate his looking out the rear window, Frank flinched, thought for an instant that he was about to be slapped in the face. His body swayed forward as Keegan put the car in reverse.

"What the hell are you...?" he said, but the car leaped forward again and Keegan turned onto a by-road which he had overshot in his anger, the tyres squealing again. "I don't like this, Eddie," Frank said loudly.

"Do you think I like it, Frankie?" Keegan shouted back. "You have put me in an untenable position."

"I'm talking about your driving, for Christ's sake! Will you slow down!"

"So," Keegan said. "So now you know how it feels, Frankie!"

"How what feels? Slow down, please."

Keegan took his foot off the accelerator. "For someone to have power over you, to have someone else in the driver's seat."

With his hand still on the dashboard bracing himself, Frank said, "I don't know what you're up to, Eddie, but that was a piece of cheap shit. Do you think you're giving a lesson to a child? Or to one of your parishioners?"

"You just found out how it feels to be in someone else's control," Keegan said, with his teeth in the words.

"Well, you don't have to treat me to a fucking demonstration," Frank snarled back. "And for Christ's sake, why the hell would I want to have control over you?"

"It's not a question of whether you want to or not!" Keegan was close to shouting. "You know I'm a… a…"

"I know you're a what, Eddie?"

"You know I don't believe in what I'm doing!"

"I don't give a shit what you believe in!" Molloy was almost shouting, too.

"But you *know*!" Keegan shouted back. He slowed the car, turned onto an empty roadside parking area large enough for ten cars.

"What difference does it make what I know? Do you think I'm going to run out and tell?"

Keegan pulled on the handbrake as if he were going to yank it out of the floor. He pulled an envelope out of his inside pocket and threw it onto Frank's lap. "This is why it makes a difference that you know," he said, "and if I get the chance I'm going to take it. Read it!" He opened the door and got out of the car.

Frank, his head full of confusion and exasperation, glanced at the envelope before raising his eyes again to look after Keegan. The priest crossed the road and went through a kissing gate in the far hedge without a backward glance. Frank leaned over so he could get a better look at where Keegan was headed. For a moment he couldn't believe he had come here without seeing what he was now looking at. The car was at the foot of Clocowen, the ruins of the ancient castle on the top like a king's shattered crown. For a few moments he remained staring, the ruins as gigantic as his memory had stored them. In the corner of his eye, he could see Keegan slowly ascending the sheep track which led to the broken, second wall of defence.

Frank brought his eyes back to the plain white envelope in his fingers. He took out the single sheet of paper. The embossed green logo was an episcopal emblem and the raised address was that of the bishop who had just died. The letter was dated, "In the event of my death," and consisted of just two lines. "Dear Father Keegan: You are one of three priests whom I have recommended to the Holy See to be my successor." The bishop had placed his seal over his signature.

Frank folded the paper and slipped it back into the envelope. For a while he stared at the pebble-dashed wall in front of the car. His mind went back to Tuesday night, to Keegan's speech about what priests would do to win the affection of people in authority. Had he been talking about all priests, or had he simply been talking about himself? Eventually, Frank shrugged his shoulders, said aloud, "Who gives a fuck," and opened the car door, the envelope in his hand.

Keegan was standing near one of the fallen walls on the summit when Frank came panting up the bare, earthen path. The priest was looking out across the flat farms, the land divided into quilt-squares by miles of criss-crossing hedges. When he heard Frank approaching, he turned around, his body prepared to deflect any assault directed at it.

"Well?" he demanded, defiance and sabre-rattling in his voice.

Frank held out the letter to Keegan. "What kind of shit did you threaten Miss Duggan with after she saw you with Kit Foley's body in your arms?"

Chapter 34

Holy Thursday – 12.22 p.m.

A MOMENT AGO HE had been a knight in armour, sword drawn, ready to defend himself against anything Frankie Molloy would launch against him. He had expected a haranguing shower of arrows barbed with sarcasm about hypocrisy. But now Father Keegan felt as if Molloy had boldly walked up to him and delivered a sharp, devastating kick. The unexpectedness of the attack, and the perfect connectedness of the kick, sent the priest's brain reeling, sent a weakness into his body, causing him to seek the support of the toppled wall behind him, the splayed fingers of the other hand across his gaping mouth.

As he held himself from total collapse, he glared at Frankie in the angry way a king might glare at a ragged peasant who has severed the royal body from the royal head with a swipe of a rusty shovel, as if to say, "A fucking peasant with a rusty fucking shovel!"

Frank saw the anger in Keegan's eyes and saw, too, the devastation his words had caused. Sadness wrestled with the anger which had been festering in him since he had read Miss Duggan's story last night. He wanted to put his arms around Keegan. But he didn't do that because, sad or not for the priest, a part of Frank wanted to punish Keegan for having sincerely told him the story of Kit Foley and Tony Donaghue while cleanly filleting his own role out of the narrative. It was all just too slick to let pass. So, instead of embracing Keegan, Frank stepped over to him and took his arm the way he would have taken the arm of an old man who needed help crossing a street. Before he responded to the gentle tug, Keegan said, "I didn't kill her, Frankie."

And Frank responded, "Miss Duggan believed you did something in the heat of passion."

Still linking arms under the huge hunk of wall which had lain on its side since the hour one of Oliver Cromwell's lieutenants had blown the fort apart, Keegan replied, "I told her I didn't do it, but she wouldn't believe me. She went to her grave believing I raped and murdered her proxy daughter. How did you find out that she saw me with Kit in my arms."

"For one thing, I had to hear that Considine man's confession yesterday, while you..."

"Oh, God! I didn't know that. I know he died..." It was clear from Keegan's eyes that he was scanning the Considine story in his head. "But you couldn't have found out from..."

"I read Miss Duggan's story for the first time yesterday afternoon," Frank cut in, "and Arthur Dimmesdale is you."

"But Arthur Dimmesdale was her name for Tony Donaghue. The initials: Anthony Donaghue!"

"Do you know who Arthur Dimmesdale was?"

"No."

"He was a minister of religion, a priest who committed adultery with a woman called Hester Prynne, and he let Hester take all the blame. Miss Duggan put sentences from a book called *The Scarlet Letter* together to construct the story. Once you know Dimmesdale was a priest there's little or no disguise in Miss Duggan's story."

With mouth ajar, Keegan looked at Molloy. "It was there the whole time for anyone to see?"

"Yes, for anyone who knew the book. Miss Duggan set Mary Delaney up to read it, to put one and one together and get two."

"God, Mary knows. What's she going to do?" Keegan was hardly able to speak.

"It's not an easy book. Mary only read the first chapter and there's nothing in it that's in the ghost story. She gave the book back to me, the one Miss Duggan had given her."

Keegan's body seemed to collapse a little farther. His breathing became audible. After what seemed several minutes, he whispered, "Jesus. And all the while I was worried about the shoes."

"What shoes, Eddie?"

Then Keegan told how the girl's shoes had been missing, and how everyone in the village went out looking for them. Only they were on the floor of his car the whole time behind the front seat.

"Come on," Frank gently tugged Keegan's arm. "Let's sit down over there out of the breeze."

Molloy was more than amazed at the change in Keegan. It was as if the priest had became instantly old, that an essential, supporting framework had been yanked out of his being. As if to verify Frank's observation, Keegan said, "I had been dreading this moment of discovery for thirty years, and I always wondered if I'd be able to bear up under it. Now I know."

They walked around the edge of the deep shaft, which local speculation had made a source of water for the ancient inhabitants of the fort, but which had, in fact, been a dungeon within the walls of the castle. The two men brushed against last summer's dead nettles standing on the rim of the hole. In silence they went around to the south side of the walls which had escaped the bombardment of 1650, Keegan walking in the narrow path, Frank swishing his feet through the long, lifeless grass beside him. With a slight twitch of his fingers he indicated the spot where they would sit in the sun.

While he waited for Keegan to explain why he had been seen with a dead girl in his arms, Frank gazed out across the quilted farmland disappearing into the gloom of the horizon.

With his hands on his up-drawn knees, with his forehead on the back of his hands, with eyes closed, Keegan felt recuperation beginning to stir in his body. But the fear that Frankie would put pressure on him once he revealed all was demanding enormous energy to begin the confession. Like a swimmer hesitating on the edge of an icy swimming hole, Keegan teetered until he suddenly made the plunge, bringing his head up and beginning to talk at the same time. For an instant he was the swimmer in the air, relieved at having jumped, but waiting with dread to crash into the frigid water.

Keegan had no need to organise the story. He knew it the same way he knew how to put on the vestments for mass.

"Kit Foley came to see me the day she was murdered. It was a terribly awkward meeting. She was trying to tell me, and not knowing how, that her two brothers were raping her regularly. The mother and father were dead. Kit had told Miss Duggan about the raping, but was too ashamed to tell her who was doing it. Miss Duggan had persuaded her to come to me. Kit was several months pregnant."

But Kit had said it differently: "I think I'm going to have a baby, Father." In the priest's sitting-room the nervous girl sat, twisting a blue-flowered handkerchief in her fingers. She had not looked at the priest since she'd sat on the edge of the low armchair. In a soft voice, which the priest strained to hear, she told him how it had begun when she was twelve. Her brothers, ten and twelve years her senior, had started coming into her room separately, had put their hands under the bedclothes and touched her body while she lay there too terrified to move or speak. Then one night one of them had taken her hand and brought it to his erection and, like a nun holding a child's hand to help steer the pen around the corners of difficult letters, he had trained her hand to move up and down, while he forced his fingers between her legs. Not long afterward– the priest didn't know if she meant the same night– the other brother had done the same thing.

"She wasn't able to go into much detail. She either didn't know the words or was too embarrassed to use them. The older brother was the first to have actual intercourse with her, but after that the brothers became a team, one to hold and one to rape."

After an hour of quiet talking, after desperate thinking and after several phone calls on Keegan's part, the priest and the girl agreed that tomorrow she should go to a home for unwed mothers; that tonight she should go to Miss Duggan and that he would go to her brothers and talk to them. The next morning Keegan would take Kit back to her house to collect some things, and then drive her to the home.

"When she left I stood at the presbytery door and waited until she was on her bike. The poor girl." Keegan moved his head from side to side as, in his memory, he saw her again, pedalling down the street, the early darkness of winter already closing in around her. "God, I hated going out there to see those two animals. What was I to say to them? I was so frightened I didn't go until nearly eight o'clock. On the way, I decided I wouldn't mention the rapes. I'd just tell them Kit wasn't coming home again and that I'd be taking her away in the morning. If they asked me why, I'd tell them they already knew the answer."

Along the muck-covered, unpaved and dark country lane that led to the Foley house, Keegan had driven his car. Fat, heavy clouds scudded across the three-quarter moon, throwing sweeping flashes of light across the countryside. He knew the house was off this lane, on a track which was in far worse condition and darker than the one he was on. He knew there was a high dung-hill in the centre of the farmyard; that he wouldn't have room to turn the car; that if he drove up the track to the house he would have to reverse his way out. The only thing to do was park on the lane, put on his wellingtons and walk to the house with the help of a flashlight and the odd gleam of moonlight.

"It was so dark and quiet except for the wind in the hedges. The wellingtons made sucking sounds in the muck and dung on the lane. A few times I stopped to listen, turned off the flashlight to see if I could detect a light in a window ahead of me. When I reached the yard I stopped again. There wasn't a light anywhere. I was beginning to feel relieved that I wouldn't have to face the bastards. They were probably in bed, I thought, not even worried about Kit not being home. I remember standing there in the quiet, the beam of the flashlight shining ahead of me and only realising when there was a break in the clouds that I was within a few feet of the dung-hill." Keegan's voice was recovering its strength as he got deeper into the story.

The moment he recognised the dung-hill for what it was, knew that he could have walked into it, fallen face first into it, Keegan was afraid the same way a child is afraid of a monster he has carved out of the shadows. The looming heap of animal manure, accumulating throughout the winter from the surrounding barns, was like a slag heap on top of a mountain, ready to slither down and engulf everything in its path. For a few moments his fear held him in thrall. He was unable to move, his boots stuck in the deep muck, the hand holding the light paralysed lest the slightest move of the beam start the dung-hill on its sweeping slide. Then the hair on his body moved and the horrid crawling of his skin caused his mouth to drop open to release the urgent flow of non-viscous saliva.

"It was a terrible sound, like a lost soul falling away into hopelessness."

Keegan was unable to move, unable to bring himself to turn to the barn on his left where the sound had come from. He heard a girl's sobbing sounds and a rough commanding voice.

What the hell? She was supposed to go to Miss Duggan.

Then he heard nothing.

"All I wanted to do was float out of there, not make a sound."

Without moving his feet, he forced himself to turn, to look at the place where the noises were. In a while he saw two faint lines of light which intersected, forming a reversed L. Eventually he realised he was looking at a closed door with a weak light beyond, the light escaping at one side and at the bottom. Without moving he took silent breaths, hoping he would not hear the sounds again, hoping he could creep away without the guilt of cowardice dragging behind him in the muck. But he heard her groaning, could hear now the rustling of straw, heard a subdued voice. He lifted his foot and started for the door.

"I knocked! Can you imagine? I knocked!"

But he was hoping no one inside would hear the timorous tapping.

"I knocked like I'd knock on a convent door. Of course no one heard me."

Tentatively he pushed on the door with his right index finger, and it moved in on silent hinges. He hesitated, stood there looking in through the narrow opening he had made, began to see faint shadows, finally making out the rear ends of five big cattle in a row. Holding his breath, Keegan stepped into the barn, moved to his left out of the opening. As his eyes began to take in the weak light in the area behind the chained cattle, he saw the shape of a standing man moving his pelvis in sexual lunges.

"No one saw me, no one knew the door had opened."

As the cattle moved their heads, the chains which bound them to the manger made low metallic rustlings. The sound of the animals chewing their cuds filled the barn the way the sound of droning fills a beehive. In his black suit, black gloves, black boots and black hat, Keegan stood motionless. A lantern was on the floor at the far side of the pile of bales on which the girl was stretched on her back. In the weak light Keegan saw the one who was raping turn his head. But he wasn't turning to look at Keegan. The man had felt a flow of cold air on his bare legs and arse. "Is de fucken door open agin, for Chrise sake? It's koult in here!" he harshed out. But he was too far gone in fucking to stop.

"It was only when he started his lunging again that I saw the other brother kneeling at the end of the bales holding the girl's arms. I had thought she was tied."

The man who was raping began to make noises like a bull grunting its way to orgasm, his noisy boots seeking purchase in the loose straw. The other brother began making noises, too. The girl was crying, "Oh, Ma! Oh, Ma!" For the priest, the scene before him was a medieval drawing of hell, the light and the dark making it all the more fantastic and terrifying. When the rapist reached orgasm the sounds from himself and the brother were the groanings of demons in the dark, the rapist slamming his pelvis into his sister until he finally fell down on top of her, she sobbing. The rapist's booted feet, with his trousers at his ankles, swung up like the end of a see-saw, the hanging trousers shaking on the tensile legs.

Keegan seemed to have missed the instant when everything in the barn changed, wondered afterward if he had moved or coughed or sneezed. The brother became deathly still on top of his sister, and the other one stopped his heavy breathing. Then the rapist was back on his feet, his rough and dirty hand sliding off his sister's unrounded breast. The penis was yanked out and the sister gasped in pain. He looked over toward the door and said, "Who's dare?" The one who had been holding the girl sprang off the floor with the speed of a big cat.

"The next thing I was aware of, before I even opened my eyes, was the smell of human shit. Then I felt a pain, like the side of my head had taken a hard wallop. I was full of aches all over me from lying in the front of my car with the side of my face resting against the back of the seat. When I opened my eyes it was like waking into a nightmare instead of out of one."

Keegan didn't know yet what he was doing in the car, did not know that the door at his back was open, that the courtesy light above his head was on, did not see Kit Foley's face within three inches of his own. For nearly a minute his unfocused gaze rested on the black gash which was her partially open mouth. He lifted his head off the seat and moved back, his withdrawing eyes pushing the girl's features into focus. Even when he knew it was Kit, when he saw the half-closed eyes through the strands of hair which had fallen over the face, Keegan's brain did not make any connections with the immediate past.

"I was still coming out of a concussion, and it wasn't until I tried to do something about being so cold that I began to function at all."

He put his left hand on the girl's shoulder. "Kit," he said, and he shook her lightly. He was shaking her again when he felt his hand was wet. He turned it over to the light. From the bloodied hand his eyes went to her neck, to the gouge that shouted death.

"Frankie, I could see no way out for myself. No matter how much I protested my innocence I would never be able to disassociate myself from the girl's death. It was two against one. It was the only way. It's easy to say I should have driven straight to the hospital in Duneamon, that I should have driven straight to the Guards. Of course I should have. For thirty years I have been telling myself 'I should'. But at that moment all I could see was me in my car with Kit's body, her blood on my hands: she was pregnant, she had just been raped. I was in a terrible state."

If Keegan had detailed the state he was in, he would have told Frank that in his anxiety he had pissed in his pants as he sat there impaled on the horns of his dilemma. The urine had run back under him and soaked into the seat of his trousers.

"There was only one way out, and that was to put her body someplace. But I couldn't bring myself to hide her where she wouldn't be found for a long time. The best place I could think of was on the golf links near the road. I gave her the last rites before I moved the car."

By the time Keegan had arrived on the road near the big beech tree he was in a state of panic. He fell out of the car onto his hands and knees, recovered and took long, hasty steps around to the other side. But the door was locked and the key was still in the ignition. Whimpering in terror, he strode back to the driver's side, leaned in across the dead body, unlocked the door, ran back again to the passenger side and pulled open the door. He had not anticipated the difficulty of manhandling a limp body, thought all he had to do was grab her under the arm and lift her out. He grunted when he tried.

"It was so hard to get her out of the car! It was like trying to lift a bag of water. She kept…"

"Slipping" was the word he wanted to say, but the memory of her slipping through his hands every time he tried to lift her made him drift into silence as he sat there beside Molloy at the foot of the thick castle walls, the sun warm on their fronts.

Keegan's panic suddenly turned into fierce anger. He gripped the girl's wrists and pulled her on her back, head first out of the car. He closed the door. The thin veneer of gentility having been ruptured, he wasn't aware of the sour smell of piss and shit. With a foot each side of her face, he bent down, ran his hands under her back into her armpits and tightly grabbed the cloth of her dress. He lifted her up, held her against his chest, her hair in his open, gasping mouth. With his feet he pushed her feet forward. Her head fell away from him and over to one side. He now had her jammed in a standing position between himself and the car. He rested for a few seconds to plan his next manoeuvre, but a beam of moonlight escaping through a break in the clouds got him going again.

"I never thought it would be so hard to lift a dead body. I almost left her there at the edge of the grass. It would have made more sense, but I thought I would be delaying the discovery long enough to let me get well away from there by carrying her a bit off the road."

Keeping her pushed against the car with his body, the priest put his arms around her middle. He twisted around to her side, pulled her hip into his crotch until his clasped hands were resting on her far hip. As if making a genuflection, he dropped his right knee to the ground and pulled her down. In the instant of her sitting on his left knee, and before she began to topple backwards, he unclasped his hands, slipped his left arm up her back and ran his right hand under her knees, conscious from the coldness that his hand had slithered through the stream of shit which had been slipping down the back of her leg. But he had her. He stumbled to his feet.

"Before I had gone twenty steps the golf links was lit up by the moon and there, not ten yards away, was Miss Duggan."

At that point Keegan lost any control he had had. He didn't know how long the two of them stood there looking at each other. And then the girl was on the ground at their feet as Keegan hysterically tried to tell the hysterical Miss Duggan that he wasn't the one. But all Miss Duggan had wanted to do was take care of the girl. She tried to pull her out of Keegan's grasp, tried to pull away from his fierce and urgent and drowning words. She couldn't hear him. But he heard her. "No wonder Kit wouldn't tell me who was doing it. And I sent her to *you*."

Then she was on her knees beside the girl, and Keegan was running back to the car for his breviary, was plunging around on the front seat, looking on the floor, in the glove compartment, in the back seat, until he finally found it and ran back to where the old woman was kneeling, the girl's head in her lap.

Then Keegan turned around and ran back to the car again to get a pen because he thought that if he got her to write her name in the breviary he would have more power over her. The ballpoint pen was on the floor where it had fallen when he had ripped open the glove compartment.

He ran back again to the dead girl, grabbed Miss Duggan by the arm and pulled her up, jammed her hand on the breviary and made her swear before God that she would never reveal she had seen him there. And then he made her sign her name on the flyleaf, told her, his face inches away from hers, that if she ever broke the vow she had sworn that she would burn in hell for all eternity. He ran to the car, leaving Miss Duggan kneeling in the damp grass, leaning over Kit Foley's body as if she were trying to put life back into the daughter she never had.

"Of course, that was only the beginning. Tony Donaghue still had to die. But once I had started to cover up my innocent involvement, the covering up became worse than the involvement. I have lied, but Erasmus said that piety requires that we should sometimes conceal the truth, that we should take care not to show it always. I have paid, repented and restituted many times for what my silence did to Tony Donaghue.

"Frankie, I died a thousand deaths over the last thirty years, fearful that I'd be found out, fearful that Miss Duggan would start talking about what had happened. Even though I knew the Foley men could not talk without incriminating themselves, there was always the fear they would get drunk and brag about how they got away with murder. When Miss Duggan died I thought the pressure was relieved, but the thing with the shoes last week almost gave away the whole thing. It was a great relief to see them burning. But then I saw the ghost story on your kitchen table. I was going to ask you for it today." For the first time since he had started speaking, Keegan looked at Frank. "The last week has been like running around from one hole to another in a dyke. And now you come along and ambush me with the whole story! Jesus, Frankie. Thank God it was you." He put his hand on Frank's shoe as if to assure himself that it was indeed Frank Molloy who was sitting there beside him.

Chapter 35

Holy Thursday – 1.05 p.m.

MOLLOY WAS LYING back against the wall, his left hand on his updrawn left knee. He was gazing into the far distance, seeing nothing.

"Now that you know everything, Frankie, will you give me the ghost story when we go back to your house?" Keegan asked.

"I have it here with me. I was going to bring it to you at four o'clock this morning." Frank pulled the story out of his back pocket and handed it over.

Keegan took the paper, opened it, looked at it for a long time without reading it, bent it back along its misaligned folds and buried it in the breast pocket of his jacket. "Thanks," he said. "When you told me you knew about Miss Duggan seeing me with the body, I almost collapsed. I'd been expecting you to say something about the bishop's letter."

When Frank did not respond, Keegan, as if he were a child talking in the dark for the sake of making noise, asked, "What were you doing up at four o'clock?"

But Molloy was trying to match up the proper words with his thoughts.

"Frank, do you want to talk to me about the letter from the bishop, call me a hypocrite?" The priest made a nervous laughing sound.

Frank said, "You've been living a solitary life too long, Eddie." He turned over onto his knees and pushed himself up, the stiffness in his joints slowing his movements. He brushed his hands together and blades of grass fell to the ground.

Keegan looked up at him. "What do you mean, living a solitary life too long?" As if to postpone hearing the response, he took a long time to stand up. He moved back a few steps until he was leaning against the warm wall beside Frank.

"Did you know that, not so long ago, Ireland had the highest rate of mental illness in western Europe?" Frank asked, but he did not wait for an answer. “One reason was that when the son in a farming family inherited the farm he also inherited the parents. Not many young women were willing to marry into a house with built-in in-laws, so the son remained single. By the time the parents died it was often too late to marry, because the son was now an old man. When I was growing up in Roongarry, there were eight houses on our lane. In four of them there were middle-aged bachelors all living alone. Each of them was very odd, if not certifiably mad.”

Keegan stirred uneasily. Threw an obstacle across Frank’s progress. “What’s the point of all this, Frankie? Are you going to tell me that I’m a mad bachelor?”

But Molloy was determined not to be sidelined. “If a person lives in isolation long enough, he will start behaving in peculiar ways because there are no boundaries, there’s no one around to tell him that his behaviour is deteriorating. One of these four men had chickens and…”

“Stop it, Frankie!” Keegan commanded. “For God’s sake, I don’t need a lecture.”

“You asked me a question, Eddie. Do you want to hear the answer?”

“What did I ask you?”

“You asked me what I meant when I said you have been living a solitary life too long.”

“Well it sounds like you are getting ready to tell me that I’m mad,” Keegan snapped.

“I’m not going to say you’re mad. What I was saying is that when people live in isolation and have no one to bounce their ideas and behaviour off, their ideas and behaviour…”

“I am not isolated, Frankie, and I certainly do not behave…”

Frank raised his voice and snatched the conversation back from Keegan. “Listen to me, goddam it!” he snapped, pushing himself off the wall with his shoulders so he could look Keegan in the face. “Listen to someone besides yourself. From what you told me since I came home you have no friend and you don’t talk to anyone about yourself. You haven’t bounced an idea off anyone since you were put on a pedestal by flocks of holy water hens thirty years ago. You’re a real Irish fucking priest! You think you know every fucking thing about every fucking thing in God’s fucking creation. Well, let me tell you something, Eddie, you have been living such an isolated life that you can’t see anything wrong with letting an innocent man's reputation rot in the grave with his body. I'm not saying you're mad, but I am saying that in your self-conceitedness, your self-delusion, self-deceit or whatever the hell you want to call it, you are no longer capable of making an objective decision about anything. You want to save yourself, but you don't care that Tony Donaghue isn't saved. You want to be a fucking bishop, but you don't even believe in your own fucking priesthood. Listen to someone besides yourself, for Christ's sake!" Frank brought his face closer to Keegan's. "Eddie! You are a conceited prick!"

Keegan pulled away from the livid face and held up a hand against the splintering words. "What I told you, I told you in confidence…" he spluttered.

But Frank Molloy shouted down Keegan. "Oh, fuck you, Eddie Keegan! Fuck you. I don't give a shit if they make you bishop. I don't care if you leave Tony Donaghue rotting in your lies. But I do know something with absolute certainty, Eddie fucking Keegan fucking priest. I don't want to see you again because you make me want to fucking vomit. You are a conceited, self-serving shit. Fuck you, Father Keegan!" Molloy spun away and took long steps down the incline away from the thick wall. When he came to the narrow track at the bottom, he turned and quickly walked out of sight around the shoulder of the hill, the determination in his steps leaving no doubt that he was trying to vacate the area as fast as he possibly could.

When he reached the gate, the tempest was still raging in his chest. As he sidestepped the swinging gate he thought he heard his name in the turbulent air around his head. He looked back up toward the castle and there, almost halfway down, was Eddie Keegan. It looked like the priest had his hands cupped at his mouth and that his face was pointed at the sky, the way a dog holds its head when it's baying at the moon.

"Frankie! Wait!"

Molloy dropped his eyes, and with elbow resting on the end of the gate he became aware of his own rapid breathing. From his remembrance of past situations when he had been full of fury, Molloy knew that at this moment he was beyond rationality. When his brain throbbed with rage, all the synapses misfired and shot out spittle-laden words shaped like arrows and knives. He knew that the gene which was responsible for this behaviour had been dredged up out of his father's gene pool, purified, put into a hopper until it was driven to the edge of explosiveness, and then carefully implanted in his own deoxyribonucleic acid. Several times when he was young he had seen his father reduced to a blithering idiot by the swirling rage in his brain; it was almost as if the man had had fits. And Molloy, as he had grown older, found himself subject to similar episodes which left him physically drained. The episodes also left him embarrassed at the things which had come out of him, even though Nina Borruso had told him he had good instincts and that he should not try to denigrate the stuff that came out at these times.

Nina Borruso had also told him that the outbursts were caused by the build-up of pieces of anger which were not released into the atmosphere properly; that the pieces became compressed until they heated up and eventually exploded in a miasma of uncontrollable invective; that the root cause of the behaviour could be traced back to the Church's designation of anger as a cardinal sin, which made it better to bury anger than burn in hell for expressing it. Intellectually, Molloy could see what the the psychiatrist meant; emotionally, he was unable to harness to his advantage the tips about anger-release she had given him.

Now, as Keegan approached, Frank wondered had his anger erupted because Keegan was reminding him too much of the priesthood he had escaped from; was reminding him of how he, too, had once believed, beyond a shadow of a doubt, that he was *right.*

What the fuck did I say to him? Jesus Christ! Am I an asshole or what?

Keegan came jerking down the rock in the manner of a person descending a steep slope in a hurry. As he drew closer, Frank's defence system went onto a heightened state of alert. He knew he had run away from the castle partly because he had been afraid of being counterpunched with angry words from the priest. He now awaited with dread the scathing retort which he suspected Keegan was about to deliver. Frank could continue to walk away, but it was better to stop and face whatever had to be faced, to get it over with. This was the kind of confrontational situation he had imagined would arise between himself and Gregory.

When Keegan was still thirty feet away, he stopped. "If for no other reason than to prove you wrong, I will listen to you, Frankie," he said in a raised voice. Then he whacked Frank with his own words, like a nun holding a child's wrist and slapping the child in the face with its own hand. "I'll prove to you that I can listen to someone besides myself, maybe even let you see that I don't think I know everything about everything in God's creation."

Frank held his position inside the gate. He looked at his feet for a long time before he lifted his head and said wearily, "If you are only listening to prove me wrong, you are not listening at all, Eddie."

Keegan narrowed the distance between them by ten feet. "I'm listening, Frankie!" There was a hint of mockery in Keegan's tone.

Frank wondered if they were feinting with each other like two old bull moose before the final charge and clatter of antlers. Frank decided to rattle Keegan's antlers. "You would not have slammed the door on Tony Donaghue if you had spoken to another human being about it."

"Frankie, in that whole episode I am an innocent man," Keegan said softly, as if afraid someone besides Frank would hear him, but with a fierceness that could wither an assuming parishioner.

"Yes, Eddie, you are innocent, but only up to a point."

"I am completely innocent. I was a victim of circumstances and I'll be damned if I will be a victim a second time."

"You are innocent, Eddie, but you know that Tony Donaghue is innocent too."

"If he is innocent, I am guilty of cowardice." Keegan retorted.

There's the word. It's finally out.

"Do you think the Foley brothers are going to let me say they killed their sister?" Keegan moved closer to the far end of the gate.

"Isn't Tony Donaghue's innocence of any concern?" Frank, unable to keep looking at Keegan's face, bent his eyes to the heel of the gate.

When Keegan responded, the defiance in his voice was weaker. "Tony Donaghue is dead, and his children got a better education than if he'd lived."

"Well, wasn't it just lucky for the children that their father was murdered."

Keegan, pierced by Frank's barbed javelin, attempted a counter-thrust. "You heard that in confession and you know that the seal of..."

"I don't give a fuck where I heard it."

Both men became silent.

As Frank surveyed the no man's land which had sprung up between them, he decided that the sarcasm and anger he was directing at Keegan were serving no purpose.

At the heel of the gate, Keegan sat down on the low wall which was the remains of what had once been the outer defence of the castle. He leaned forward and put his face in his hands.

It suddenly became clear to Frank that Keegan was using him to guide himself out of the state of turmoil in which he was floundering. That's why Keegan had come for him this morning and showed him the bishop's letter. That's why he had followed him down from the castle still wanting to talk. Even though Keegan had not intended speaking about the Tony Donaghue matter, now that the subject had been introduced by Frank it was obviously a substantial part of the quagmire in which Keegan was plunging. Frank raised his head and looked over at the sitting Keegan. Again, his emotions mercurial, he had the urge to go to the priest and put his arms around him.

Fuck and a half, as Padrake would have said.

"Eddie," he said, with more gentleness than he'd used in the last hour. "I think you already know what you have to do, and I think you have made up your mind to do it." He paused to see if there would be a reaction, but Keegan did not respond, did not move his hands away from his face. "You are afraid to take the first step to freedom." Frank started winging it, not sure at all if what he was saying was correct. "You think you were a coward because you were afraid when you saw the girl being raped; you think you were a coward because you didn't save her. You knew Tony Donaghue was innocent, and afterwards you persuaded yourself it was your cowardice that allowed him to be murdered. And that's what you've been protecting from the very beginning; you're afraid your cowardice will be discovered."

Keegan pressed his fingers into his forehead as if to invade his skull and rip out his memory. He brought his hands down to his cheeks and squeezed his face out of shape, his mouth looking like a stepped-on doughnut. He stared out at nothing in the distance. Frank waited.

He would not have known Keegan was sobbing had he not seen his shoulders shaking. There was no sound from the man. Frank wondered how Eddie was able to do it. But then he remembered a time, before he met Padrake, when he himself had been ashamed to be seen crying. He had attended funerals where the effort to suppress the urge to cry did dreadful things to his throat. It was as if he had been crying through his tonsils.

Leaning on the gate, Frank did not move. He gazed at the shaking priest with the same remoteness as if he were looking at a goldfish circling in a small bowl. And then his eyes slipped into a twelve-mile stare when his memory presented the remembrance of his own crying the night Padrake had been murdered. But from this distance he wasn't sure anymore where his tears for Padrake had ended and where his screaming at the asshole with the gun had begun.

When a white handkerchief fluttered in front of Keegan's face, Frank's eyes returned from the past. The priest pushed his glasses up on his forehead. He loudly blew his nose and quickly swiped at his eyes before putting the handkerchief away. He cleared his throat. He looked over at Frank. When he spoke, his voice came out strangulated in stringy saliva. "What am I going to do?"

Molloy let the question rest in the air for a while before he responded. He knew that what Keegan thought he should do, and what he, Frankie, thought Keegan should do, were two different things, simply because they were approaching the same spot from two different directions. One was seeing the likely disintegration of his own reputation, the other was seeing a breach in a prison wall, the chance of a dash to freedom.

Molloy tried to put himself in Keegan's place, tried to imagine what the last thirty fearful years had been like: the constant fear of giving himself away; the fear of Miss Duggan; the fear of the Foley men; the fear, unmentioned by Keegan, that the day would come when Dervla Donaghue would know he had been protecting himself by damning her husband; the fear that some day he would have to stand up and admit that it was he who had been blocking the truth, the truth that would free the people of Davinkill from their suspicion of every man above a certain age. Frank stopped imagining and decided he would have chosen his own life, Padrake and all, Cotswold and all, over the misery Eddie Keegan must have endured.

Then he remembered his own feelings of freedom when he had faced the truth and finally walked away from the Church. This sense of freedom, and his imaginings about Keegan's years of fear, made the words fall out of his mouth.

"Get free, Eddie."

He said it almost to himself. Then, still looking at the bottom hinge of the gate, he spoke loud enough for Keegan to hear, each word chopped out individually. "Get fucking free!"

Then, remembering the day when he had finally shaken the dust of the priesthood off his sandals, to himself he said aloud, "I am free!"

Up Clocowen his voice went, across the throbbing fields ready to burst forth in the first greening of spring, back across his whole life to all the people who had, in the love of their hearts, enslaved him to the Church.

He returned his hands to his pockets and hugged himself. "I am fucking free," he said quietly, and he lay back against the wooden fence. He felt anger wisping around inside his brain, and knew it was the residue of the anger at himself for not having turned away from Cotswold and the Church that first day in Falworth many years ago. *But I did leave. In the end I grabbed at freedom the way an acrobat grabs at the metal bar that will stop the plunge to the ground below.* "And fuck you, Cotswold!" The sound of his own voice surprised him, and he looked over to see if Keegan had heard him. He left his eyes resting on the side of Keegan's head.

As one who had walked to freedom by giving up everything he had ever believed in, by rejecting the beliefs inherited from his own family, by rejecting the beliefs which his forefathers had died for, Frank longed to go over and wrap his arms around this prisoner, to tell him that freedom was worth the last penny of whatever pain it would cost him. He pushed himself off the gate, and walked over to where Keegan was sitting.

Two hours later, the two friends walked back to the car. In three days time, on Easter Sunday, Keegan would stand before the people of Davinkill, bare his soul, and at long last set Tony Donaghue and himself free.

The irony was not lost on Frank that on the other side of the piece of paper on which Keegan had written out the plan of his proclamation was Miss Duggan's ghost story; the story in which the soul of that sufferer was finally flowing forth in a dark, but transparent stream, bringing all its mysteries into the daylight, dragging all iniquity out into the sunshine, about to send its own throb of pain through a thousand other hearts, in gushes of sad, persuasive eloquence.

Chapter 36

Good Friday – 8.15 a.m.

ON THE SLOPING top of a low conical hill above Davinkill, the cemetery sat. From a distance, the irregular headstones were the symbolic ornaments in the ancient crown of a many-titled sovereign.

In the sunlight of early morning, Gregory Molloy could see the two tall yew trees. It was only from being familiar with the cemetery close up, that he knew the yews shadowed the life-size Calvary, white figures on black crosses, the trees shaped like the tops of Norman-styled church towers. He could also distinguish the row of tall, slender cypresses, pleading to the sky at the back of the nuns' plot; at the head of each narrow cell, a short, black iron cross with a name and two dates in white relief.

This morning, while waiting for a half-interested stallion to mount a reluctant mare, he had glanced at the ancient crown two miles away and decided to visit his parents' grave. He liked going to the cemetery early in the morning. Knowing no one else was there allowed him to give free rein to the sadness which sometimes overwhelmed him even though his father and mother had been dead for a long time.

Ten minutes after he and Barry Curry returned the stallion and mare to their still-chaste stalls, Gregory brought his car to a stop before turning left onto Downs Road. He slipped the car into first gear, but as he raised his foot off the clutch he heard a vehicle approaching around the corner to his left. As he looked to the noise, Saint Willie Gorman's tractor came roaring into view, the manure spreader behind the big tractor wheels like a terrier nipping at the heels of a frightened cow. Gregory responded mildly to the Saint's salutation of raised hat and grinning face. He turned onto Downs Road.

The cemetery disappeared behind a high leafless hedge, and Gregory felt his insides contracting. There was something about the road to the cemetery.

He had noticed before that the moment he made the turn onto the Derrysheer Road, juices were pumped into his digestive system for which his system had no digestive purpose. It didn't matter whether he was attending a funeral, visiting his parents' grave, or just using the Derrysheer Road to get from one place to another, his stomach still reacted in the same way. It was as if the hasps of a tightly packed chest suddenly burst apart, releasing in one short, concentrated burst, all the emotions associated with the cemetery road since he was a child. It was difficult to pick the emotional burst apart, to separate one strand from another. He knew his grandmother's death was in there. Although the funeral itself was not clear in his memory, he could recall her wooden coffin sitting atop the open grave, two pieces of wood holding it above the waiting hole, Father Kelly saying a long prayer in a voice which had said the same prayer too many times. As the weary words fell among the people and the headstones, the child, Gregory, had been unable to pull his eyes away from the dark hole beneath the coffin. Even though he was holding his mother's warm hand, the dark hole called to him, emanating a safeness which he found comforting. The hole, like the cave made with the kitchen table and two blankets, was a safe place, shutting out all anguish, all anxiety, all pain, the weather. And Granny would be there with him. No one had told him she was sick. No one had said she might die. She was suddenly dead, and she had not said goodbye. His childhood had died with her.

He remembered being wheeled to funerals on the bar of his father's bike, and then standing near the back of the crowd, holding his father's hand, feeling the callouses. He felt shame when his father invariably asked why he was crying, the tone of the question telling him he shouldn't be. But it was hard not to, when the big people beside the open grave were crying. It was for them he was sad, not their relative being buried. Most of the time he hadn't even known the person in the coffin.

There was his father's own funeral: the sight of the hearse in the farmyard, its hatchbacked door open like a ravenous mouth waiting to devour, his mother asking no one what that thing was doing there – not even naming the hearse, not even looking at it; the grunts of the men from inside the house as they manoeuvered the coffin around sharp corners, having to stand it on end to get it into the kitchen where his father used to kneel on the bare concrete floor at a chair to say his prayers, the sole of one bare foot rubbing the top of the other, the dry, scratchy sound making a listener's teeth fret; the sound of big men talking softly to each other as they followed the hearse at walking pace along the hilly and narrow cemetery road; the sound of their uneven tread behind him on the hard surface; the coffin looking small through the back window of the purring hearse, the sparkling crucifix and sparkling nameplate with its two dates, the sparkling ornamental handles – and he imagining his father lying on his back in the eternal darkness inside the pine box; what was being buried with him: what about all the back-breaking work, his pain, his anger, his tears, his curses, where was all that stuff? Was it being buried with him? Seedy Uncle Eamon, smelling of free liquor in his greased mackintosh, walking beside Gregory, Eamon making verbal noise, which he imagined communicated empathy for Gregory; Gregory pretending he wasn't hearing the questions, because he wanted to be left alone with his sadness for his dead father, for his sad mother travelling in a car not far behind, and for Frankie who didn't even know his father had died, could not be told because he was lost somewhere between addresses in North America; the sadness for the unwitting Frankie tempered with relief, since he and his mother were the only ones who knew that Frankie had left the priesthood.

As he pulled into the sloped and gravelled parking lot at the side of the cemetery, Gregory questioned again the wisdom of his mother's decision not to tell his father the truth about Frankie. As he got out of the car, he wondered if it was to spare herself the non-stop, loud fretting at what the neighbours would think.

From the parking lot, Gregory took the three steps to the wicket gate in the pebble-dashed cemetery wall. The six-acred field of graves was spotted with polished black Carrara marble headstones, shaped to look like crosses or open books or scrolls; the indented, gold-leafed lettering telling of names and dates, the marble and the gold disproving the notion that death is the great leveller.

As Gregory turned to close the black iron gate behind him, his eyes, out of habit, drifted down to his own farm. And it was as he was distractedly gazing – the very distraction acting as the attraction – that a flash of insight, as blinding as a bolt of lightning, struck.

The instant of denial which followed the searing revelation was followed by a deluge of acceptance so powerful that Gregory was staggered. His grip on the iron gate tightened, and the feeling which overwhelmed him was one of self-loathing. It was he who had betrayed.

It was he who had collapsed under the perceived communal pressure; he who had taken sides against his brother when his brother needed him most; he who had taken care of his own survival within the community and who, in the process, had not only abandoned Frankie, but had let it be seen that he was out on the front line throwing stones at him.

Gregory had always been critical of families which abandoned unmarried daughters who got pregnant. He had done the same thing – abandoned Frankie when he needed a brother most.

Slowly he turned and leaned against the gate he had just closed. He did not see the tall and smooth and clean limestone monuments, strewn with stony hearts and thorns and tears, keeping alive the memories of their graves' occupants in black-painted indented lettering; the limestones at older graves scarred with blotches of lichen, the letters blind without their black paint – the first thing to fail in the march toward final obscurity.

Now Gregory admitted to himself why he still wept at his parents' grave. For the past few days, knowing that Frankie was within a couple of miles of Roongarry, Gregory had had an ineluctable urge to go to his brother, to embrace him. His head had stopped him. But now he saw that, in some way, he had been readying himself for the bolt of insight. He may even have created it. It had not been a flash at all. It was an acceptance of him, by Gregory, of his own weakness in the face of real or imagined social pressure.

He fantasised flinging himself to the ground, prostrating himself before his brother, and saying, "I have sinned. You are not the prodigal returning home. I, the one who stayed, am the prodigal son. Forgive me."

With the iron of the small gate pushing unheeded into his back, Gregory gazed in a stupor across the graved field where, sprinkled among the Italian marble and Irish limestone, were feebler attempts, born of poverty, to keep disremembrance at bay.

He was remembering his mother's funeral, acknowledging the source of the overriding sadness. It had been the terrible sadness that Frankie was not there.

God, the emptiness he had felt, the desolation! And there had also been the unacknowledged, yet nonetheless painful, feeling that he himself was the obstacle to Frankie's presence. But when the emotions which had surfaced with the death of his mother had subsided, Gregory's prideful anger had gradually re-emerged, sinking him back into the rut from which he had briefly emerged. It was during the cemetery visits, when he was overcome by tears, that his love for Frankie had been trying to resurrect itself; it was for Frankie he had been weeping.

But now he must seize the moment. Now he must swallow his pride, his self-righteousness, his blindness, his stupidity at choosing the wrong side out of weakness.

He pushed himself off the iron gate. With head down, he pensively walked along the gravel path, buoyed by the knowledge that he was going to welcome his brother, that the pretence was at long last going to end. But beyond his joy he was already planning damage control to his own pride. What face would he be able to put on this complete turnaround in his behaviour? What explanation should he devise, so that people would understand why he was suddenly inviting the reviled brother into his own home?

As he pondered, he moved up the slope which brought him to the main cross-walk – the smaller yew tree in the corner in his downcast and distracted eye like a beacon directing him. He passed by the little garden of nuns' black iron crosses, their barren white pistils not catching his eye. Like a blind and slow-moving space probe, he was swung on his way by the nuns' cemetery, across the front and around the far side of the Calvary. The circled path around the base of Golgotha swung him deeper into the cemetery, to the second row of graves on his left. Two graves in stood a white marble headstone with his grandparents' names and dates, his father's and mother's names and dates, all in black letters, a heart encircled with thorns on the top.

When Gregory came to an instinctive stop at the family plot, he paused in his walking and thinking. He had not devised an acceptable way of saving face. He raised his head and, for a moment, he was surprised at where he was, surprised that he had negotiated his way out of force of habit.

He looked over at the family plot, and he wondered how long it had taken him to see an older Frankie kneeling there, kneeling on the curbstone at the foot of the grave, his face turned toward him.

Chapter 37

Good Friday – 8.35 a.m.

FRANK AND GREGORY looked at each other for a long time, neither one hearing the uh-uuhing of a nearby mourning dove as it pecked on a gravelled path; neither feeling the edge of the April breeze blowing off the headstones, abrading their cheeks; neither seeing the dandelions dancing among the short daisies, their yellow faces held in joy above the green grass between the graves.

Gregory stood with his mouth open, his mind flooding with memories of childhood and adolescence. The images bubbled up with such force that he could only catch speeding glimpses. Clay pigeons and shotguns. Birds' nests. Fishing in the lake. Castles. Free-wheeling down the mountain. Exploding carbide cans. Robbing Mrs Murray's raspberries. Mares foaling. Sunny hayfields. Hazel nuts and long poles with hooks. Rabbits. Going to the pictures. Singing in bed. Apple picking. Pellet guns. Working the turf. Swimming in two feet of cold river water.

And while Gregory gaped and remembered brotherly times, Frank gaped back at him, his memory shovelling up stuff which was not synchronised with the present circumstances: walking away from his first job interview, his self-confidence in tatters around his ankles; the gagging, greasy smell of the cheap rooming house in Shockapee; the suspicious farmer in Ledyard poking behind Frankie's lies as they stood in the flies beside a heat-stroked, dead steer; waiting, hoping for a tip as he held the elevator door when he worked as a doorman in New York city; standing at a roadside, giving up, giving in, trying and failing to summon whatever it took to step out in front of a truck; the letter finally catching up with him, telling him his father had died six weeks earlier; his mother's distant death and funeral; Padrake, through the train window, slumped, unmoving on the seat – "Nobody allowed in, sir," "But only to hold her!" "No, sir!" "But she's my wife!" – screaming, the four men carrying the body bag, passing him, not knowing it was his wife they had. All times when Frank had called out in his soul for Gregory.

At the foot of the grave, Frank put his body in motion to stand up, pressing down on the curbing stone with one hand, his rear end in the air. At the same moment Gregory started toward him. When Frankie straightened and turned in the same movement, his brother was almost on him, and without hesitation, as if they had practised it a thousand times before, they walked into each other's arms.

After a long time they heard the mourning dove, felt the edge of the morning breeze, saw the dancing dandelions in the grass.

At first they were unable to talk. They didn't know how to start, where to start. Eventually, they sat on the low shoulders which projected from either side of their parents' monument, their feet on the grave, the sun on their backs. In a low, unemotional voice, Frank spoke, not defending past behaviour, just telling; Gregory just listening.

The priesthood had been a romantic thing, the attaining of it, the great adventure of it. The brotherliness of the priests would be the only emotional support needed. He would be dressed in a white soutane, preaching to an open-air class under an African sun. Everyone would listen, and everyone would go away converted, changed so completely they would never utter a nasty word again, never have a nasty thought. There would be no dampness, no cold rain, no cold puddles, no chilblains. But he had only made it as far as Falworth. The presbytery was a cold, musty prison, glistening rivulets of bile running down the walls. No sun shone. Whatever is the opposite of brotherliness abounded. He never once came within shouting distance of brotherliness. There had been living death, no joy, not a hint of humanness. The priests were not of this world, and the world they lived in could never be his. It didn't take long to realise he was wading knee-deep in intellectual, spiritual and emotional rot.

"But I couldn't leave. I couldn't disappoint you and Daddy and Mammy, not after all the effort the three of you made to help me be a priest. It was like being trapped in a ward with barred windows, full of forever-babbling lunatics."

One time, when he and Gregory were young, the cow they called Three Spin couldn't stand up after it calved. After a week, their father went off and borrowed a sheepskin somewhere, and everyone said it was only superstition, that it would not cure the cow, that her bones had been hurt and she would never stand again. But Peter Molloy had spread the sheepskin on her back anyway, feeling very foolish he told his family afterwards, but desperate enough to try anything to save the cow, tied the skin on Three Spin so it wouldn't slip off. And the next morning Three Spin was standing, the sheepskin in the straw at her feet. There had been nothing curative about the sheepskin. The need to escape the maddening itch overcame the cow's inability to stand.

"That's what happened to me. There came a point when it didn't matter any more how bad I felt about you and Daddy and Mammy. Only one thing mattered, and that was to get out, get out, get to hell out of the priesthood before I went insane. God! I was so angry at myself for the lack of courage which kept me in so long."

During the years it did take him to leave, he was an angry pain in the ass to everyone. Every sermon he gave raised at least one set of hackles. The bishop was kept abreast of everything he said from the pulpit, and had written letters of reprimand when he thought it was necessary.

"But I didn't give a shit. I had never once met my bishop."

He had acted out his adolescence in the most shameless way; brought women to his rooms, had sex with most of them; smoked dope, drank. He was a hypocrite calling hypocrisy by its name at every opportunity. There was fighting at the dinner table, and on occasion he was abandoned to stew in his own insolence and rudeness. The more obnoxious he became to the professionals, the more he had in common with normal people.

"But I wasn't normal anymore. I was too bitter, not a priest at all, someone full of anger because he had been given a scorpion when he had expected bread. Even though I was seething with bitterness when I finally left, I still, today, resent that I was forced to jump up like Three Spin, to shudder the horror out of my soul. I had wanted to be a good priest, but the Church wouldn't let me be a human being. I left England because I still hoped, even after several years of disillusionment, that I could salvage the whole thing in America, that everything would be different and better."

In fact it was different enough to keep him in for two more years, but it was no better. The corruption over there was worse, just that it was carried off with more panache. There was more money, and the women didn't take as long to get out of their clothes. But there was the discovery again of these isolated old men, retreating all their lives, socially comparable to a spare prick on a honeymoon, eventually living in a realm of insanity which only they inhabited, each in his own solitary company.

"If I was ever going to be acceptable to the professional Church, I would have had to live a life which would finally make me one of them."

The old priests were so removed, so haughty, that they could not understand, could not hear anyone telling them that they did not have a monopoly on wisdom and that they were not entitled to lobster and wine on their tables whenever that was their whim. They never questioned their own way of living, their lives so riddled with idiosyncrasies that people smiled, attributing the priestly eccentricities to sanctity. The people had a need, too, to call the obvious eccentric behaviour by another name. It was not only the priests, but also the people they served who used fabrications to protect themselves against the collapse of the beliefs they supported between them.

"What a tremendous relief it was when I shook it all off. I knew how Three Spin felt when she jumped up, aching bones and all. I suppose my aching bones was my guilt. The first great windfall profit from leaving the priesthood was the knowledge that I was never going to become one of them."

He had escaped spending the rest of his life training to be a sitting-up corpse draped in old cobwebs in the corner of a dimly lit room with dirty windows.

"God! Gregory! You can have no idea of the sense of freedom I felt then, and can still feel now, still feel with the same intensity."

He had escaped from a prison inhabited by mummified men who still moved, who played golf, who said mass, who told prurient and dirty stories, but who had become embalmed from the deadly loneliness, the separateness, the apartness. They were emotional mummies. There wasn't even a trace of spirituality anymore, just insanity which was incorrectly, but conveniently, interpreted.

"No matter how bad things would become later on, I never lost the feeling I felt when I finally stumbled to my feet and threw off the cloak of the Church and cheered for my freedom. I still cheer for it, still cheer for it after all these years."

It had been an imprisonment of the soul, an imprisonment of the mind. It took Frank a long time to get his bearings in the real world, but that didn't matter.

"In my ignorance and self-delusion I thought all I had to do was walk in, tell them I'd been a priest, and I'd be made president of the company."

The mind-set of priestliness had rubbed off on him. He still thought he was that little bit more special than everyone else.

"In fact, I didn't know my business ass from my business elbow. I didn't know how to balance a checkbook. I didn't even have a checkbook."

Up to that time someone had taken care of him. A roof was put over his head. His meals were put on the table. His clothes were laundered. He was given pocket money, health coverage and four weeks' holidays.

"God, how naive I was! I thought everyone had the same standard of living I had, the naked evidence notwithstanding."

As quickly as ordination had boosted him through many social layers, the abandonment of the priesthood had stripped them away. Most of the people who had been friends suddenly developed a new attitude. It was as if the safe extra prick was suddenly no longer safe. The sycophants who had only been interested in rubbing shoulders with priests didn't know what to do with Frank Molloy. Without the cloak of the priesthood he was a nobody.

"That was the second great benefit of quitting. I was anonymous. I was no longer a local celebrity. I wasn't a magnet attracting all kinds of wounded and damaged people to whom I had nothing to offer. Gregory, I was free, and that's all that mattered. I finally got on my feet, got a job teaching in a college and lived my life like a normal human being. I imagine Elisabeth has told you what happened to Padrake...."

Padrake had been a survivor of the Church, too. She had taught him how to live, the same way physical therapists teach a damaged body how to walk and talk again. When she died, something gave way on the inside.

"Does it ever happen to you, when you think of a sadness from the past, that you instinctively call on someone, like God, or Daddy or Mammy? Whenever I was faced with real bad things, sad things, it was your name, Gregory, that came out of me; I always called on you for help."

With the saying of these last words, Frank's face suddenly erupted.

Before he had time to drop his head into his hands, there were tears in the air and a sound like "Oh! Gregory" had escaped his uncontrollable lips. Still sitting, he bent, face first, into his hands at his knees. The loud sobbing shook his shoulders and when his brother touched him, the words and his sobs mixed with each other and made the sound of a lost boy calling in the dark. But what Gregory heard was, "Oh! Greg. Oh! Greg."

Chapter 38

Good Friday – 9.52 a.m.

At the foot of the Calvary, the two brothers parted, Frank to go to his motorbike which was outside the main gate, and Gregory to go to his car in the parking area. With their reconciliation and Gregory's invitation to Easter dinner buoying him up, Frank felt he was bouncing down the sloping main path of the cemetery. He knew if he could ever fly, take off like a bird and soar around the windy sky, this was the time. He remembered himself as a child on long summer evenings lying on his back in the grass, watching high-flying birds, wishing he could soar with them over the blue mountain.

Before he reached the cemetery gate, he wished Padrake could have known about this moment. She, too, would be flying with him, laughing.

Without thinking of Cotswold, Frank got on his motorbike, and without starting the engine, he pushed himself off onto the steeply sloping road. The rushing air was all he heard, the cool air on his face like the palms of his mother's hands drawing the fevers of childhood off his forehead.

He was still astonished at the depth to which he had sunk in the well of his tears at his parent's headstone; he had gone down to the very source of his sadnesses, to the dark place where tears trickled off fields of memories which had been hidden away; the trickles joining to make streams until they became a river in whose curative waters he had washed his scars. He had cried for his father, bathed him in tears of regret, held him and told him he loved him. He had wept too for his mother, held a poultice of warm tears against her distress the same way she had eased his childish aches and sprains with folded cloths full of hot, ground barley meal and mustard.

His trailing mind's eye saw Miss Duggan under a tree on a moonlit night, looking at a man holding a dead girl in his arms, a girl she regarded as her daughter. A river of tears must have flowed off that glacial memory for the remainder of Miss Duggan's years.

As the motorbike came to the bottom of the hill, Molloy switched on the key and slipped the engine into third gear. The motor sang itself alive and the light bike surged forward on the new energy.

As he had heaved himself up out of his sadness in the cemetery, Frank had seen a parade of dead family members rising up with him, raising hands in benediction, men and women who had had their own turns at trying to find the signposts which would have given order to their lives. Some waved like drunks wave, gone to their graves never having penetrated the alcoholic haze in which they'd lived. Others had swallowed Irish Catholicism, hook, line and sinker, the teachings altering their reality as effectively as the liquor had changed that of the imbibers. There was one suicide, dripping the ditch water in which he'd done the deed – depressed, Frank's father had said, about the land-grabbing behaviour of his family. The young great-aunt, who had died in 1906 in San Francisco, waved a small white hand – Frank had seen her black-trimmed memorial card once. She was dressed in black, a black veil pulled up off her face. Her name was Theresa. At the end of the line he saw Padrake wrapped in fat winter clothing, only her face visible, her laughing smile and gloved hands cheering on himself and Gregory.

The location of our meeting was propitious. If dead people can cheer, then we had a whole cemetery cheering for us.

Frank braked as he approached the junction with the Maybridge Road, took his feet off their rests and let his soles glide within an inch of the road's surface. He didn't come to a complete stop, and he brought his feet back to their places when he turned right and increased the throttle.

The way Molloy's mind was jumping all over the place reminded him of how it had run away, had got away from him, when Padrake died. Then, it had been medication which had slowed him down, had stopped the ever-bouncing brain aching with the same sizzling and searing pain endured by something live in a frying pan. But he knew he would never lose control like that again. Nina Borruso had taught him how to identify the early warning signals, and what to do once they were recognised. But he wasn't concerned for his careening brain now. He knew it was dancing out of happiness.

His head was light with the giddiness in which his soul was marinating. The catastrophic expectations, as Doctor Borruso would have called them, had collapsed in the face of Gregory's unexpected display of affection. The pressure which had been containing Frank's emotions had been suddenly lifted, the pent-up anger floating off into space with the suddenness of a helium-filled balloon exploding its gas into the stratosphere when the outside pressure can't contain it anymore. The world was a nicer place than it had been for a long time. If only Eddie Keegan had his public confession behind him.

The poor bastard. But once Sunday is over it'll be all over.

Nathaniel Hawthorne's puritanical New England slipped across Frank's mind and left behind fading images of the Reverend Dimmesdale and Hester Prynne.

Jesus! Mary Delaney! She said ten! Molloy pushed his wrist out of its sleeve. *Two minutes to. She'll wait.*

He saw her again inside his front door, her overcoat open to reveal a body as barely clad as Eve in Eden in renaissance paintings, a leaf here, a leaf there.

Jesus!

Molloy changed up into third gear and adjusted the throttle. He saw a man walking along the road ahead of him, and his mind slipped off Mary Delaney and back to Gregory. There had been a dam of anger and shame and misunderstanding between them, and in the end only a few words had been needed to blow the obstruction out of the water. Without even knowing that it was because they had loved the same people, he and Gregory had taken the steps toward each other, had ended up so physically close to each other that words weren't necessary.

Gregory simply held out his arms. It was so decent of him.

In his relief, Frank pushed down on the foot rests and raised himself off the saddle. He would have let rip with a loud "yah hoo" had it not been for the presence of the man on the road ahead with a pitchfork over his shoulder. As Frank neared him, the walking man turned around to face the approaching noise. He lowered the handle of the pitchfork to the ground near his feet, the two iron prongs against his right shoulder. For a fleeting instant Frank was reminded of the man and woman standing in front of the window in *American Gothic.*

Grant Wood.

In high and joyful spirits, Molloy leaned over and swayed the bike into the middle of the road, calling "Good morning!" as he passed. But

Paddy Dillon, on his way to the old Duggan house, was too taken up in his alcoholic want to respond to the greeting.

Just after he passed the walker, Molloy began to slow down as he approached the stop sign where Maybridge joined Downs, the two roads forming a sweeping calligraphic Y rather than a sharp T-junction. With the wind gone from his ears and the motorbike quietly ticking over, the loud sound of an engine dissolved Molloy's remembering as effectively as if someone had dropped a stone in a pool of reflecting water. He brought the bike to a rolling stop with the front wheel projecting out onto Downs Road. When Frank looked to the sound, he saw Saint Willie Gorman's tractor swinging around the bend. He moved the motorbike back with his feet until he was completely off the main road. The clump of whitethorn bushes on the corner was now between him and the tractor and its trailing dung-spreader.

Despite the noise, Frank's careening brain once again found Mary Delaney in her state of undress inside his front door, and he remembered how he had moved toward her, after viewing her near-nudity, his right hand raised to descend on her breast.

Through the thickening sexual fog a new sound pierced Frank's consciousness. It was a sharp scraping noise coming at him in irregular intervals, the noise of a huge fingernail on a blackboard. He looked up and when he saw Saint Willie Gorman's tractor whizzing past on the far side of Downs Road, the Saint waving a greeting hand, Molloy knew something was amiss. The huge fingernail made one more scrape, and at that moment Molloy knew what was wrong.

The dung-spreader, detached from the speeding tractor, came crashing through the whitethorn bushes fifteen feet from where Frank was sitting. All the hairs on his body seemed to stand on edge and fright immobilised him. All he could do was tighten up the flesh on the left side of his body, the way he would have instinctively tightened his face against an imminent slap. Just before the dung-spreader hit him, he brought his hands off the handlebars and held them out against the oncoming pain.

Because his brain was taken up with the defence of his body, and because his nervous system was trying to cope with the wave of pain threatening to overload it, Molloy's awareness mechanism momentarily shut down. When it started up again, he found himself on his back. He had no pain, but neither could he feel anything else.

He didn't know that he and his bike had been pushed across the road onto the grass verge at the far side. The mangled bike was lying on top of Molloy's equally mangled legs. The tail end of the dung-spreader was sticking out of the wide ditch just beyond where he was lying, the air slowly hissing out of the fat wheel which had dragged the motorbike and its rider.

Frank Molloy looked up at the blue sky and saw high-flying birds sailing on lazy wings. The birds were mere shapes composed of lines of light and shadow. He thought they were seagulls.

Suddenly a man's face came between Frank and the birds, an out-of-proportion face with an out-of-shape hat on its head, a clown's head from Duffy's Circus when he was a child, the clown doing somersaults, standing up and taking glasses of water out of his inside pocket. A second head appeared. It was the man out of *American Gothic*, but there was something different about the fork. The clown and the *American Gothic* man looked at each other, their faces so close together in the sky that they became two boxers intimidating each other before a fight. The two heads went away, and the seagulls in the high sky floated around in lazy circles. Molloy began to feel a pain in his right leg. For a moment the pain made him flinch, but then it was gone. A pain in his left upper arm came and went. He felt as if he were lying on damp earth, and he heard his mother saying, "Don't lie on the grass, Frankie, even if it looks dry. The dampness in the clay will make you sick." He tried to get up, but his body wouldn't move.

As the seagulls wheeled in the high distance, the head of the *American Gothic* man floated into the sky again. He moved the fork in a way that reminded Frank of a cheerleader twirling a baton in slow motion. The *Gothic* man clasped the fork handle in both hands, raised his hands into the blue sky, and then brought them down with force. Frank saw Uncle Billy standing on the side of the river with a long pole in his hands, a barbed trident on the end of the pole, a salmon squirming on the prongs of the trident. Uncle Billy had black curls in his hair.

The moment the *Gothic* man pulled the pitchfork back up into the sky, Frank had the peculiar sensation that he had sunk into water. He closed his eyes against his panic, told himself he wasn't in water, that he couldn't be drowning. When he opened his eyes again, there was another head in the sky above him, a woman, his mother. He was trying to cough the water out of his lungs, and his mother was undoing the buttons of his shirt. But he wanted her to lift his head off the pillow so he could get the water out, to help him sit up. Again, he closed his eyes, told himself there is no water. How could there be water in his room, in his bed? There is no water. He had difficulty opening his eyes, he thought that maybe there is water, maybe the water is keeping my eyes from opening. Mammy. Padrake loved the ocean, and I hated strong sunshine. When she went to the beach in the summer, I would sit in the garden under the maple trees. She was great in the garden, Mam, always experimenting with new flowers. The girls adored her. You would have loved her, too, Mam.

He opened his eyes again and the seagulls were gone. The sky was dark, but after a while he realised he was looking at a group of heads near his face, all moving away and toward each other without rhyme or reason. And he became aware, too, that he wasn't hearing anything. How strange, he thought, with all those people and not a sound out of any of them. What are they doing? There seemed to be more water in his lungs, but he was calm now. Mammy and Padrake were here, and he remembered the time he took medicine that... His eyelids were too heavy to keep open, and as they closed down he saw the heads near his face moving frantically. But it was all right. Great-Aunt Theresa from San Francisco was here, and Granny and Daddy and Uncle Eamon. Padrake. Padrake. He knew he was too tired ever to open his eyes again, and he knew Mammy and Padrake would take care of him while he slept. Oh, Greg!

As the green and yellow ambulance pulled to a stop, Doctor O'Leary took his thumbs off the two holes in Frank's chest. "You can stop that now," he said to the two women kneeling in the grass, each with a hand under the body, each pressing a finger on one of the two holes in Frank's back. When they did not respond immediately, the doctor snarled at them, "He's dead." Then in a less abrasive voice he said, "Maybe Dillon's pitchfork was a blessing. His neck and back are broken along with everything else."

Elisabeth Molloy looked up at her husband. Mary Delaney looked at the doctor. Saint Willie Gorman, kneeling in the damp grass near the tail of his dung-spreader, slipped the rosary beads through his fingers, his eyes closed in meditation. Maura Gilligan, standing beside John O'Brien, looked at the praying saint and silently canonised him an arsehole of the first degree. As Doctor O'Leary stood up without putting his hands on the ground, Father Edward Keegan came striding across the grass, a small stainless steel container in his fingers, the ends of a narrow purple stole whipping in the wind near his elbows. He plopped down on both knees and looked at the battered head of his friend where the corner of the dung-spreader had caught him. His eyes slipped down to the bare chest, to the two purple holes surrounded by two blobs of bubbly blood. He unscrewed the top of the stainless steel container, and dipped his thumb in the oil of the sick.

As the priest brought his thumb to Frank's forehead to administer the last anointing, Mary Delaney reached out and caught his wrist.

"Don't!" she said.

Chapter 39

Easter Sunday – 7.55 a.m.

THE WHITE LINEN amice, starched and ironed, was as smooth as an icicle, its two tying strings in neat coils sitting on the two far corners. Because it was the first thing to be put on, it lay on top of all the other vestments. Without ever considering that the nun-sacristan had spent almost two minutes of her life laying out the amice and winding up its strings, Father Keegan stepped up to the vesting bench, took the piece of rectangular cloth in his hands and flicked it over his shoulders. He crossed the strings in front, brought them around his back, exchanged the string in each hand, and brought the ends around to the front. He tied a bow knot. Then he pushed the edge of the amice down inside his collar.

The nun-sacristan had spent two and a half minutes laying out the next vestment – the alb, always as white as its name, shaped like Ebenezer Scrooge's nightdress. The nun had put the alb face-down on its sleeves on the vesting bench, had gathered up the back as far as the shoulders. Without thinking at all about the sacristan's work, Father Keegan ran his fingers under the rolled-up cloth and flipped the alb over his head. He pulled at the shoulders until he thought it was hanging evenly, and then he tied the two short strings at his neck.

The nun had used two and a quarter minutes of her life-span to lay out the cincture, had shaped the long white rope to look like the letters IHS. "I Have Suffered" were the words the laity attached to the monogram, and Father Keegan would not have bothered to inform them that the letters stood for *Jesu Hominem Salvatorem*: "Jesus, Saviour of Men". Without hesitation, after tying the strings of the alb, the priest shattered the nun's handiwork, took the doubled cincture, ran the looped end around his back, brought it to his front and made a simple knot. Then he let the two tasselled ends fall toward the floor.

Before the tassels fell as far as they could, Father Keegan had taken up the sparkling white stole. He was not aware that the stole only looked whiter than it actually was because for the six weeks of Lent the vestments had been purple every day. Nor did Father Keegan know that the nun-sacristan had spent forty-five seconds arranging the stole, had used her own special little trick to straighten out the gold threads at each end. While the tassels of the cincture were still jerking around after their sudden stop an inch from the floor, Father Keegan brought the middle of the stole, marked with a little cross, to his lips and kissed it. Then he threw it over the back of his neck like a scarf. He bent forward from the waist and let the stole swing out so he could see if the ends were even with each other. Satisfied, he straightened up and, with the spare ends of the cincture, he trapped the ends of the stole against his belly.

The nun had laid the chasuble down on its front, too, and had rolled up the back, the strings for tying it to the body coiled like the strings of the amice. From so much repetition, that he did not even know he was doing it, Father Keegan threw the back of the chasuble up and, at the same time, he took a small step forward. Without touching a hair on his head the chasuble came down on his shoulders and, before it had fallen into place, Father Keegan had the tying strings in his fingers and was bringing them around his waist. He tied a bow knot.

The moment Father Keegan had tied the strings of the chasuble, the door of the boys' sacristy opened. A single line of altar boys came silently into the priest's sacristy, each boy wearing black, soft-soled shoes, white surplice and red cassock, hands joined at breast with fingers pointing to the ceiling. The nun silently closed the door between the two rooms. The boys came to a stop behind the priest, the nun dropping her hands to her sides and bowing her face to the floor. Father Keegan looked at the big-handed clock on the far side of the vesting bench. The red hand showed forty seconds to eight. The priest bowed his head slightly and brought his joined hands to his mouth, the nail of his right index finger pushed into the shallow space between his two false front teeth. He watched the red hand swinging around the bottom of the clock's face and begin the climb to twelve.

At ten seconds before the hour Father Keegan bowed to the crucifix. He turned around and the well-trained boys, with a minimum of confusion, fell into two lines and preceded him to the sanctuary door. The nun was there to open it and, as the feet of the first two boys made contact with the sanctuary floor, the bell in the church tower pealed out the first stroke of eight. As he stepped out of the sacristy, Father Keegan felt the strap of his wristwatch with the fingers of his right hand to assure himself that the notes of his sermon were there.

After the dreariness of the Lenten and Holy Week liturgies, the mass of Easter Sunday was truly a celebration. Through the penitential rite, the introit, the prayer, and the readings, Father Keegan drifted with the assistance of two lay readers and the choir. After the congregation had stood and joined in the singing of the Responsorial Psalm, adorned with the first alleluias in six weeks, Father Keegan went to the pulpit to read the Gospel. It told the wonderfully uplifting story of the two disciples going home to Emmaus from Jerusalem after all their dreams had died with Jesus on Friday, and how Jesus, coming as close as he ever came to playing a magic trick, joined them on the dusty road but withheld his identity, tut-tutting with them about their disappointment, until he finally revealed himself and promptly disappeared. All that was missing was a puff of smoke.

When the congregation sat down after the Gospel, Father Keegan read out the notices. There would be a meeting of the Pioneer Total Abstinence Association next Sunday to plan the year's annual excursion. Then he announced that the boys' school and the girls' school would re-open on Tuesday. He requested the prayers of the people for the souls of Kevin Clinton, Mary Donovan, John Cummins, Mary Dunne, Sheila Feeney and Philip Quigley whose anniversaries occurred around this time. Then he asked for prayers for the repose of the soul of Francis Molloy who had died on Friday as the result of an accident.

As the people joined him in saying, "May their souls and the souls of all the faithful departed through the mercy of God rest in peace. Amen," Father Keegan pulled the notes of his Easter address out from under his watch strap. As he smoothed the page on the rim of the pulpit, he wondered if anyone in the church would remember that he had given the same sermon three years ago. He liked the sermon, liked the way he described the two disciples running back to Jerusalem, after Jesus had disappeared, to tell the others how everything that had been foretold had come to pass. And how, after the long run back to Jerusalem from Emmaus, they were told, "We know. He appeared to us, too."

After the sermon, Father Keegan waited at the altar while one of the lay readers led the congregation in the Prayer of the Faithful. Then while the choir sang a motet, he prepared the bread and wine for consecration. He sang the Our Father without falling off any note and then invited the people to extend a sign of peace to one another. But Father Keegan did not extend the greeting of peace himself because he did not like squeezing flesh that was not as clean as his own. When it was time to give out holy communion, he noticed that his apprehension was less intense than usual. Maura Gilligan was the only person to rattle him, and he managed to avoid her slobbering tongue and spittled lips.

Father Keegan purified the communion patens, his fingers and the chalice. When he had put the dressed chalice aside, he read the last prayer.

He kissed the altar before the final blessing, and as he straightened up he imagined himself standing in front of the altar in the diocesan cathedral, waiting for an assisting priest to place the mitre on his head, doing it with a flourish because he was in the penumbra of the bishop's spotlight. Then he saw an acolyte coming up the steps holding in his veiled hands the ornate crozier, the ultimate symbol of episcopacy. He saw himself taking the crozier in his white, silk-gloved left hand, saw himself standing there for a moment in the full dress of a bishop before intoning the words of the blessing he was about to bestow on the people of the cathedral and the diocese. He saw himself from the back, saw the the two-pointed mitre, saw the gleaming crozier, saw his ringed and gloved right hand rising up over the congregation, and in the choir stalls around the altar he saw all the priests of the diocese bowing their heads.

Father Keegan blessed the people of his parish, picked up the dressed chalice and went down the altar steps to the floor of the sanctuary. He swivelled back to the altar on the ball of his right foot, and the bottom of his chasuble at the back swayed out like the gown of a graceful, distant and mysterious dancer. When the altar boys were ready, he genuflected with them, stood up and followed them off the altar.